Born and bred in Sydney, Lynne Wilding worked at a variety of office jobs and as a cabaret singer under the name of 'Linda Gaye' in the sixties.

She began writing seriously in 1981, and her first novel, a romance titled *The Sheikh*, was published internationally in 1991. She continued to write bestsellers, with *Heart of the Outback*, *Whispers Through the Pines*, *Turn Left at Bindi Creek* and *This Time Forever* being outstanding successes.

Lynne was the inaugural president of Romance Writers of Australia Inc. in 1991, an association that grew considerably under her commitment and expertise.

G000153483

To Janet,

Heart of the
Outback

Hope you enjoy reading this!

Lots of love
Deborah and
Ros xxx

Lynne
WILDING

Heart of the Outback

HarperCollins*Publishers*

HarperCollins*Publishers*

First published in Australia in 1998
This edition published in 2013
by HarperCollins*Publishers* Australia Pty Limited
ABN 36 009 913 517
harpercollins.com.au

HarperCollins*Publishers*
Level 13, 201 Elizabeth Street, Sydney NSW 2000, Australia
31 View Road, Glenfield, Auckland 0627, New Zealand
A 53, Sector 57, Noida, UP, India
77–85 Fulham Palace Road, London W6 8JB, United Kingdom
2 Bloor Street East, 20th floor, Toronto, Ontario M4W 1A8, Canada
10 East 53rd Street, New York NY 10022, USA

National Library of Australia Cataloguing-in-Publication data:
Wilding, Lynne.
    Heart of the Outback.
    ISBN 978 0 7322 9760 2.
    Ranchers – Queensland, Northern – Fiction.
    Man-woman relationships – Fiction.
    Police, Rural Queensland, Northern – Fiction.
    Women architects – Queensland – Fiction.
A823.3

Cover design by Darren Holt, HarperCollins Design Studio
Cover images: Woman © Steven Lippman/ Getty Images; Windmill and water
tank by Peter Walton Photography/ Getty Images
Typeset in Sabon by Kirby Jones
The papers used by HarperCollins in the manufacture of this book are a natural,
recyclable product made from wood grown in sustainable plantation forests. The
fibre source and manufacturing processes meet recognised international
environmental standards, and carry certification.

5 4 3 2 1   13 14 15 16

To my daughter, Karen, her husband Stirling, and especially to my first grandchild, Liah Rachelle Davis, born 11 November, 1996.

PROLOGUE

The rider sat astride the dun-coloured horse on the western ridge in the pre-dawn light, waiting. The Drizabone collar had been raised as protection against the early morning coolness and the weather-beaten, broad-brimmed hat was angled low.

In the valley below, the cattle were stirring. The sounds of their gentle lowing echoed and mingled with the wake-up calls of a flock of cockatoos. Two grey kangaroos grazed near the edge of the muddy waterhole and on the other side of the stretch of water a dark-skinned jackeroo stirred the embers of last night's fire into life. A wisp of smoke began to trail upwards until it dispersed against the lightening sky. A second man wearing fawn moleskins, a checked shirt and a red bandanna tied around his neck removed the nobbles from his horse and saddled it, getting ready to drive the mob forward before the heat of the day became too intense.

The mustering was on schedule, Richard Ambrose thought as he looped the bridle over his mount's ears. They'd make it in time to the holding pens before the herd was to be picked up by a road train. That would give him and Billy a full day and night to recuperate from the rigours of the trail.

The rider on the ridge watched the sun peep over the eastern hill. Rays of golden light stole like stretching fingers across the grey shadows of night, across the rocky outcrops, across the termite hills – some standing more than a metre high – across scrubby spinifex and across the earth, anointing it a dull, lifeless red. The land would remain that colour until the annual rains came, if they came at all. Then the land would change miraculously but briefly to a carpet of green complete with a profusion of multicoloured wildflowers.

Richard, tall and rangy, his fair hair flopping down over his forehead, hunkered down on his heels near the fire's edge. Billy Wontow, the Aboriginal stockman, handed him a steaming mug of tea and a thick slice of bread toasted over the open fire and smeared liberally with raspberry jam.

As Richard bit into the toast and then washed it down with the near boiling black tea he silently reflected on their muster. They'd tracked and mustered over one hundred and fifty head of cattle – his father would be pleased. Their swag of food had diminished to this – he bit into the toast again – the bare essentials. Still, it was enough to get them to the Isa without their bellies griping emptily.

His head shook almost imperceptibly as he thought of his Aunt Shellie. She sure knew how to pack a swag but, as she always said, a finger waggling at him for extra emphasis, they had to make it last. If they gobbled everything up too fast it was their own fault. Richard had done that just once in the four years he'd been moving cattle on Murrundi Downs station. Two days on a ration of black, unsweetened tea had taught him not to let his stomach rule his head.

Through a gaze narrowed by the morning light and camp smoke he glanced across at Billy. The Aboriginal stockman could always find himself a feed in the bush but, sometimes, Richard couldn't quite stomach what Billy turned up.

"What I wouldn't give for a decent breakfast. Sausages, eggs, bacon. Brewed coffee," Richard complained good-naturedly.

"Sure, boss. Wait'll we get to town. How about the biggest, juiciest rump steak, chips and eggs? That'd be a real treat."

"Shut up, you bloody torment."

Billy continued to grin at the younger man as he gulped down his tea. He knew the young boss liked his tucker as much as his old man CJ did.

The rider on the ridge stood up in the saddle's stirrups to get a better look at the cattle and camp over a clump of mulga shrubs which partially obscured the view. The cattle were all standing now and had begun to move towards the waterhole. A gloved hand reached for the rifle and slid it out of its leather scabbard. The barrel rose skywards, the butt rested on the rider's left thigh. The index finger slipped into place in front of the trigger and squeezed. Slowly.

A shot rang out like a bolt of thunder in the morning's silence.

The recoil from the discharge pushed the rifle butt down hard into the rider's thigh. The horse reacted, skittishly prancing until the reins were jerked hard and knees were pressed into the animal's flanks to bring it under complete control again. A gloved hand jerked the pump action, dislodging the spent case.

The cattle's gentle lowing suddenly changed to screeches of panic as a second shot rang out and then, within seconds, their placid milling galvanised into an all-out stampede.

"Shit!" Richard Ambrose threw his mug of tea into the fire and raced for his horse. "Must be tourists out shooting roos or wild pigs. Bloody idiots!" He grabbed the reins and vaulted into the saddle. "Billy," he shouted, "I'll try to turn them at the waterhole. You go down the left flank and slow the stampede as best you can."

With a savage pull on the reins, Richard dug his heels into his horse and took off. His heart was racing inside his chest as he saw the turmoil of the mixed breed of Brahman and Texas shorthorns his father had bred for the harsh conditions of the far north. The whites of their eyes clearly revealed their fear as they pressed against each other in an animal hysteria caused by the rifle shots.

Richard knew from experience that the likelihood of stopping them from going through the water was slim. If they weren't brought quickly under control, they'd run for kilometres and scatter in so many different directions that it would be impossible to re-herd them in time to meet the road train. He reached for his stock whip and uncoiled it as he galloped along the edge of the stampeding animals, cracking it in a fluid motion as he yelled at the top of his lungs in an effort to turn the mob, to bend them to his will.

Another shot rang out.

The rider whispered a curse as the bullet went slightly askew and lodged in a spindly eucalypt, splintering half the trunk.

Richard didn't have time to utter a curse. A third of the cattle changed directions again. Clouds of dry, red dust rose until it began to choke him, forcing him to pull his bandanna up over his nose. Blue eyes scouted the other side of the mob, trying to locate Billy, but the noise,

4

compounded with the dust made it impossible. Still, he had faith in the stockman. Billy knew his job, knew what to do.

A crazed Brahman-cross lurched out of the melee, bringing half-a-dozen steers with him. Richard used the pressure of his knees and a flick on the reins to urge his horse sideways. The animal obeyed instantly but as they moved, Richard felt the saddle underneath him slip sideways.

As the saddle's girth strap snapped and he lost his balance, Richard grabbed for the horse's neck, his fingers tangling in its mane as he tried to regain his seat. Out of the corner of his eye he saw the lead Brahman charge the flanks of his horse, knocking his mount sideways. The jolt caused him to lose his balance again and he fell off, his feet scraping along the ground. The last thing he saw as his eyes widened in comprehension of what was happening was the slobbering mouths and crazed eyes of the animals and their dust encrusted flying hooves as they ran over him.

The rider on the ridge returned the rifle to its scabbard and stayed to watch the progress of the stampede through a pair of powerful binoculars, focusing in on the red bandanna. When the eye-catching colour could no longer be seen, the gloved hands reached for the horse's reins. A satisfied smile stretched across a pair of dried lips and with pressure from the knees the horse was urged into a canter, away from the scene of destruction.

Richard Michael Ambrose, twenty-five years old and heir to CJ Ambrose's fortune, was laid to rest beside his mother, Brenda deWitt-Ambrose in the family plot on Murrundi Downs, the family's cattle station on March 3, 1996.

CJ stood dry-eyed beside the grave, separate and aloof. More than two hundred mourners had come to pay their last respects to the son of the man known unofficially and not always with affection throughout Queensland as "the man with the golden touch". The nickname had stuck over the years because almost everything CJ touched turned to money – lots of it.

People left him alone after the funeral and during the Aussie wake where drinks and plates of food were served on the lawn and garden which bordered the swimming pool of the modern homestead. CJ, who considered the pretence of being cordial and controlled after the internment of a loved one as something barbaric, retired to his study and locked the door behind him. He knew that his sister Shellie, his adopted daughter from Brenda's first marriage Natalie, and Les Westcott, his right-hand man, would play host to those who'd come. Less than half of them were genuine mourners anyway. Many had come to be seen to be doing the right thing and, hopefully, to impress him.

He slumped heavily in the leather armchair and tried, as he had tried every waking moment since learning of Richard's death, to make sense of it all. A stupid bloody accident had taken the life of the one person he loved more than life itself. A bitter grin creased the corners of his mouth as these thoughts ran through his head. Some of his so-called friends and business colleagues believed him incapable of loving anyone. They saw him as he wanted them to. A man who ruthlessly cut down or worked around those who opposed his plans and business schemes. But he had loved Richard unequivocally, even if he hadn't always shown it. To him, his son had been a ray of light, all that was good in what he considered a crazy, sometimes unacceptable world.

A wave of emptiness engulfed him as he contemplated the adjustment to a world that no longer contained his son. Richard had been well on the way to understanding the complexities and vastness of the business empire CJ had carved for himself out of the far north in a mere twenty-six years. It was an empire his son had shown the capacity to embrace and understand. Oh, granted, the boy hadn't been perfect, didn't have *his* killer instinct to close a deal, but he had been a good son. Intelligent, eager to learn. They'd got on. Really, got on. Which was more than he could say for his adopted daughter, Natalie. Something about her didn't sit comfortably with him, even after all these years.

He looked about his study, his eyes blue and faded but still similar to Richard's own colour, and his nostrils dilated as he breathed in deeply. A pleasant smell permeated the room, his own personal preserve. A mixture of furniture polish, cigar smoke and a mustiness which came from storing row upon row of books, most of them heavy, intellectual tomes. Not that he'd read any of them. He'd always been a man of action, too busy making money, doing deals, but they impressed the people he chose to do business with.

His sister had seen that all the photos of Richard were removed. Damn her interfering ways! Probably thought she was doing the right thing, making it easier for him. He'd tell her to put them back even though he knew that every time he looked at a photo it would stir up the pain; but the pain made him feel alive. Pain helped numb the other emotions, the sense of loss, the desolation. Christ Almighty, he couldn't let people see that. They'd think him finished. Try to take advantage of him.

A loud sigh cut the silence of the room and he eased back into the chair. Stillness. Keeping still helped to absorb the pain. It allowed it to move through his tissues and muscles, along the veins, pumping it through his heart, his mind. Richard. He silently screamed the name. Emptiness. Gone. Forever. The words kept repeating until they became chant-like.

He shut his eyes and let the memories dance before his closed lids. Richard in various stages of childhood and growing to manhood, and then his late wife Brenda who'd died three years ago. A single tear forced its way out and slid unimpeded down a time-lined cheek. He had to do his mourning now. Alone.

Darkness had invaded the room when CJ next opened his eyes. All was quiet, the milling sounds of guests and their vehicles gone, finally. He reached forward to the desk and flicked on the lamp. The light highlighted the coloured photograph of the largest opal he'd found when mining at Coober Pedy years ago. "You little beauty" was inscribed on a brass plate beneath the photo. Staring at its irregular shape, roughly the thickness of a man's little finger, triggered something, and his thoughts – which till now had been immersed in Richard – suddenly harked back more than twenty-six years. To a very different time and place before his son had even been thought of. To Mary ... the one person he had, over the years, strenuously kept out of his conscious memory.

But the memories, once set free, destroyed the layers he'd spread over that time, trying to keep at bay the images, and the guilt. A pair of brown eyes that could haunt him even now, after so long. What a bastard he'd been.

CHAPTER ONE

From the age of six C.J. Ambrose had been known as "CJ".

On his first day at the regional outback school in Longreach, the school bully, Reggie Dent, had challenged him saying that Cyril Jedediah was the stupidest name he'd ever heard and he was going to thrash the living daylights out of young Cyril just for having it. Unfortunately for Reggie, who was two years older than Cyril, he hadn't taken into account one simple fact. Cyril also hated the name his parents had saddled him with and, with an instinct that would become part of his future trademark, he knew that to have any peace at school he had to stand up to the bully and earn the other school kids' respect.

Another thing Reggie didn't know about Cyril was that he had a mighty fine temper and when it reached boiling point – which it did when his given name was mentioned – then Cyril became a force to reckon with.

After school at the back of the schoolhouse the unequal duel took place. The bully, a stone heavier went home the worse for wear, sporting a black eye and a bloody lip.

Cyril went home too and announced that from that day on he'd be known as CJ and, as his reputation as a fearsome scrapper grew, no-one there or for that matter anywhere else, queried the shortening of his name to his initials. As he grew to manhood some people may have raised an enquiring eyebrow at the unusualness of it, but on seeing the warning light in CJ's eyes, any questioning quickly died a timely death.

The Ambrose family had for three generations worked their own piece of land in north Queensland until the early fifties when CJ's grandfather, Percy Ambrose, went bankrupt. The family lost everything in a punishing drought. The loss of their medium-sized cattle station, Amba Downs, and the subsequent hard life drove CJ's gentle mother Rachel to an early grave. His father Neville had been forced to look for work as a station manager-cum-jackeroo wherever he could, earning, as he moved from town to town and station to station, the nickname of "Walkabout" Nev. His children, CJ and Shellie, tagged along wherever the search for employment took them.

CJ, a lanky thirteen-year-old who'd learnt to ride almost before he could walk, hadn't minded the harsh, semi-nomadic life, but he certainly had minded the family's fall from being landowners. He'd minded it like the very devil. One day he would have inherited Amba Downs and he was secretly angry with his grandfather and father for not having been better prepared to survive the years of drought – a common occurrence in the Australian outback.

Possessing a high intellect but little patience for book learning, CJ happily left school at fourteen to strike out on his own. He worked up in the Gulf country shooting crocodiles and wild buffalos, then he cut cane on a sugar plantation south of Cairns to see if he liked it, and by his late teens he had jackerooed the length and breadth of far north Queensland. During his years of work and travel he came to an important conclusion. If he was to get back on the land he loved and own a station again, he had to make money, big money. That's what it would take to buy a reasonable-sized property, stock it and then build up the herd.

Leaving Shellie to look after his ailing father, CJ's quest for wealth took him first to Broken Hill to learn about mining then across the country to Mt Lyell and to Kalgoorlie panning for gold. Finally, by the time he'd reached thirty, he found himself at Coober Pedy prospecting for opals. All the while his bank balance was growing but not fast enough to put him where he wanted to be – on his own piece of land with the finest breeding stock in far north Queensland.

He and Mickey Edgars (the two had met in a gold mine at Kalgoorlie) had agreed to fossick for opals at the Coober, initially around the mullock heaps to see what missed gems could be picked up. Mickey had once mined opals at Lightning Ridge and he taught the eager, quick-to-learn CJ everything he knew. From their first meeting they had forged an easy-going friendship even though the two men were vastly dissimilar in nature and builds. For some inexplicable reason a friendship had developed as they'd worked "Kal's" gold fields and now the Coober Pedy's opal fields which to them held the promise of great, and if they were fortunate, quick wealth.

One Saturday night they left the rough camp they'd made on the fringe of the diggings – they'd been noodling the dumps for small opals overlooked by other miners – to go into town. And maybe, after a beer or two, and if they were lucky, one or both of them would come across an unattached, willing woman as well.

Instead, CJ found a poker game and played the game of his life. He'd taken the pot which included eighteen hundred dollars in cash, a registration slip for a rust-encrusted VW kombi-van and a miner's right to a "supposed" opal mine west of the town's limits.

"That mining lease is no good to you," the cigar smoking player who'd lost everything told CJ.

"Why's that?" Mickey wanted to know. A little man, ex-jockey and ex-army, he often made up for his lack of height by a strutting belligerence. He was dark-haired, with upslanting grey eyes and unremarkable features but prided himself on his forthrightness. He didn't like people who were cruel to children, or poor losers like the man opposite him.

"Opals there are played out. Everyone knows it. But," the card-player added, his tone soft so few could hear the words. "I'll take if off your hands for two hundred dollars."

"Don't listen to him, mate. You can never tell with opals. Could be a fortune down there," a grizzled miner said. "Been proved time and time again. Someone mines for a while, finds nothing and lets his lease run out. Then a new bloke comes in and finds good opal."

"Yeah. You've got to work it to find out," said another.

CJ listened to all the comments. A thick-set, broad shouldered man with blonde hair that had the tendency to curl and then flop over his forehead, he was by no ways handsome. CJ had been involved in too many punch-ups in which his nose had been broken twice and he'd had his left cheekbone shattered. But something about him caught people's attention. A certain presence, an air of command. By the age of thirty, there was a hardness in him which bespoke the background from which he'd pulled himself up. And along the way he'd acquired an aura that fitted in with the tough men of Coober Pedy. People may not have liked him but the tilt of his head, the expression in his cool blue eyes said I don't give a damn, so long as you respect me. His single-minded goal in life, he jokingly called it his magnificent obsession, was to acquire great wealth, legally if he could, to keep his family happy.

He had come a long way in that regard. On one of his many visits to Townsville (where his father and sister Shellie lived since she'd married a businessman named Peter Kirkby) he'd met and courted a young widow, Brenda deWitt. Brenda was an only child and her father, Miles deWitt, owned a score of sugar cane plantations which stretched from Nambour to Cairns, as well as a couple of commercial buildings in the heart of Brisbane. Miles wasn't overly pleased that his daughter had fallen head over heels for the brash, opinionated Ambrose. He suspected that CJ was an opportunist looking to marry a woman of means. Knowing deWitt's suspicions were fairly accurate, dented CJ's pride, so he intended to prove his future father-in-law wrong by making it on his own.

CJ convinced Brenda that they shouldn't marry until he had substantial funds behind him, so they had become engaged on the understanding that he would take a year, no more than two, to establish himself. Soon after he'd left for Kalgoorlie eager to find the riches that would put him in a better light with Miles deWitt.

CJ studied the cigar smoking card-player. CJ's blue eyes were startling, an electric kind of blue capable of staring with disconcerting intensity, often making people squirm. "If it's no bloody good, why are you willing to pay good money for it?" CJ asked sternly.

"Oh, among the potch there might be a few small stones, enough to warrant the investment."

"I'll have a look at it first, then I'll let you know if I want to sell."

The next day, in his newly acquired VW van, CJ and Mickey found the M45 mine using a hand-drawn map the previous owner had grudgingly made for them. That the previous owner had said there was little chance of discovering traces of precious opal only increased CJ's resolve to have a damned good look for himself.

The mine was no more than a hole in the ground with several piles of mullock surrounding it. Near it stood a crude, but liveable dugout which had been hacked out from the hill. The dugout had a galvanised tin front wall with a door – no windows – and the inside was hollowed out like a cave to make one large room. The floor was hard-packed earth, the furniture basic and half of it homemade. A single burner spirit stove, a gas bottle fridge, a rickety table and two chairs and two bunks, one without a mattress stood inside. A kitchen dresser held an accumulation of mis-matched crockery and saucepans all of which were covered with a fine layer of dust.

Both men knew that the aridity of the landscape meant there would be little water around but a galvanised iron water storage tank stood at the side of the dugout to catch whatever rain might fall. It was, of course, empty! They knew that they would have to buy and haul their water from the general store, like everyone else did on the diggings.

CJ didn't know as much about mining opals as he did about iron ore or gold but some sixth sense – he had developed an innate ability to make decisions that led to him bettering himself – told him to give this mine a shot.

The price of quality Australian opals on the international gem market was rising, and if he found a decent vein it could make him rich overnight.

"The bloke's equipment's still here. I'm going to give it a go."

"What, full-time?" queried Mickey.

"Why not? I've the nest egg of those poker winnings. That'll tide me over for several months. Want to come in with me, Mickey? Two will get a lot more done than one."

"As a full partner?"

With eyes narrowed, CJ thought about it for two seconds. "Of course, what else?"

That was how the Ambrose-Edgars opal mining partnership was formed at the M45 mine.

The two men worked well together and had no trouble putting in ten to twelve hour days digging, hand gouging and detonating for the elusive opal-bearing seams. They'd cart the potch – useless opal and soil – out of the mine, sort it again for stones they may have missed and then dispose of the worthless material. After no time at all more cylindrical pyramids of mullock began to form around the site.

CJ and Mickey read what books they could find on mining opals but listening to the miners talk, around campfires, the general store and the pub, was the best education. Bit by bit they picked up the knowledge needed to differentiate precious opal from common opal, and to recognise the many varieties. One book said there were fifty-seven different kinds of opal but the important ones worth finding were crystal, water, pin fire, matrix, harlequin, girasol, milk and moss opal.

After two months their cache of a few quality opals of the harlequin, milk and fire variety had grown sizeably, enough for them to take a few days off and venture into town again for some relaxation and entertainment.

Young Mary Williams was getting used to the work in the bar. At first the noise of plain-speaking men, some with funny accents who could hardly speak a word of English, and those who didn't ask politely for a beer but yelled for one at the top of their lungs, had alarmed her. She knew they had to shout to be heard over the noise but she just wasn't used to it. After all, this was only her second week of employment at the hotel as an assistant barmaid, the only job the nuns from the mission school had been able to get her. The job included her own room at the back of the hotel, board and a poor weekly wage of seven dollars and fifty two cents.

There wasn't much to spend one's money on in Coober if one didn't drink or gamble or buy opals, which she didn't, so she was happy to sock most of her earnings away for the future. Perhaps for a visit to Adelaide. She'd heard it was a wonderful city with tall buildings, churches, lovely green parks with flowerbeds beside the Torrens River. She had seen pictures in books and longed to see the ocean and the beaches one day too. So different from Coober Pedy.

Fresh from the mission and not knowing how to react or behave, keeping the men who had shown interest in her at a distance had been hard for her at first. The nuns had forewarned her about men and, thank goodness, Gustav Farber the licensee and his thickly-accented, hard-working wife, Rita were God-fearing, kindly Germans. Gus kept an eye on Mary, as he'd promised Sister Magdalena he would, and if any of the young bloods got too bold he quickly told them to piss off.

Tall and slender and quietly spoken, Mary had been raised at the mission school never knowing either of her parents. She did know that her father was white and her mother part Aboriginal. She had been left on the mission's doorstep at the age of nine months with a note that begged the nuns to take care of her. They had, but when she reached eighteen they were obliged by the mission's rules to find her work and send her out into the world.

On Saturday night the din from the cream-tiled bar with its beer-stained counter reached monumental proportions by seven o'clock. Two men, egged on by a cluster of miners, were arm wrestling at one end of the bar. A darts competition was in full swing towards the side entrance door and a pall of cigarette smoke floated about fifteen centimetres above everyone's head. In the far corner a group of six men, glasses in hand, were vigorously debating some political matter, and another group were arguing about the estimated value of the iron ore deposits found in the Pilbarra. Several were talking about pulling up stakes and moving to Western Australia.

Mickey and CJ stood in the open doorway to the bar. Mickey recognised a bloke from down south and stopped to talk to him so CJ entered the fray alone. Almost immediately his eyes began to water from the cigarette smoke and the smell of stale beer. He elbowed his way through the throng to the front of the bar ... and then he saw her.

Her cheeks were flushed with exertion, her lightweight summer frock clung to her like a second skin, and a fine sheen of perspiration covered her neck and arms. Jet black hair curled and bobbed attractively around a face he could only describe in his head as angelic. She was attractive but not beautiful, not in the accepted sense. Her mouth was a little too wide and too full and her eyes were too large in a slightly narrow face that had a pointed chin. Who on earth would send such an innocent to work in this rough place? he wondered. Looking at her was like discovering an oasis in a desert, or the joy he felt at seeing a shooting star on a moonless night. Unexpected, wonderful. Absolutely splendid.

For once CJ didn't mind waiting to be served because he could watch as she moved along the bar filling orders. He was quick to note the admiring gaze of several of the men and something alien tightened inside his chest. He tried to think logically. She was young, pretty, *new*. Out of the corner of his eye he spied the licensee giving him a once-over. There was a very definite meaning in the older man's eyes. Okay, he could live with that.

"Yes?"

He blinked as she stopped in front of him. "Hello, you're new here?"

"Yes. What can I get you, sir?" Mary asked in a harried tone. She had long ago lost count of the times she'd been asked such a question. The back of her legs ached like the devil because she still wasn't used to standing for ten hours straight. Even after two weeks of it her body hadn't adjusted.

"I'll have a schooner of old, miss?" He should get something for Mickey, he realised. "Make that two, please, miss."

"The name's Mary," she said with a shy smile. Something in his eyes made her look at him again. They were so blue. She could hardly break her gaze away from him. He had a nice sounding voice too, not rough and loud like some of the other men.

CJ put his money on the bar, picked up the glasses and elbowed his way back to a position from which he could enjoy his beer and still observe Mary as she worked. She was diligent, he observed, the ever-watchful licensee couldn't fault her in that.

It was only after the second schooner that Mickey noticed the cause of his partner's distraction. "Yeah, she's a bit of all right, mate." He nudged CJ in the ribs. "But you could have competition. I see at least four other blokes drooling over her too."

CJ winked. "Only four! Hardly any competition at all."

Curious, Mickey asked, "So what are you going to do?"

"Absolutely nothing."

"Nothing?"

"Well, not right now. Mary's the kind of girl you don't rush. She'd run a million miles if I came on strong to her. No, the way to Mary's heart is," he grinned at his shorter mate, "I think, the slow, safe route. Get to know her first."

"What if one of the others beats you to her?"

"They won't," CJ said confidently. Thank God he hadn't told Mickey about Brenda. For some inexplicable reason he had held back disclosing his engagement to the Townsville widow. Just as well. Mickey was a bit straitlaced for all his rough living ways and his colourful past. Brenda. A pang of guilt flooded through CJ. There she was, waiting patiently with her young daughter, Natalie, and here he was with the hots for a dark-skinned, naive youngster. He should know better. He did, but something about Mary drew a response he couldn't deny. She was quite irresistible.

The following week CJ worked the mine like a man possessed, putting in twelve to sixteen hour days without complaint. He had this great surge of energy and he knew its origins. Thoughts of Mary sexually and physically stimulated him and he couldn't wait to see her again. Neither could he get her out of his mind. Awake he thought constantly about her and when he fell asleep, exhausted, in his narrow bunk, he dreamt of her.

On Friday afternoon he found the best indication yet that they were on the right track. He had chased a promising level of potch. Mickey set and exploded several sticks of gelignite along the drive and after disposing of the mullock, down a disused drive, both men had seen the first real sign of precious opal. The level ran horizontally along the mine wall, maybe ten metres below the surface.

CJ's work-roughened fingers followed the milky white trace and he began to chip delicately at the colour. This was when it got nerve-racking. Too hard a blow could shatter the opal, wasting hours of effort. But not this time. An hour's gentle tapping revealed a good-sized milk opal. He licked it and then held it up to the light on his miner's hat. Colours sparkled and danced. Beautiful. By the end of the day he'd liberated four fair-sized stones. A good day's work in any opal miner's language.

Mickey wanted to keep on working the level but CJ insisted they celebrate. He wanted to see Mary again even though he could only watch her from a distance. She was too busy to indulge in a mild flirtation with him, even if she knew what a mild flirtation consisted of.

More by luck than design CJ saw Mary walking home from St Peter and St Paul's Catholic underground church in Hutchison Street on Sunday morning. Dressed in a light-blue cotton dress with short sleeves and a mid-calf skirt, white sandals and white netting gloves and a straw hat with a daisy chain around the brim, she looked delightful.

Considering the straight-out approach best, CJ walked up to her and began keeping step with her strides until she turned her head sideways to look at him.

"Hello. We haven't been properly introduced. My name's CJ Ambrose."

"Oh." She remembered him. The man with the wonderful blue eyes. She remembered how he watched her all the time too. But so did several other men and she had become very good at ignoring their pointed stares.

"My name's Mary Williams," she said politely. To do otherwise, to ignore him would have been rude. "Did you say, CJ? Just CJ?"

He smiled at her, aware that when he did so it showed his even white teeth and the slight dimple in his cheek. "That's right. Everyone calls me CJ." He held out his hand. "Pleased to meet you, Mary Williams."

Something made her respond and she gripped his hand in return. It was firm, and warm and she could feel rough calluses on the inside of his fingers through her gloves.

"I'll walk you home."

His offer made her brown eyes sparkle. "Home is just down the street, at the back of the hotel." It was only about thirty-five metres away from where they were standing but somehow, though she knew it wasn't necessary, his attempt at gallantry pleased her. CJ looked like the kind of man, with his self-confidence and rugged good looks, who could have anyone. So, why did he want to be bothered with her?

"Thank you, I'd like that," she replied finally.

"Do you have today off?"

"I'm expected to help with lunch for the guests staying at the hotel, then I have the rest of the afternoon off."

"Perhaps you'd like a spot of afternoon tea at the cafe down the street?" CJ knew it was the only place in town, other than the hotel, which served food. Mary's indecision was palpable. CJ could almost hear the nuns' words of warning running through her head. Slowly, old man, don't rush it. "Another time then," he said, letting her off the hook. "Perhaps next Sunday would be more suitable."

Should she? Mother Magdalena had told her to be very careful of men. Not to trust them. That they only had one thing on their mind when it came to young women. He *was* nice though, she decided. Not like some other men who'd been after her, who'd pawed and whispered suggestively in her ear when Gus wasn't watching, which he couldn't be all the time. "Yes. Next Sunday would be fine," Mary said with a smile.

That was how Mary and CJ's relationship began. CJ courted her with old worldly charm, taking her wildflowers he picked himself when the desert bloomed after a spot of rain and boxes of chocolates which he said she had to eat straightaway, before they melted. And, when he learnt that she liked to read, he plied her with books; some new, some bought second-hand, to read at night while she listened to the radio.

Six and a half days a week he laboured in the depths of the opal mine with Mickey, and they made some good finds. Not enough to make their fortune though, but each gem they discovered led them to hope that somewhere in the claystone and dirt that was forever in their clothes, in their eyes, even in their mouths, there'd be a big strike. They both believed wholeheartedly that one day it would happen to them too.

Mickey, something of a daredevil in the way he casually handled the gelignite and fuses, nevertheless possessed the patience to go on. And CJ had the drive – the relentlessness to work long hours at a stretch, digging, hauling the claystone out, sifting through it and then discarding the useless earth in a heap near the mine. Often he worked long into the night, indeed the difference between day and night counted for little down the mine. His dream pushed him on and the most profitable cattle run in far north Queensland was his first goal. He'd have the best homestead, the best mix of cattle and then he'd diversify into other businesses, property, sugar cane and overseas investments.

That's where his grandfather had gone wrong. Old Percy had put all the profits back into the land and when the hard times came – one of the longest droughts on record – there'd been no reserve and eventually the banks had reclaimed Amba Downs. Damn those fastidious number crunchers, they had presided over many a family's downfall. Well, they wouldn't preside over his. With his bare hands and his brains and the energy he possessed he would carve an empire such as had never been known in Queensland.

"If Gus finds you here, I don't know who he'll skin first, you or me," Mary giggled as CJ took her in his arms.

They had never gone to her room before because she was afraid Gus or someone else might see CJ coming or going, but he'd entreated and cajoled her until she had agreed. How could she resist? CJ was marvellous. Warm, caring and considerate, she couldn't deny him anything.

His blue-eyed gaze darted around the plain room. The floor was of worn linoleum, the walls were unpainted galvanised iron and from the ceiling a bare globe hung without a shade. An old wardrobe with a mirror stood near the window and beside the single bed was a small bedside table with a reading lamp. Next to the door stood a second-hand bookshelf in which Mary kept her growing library of books.

"I made sure Gus had quite a few tonight and doesn't he sleep on the other side of the hotel?" CJ asked. He watched her nod her head affirmatively. "Then we've nothing to worry about, unless old Gus's snores blow the roof off."

Mary disengaged herself from him to go and pull down the shade and draw the curtains, though it made the room suffocatingly hot. She then turned on the oscillating fan she had bought last week, it would at least move the warm air around the room.

"I've something to show you," CJ said as he sat on the bed, which squeaked under his weight. "Look!" He took a piece of cloth out of his back trouser pocket and laid it on the cotton bedspread. Slowly he undid the soft cloth to reveal several stones. He turned the stones over so that Mary could see the opals and the shimmering colours trapped within.

"They're beautiful."

"Aren't they. They're the biggest and best we've found." He turned the reading lamp on, picked up the largest stone and held it to the light, turning it in different directions. "See the colours. Magnificent. Mickey reckons it's worth a thousand dollars by itself."

"A thousand!" Mary had never seen anything worth that much money in one piece. "The colours, they're like a rainbow. CJ, tell me about opals. How are they made?"

CJ thought for a moment, trying to think of a simple, uncomplicated explanation for the gems. "According to what I've read and heard from the other miners and Mickey, precious opal occurs in rocks affected by weathering. Sun, wind and rain, can start the process which may have begun up to seventy million years ago."

"Gosh, I had no idea they were that old."

"Well, the stones aren't – it's the process that's old. Weathering makes the country rock produce something called kaolin and soluble silica – the main ingredients in claystone and other rocks. As the weathering continues, cavities are created in the rock by dissolving minerals and fossil shells. These cavities provide pathways for underground water containing the soluble silica."

A puzzled frown feathered across her young forehead. "But how does this create the opal?"

"Experts reckon that as the water table rises and falls, probably because of changes in the weather, the silica-rich solutions are carried downwards, depositing opal containing stone in the cavities." He grinned at her. "And now they're down there just waiting to be dug up."

"I think I understand. It's a bit like the way silver and gold are formed, but how do the stones get their spectacular colours?"

"From the silica and water, which over millions of years, goes rock hard. Generally, precious opal contains six to ten per cent water. It's that plus the silica squares arranged in a regular pattern that make the colours. The colour you see in them, the reds, blues, yellows and greens is caused by the regular array of silica spheres diffracting white light." He paused for a breath. "If you didn't shine light on them, or see them in the sunlight, you'd have no idea of the brilliant colours contained in the stone. Colour also depends on the angle of light. Rotating a stone can make the colours change and even disappear."

Mary shook her head. It was complicated and she didn't understand all of it, even though CJ had explained it well. "It is a little difficult to understand ..."

"Don't worry too much about it," he told her. He took her hand and placed the largest uncut stone into her palm. "I want you to have this, Mary." He pulled her onto his lap and stroked her dark hair. "I'll have a jeweller in Adelaide polish it and make you a pendant, or a ring. How does that sound?"

"CJ, I couldn't. It's so valuable, I'd be scared to wear it."

"Nonsense," he assured her. He studied her dark-skinned face for a moment. Her parentage had bequeathed her the dark hair and complexion of her mother, but he guessed that her eyes came from her father. They were an interesting mixture of light-brown with greenish flecks. "You know, your eyes are like brown opals. I'll have to find a good one for you, maybe enough to make earrings as well."

She smiled back at him. "You're too good to me, CJ." Then she frowned. "What if ..." He kissed the side of her neck and she suddenly found it hard to think, "I lost it?"

"You won't." He continued to feather kisses down to her bare shoulder, his lips tasting the slight saltiness of her skin while at the same time his hands caressed her body, feeling it stir to his touch. She was a sensual little creature and responded almost immediately to his demands. His mouth found hers in a searing kiss of possession and he teased her lips with his tongue until she opened to him. He sank his tongue deep into her mouth and ravaged it, his body hardening as he heard her throaty moans of delight. "Oh, baby," he whispered close to her ear. "I want you so much."

"Me too, my darling." Mary helped him strip off her flimsy clothes and she tingled all over with delight and need as his ambitious hands and mouth roamed over her, bringing her to an anticipatory peak in just a few minutes. How she loved him. CJ had filled her thoughts, her dreams ever since the first time they'd made love, on a rug out at the Breakaways, with the moonlight anointing their bodies and a million stars twinkling down on them as unbiased observers. It had been so romantic and absolutely wonderful.

All her life Mary had yearned for someone to love. At the mission school she had been fond of the nuns, but they always stayed somewhat aloof. There had been the children though. One girl, Paula, whom she'd loved like a sister. Paula had been fostered out last year and since then, the only creature she'd pinned her affection on was Sister Magdalena's dog. Bitsy, a part dingo, kelpie and labrador cross, was named appropriately. Leaving Bitsy behind when she left the mission had made her cry more than any other reason, though in hindsight she now realised that many of her tears had been for fear of the unknown.

Now shirtless, CJ laid her back on the bed and stripped the rest of his clothes off. He leant back to look at her, as he liked to do, and smiled as he marvelled at the beauty of her body. She'd been almost pitifully thin when she'd first come to work at Gus's but she had filled out nicely. Her breasts were round orbs of delight, her waist so narrow he could almost span it with his large hands and her shapely thighs and the dark triangle of her womanhood made him wonder, suddenly, what the hell he was waiting for. An invitation? He smiled to himself, he had that. She was ripe, ready for him and the straining nature of his erection told him he was more than ready for her too.

He reached forward to turn off the reading lamp. "Baby, you got that script, didn't you?"

"The pill? Yes." A wave of heat rushed through her body as she remembered the discussion with the visiting doctor. It had been embarrassing to have to ask for the contraceptive pill and then listen to the doctor's lecture on morality and the possible side effects of the medication. "I've been taking them for ten days, but sometimes it's hard remembering to take one every day."

He laughed that deep throaty laugh of his. "Don't forget, baby. We don't want any little accidents, do we?"

"No, but ..." In the darkness his mouth unerringly found hers, cutting off what she'd been going to say. And then, as his body covered hers she gave herself up to the passion CJ could arouse in her, and welcomed his sensual, satisfying domination.

CJ climbed down the eight metre metal ladder into the darkness of the mine. The horizontal drive ran in a straight line due north – he'd checked the compass so that they didn't run into the adjoining claim which ran due south. The work was tougher than jackerooing, tougher than gold mining. At least over in Kal they had machinery to take away the mullock and do the drilling. Here they had to hand gouge to find traces, then use a wheelbarrow to bucket the potch in, and then hand haul it out of the mine. Slow, sweaty, backbreaking work.

Mickey's enthusiasm was one thing that kept him going. Whenever they found a slim opal bearing seam his partner would dance about as if they'd won first prize in a lottery. CJ smiled to himself. And then Mickey'd remind him that the regular finding of opal bearing deposits was a sure sign they were getting close to a productive seam.

CJ flicked on his miner's hat and followed the well-worn track to the end of the drive where he could hear Mickey drilling holes to place the gelignite. "Time for a break, Mickey. Here's a thermos flask of cold water."

"Thanks, mate, I could drink a bucketful."

Mickey dropped the hand drill and promptly squatted on the mine floor amid the debris of broken rocks and claystone. "Take a look at that one," he pointed to a clump of whitish-yellow claystone.

Thumbing away the loose stone, pinpoints of light and colour were picked up by the light. CJ whistled in appreciation. "It's beautiful." The find began to glow a pale yellowish-blue.

"What's it like up top?"

"So bloody hot you could fry eggs and bacon on the VW's roof. The thermometer says it's 108 degrees, but I think it's shot. Have you noticed, it doesn't go above 108 or drop below 95 degrees?"

Mickey grinned cheekily up at him. "Well, I'm glad I'm in here and you're working up there."

Both men knew there was little difference in the physical energy needed to work either in the mine or above it. The real difference was that the mine stayed approximately fifty degrees Celsius where on the surface it did not.

"Lucky bugger." C_ _ _ _ _ _ _ _ _ _ _ _ _ _ _ _ _ position against the mi_ _ _ _ _ _ _ _ _ _ _ _ _ _ _ _ you dehydrate."

"Okay. I'm setting n_ _ _ _ _ _ _ _ _ _ _ _ _ _ to the thin milky whit_ _ _ _ _ _ _ _ _ _ _ _ _ level. "This one looks _ _ _ _ _ _ _ _ _ _ _

CJ laughed. "That's _ _ _ _ _ _ _ _ _ _ _

Leaving Mickey to _ _ _ _ _ _ _ _ _ _ _ and started to load _ _ _ _ _ _ _ _ _ _ fourteen bucket loads

sh_
Wh_
and rap_
Particles o_
throat, making_
his pocket for a ra_
"Mickey! Mickey.

getting the mullock up to the surface then painstakingly noodling for small pieces of colour.

All was quiet above ground, the barren landscape with its mullock dumps resembled what CJ imagined could look like an alien world. Not a bird, a breath of breeze or a sound broke the silence. And as always, the unrelenting sun beat down from a cloudless sky. The only noise CJ was aware of was his heavy breathing as he hand winched up the load. The sturdy timber frame which held the pulley creaked protestingly, like the rope, as it wound around and around. He locked the device and as fast as his aching muscles would allow removed the buckets from the platform.

In the process of returning the platform to the mine floor he heard a noise. The sound was completely foreign to him and in the stillness, he couldn't identify it. Until a whooshing sound and a cloud of dust shot up the shaft. Then came another sound, a scream. CJ froze as realisation hit him.

Cave-in!

By tradition, opal mining in Coober Pedy, compared to gold and silver mining, was relatively safe from cave-ins. The clay and claystone hills were so stable that timber shoring wasn't necessary. Occasionally, rarely, gelignite would displace a pile of loose earth behind the claystone mine wall or roof resulting in what opal miners called a
ide.

th his heart pounding, CJ grabbed his miner's hat
idly descended the ladder into the darkness.
 dust flew into his mouth and clogged his
him cough. Automatically he reached into
ged handkerchief to tie around his face.
Where are you?"

CJ's ears strained to catch some sound, anything. The light hit a mound of claystone across the drive. It rose about one and a half metres to half block the rest of the mine. *Shit.* Comprehension came quickly. Part of the roof had collapsed into the mine leaving a gaping vertical shaft. But where was Mickey? He stared at the pile of rubble and then he lunged forward and began to dig furiously with his hands.

"Mickey, Jesus Christ, where are you?"

CHAPTER TWO

CJ's hands touched something soft. Material. Grunting with the effort he grabbed a handful and pulled with all his might. The claystone and rocks fell away to expose Mickey's head and torso.

In the weak light CJ saw blood oozing from a head wound encrusted with earth. Silly bastard hadn't been wearing his hat. Damn his casual attitude. He tugged some more and Mickey coughed then groaned. Thank God, he wasn't dead. With more hand digging and tugging, enhanced by a series of voluble curses, CJ released his partner's unconscious body from its premature grave.

He lay him on the dirt floor and checked him over. To the best of his limited medical knowledge there were no broken bones. The wound on his head looked bad though, the blood now flowing freely, staining the earth. CJ ripped off his shirt and wrapped it around Mickey's head as a make-do bandage. He trained his light on the roof above the cave-in. Pieces of rock and sand continued to rain down intermittently. He knew he had to get him out of the drive quickly, in case another cave-in occurred. The platform!

Half carrying, half dragging him, CJ got his burden to the shaft. He looked up to the circle of blue sky eighty or so metres up, wondering if he could fit Mickey's body on the platform. He'd need ropes to tie him to it. Scampering up the ladder at top speed he found what he needed and went back down with the platform. It took a precious fifteen minutes to manoeuvre the unconscious Mickey onto the platform and another fifteen to haul him to the surface.

Mickey's groans had stopped and CJ noted that his skin had turned deathly white. Shock. How much blood had he lost? Too much probably. The dark colour began to seep through the folds of his shirt. He needed to put something else around the wound. Running into the dugout he tore a sheet off the bunk, ripping it into a wide bandage strip. Somehow, later on, he couldn't quite remember how he carried Mickey to the VW and laid him in the back.

Don't die, Mickey. Don't die, he chanted as he drove at breakneck speed towards town.

For two days Mickey Edgars hovered between life and death. The Flying Doctor Service had advised Sister Damien at the hospital on what to look for and if his condition failed to stabilise they'd fly in and take him to the closest hospital with medical staff. CJ stayed almost constantly at Mickey's bedside and Mary, who'd come to know and like CJ's partner over the past few months visited too, keeping the man she loved company and praying for Mickey.

On the third day Mickey showed signs of regaining consciousness, coming out of the deep coma his head injury had caused. Everyone breathed a sigh of relief.

"Go home and get a good night's sleep," Mary suggested to CJ from the other side of the hospital bed.

Her dark eyes studied the man around whom her life revolved. CJ looked awful. His eyes were bloodshot, he hadn't shaved in days and he was still wearing the torn, dirty clothes he'd been in when he had dug Mickey out of the mine.

"Soon," he promised. "When Mickey wakes up and recognises me." Throughout his vigil the one thought dominating his mind was that it could have been him lying in the hospital bed. If he had been placing the gelly instead of removing the potch he would have collected the cave-in. Talk about luck.

He'd always been a lucky bastard though. A wild buffalo had gored him years ago up around the Daly River and missed ripping his liver out by a couple of centimetres. And that fight in Kalgoorlie with the dago – he could have been cut to ribbons. Not to mention all the spills he'd had off horses. Christ, he'd never even broken a bloody bone. His sister said he was like a cat, had nine lives, at least.

"Let's go to the hotel and have something to eat," Mary suggested. "You haven't had a decent meal for days."

CJ allowed himself to be convinced that was the right thing to do. Just as they were leaving a faint moan from the bed stopped them in their tracks.

"CJ, that you?" came weakly from the bed.

For a big man CJ swung around fast and returned to Mickey's side. He gripped the older man's hand firmly. "Mickey, old mate. You've finally woken up. I thought you were trying for the Rip van Winkle record. How do you feel?"

Mickey opened one eye for a second or two and squinted against the light. He saw Mary standing beside CJ and grinned weakly. "Can't tell you, mate, there's a lady present."

"That's okay. I've probably heard more colourful language in the bar anyway."

"Yeah, right. I feel like shit." Mickey's eyes closed and he drifted off again.

They tiptoed from the room and CJ heaved a relieved sigh. "He's going to be all right." Knowing that made him suddenly aware that his stomach was growling ominously. "Now I could do justice to a good feed. Come on," and he grabbed Mary by the forearm and ushered her out into the late afternoon sunshine.

The first time CJ went down the mine after the cave-in a chill ran from the top of his neck to the end of his spine. The silence was eerie and he could have sworn there were ghostly shadows playing at the edge of the light waiting to claim him too. He knew such thoughts were fanciful nonsense but he had them anyway as he cautiously picked his way along the eighteen metre drive using a powerful torch combined with the light from his miner's hat. The last nine metres or so, where Mickey had been working before the cave-in, was full of debris. He grunted with disgust as the torch light ran over the amount of sand and claystone, estimating that almost half a ton had collapsed into the drive. It would take more than a day's work to clear it. But before he could do anything he had to make the drive's roof safe. Probably have to shore up a rough ceiling to protect them from more trouble too.

He shone the torch along the wall towards the gaping hole. Something caught the light. Quartz? Agate? Maybe. He checked all around the hole to make sure there was no active crumbling and then he scrambled to the top of the claystone heap to investigate the glint. Gently brushing the dried, sandy soil aside he found a horizontal trace of potch. Something in the rock sparkled; tiny mosaics of colour winked at him.

Shock caused him to almost topple off the heap. There, exposed by the cave-in lay a level of opal. It ran a good fifty centimetres upwards then disappeared into solid claystone. Contrary to normal the vein ran vertically, not horizontally. With a patience that belied his excitement, his trembling hand exposed a small part of the vein. The colours were magnificent.

He dislodged a piece, held it up to the torch light, then licked the rough stone and held it to the light again. Prisms of colour sparkled at him. A fire opal, one of the most prized types of opal and, from the look of it, the vein was huge. Rich.

"Yippee. *You little beauty*!" His voice echoed hollowly along the shaft.

CJ scampered down the pile of rubble and did a stomping dance of joy in the narrow drive, scraping his arms and shoulders against the solid walls. You lucky, lucky bastard. Fascinated, his torch light danced on the exposed vein of opal again. You've done it. Well, actually, Mickey had done it … and it had almost cost him his life. He did a rough calculation of what the discovery could be worth. Forty, maybe seventy-five to eighty thousand dollars. He and Mickey – who'd never owned much more than the clothes he stood up in – were going to be rich. Filthy, bloody rich.

Work, man. Get to work. *Think*. First he had to shovel the debris out of the way so he could get a ladder up to the vein. Then he'd shore it up and by God, a grain of claystone wouldn't move unless he gave it permission. But he wouldn't tell Mickey until his condition had improved. The fewer people who knew the better. Their valuable find wasn't going to be ratted by some enterprising lowlife around the diggings.

He ran back to the shaft and found a shovel, his thoughts going this way and that in a flurry of activity. He could fill up one of the useless drives they'd previously explored – even though the practice was illegal – instead of taking the mullock up to the top. That would save time and energy. Now, he grinned hugely into the near blackness of the drive, CJ Ambrose's dream had come true. He was on his way.

CJ and Mary were taking a walk after seeing Mickey and then enjoying a meal at the one cafe in town. On impulse CJ turned to her and said, "Come on, I want to take you out to the mine."

"Now?" Mary knew it was an hour's drive there and back. In truth, she'd rather they spend the time here, together, rather than travelling along a bumpy dirt track into the hot, dry desert. But tonight she'd noted that he seemed wired tighter than a spring, as if he was bursting to tell her something but couldn't. He kissed her full on the lips and she blushed because a couple across the street saw them. "CJ ..." she whispered in that gentle, warning way of hers.

"Do come, Mary. It's important," he pleaded, running his fingers through her hair.

When he asked so nicely how could she say no? Besides, she had something to tell him too. "All right, but I can't be too late. I'm rostered on for breakfast duty tomorrow."

"You're so conscientious," he said with a chiding laugh. "What would the Farbers do if you just didn't turn up? They'd survive."

"I couldn't do that. They're my employers. I have a duty to them."

He shook his head with amusement as they made their way to the VW. Mary was a funny little thing. She had firm ideas on correct behaviour and what was right and wrong – no doubt drummed into her by the nuns at the mission school. Yet when he held her in his arms, she melted like liquid fire. Just thinking of her responses made him go hard with wanting. When they were at the dugout …

By the time they reached the M45 mine, darkness had fallen like a blanketing fog over the desert landscape. Mary had only been to the mine site a couple of times, once to celebrate Mickey's thirty-eighth birthday. Illuminated by the van's headlights, the starkness of the countryside pockmarked with its mullock dumps from the various opal mines, the lack of colour and the dryness didn't appeal to her at all. Where she'd been brought up, there had been trees and shrubs and the odd patch of grass. The topography of the opal fields was like no other place on earth that she had seen or read about.

CJ jerked the van to a halt with a squeal of brakes and jumped out with his torch already in hand. It was a moonless night and with the torchlight to guide him he strode over to the petrol generator and fired it up. Immediately two beams of light lit up the area, outlining the make-do timbers and galvanised iron wall of the dugout, and the circular hole which was the entrance to the M45 mine.

"Come on, out you get," CJ commanded as he opened the van door and without waiting for her he moved in the direction of the mine shaft. "You're not worried about dark narrow places, are you? I mean, you're not claustrophobic?"

"I don't know," Mary shrugged her shoulders. The hole yawned gloomy and uninviting with just the top of the ladder visible. "Why do you want me to go down there, CJ?"

"I've something to show you," he said, barely able to contain his excitement. He had worked the level for two days, with very little sleep in-between, exposing the vein and marvelling at the extent of the find. Mickey still didn't know that he was going to be a rich man. Disappointingly, his recovery was slower than expected, but CJ had an idea that it was because Sister Damien was young, attractive and unattached. The skull fracture had been severe and Mickey had to spend several more days resting up, according to the sister. CJ champed at the bit to tell him the news and tomorrow he intended to take what he'd chipped out to show his partner. That would buck Mickey up and, he had no doubt, speed his recovery.

Mary peered into the hole. "It looks pretty dark down there. I don't think ..."

CJ flicked a switch on a board and a series of lights lit up the shaft. "I bought these from the general store yesterday. They work off a twelve volt battery. It's as good as daylight down there now."

He gave her a hug and a brief kiss on the cheek, then he proceeded to climb down the ladder until he'd reached the main horizontal drive. With some reluctance Mary descended, trying not to think of Mickey and the cave-in, or whether spiders or other nocturnal nasties inhabited the place. She was relieved when CJ took her hand and half dragged her along behind him. Finally they reached the drive that contained the opal vein. It too was lit by the light.

"There. See."

Mary looked up and her eyes widened. Opal, illuminated by the strong light, stood out clearly. The colours were wonderful. Milky-white, red, blue, yellow and green sparkled inside a translucent coating. Through Mickey and CJ and overhearing conversations at the bar, she had picked up quite a bit of information on opals. She knew she was staring at a considerable find.

"Oh, it's so beautiful, CJ. I can't believe it."

"I wanted you to see it before I started chipping the stones out. Tomorrow I'll take some to show Mickey. Boy, is he in for a surprise."

Exuberantly, she threw her arms around him and kissed him full on the lips. "Congratulations, CJ," she whispered. "Now you can do the things you've planned to do, those things you told me about."

"Yeah." CJ stilled in her arms. Maybe he'd talked too much to her about his future plans for a station and breeding cattle, and other things too. But she'd been so damned easy to talk to and interested, making him want to pour out his dreams to her. Suddenly a mental image of Brenda came to him, followed by a rare sense of guilt. Guilt for deceiving both of the women in his life. Brenda, to whom he'd promised marriage, and Mary, to whom he'd made no promises though he knew she had expectations.

With an effort he shrugged the feeling off, as well as the anxiety caused by a decision he'd soon have to make. "Let's go up top and celebrate. I've a bottle of French champagne in the fridge, the best Gus can get."

"I've never tasted champagne," Mary admitted as she watched the ritual of CJ popping the cork. She giggled with amusement as it fizzed over the top of his hand and onto the floor to be quickly absorbed by the hard-packed earth.

"There'll be lots more of this," he promised as he clinked their glasses together. He studied Mary as she drank her champagne and smiled at her simple enjoyment of it. There were no pretensions, no airs and graces about her, but then she was very young. She hadn't had time or enough exposure to life in general to have picked up any sophistication. Besides, there was precious little in a place like Coober Pedy. How would she fit into the life he planned to have one day? Could he see her greeting wealthy businessmen and society folk? Would she be able to cope with the demands of organising a dinner party for twenty? Would she want to? Christ, he didn't know the answer for sure but in his heart he doubted it. But ... she was lovely. Watching the shadows at play on her face and hair, he saw the beginnings of a beauty that was as much physical as it was spiritual. Yes! Like the precious opal he'd sought and found, Mary's beauty was internal and it enhanced her visual attractiveness tenfold.

He reached for her and led her to the bottom bunk on which he'd thoughtfully put clean sheets that day.

"So, this is the real reason you brought me out here, to have your wicked way with me," she teased.

He kissed her with a passion that was suddenly fierce. "Too right ..."

In the aftermath of their lovemaking CJ lay on his back with Mary pressed into his side cuddling him.

"CJ?"

"Mmmm," came his sleepy response. His sexual appetite sated, tiredness from a hard day's work and a hard hour's loving was taking its toll.

"I've something to tell you, and you've got to promise not to be angry."

"Why," he said with a yawn, "would I be angry?"

"I'm not sure." She hoped his delight would equal hers. "You might be."

"Tell me and we'll see."

"Well, I'm late." She held her breath and waited but the response she expected didn't come.

"Late for what?"

"You know," she elbowed him gently in the ribs to bring him to a higher state of wakefulness. "My monthlies. I'm two weeks overdue."

His body stiffened. "What!" He sat up and dragged her up to face him. "What do you mean? You haven't had your period? But ... you're on the pill. You've been taking it, haven't you?" In his growing anger he gave her a little shake.

"Yes, yes. I don't know what's wrong. I followed the instructions on the leaflet but," her huge brown eyes pleaded for understanding, "I think I'm pregnant." She had other symptoms too. Like morning sickness and sore breasts and for some strange reason she had a craving for strawberries which were unattainable this far north of Adelaide.

His blue eyes hardened. "You might just be late. Have you seen a doctor?"

"Not yet. The regular doctor's visit isn't until next week. I wanted to tell you first. I don't want other people to know. It's a small town and you know how everyone gossips."

"Yeah, well, it'll be a bit hard to hide that sort of thing after a couple of months, won't it?"

He couldn't look at her. At the same time he tried to hold his anger and disappointment down, with difficulty. "Christ Almighty, this is what I didn't want to happen. Damn, damn, damn." He got up and, still naked, stomped around the dugout.

This development complicated matters more than he cared to think about. It soured everything. Discovering the opals, knowing that he was going to be rich. His dream.

Damn her stupidity, and her innocence. *He* hadn't done anything wrong, she had.

He saw her crying softly, quietly, and grabbing his trousers he got dressed and sat on the bunk next to her. "Don't." He took her hand. "Look, Mary, the first thing is to have it confirmed whether or not you're pregnant. We'll take matters from there. There are options, you know." Yeah. Someone must know some place where it could be gotten rid of. That would be best for both of them. Hardening his heart to the appeal in her eyes he made the decision he'd hoped to put off for a while. For too many years he'd dreamt the dream and the power of it was too strong for him to be turned from it. Mary wasn't right for him, kid or no kid. Brenda deWitt fitted into his future needs more than Mary could ever hope to. And, he wasn't going to marry her to give the baby a name and a home. No, sir! With bullheaded determination he pushed the guilt from his mind. Mary was young, she'd get over it.

"Come on, get dressed, love. I'll drive you back to Coober."

Mary did so in a state of shock. He hadn't said what she'd desperately hoped he would. That he was overjoyed, that they'd get married straightaway. She could feel him retreating from her, sense the hardness in him coming to the surface. Dear God, what was she going to do? She couldn't make him marry her. CJ was the type of man who liked to run things, to call the shots and if he didn't ask her ...

Without conscious thought she dressed and combed her hair and with the jerky movements of a sleepwalker followed him out to the van.

CJ was up the ladder carefully chipping away at the opal bearing level – as he had been for the past week – when he heard the repeated bipping of a car horn as it approached the mine. By the time the car halted he was on the last rung of the ladder staring curiously at his visitor.

Gus Farber. Why on earth would he be visiting CJ?

"Hi, Gus. Didn't know you were interested in opal mines," he welcomed him with a grin. "Want a beer?"

"I'm not, and there's no time for a beer, CJ. I," the German stumbled over his words. "There's trouble. Mary asked me to come and tell you about Mickey."

CJ wiped his dirty hands on a rag he kept in his back pocket. "I saw him last night. Sister Damien said she'd discharge him tomorrow. What's wrong?"

Gus shuffled from one foot to the other and thrust his huge hands into his trouser pockets. "He had a fall this morning, in the shower, so the sister said. Cracked his skull open and," he glanced across at CJ and saw that he had his full attention, "it doesn't look good, mate. The sister thinks he's had a … cerebral haemorrhage. Gone into a coma again. The Flying Doctor Service is coming but she thinks he's not gonna come out of this one."

"Christ Almighty!" The breath whooshed out of a shocked CJ. He tried to grasp what Gus was telling him. "I can't believe it."

"Sister Damien says to come quick. Mickey's breathing's all funny. She don't reckon he'll last till the FDS gets here."

CJ turned away from Gus and slowly exhaled. A chill ran all the way through him. Mickey. *No.* Fighting to control his emotions he balled his hands into tight fists. He'd experienced this sense of helpless frustration before. When his grandfather had died, and then his mother. For God's sake get a grip, he ordered himself. But Mickey Edgars was the closest thing he'd had to a real mate in years. He blinked rapidly to push back a suspicious moistness. Tough men don't cry, he remembered his dad telling him at his mother's and grandfather's funeral.

Groaning, CJ grabbed the blue checked shirt he'd hung over the mine's winch, he pulled it on in a jerky movement. "Let's go then."

Mickey's death hit CJ harder than he would have thought possible. He was utterly distraught. To him it was inconceivable that the little man with the perky ways, energy, and love of life was now forever quiet and still.

The day of the funeral CJ got roaring, fighting, mad drunk – his way of dealing with the pain – until Gus had to restrain him by locking him in one of his storerooms until he sobered up. In the light of day and with a massive hangover he seemed to recover his self-control and went back to the M45 mine to work the grief out of his system.

Mary watched as he retreated into himself, and was at a loss to know what to do to help him. He had distanced himself from her since she had confirmed her pregnancy as if, by pretending it didn't exist, the problem would go away. She knew they had to talk but CJ wasn't in a talking mood. He had become consumed by an all encompassing passion to gouge the precious opal from its earthly hiding place, day in day out.

Two weeks after Mickey's funeral CJ came into town on Saturday night and waited until Mary had finished working. They sat in his van afterwards, talking. Mary sensed the tension in him as if it were a tangible thing, and in her naivety regarding relationships, she didn't know how to bridge the gap that had developed between them. He had stopped touching her too, which hurt immeasurably. It was as if she had become an acquaintance instead of his lover. That hurt too. But, unbearable as it was, she bore it, hoping against all hope for a change in him, a softening.

"New people have bought the general store," she told him, trying for an impersonal topic to break the ice. "Gus says they're immigrants and that they plan to open a cafe as well. I might try for a job with them." Waiting on cafe tables had to be better than serving alcohol in a hotel bar.

"Immigrants, hey? They'll fit right in here," CJ said with a disinterested grunt.

She acknowledged that with a nod of her head. More than half of Coober Pedy's inhabitants were foreigners who'd come here with the dream of finding their fortune in the desert town, which some likened to a twentieth-century version of an American frontier town.

Out of the blue, CJ said, "I think we should get away for a while. You'd love Adelaide, Mary, it's a real pretty city. You've always wanted to see the place. You could buy some new clothes and shoes and we'll take in the sights. Come with me, Mary."

Hope began to beat inside her breast. Perhaps he was suggesting a new start for them – together. She allowed herself to hope again. "I'd love to go. When?"

"As soon as you can fix it with Gus. You've been working for him for more than six months. You'd be entitled to a week's holiday, I guess."

"I'll ask him tomorrow." She looked across shyly at him, still unsure of his motives and his mood. "Are you staying in town tonight?"

CJ shook his head. He didn't tell her that the level of precious opal had just about petered out, or that he'd lost the will to start a new search. It was time to move on – sell his cache of opals and make his dream come true.

"I've work to do at the mine. I'll come in tomorrow afternoon for a bite to eat and you can tell me what you've organised. We'll drive to Tarcoola and get the train to Adelaide. How does that sound?"

Her eyes sparkled. "Wonderful."

CJ took Mary to Glenelg, the most popular beach in Adelaide. They travelled there on a rattly old tram which had delighted Mary. Being late autumn it was too cool to swim but despite the cold she removed her shoes and paddled in the Great Southern Ocean as they walked along the shoreline.

Her eyes were wide with amazement as she gazed out beyond the line of breakers. "I had no idea the ocean was so huge. It just goes on forever, doesn't it?"

"Yeah. All the way to Antarctica."

"It's beautiful and scary."

He frowned. "Why's that?"

She watched a two metre wave peak and crash into the surf. "It's so fierce and untameable."

"It is that." He laughed briefly. "I went to sea once, to see if I liked it. I didn't. I spent half the time in my bunk being seasick and the seas weren't that rough. That helped me decide that a landlubber's life was for me." He looked down at her feet. "Mary, your feet are turning blue. We've time for a walk along the wharf and an ice-cream then we'd better be going. I promised to take you shopping, don't you remember? We'll dine out in style tonight so you'll need a new outfit."

The thought of dining out in a posh Adelaide restaurant filled Mary with a sense of dread and nervousness. She feared she would touch or do or say the wrong thing. But really she knew she shouldn't worry. Since they'd arrived

CJ had been almost his old self so she was trying hard not to annoy him.

"Of course. I want to buy some things to take back to Coober Pedy." Baby things, but she didn't tell him that. There was little to be gained by mentioning the baby and possibly starting an argument. Perhaps CJ just needed time to get used to the idea of being a father. Some men did, she'd heard.

The city of Adelaide was a revelation to Mary Williams. Coming from the bush she had never seen the like. The roads were wide and straight, the buildings majestically tall and the many churches – of several denominations with their fine architecture, spires, and limestone carvings – were wondrous to behold. So were the parks and the diverse shrubs which grew profusely. She had never seen such colour or beauty in anything other than books. And there were streets and streets of shops with all kinds of merchandise for sale. She went about goggle-eyed at the variety of wares, and at the prices asked. CJ insisted on paying for everything. That rankled a little. She was independent enough not to want him to, but deep inside it pleased her that he offered, and she chose to believe it was a further sign of commitment.

They were staying at an expensive hotel in separate rooms with an inter-connecting bathroom between them. They went everywhere in taxis. And if the truth were known she was enjoying being spoilt and cosseted. No-one had ever made a fuss of her before but CJ made her feel special. So, perhaps naively, she saw that as a sign that he was coming around and would, she hoped, before they returned to Coober Pedy, ask her to marry him.

They spent three leisurely days exploring Adelaide. CJ crammed so much into their daytime activities that straight after dinner fatigue overtook Mary and all she'd want to do was climb into bed and sleep.

On the fourth day, after breakfast in the hotel's dining room, CJ broke from their topic of conversation to say, "I want you to see a doctor, Mary. Just to check things out."

"Why? The doctor comes to Coober Pedy regularly and there's the FDS for emergencies. As well, Sister Damien's a midwife. That's enough, surely?"

"Just for me. Please?" he coaxed, smiling.

CJ was irresistible when he smiled. "Very well." Besides, wasn't this another sign that he cared and that he wanted everything to be right for her and the baby?

They took a taxi to the address: a neat, unassuming claystone house in the suburb of Frewville. Inside, in the foyer, a nurse in white showed them to a small waiting room.

Mary wrinkled her nose at the lingering odour of methylated spirits. It reminded her of the hospital and Mickey. She missed Mickey Edgars and his bright ways. The little man had been blessedly uncomplicated, not like CJ. The man she loved seethed with ambition and energy and continual schemes for making money. Even now when the M45 mine was making him wealthy she sensed that he wanted more. With a wisdom beyond her years she realised CJ would always be that way, driven by the need to be bigger, and to have more than the next man.

A squat, bespectacled man wearing a white cotton coat came into the room and introduced himself. "I'm Doctor Becker." He looked at Mary and smiled reassuringly. "Tell me, my dear, how far are you into the pregnancy?"

"Twelve weeks, doctor."

"Good." The doctor nodded meaningfully at CJ. "Any further along and there would be considerable risk."

"What risk?" Mary asked, perplexed. "What do you mean, doctor?"

"Err, Mary," CJ took her by the elbow and motioned her towards the window. "Doctor Becker is a special kind of doctor." He looked into her eyes as he held both her hands, as if compelling her by his will alone to obey him. "I don't want this baby, you know that. I'm not in a position to offer you anything official or legal. You understand? I have a commitment to someone else up north. Do you understand what I'm trying to say, Mary?" Without waiting for an acknowledgment he rushed on. "But ... I am concerned about you and your welfare. Having a baby could ruin your life. The stigma, you know, on unmarried mothers is still severe, especially in country towns."

"CJ ..." The revelation hit her hard – *he was engaged to another woman*. Oh, God, no!

"Listen to me, Mary. You're very young. You'll get over this and find someone who's just right for you. You'll get married and start a family then – not now."

"I don't understand, I thought ..." What had she thought? She had thought this trip meant something special to him. It didn't. It was his way of saying goodbye. *Another woman*! The harsh reality of what he'd said drummed into her brain. The nuns had been right, it was foolish to trust a man. Another thing was true too, they only had one thing on their mind.

"It doesn't hurt too much, Miss Williams. Just some discomfort and a pricking sensation. That's all. Then everything comes away naturally," Doctor Becker said matter-of-factly. "I'll give you a light anaesthetic – you'll hardly feel a thing."

Mary stared at CJ and suddenly understood what kind

of a doctor Becker really was. "You brought me here for an abortion?" she cried.

He nodded affirmatively. "It's for the best, Mary. You mightn't see it now, but later on you will. Of that I'm sure."

"Well, damn you, CJ Ambrose, I'm not, I won't do it! How could you ask me? I'm Catholic, for God's sake – it's a sin." Her wits were scattering to the four corners of the room. She couldn't believe he wanted this. "Don't you have any feeling for me or the child? Your child," she reminded him pointedly. An intense pain tore into her heart and squeezed it violently. How could she love such a cold, calculating man? Didn't he care for her at all, didn't he have any sensitivity as to how she felt, or what she wanted?

Sensing the matter was getting heated the doctor moved to leave. "I'll wait in my office until you finish your discussion."

"I'm thinking of you, Mary –"

"Bullshit!" She never swore but now, suddenly, she was beside herself with anger. All those months, thinking he'd loved her as she loved him. Lies. Lies! "You're thinking of yourself. Solely of yourself. All right, so you don't want to marry me, that's pretty clear. I see *everything* clearly now. I was just a source of amusement for you, while you were away from your precious fiancée. But," her chin lifted, "you are not going to make me give up my child."

"Listen to me," he shook her by the shoulders, "it's not my life that'll be ruined, it's yours."

"I don't care." She raised her hand to prise his fingers away from her. "Don't touch me. I love this baby we made together and I will have it, with or without your support." She looked him up and down as if she were seeing him clearly for the first time, and disliking what she saw. The trouble was she still loved him, even though she now saw him in his true light. More fool her!

"You've made your fortune and you didn't even have to share it with Mickey," she reminded him. "Why don't you take your precious opals back to your sweetheart? Show her, I'm sure she'll be impressed." Her brown eyes moved about the sterile environment and when they returned to CJ they were full of loathing. "I want to get out of here. This place and *you* make me sick to my stomach."

The next day Mary returned to Coober Pedy on the train without CJ. She never saw him again.

"CJ. CJ, are you awake?"

A voice roused CJ from his memories. He jerked upright in the chair. His hand ran through his thinning grey hair and then stroked the stubble on his cheek. He listened to the rasping sound beneath his fingers.

"CJ?"

"I'm all right, leave me alone." He heard Natalie's purposely loud sigh through the solid oak door and grinned. His stepdaughter would hate being discharged like this, but he didn't care. He'd needed time alone. Things to come to terms with. Memories to put into their rightful place.

"It's getting late. Shellie thought you might want something to eat. She's worried about you."

"Well, I'm fine. Go away." CJ's tone was deliberately dismissive just to annoy her. He liked getting Natalie's dander up. Always had. Ever since he'd married Brenda and become Natalie's stepfather, he'd enjoyed getting under her skin. In many ways they were alike, too alike. Quick-tempered, ambitious, ruthless. Unfortunately, she had other character traits that weren't to his liking – cattiness, a common tongue and she lied – and in all her thirty years of living with him a subtle cold war had gone on between them. The verbal skirmishes had escalated since Brenda's death as his wife had been the only one able to keep Natalie in line. And now ... and now, with Richard gone she would be regarded by all and sundry – including herself – as his rightful, his only heir.

Hell and damnation. A deep-seated growl, like that of a discontented lion, rumbled from his throat and his lined features expressed his distaste. The thought of Natalie ruling his empire was not palatable, by any stretch of the imagination. At one time he had hoped that she and Les Westcott would make a match, but now they seemed totally incompatible. In deep contemplation the fingers of both his hands drummed staccato like on the sides of the chair.

With his gaze focused again on the photo of the opal, for the first time in twenty-six years he *allowed* himself to consciously think about the child, Mary's child, as a real person. What would he, or she, be like? The child would be about a year older than Richard. How had Mary fared raising him on her own? He'd sent her money before he'd left Adelaide, a bank cheque for ten thousand dollars. That would have set her up well enough, if she'd used it carefully. She never had. The bank had informed him the cheque had been returned and the money credited back to his account. Damned independent woman, Mary Williams. Then, in the wink of a mere second he was swept by an aching, desperate longing to know about the child. About Mary. To try to make amends for the wrong he'd done both of them, but that was impossible. Too many years had passed and, for all he knew she was most likely happily married to someone else.

Even so, his right hand reached for the bottom drawer of the desk. He opened it and retrieved an old tin. Rummaging through the contents he found a photo and pulled it out. The photo was dog-eared and badly faded. It showed a young woman in a cotton dress. *Mary.*

It wasn't often he admitted the error of his ways, he was too bullheaded and ruthless to dwell on them and the finer points of life. But in Mary's case he should have done more. Made her take the money and seen her set up so that she'd be comfortable, only at the time he'd felt so damned guilty over what he'd tried to get her to do, he'd wanted to get as far away as he could from Coober Pedy. She had once been very important to him but not as important as his dream of being successful. He had allowed nothing, not Mary, not Brenda, not even his son Richard to come before that.

Nostalgically his thoughts returned to his son, gone, forever. His mouth turned down in a travesty of a smile. Perhaps God was finally getting even with him for what he'd done to Mary. Well, he was paying a higher price than he'd ever thought possible.

CHAPTER THREE

Aden Nicholson leant his tall, trim frame against the office door jamb to better observe the woman bent over a large drawing board. A fax sheet lay loosely in his right hand and he slid his left hand into his trouser pocket. A contemplative smile hovered around his mouth as he watched her, while silently he marvelled that she could remain so still, or relatively still, for so long.

Francesca Spinetti, Francey to everyone, Chief Assistant Architect at Nicholson, Drew and Carlyle, was such a bundle of energy and Italian volatility that her ability to concentrate when she was drawing up a plan constantly amazed him. Aden had enough nous though, considering her capacity to speak her mind at an instant's notice, not to mention it to her. Francey had come to work for the firm after graduating with honours from Sydney University. In a few short years she had livened up the traditional thinking of his architectural firm more so than any other architect had done in Sydney for years with her *nouveau* architectural designs, her love of colour and of mixing the traditional with the ultra modern.

"You know I don't like people looking over my shoulder when I'm working." Her tone was soft, a touch husky, and she spoke without lifting her head from the drawing board.

"Is that the thanks I get for lobbying the partners to let you have your own office with good light?" Aden retaliated as he came into the room. "I'm not watching what you're drawing," he added softly, "I'm watching you."

Francey's mop of long dark curls that swayed at every twitch and turn of her head jerked up from the drawing board as she turned to look at him. "Well, it's nice to know that the boss has so much leisure time." Her direct gaze studied his angular features, the dark hair, the wide shoulders. He would strip well, she thought. Yoicks! What on earth had made her think that? He was her employer, for God's sake. His remark, personal without a doubt – I'm watching you – had set her thoughts along lines not at all related to work.

He grinned boyishly as he sat on the side of her desk. "Mmmm, one of the perks of being the boss, wouldn't you say?" He liked the way they fenced verbally with each other and especially liked the undertone of attraction that shivered invisibly between them. It had become more pronounced since they'd worked together on a few projects. There. Just below the surface. Not that he'd made a move in that direction. Yet.

Actually, why he hadn't he still didn't understand. Maybe he hesitated to step over the employer/employee line or the obvious social differences between them. There wasn't much he didn't like about Francey Spinetti though. She was easy on the eye, as the saying went. Wide-set, huge blue-green eyes, lustrous black hair that seemed to have a mind of its own, just like its owner, and she was unusually tall and slender for someone of Italian extraction.

He shook himself out of his reverie and became all business. "How's the plan for the Monroe building going?"

"Slowly." She gave him a droll look. "Mainly because Mr Monroe and his board of directors keep changing their minds about what they want."

"Problems?" She shrugged her shoulders, giving him a tantalising glimpse of pink lace between the vee of her deeper pink blouse. Her just-a-fraction-too-wide pink lipsticked lips pursed in contemplation. They were very kissable lips. Oh, yes, he'd fantasised about them often lately.

"Nothing I can't handle," Francey told him. "Their indecisiveness slows the process, that's all."

"Well, make the best of it. We don't want Monroe upset. He's too important a client. This," he passed her the fax he'd been holding, "might cheer you up."

Francey read the fax and grinned, well, it started as a grin and then it became a wide, radiant smile that lit up her whole face. She re-read the most important part again out loud. "Your design: the one hectare Swayne's apartment building, shopping complex and marina is confirmed as one of the finalists in the medium density under three point five million freestanding Australian Architectural Design awards."

"Aden, this is wonderful." Her hands went into action and she began to gesticulate wildly. "I can hardly believe it."

The Swayne's complex had been her most ambitious and successful project to date. Completed six months ago, after eighteen months building time, she was inordinately proud of the design which combined the latest building materials and blended them in such a way that they harmonised with the surrounding neighbourhood and the water views of Tambourine Bay. Matthew Drew and Tony Carlyle, Aden's other partners, had been critical of the innovative design, wanting to opt for something more traditional, but Aden, the senior partner, had the ruling vote and had backed Francey up. He'd given her her head and Alex Swayne had waxed lyrical far and wide about the finished product. The apartments and the small, exclusive stores had sold in record time and the ultra modern marina was filling with permanent berths fast.

"It is good news. You're a contender for an award, Francey. Pretty fantastic, considering you've not been working that long." His grey eyes began to twinkle with mischievous anticipation. "Which means you must wear something outrageously sexy when accepting the award."

She shook her head from side to side, causing her curly tresses to sway and curve around her face. "Aren't you being somewhat premature? I have to win it first."

"I have the utmost confidence that you will. You see, I've seen a couple of the other entries."

"Now you've done it!" She waggled an accusatory finger at him which made his features take on a bewildered look. "My concentration's shot for the next half-hour, just thinking about Thursday night." The venue for this year's awards dinner was The Regent. She'd been last year and it had been a huge yawn. However, she knew she wouldn't be bored this year. But she wouldn't enjoy herself either because all evening she would be a bundle of nerves. Wait until she told mamma and papà. They wouldn't believe it.

"Take an early lunch," he suggested.

Eat? Who could think about food? But she said as a matter of form, "Good idea."

She rose from her stool and stretched. In low heels and standing to her full height she was twelve centimetres shorter than Aden.

"Would you like me to pick you up Thursday evening?" Aden offered.

"Thank you, but no. I'll get a taxi."

She went behind her desk and picked up her handbag while at the same time she reached for her navy blazer which lay casually over the back of her desk chair. She could just imagine what her father would think if he knew that Aden Nicholson, her boss, was showing a personal interest in her. He's very good husband material, her father would proclaim, and then she'd never hear the end of it. The situation was bad enough as it was. Every opportunity he got her father reminded her that she wasn't getting any younger. That she should be looking to settle down, get married – like her cousins. Since she'd achieved her degree he'd become the perennial nagger, wanting her to find a good man and give him and Lucia, her mother, a tribe of grandchildren. What a thought! She had too much to do career-wise. Her dream was to one day have a full partnership with Nicholson, Drew and Carlyle. And she'd never travelled. Before she turned thirty she wanted to see the ancient architecture of places she'd read about – Italy, Greece, England – as she had studied for her degree.

They walked together to the outer corridor beyond the large room in which four draughtsmen were employed to draw up the detailed plans of the architects. Aden left her at the foyer and went towards his own office. Like Francey, he knew it would be hard to concentrate for a while. Lately, Francey had that effect on him. Soon, he sensed, almost fatalistically, he'd have to do something about it.

"But Francey, *amore,* I don't understand. This drive, this ambition you have. Why you not want to marry a good man and have lots of *bambini*? That's what your mamma always wanted to do but," Carlo Spinetti shrugged his shoulders sadly, "we were only blessed once. With you."

Francey's throat muscles tightened. She regularly ate with her parents on Wednesday nights and this particular turn in the conversation always had the same effect on her, no matter how hard she tried for it not to. She'd tried over the years to make her point but her father still didn't understand.

"Papà, we've had this talk before. Many times. I don't know why I have this need inside me, this desire to be the best I can be at something. I can't explain it, but I can't ignore it either." She tried not to let the hurt show in her voice. "I thought you'd be happy for me. Being in contention for a national architectural award is quite an honour. Think of all the architects around Australia trying to win this award – hundreds! And even if I don't get a place just being short-listed will increase my value with Nicholson, Drew and Carlyle. Maybe they'll offer me a junior partnership next year."

Carlo shook his silver head, a mixture of consternation and frustration etched into his lined features, the expression in his dark eyes undecipherable. "Aahh, Francey, you'll end up an old maid. Alone and unloved," he opined as he slurped his minestrone soup.

"You'd rather I be like Rosa or Daniella?" They were her cousins, her Aunt Josie's children. "They've each pushed out a baby a year for the last three years. Well, no thank you. I don't want to be a baby factory, or be tied to a husband and live off the crumbs he graciously throws me." This was something of an exaggeration but her father's words stung, even though she knew that Rosa and Daniella were happy with their respective husbands, and they were wonderful mothers too.

"You're not getting any younger," Carlo pointed out. "One day you'll wake up in bed alone and you'll want those things. Marriage. Children. You might be wealthy and successful by then, but you'll be too old. And you'll be by yourself."

"I date," she said with a bored sigh. "Didn't I go to a wedding last week with Rocco Biviano?"

Carlo's head shook slightly. "Rocco is your second cousin. Big deal, as you young ones say."

"Papà, I've got plenty of time to settle down. I'm nowhere near thirty yet." Francey forced herself to breathe deeply, slowly, and not take offence because he didn't *mean* to hurt her. It was just that he had this thing about her getting married, and unlike some Italian-born fathers who tried to hold onto their single daughters, Carlo Spinetti was quite the opposite.

God, if she had a dollar for every time he'd made a comment about finding a man over the last four years, she'd own her much-loved VW beetle outright. For a moment her blue-green eyes snapped with the light of battle – she enjoyed a confrontation – and then her gaze darted about the kitchen her mother was so proud of. Finally, after years of agitating and not-so-gentle arguments Lucia had convinced her tight-fisted husband to have it modernised. And now, her mother, who loved to cook, while Francey did not, happily spent a good part of her days conjuring up wonderful food for her husband and daughter. No, she decided, no arguments tonight, she was too happy about being on the awards short-list.

Still, she had some understanding of her father's reasoning. Carlo and Lucia Spinetti were from Murge, a village near Minerveno, not far from Bari, on the south-eastern side of Italy. A few years after World War II they'd come to Australia to start a new life, and had brought many reminders of the old country with them. Family photos, hand-stitched linen, mementoes and the old ways with which they were familiar. And in her father's case, the traditional belief that women should marry early and devote their lives to their husbands, home, cooking and raising many *bambini*. Poor Papà. A well of compassion flowed through her as she remembered some of the stories he'd told her of his relatives, and where he'd grown up. The poverty had been unbelievable. Now, Carlo Spinetti was caught in a time warp, unable to catch up with twentieth-century technology, let alone the coming third millennium.

"Carlo, leave Francey alone," Lucia entered the debate as she dished up three plates of spaghetti marinara and placed a bowl of salad on the table. "We only see our daughter once a week. You stop the scolding. *Va bene?*"

Francey grinned at her mother, her mouth twitching to hold down a brief smile. Lucia Spinetti was one hundred and fifty two centimetres of Italian volatility. Packaged in a comfortable, still curvaceous figure and with greying hair arranged in a neat bun and dark, almost black eyes, she wasn't afraid to stand up to her larger, bombastic, sometimes overbearing husband. People said she got her temperament – if not her looks – from her mother.

"Thanks, Mamma." She dropped a grateful kiss on the top of her mother's head as she sat at the dinner table and put a serving of salad on her plate.

"Francey," Lucia said, "Meredith rang here earlier on. She and Brett are sailing on Sunday. She said if you want to come, you give her a call. *Va bene?*"

"Right, I'll ring her later. After dinner I'll show you the gown I'm going to wear to the awards dinner." And then she made a mental note to steer the conversation away from herself. She could always get her father to talk about the shop, how expensive fruit and vegetables were getting, how much more selective and critical the customers were. Yes, that was the safe way to go.

Francey smoothed down the black crepe tight skirt and posed this way and that in her parent's bedroom mirror. Yes. She was sure Aden would approve of her choice. What a good buy she'd made – off the rack too.

Carlo Spinetti looked up from the television where the ABC news was in progress. He sat in his favourite armchair, his hands wrapped around his coffee cup, waiting for the liquid to cool.

"*Porco cane.* Francey, where is the rest of your frock?"

Francey winked at her mother. "What do you mean, Papà?"

"It is indecent. You show too ... too much." His right hand gestured wildly across his chest. "You know."

Francey smiled. "Oh. Cleavage." The sophisticated black dress was a little more low-cut than she usually wore but not as scandalous as he tried to make out. "It's the fashion," she said airily, thinking, if he had his way she'd be buttoned up to the neck, with long sleeves and in high stepping lace-up boots. She hoped he wouldn't notice the thigh length side-split. That would set him off again. Then, sheer mischief made her add, "You say you want the men to notice me. Well, in this they will."

He shook his head and waggled a finger at her. "Disrespectful girl. I didn't raise you to speak that way to me."

"Oh, Papà, I'm only joking."

"Of course she is," Lucia came to her defence. "Pah, you are too old-fashioned, Carlo. You need to," she frowned as she looked at Francey, "how do you say it, *cara*?"

"Update yourself. Get in tune with the nineties. Get with it. Any of those phrases will do, Mamma."

"Two women in the house. What can a man do? You gang up on me," he complained half-heartedly.

"You look beautiful, Francesca," Lucia said as she reached up on her toes to kiss her daughter's cheek. "On Thursday night you will knock them dead, no?" she added with a smile. Her little girl had become a beautiful young woman with the fire, the spirit in her like she had once had. She glowed with good health and she had a body, oh, yes, and what a body. Not as voluptuous as Lucia had been in her youth, but more like a modern model only with more curves, thank God. She had watched the way male customers looked at her when she walked through the fruit shop to their flat. As if they could eat her right up. But a sudden sadness ran through her. Francesca wasn't interested in romance.

A strange need had taken possession of her as soon as she had graduated. She *had* to have a career. She *had* to be successful. The goal consumed her. Maybe because she had come from humble origins, she thought, and had something to prove. It was true, she and Carlo had never had much money. They made a living, worked long hours to do so and the truth was they came from a peasant background. Of that she was not ashamed, and she knew that her Francey was no snob. She just wanted different things. Back in the old country, she remembered, being a fruiterer was a time-honoured form of work for a man, although there was nothing high-class about it, in Italy or Australia.

"I'd better get changed then ring Meredith. I don't want a late night tonight."

Sitting at the kitchen counter she dialled the number she knew off by heart. "Meredith?"

"Francey. You're getting harder to catch than a taxi in George Street at peak hour. How are you?" came Meredith O'Connor's breezy voice through the receiver.

Francey smiled at her friend's sense of humour. "Too busy to be bored," she quipped back. "I'm in a rush, love, but how are you feeling? Is that baby you're carrying still kicking you half to death?"

She and Meredith Brooks, now O'Connor, had been best friends since year seven at St Scholastica's. And the friendship hadn't lessened when Meredith joined the police service and Francey had gone on to university. Somehow they always found time for each other in their busy schedules; meeting for lunch, seeing movies together and even getting each other blind dates. One such blind date, with Brett O'Connor, had led to Meredith marrying him, which gave Francey a proprietorial air towards them. She had been the unofficial matchmaker.

"Too right. Brett reckons it's gonna come out in a Tigers' uniform. The kicks are fullback material at least." Meredith giggled briefly. "Are you free Sunday? We're sailing, maybe up to Middle Harbour."

"Sounds wonderful. Yes. What time? What about food, drinks?" A day on the harbour. Just what she needed to alleviate the stress of this week's heavy workload. Brett and Meredith were trying to teach her how to sail their eight-metre yacht. Then, without prompting, an idea popped into her head. "Be okay to bring a friend?"

"Sure," Meredith said without hesitation. "And if he or she knows how to sail, even better. We'll bring the food and refreshments. Could you be at Waverton marina by 8 a.m., please? You know how Brett hates to be deprived of his time on the boat. Oh, and good luck for tomorrow night. Your mum told me about the award."

"Thanks. Bye."

As Francey closed the bedroom door of her Potts Point apartment, she sighed with contentment. The bedroom in particular was her haven, it always had been even when she'd lived at home. Here she could be herself, indulge her dreams, her fantasies and her hopes without fear of criticism or derision. She was about eleven when she'd begun to daydream about what she wanted to do with her life. When she'd been doing chores in the fruit shop, mopping the floor, stacking or picking out bruised fruit for her mother to stew, she'd think about the future.

Seeing her parents struggle to earn a good living – competition along Glebe Point Road was strong, and there were the supermarket chains – had been a salutary lesson for her. She knew she wanted more. Not necessarily to be rich and famous but the best she could be, but at what?

Her daydreams would start with: once upon a dream I dreamt I wanted to be a ...

Would she become a renowned scientist inventing cures to save mankind? Or a rock star? though her singing voice was a trifle suspect in that regard. Perhaps she'd be the first female racing car driver to win a grand prix, or the managing director of a multinational company.

By the time Francey turned fifteen, with her passion for drawing plans and imagining new structures she had chosen architecture as her vehicle for success. She wanted to be the finest architect she could be and after four years she was steadily working towards her next goal: to become a full partner at Nicholson, Drew and Carlyle.

After finishing university, with her first pay cheque she had immediately begun to save obsessively. Independence was what she needed – a place of her own. She loved her parents dearly but she needed the privacy and peace of her own space, away from the demands of a large Italian family with hordes of noisy relatives calling in for impromptu visits. Within three years she had a deposit and the contacts she had made in the real estate business had allowed her to do a good deal.

The apartment block in one of Potts Point's narrow back streets was old but the rooms were large, with high ornate ceilings. Initially, she and her cousin Tony had painted the four room apartment. The ceilings were white, the walls a soft dove grey and the skirting boards, door and door frames a brilliant turquoise.

She had renovated the galley style kitchen and next year she planned to strip and fix up the antiquated bathroom. Gradually, as her pay packet allowed, she decorated the living room the way she wanted. Two modern patterned sofas, a coffee table and against one wall she had indulged her love of music. A shelving system housed a TV, a hi-fi stereo and, on the wall facing the kitchen, hung an arrangement of her favourite black and white photos.

Francey threw her briefcase and jacket onto the double bed whose cover had a bright geometric pattern and then closed the vertical drapes for privacy against the possibility of prying eyes from neighbours in the apartment building across the street. In one corner of the bedroom stood a draughtsman's board, a computer on a laminated desk and a swivel chair which could be used for drawing or working on the computer. Above the computer hung a very large black and white print – a study of children at play in a city park.

A budding amateur photographer, Francey loved escaping into various parts of the city – the beaches, the suburbs – and photographing a wide variety of subjects: children, houses and all manner of objects that took her interest.

That was something else her father didn't like. Her photography hobby. He said it was dangerous to roam around Sydney early in the morning or at sunset. That there were too many weirdos around. She knew he'd prefer her to spend her leisure time going to parties or barbeques seeking out young men – future husband material! She shrugged her shoulders casually as she peeled off her work blouse, her skirt and then her pantihose. Papà was right about the weirdos. So, for safety's sake she'd taken a course in self-defence and when she went out on a "photo shoot" she dressed in her daggiest clothes so as not to arouse attention.

Glancing at her bedside clock she decided she had time for a quick shower before she dressed for the awards dinner. A flutter of nervousness rippled through her stomach as she draped the terry towelling robe around herself. Tonight could be eventful, in more ways than one. There were the awards of course. But also there was Aden Nicholson ... whose personal interest in her was becoming more apparent with every passing day.

Twenty minutes later, warm and slightly flushed from the shower, Francey slid open the mirrored wardrobe door and took out the black gown. With her colouring she could wear just about anything but tonight was so important. She had to look right.

The computer desk doubled as a dressing table so she perched on the edge of the chair, brushed her curly hair out and drew it up into a chignon, allowing a few tendrils to frame her face. Aden had never seen her with her hair up before, the thought came to her. At work she wore it loose, casual, because it was easy to look after. She smiled at her reflection in the mirror as she made her face up. Aden. Did she like him? Yes. Her mouth curved into a contemplative smile. Somehow, over the years she'd worked at Nicholson, Drew and Carlyle, he had infiltrated the defences she'd built around her emotions.

The smile faltered, then faded. A necessary survival mechanism because of ... Bryan Steinberg.

Her mouth tightened noticeably as her mind, unable to control itself, rushed back in time to happier days. Memories. Images. To the thrill of being really, *seriously* in love for the first time. For perhaps thirty seconds she closed her eyes and relived the feelings, the joy and the happiness being in love had initially brought. But all too soon her self-control shifted into protection mode and pushed the memories back. She couldn't afford the luxury or the pain; remembering still hurt.

The expression in her eyes was bleak as she studied her image. What a naive innocent she had been. Stop! Don't go down that road, Francey. It's history. Let it go. With jerky hand movements she regained complete self-control to finish her face, check her hair and then stood, in bra and lace-edged panties to dress.

For a minute or two she studied her finished reflection in the mirrored wardrobe door. The black gown fitted her perfectly, as if it had been made expressly for her. She picked up her evening bag and placed the lace bolero jacket around her shoulders just as the taxi she had ordered beeped its arrival down in the street. Perfect timing. She only hoped everything else about tonight would be as perfect.

"And the first place for the category B2 of the Australian Architectural Design Awards, for an architectural development under three point five million dollars is ..."

Aden stretched across and covered Francey's hand with his own. He gave her fingers an encouraging squeeze for just an instant and grinned confidently at her before removing his hand again.

The presenter paused, milking the moment for as long as he could. He slashed the envelope and brought out the card. "The B2 award goes to," pause, "the Swayne Complex at Tambourine Bay, Sydney, built for three point two million dollars. Architect Francesca Spinetti of Nicholson, Drew and Carlyle, North Sydney."

"Congratulations!" was chorused by those around Francey's table.

Aden leant across and kissed Francey's cheek so softly she barely felt it or had time to analyse her response to it. Her heart began to beat double time as she rose to walk to the stage. Matthew Drew and Tony Carlyle beamed at her. She felt her mouth go dry, and a wave of nervousness rose in her stomach and then worked its way along her limbs. She had heard right. She had won!

Somehow she managed to get to the podium without tripping, make her acceptance speech without mumbling to what seemed to be tumultuous applause and collect her plaque without dropping it. Then Aden was there, with that lazy, wide smile of his, one hand at her elbow, assisting her back to the table.

"Marvellous. Bloody marvellous," he whispered in her ear. "You're radiant and," he let his admiration show, "you looked terrific in the spotlight."

It took another hour for the remaining awards to be presented and then the crowd started to thin out. Well-wishers hovered around the Nicholson, Drew and Carlyle table. A photographer and journalist from the *Daily Telegraph* took relevant details and after what seemed an eternity, the hullabaloo began to ease.

"I've just been talking to a freelance journo, Sue Williams. She wants to do a profile on you for one of those career women's magazines," Aden said as he eased himself into the chair next to Francey. "It'd be good publicity for the firm, and for you."

She smiled her agreement at him. "When?"

"The sooner the better." He grinned back. "How do you feel?"

She shook her head, her long drop earrings swayed against her neck and the tendrils of loose hair fluttered. "I still don't believe it. Even though my name's on the plaque and everything. I really didn't think ... I mean, I thought it would probably go to someone more established, with more experience."

"You deserved it, Francey. Your designs have been like a breath of fresh air for our company – visually and financially. Now, just wait and see, rank and file architects will be copying your every move." His grin turned a touch cynical. "Mark my words. In about twelve months you'll see variation copycat developments springing up all over Sydney."

"I don't mind. Isn't it good to be a trendsetter?"

"Of course," he agreed, "I think more champagne is required. I haven't had the opportunity to toast your success properly."

"That's nice, Aden, but as soon as I can get away, I want to go tell my parents."

"Isn't it a bit late for them?"

She shrugged. "Doesn't matter. This," she patted the plaque affectionately, "is worth waking them up for."

"Very well. As soon as we decently can, we'll get away."

An hour and two glasses of champagne later, the crowd had thinned to the hardened stayers and Francey was still mentally pinching herself that she hadn't dreamt it. She'd have to make sure the attention didn't go to her head, Francey thought to herself as people stopped by on the way out to congratulate her. Two architects, one from Transfield, even dared to whisper something about a job offer. She wasn't interested. Loyalty was important to her and she was happy with Nicholson, Drew and Carlyle. Aden had seen her creative potential and had let her run with it.

"We'd better call it a night," Aden finally said. His gaze studied Francey's flushed face, her sparkling eyes. "Not that I really think either of us will do too much productive work tomorrow."

"You're probably right."

"I'll see you home."

"There's no need. I'm getting a taxi to Glebe."

"I haven't got my car so we'll share a taxi. Is that acceptable, *Miss Independence*?"

Aden shook his head in the way she had come to know as meaning he was bound and determined to have his way. Secretly, and because the champagne had mellowed her defences a little, she was pleased that he wanted to see her safely home. "Sure. Perfectly acceptable."

Twenty minutes later the taxi deposited them outside the Spinetti's fruit shop on Glebe Point Road.

"Thanks, Aden. See you tomorrow." No, that wasn't right, she decided, it was already tomorrow. "Umm, in the morning."

Aden looked around, there were lots of shadows around this part of the street, hiding places. "I'll see you to your front door." He saw her expression and added quickly, "Don't argue with me." As he got out he poked his head back in the taxi's half open window. "Here's twenty dollars on account. Wait for me."

For once Francey didn't argue. They walked down the narrow alley sprinkled with graffiti which ran between the fruit shop and the butcher's shop. Halfway down there were three steps, an alcove and then the Spinetti's front door with a low wattage globe burning.

Aden's gallantry made an impression on Francey, and she felt obliged to ask him in for coffee and to meet her parents.

"Love to."

Francey settled Aden into her father's favourite chair and then went upstairs to tell her parents the news. Ten minutes later a sleepy-eyed Carlo came down in his dressing-gown to give her boss a thorough once-over while Lucia and Francey bustled about in the kitchen.

This was where Francey Spinetti grew up. As Aden traded bland conversation with Carlo Spinetti, his gaze roamed about the room. Pieces of furniture were crowded into every available space. He noted the patterned wallpaper, heavy, dark colours and as he inhaled he could smell the faint fragrance of furniture polish mingling with the aromas of cooking. Italian, no doubt. Maybe cannelloni or fettuccine. Fresh flowers: daisies, carnations and something green rested in a vase on the dinner table. A stack of photographs of different sizes and shapes sat on the mantelpiece over a wooden fireplace. A large photograph, a black and white seascape, stark, the aftermath of a storm, hung on the wall above a china cabinet.

Carlo caught Aden's attention when he said, "Francey took that picture. She is a good photographer, you know."

Aden smiled. "It's a great shot. I didn't know photography was her hobby, Mr Spinetti. It seems your daughter has talents other than being a fine architect."

"*Sì*." Carlo's voice was proud. "She could be a professional if she wanted to be."

When Francey and Lucia returned to the living room with a loaded tray her parents insisted that she give them a blow-by-blow description of what had happened at the dinner. As she did so she handed Aden his coffee and sat on the lounge opposite him.

"Tonight was wonderful," she told her parents as she sipped. "Now I know what it's like to be a princess. All that fussing. It's nice."

"Gone to your head, hey?" Aden queried. Even under her father's watchful gaze he found it hard to keep his eyes off her; it had been that way all evening. She had been a big hit and even his two partners had finally seen her in a new light. He knew he wouldn't have any more trouble from them when he pushed future projects in her direction.

"Not for long, I'll be back to normal tomorrow," she promised.

"It's wonderful, *cara*," Lucia enthused. "I can hardly wait for morning so I can call Josie and the family, and Guiseppe in Dubbo, and tell them our daughter is famous."

Francey laughed and shook her head. "Not exactly famous, Mamma," then, her eyes sparkling, she added, "not yet."

Carlo grunted disapprovingly at his wife. "You are not to spend the whole morning on the phone, Lucia. There will be too much work to do in the shop."

Lucia's eyebrows rose. "Oh, Carlo, you are always the slave driver. So what if the work takes a little longer to get through. Our Francey, it shows that all the study and the work she's done has been to some purpose. Your father and I are so very proud of you." And in her enthusiasm, Lucia jumped up and gave her daughter yet another exuberant hug. "It is very good, is it not, Mr Nicholson?"

"Yes, it is. Please, call me Aden." He already knew Francey had worked her way through university because her parents hadn't been able to pay for her tuition and books. One day they'd been at a business lunch and she'd said she had a good deal of compassion for waitresses because she'd been one herself. He also knew she had worked as a housemaid at one of the hotels in the city.

They spent a half-hour in the Spinetti's living room, until Carlo's persistent yawning caused Francey and Aden to be on their way.

In the taxi, on the way to Potts Point, Aden became consumed by what had been niggling at him for some time. He had to know. Office gossip! His secretary, Marg, said Francey had a thing about men, that she liked to keep them at arms length or even further. Aden prided himself on being a practical man and what was the point in harbouring a dream if there was no chance it could come to fruition?

"The partners wondered why your boyfriend, someone special, wasn't with you tonight."

"Did they?"

He decided to come clean. "Well, actually, it was me. I wondered why."

She didn't hesitate. "I don't have anyone special in my life right now, Aden. I haven't for a long time."

It took a moment for him to digest that and then he said quietly, "I see." Although he didn't really, and he longed to ask why. That Francey Spinetti didn't have a man in her life made no sense at all. She was too lovely for members of the opposite sex not to be interested in her. But he was glad no-one was at present. Damned glad.

"One day I'll tell you why."

He jumped at that. "Why not now?"

She shook her head at him and gave him a slow slightly mysterious smile. "Because it's late and it's a long story. Besides," the taxi pulled up outside her apartment block, "the meter is ticking over."

He wanted to say to hell with the taxi meter, however, he knew her nature well enough to know that she, not he, would choose the time of the telling. "I look forward to it."

After he'd seen her to the door and she was safely ensconced in her apartment, she leant against the closed front door and mentally recapped the evening. First place. *Recognition.* Again she shook her head at the wonder of it. And then at the wonder of Aden. For a second or two she had thought he would kiss her goodnight, but he had hesitated and the moment had been lost. A pity. Still, recalling the way he had looked at her all evening sent a shiver through her, a feeling she hadn't had since, she sighed, way back then. It was early days yet.

CHAPTER FOUR

"Where's CJ?" Shellie Kirkby, bringing a loaded breakfast tray out to the patio table on the screened-in verandah of the Murrundi Downs homestead, asked Natalie deWitt-Ambrose.

"In his study. Talking to a journo, I believe," Natalie said as she dried herself. When at home she swam regularly before breakfast in the pool which was visible from the high verandah.

A two metre hedge of green conifers ran around three sides of the pool and the tennis court, for privacy and protection from wind and dust storms. Past the hedge and the profusion of mostly native shrubs in the landscaped garden lay the beginning of CJ's vast cattle station, now just one of his business interests. The land beyond the range of the bore water sprinklers was reddish-brown, the grass yellow and sparse even though there had been unusually good rain recently.

"They seem pretty thick at the moment, CJ and this journo." As she spoke Natalie slid into a silk robe and knotted it around her waist before sitting on one of the cushioned cane chairs. "God knows what mischief the two of them are concocting. Probably some politician or big name about to bite the dust." For a tall woman Natalie had small hands and feet. She deftly finger-combed her boyishly short platinum-dyed hair back off her face. On many the style looked harsh but it suited her striking, sharp features and olive skin.

"Don't CJ and Les have a business meeting with that sea cat company in Cairns today?" Shellie asked in the servile manner she'd grown into over the years as she poured Natalie a glass of freshly pulped pineapple juice.

"They'd better have. This afternoon, I think. I plan to cadge a lift to Cairns so I can drive up to Port Douglas. I want to check on how my art gallery in Macrossan Street is shaping up." Her tone hardened. "I don't trust the bloody builder. I reckon he's screwing me. Dollar-wise, that is."

That wasn't the only reason Natalie was anxious to reach Cairns. She had planned a rendezvous with a certain person, but she had no intention of mentioning with whom. It would shock Aunt Shellie too much. Out of the corner of her eye she noticed Shellie shake her head. Her stepaunt didn't like the way she spoke, so when CJ wasn't around to berate her for her common tongue she quite enjoyed seeing Shellie squirm. In fact, her lips twitched slightly as she thought about it, she enjoyed making lots of people squirm.

Grey eyes sighted Les Westcott coming from the direction of the jackeroos' bunkhouse at the rear of the homestead. A fine layer of dust lifted as his boots scuffed the earth. She licked her lips and then let them stretch wide across perfect teeth. Natalie liked to see Les squirm too, only it was harder to achieve because of his laconic manner and perennial poker face. Still, she chuckled inwardly, in the past she'd managed to get him going a few times.

"Morning all," Les greeted the two women as he removed his hat and dropped it onto an empty chair. "I'm so hungry I could eat a –"

"Horse," the women said in unison.

Natalie laughed, the sound a touch brittle. "God, you're so predictable. You make the same comment every morning, no matter what's served for breakfast." He shrugged and stared at her. "So I'm a creature of habit. That's not a crime, yet, is it?"

Shellie could almost physically feel the tension between the younger people. Everyone at Murrundi Downs knew they'd had a falling out over something and, where once they'd been good buddies, now they could barely speak civilly to each other. "No, it's not, Les," she acknowledged his question. "What would you like?"

"A bit of everything, Shellie. You know me."

"I have to go to Cairns. Okay to grab a seat on the plane, Les?"

"Sure, it's big enough."

Les Westcott just managed to disguise his annoyance. That's all he needed. A two hour plus plane flight with Natalie rabbiting on in his and CJ's ears. He wouldn't mind if her conversation didn't centre so much on herself or her damned art galleries. The Ambrose heir, he grudgingly admitted, had become quite the successful businesswoman. Six years ago CJ had loaned her the money to set up an art gallery in Brisbane and since then she had successfully developed galleries in Noosa, Cairns and now Port Douglas. In fairness though and to her credit and everyone's surprise, she'd insisted on paying the original loan back to her stepfather, with interest.

Thinking of the flight ahead he decided on an extra hearty breakfast to fortify himself so he added two extra rashers of bacon and a third slice of toast to his plate. "Takeoff time is zero nine hundred hours."

Hearing his terse tone, Natalie's mouth tightened slightly and her gaze ran over him with clinical precision. Heeled boots, jeans, a lightweight checked shirt rolled up above the elbows. Typical jackeroo garb, but she also knew he could dress differently, smartly, when the occasion arose. It was the coldness in his eyes and the stubborn set of his jaw that amused and at the same irritated the hell out of her. He was an unforgiving bastard, that was for sure. So they'd had a major difference of opinion. It hadn't been the first time they'd disagreed on something but when, in the past, they'd forgiven and forgotten, today after many weeks they remained alienated.

Natalie arched an eyebrow at him. "That's aviation talk for 9 a.m., isn't it?"

"Yeah, just try to be ready," he said sourly. "You know CJ hates to be kept waiting."

A silent Shellie, hearing the harsh edge in Les' voice, tried to remember him as she'd first met him: a sixteen-year-old who had turned up at the homestead begging for a job. Tall and skinny, clothes worn and patched, the station hands had joked that a strong puff of wind would blow him over. An unwanted, unloved, damned stray cat. That's what CJ had said about him. But in some indefinable way Les had struck a sympathetic chord with her hard-nosed brother, and CJ had given the teenager a chance to prove himself. Les had.

Ten years older than Richard Ambrose, Les had also become his and Natalie's unofficial brother and it was he, not CJ, who had taught Richard all he'd needed to know about raising and driving cattle and running a station as large as Murrundi Downs. The two had camped out and had gotten drunk together, even holidayed overseas together and unashamedly been best friends, in spite of the age gap or the difference in their circumstances.

A loner by nature, Shellie recalled when Les had fallen in love with the first girl who'd given him a kindly smile. His marriage to Nancy O'Shea had been a disaster. CJ built a small cottage for Les and his wife to live in, at the back of the homestead, but Nancy couldn't adjust to the harshness of life on the land. Two years and many arguments later, she and their baby son, Mark, had left to live in Brisbane. The resulting divorce had been amicable. Nancy had happily remarried but Shellie knew that Les missed his son. He saw him as often as he could and, occasionally, Mark came to the station for school holidays. Since the divorce Les had devoted himself to becoming CJ's right-hand man, his CEO, and now he knew as much about CJ's business empire as CJ did.

Les had taken Richard's death hard and afterwards he seemed different, harder, less patient, especially towards Natalie.

"Speaking of waiting," Shellie muttered a little crossly, "if CJ doesn't hurry up and appear for breakfast, I'll have to reheat everything."

"You spoil him," Natalie said. "I doubt you'd bother reheating breakfast for Les or me, but when CJ says jump," she added slyly, "you ask 'how high'?"

"Cute, but not very original," Les grunted from across the table. He folded yesterday's newspaper back and continued to read as he munched his way through his enormous breakfast.

"There he is." Natalie pointed towards the hedge on the far side of the pool as CJ came into view. Her gaze narrowed, and focused totally on him as he approached the verandah.

At fifty-nine CJ cut an impressive figure. Not overly tall and with his hair thinning and greying, he nevertheless walked with the gait of a man who had supreme confidence in himself. He wore locally made embossed cowboy boots – something of a trademark with him – and off-white moleskins held up by a plaited leather belt with a pewter buckle. A hand-tailored, crisply ironed blue denim shirt showed the breadth of his shoulders and chest, making him look the archetypal man on the land.

CJ was the only man Natalie deWitt-Ambrose feared. Not physically but for the power he could wield. Over the years he had accumulated great wealth and power from his own hard work and her mother's inheritance. She'd watched him break politicians who'd opposed him, undercut tenders to get what he wanted; he had dealt with criminal elements and generally wreaked economic havoc on others to get his own way. Success had come to him like a dutiful magnet and Australian as well as international businessmen and companies courted him with due reverence. He was what her friend, journalist Trish Pentano, called a financial enigma of mega-watt proportions. She smiled smugly to herself as he sat beside her at the table. One day all that CJ Ambrose owned would be hers.

"How's everyone this morning?" CJ asked with unusual affability. Since Richard's death he had had to force himself to be pleasant and civil, even to these three people who were closest to him.

"Fine," Shellie said as she poured him a cup of coffee.

"Great," Les Westcott answered. He folded the newspaper in half and put it on the cane coffee table so that he could give CJ his full attention. "I've been to the bunkhouse and given the crews their orders for the next few days. That new foreman, Mike Hunter, seems to know his stuff. Gets on well with the men too."

"Good. What about Lisa in the office? Did you tell her I wanted the report on that Hong Kong deal faxed to me as soon as it comes through?"

"Sure did. It should be at the Hilton by the time we reach Cairns."

"I'm coming to Cairns too, CJ," Natalie put in with a defiant glare at Les.

"That's fine." CJ paused to look his stepdaughter up and down. He frowned. "Natalie, haven't I said before that you should come to the table dressed. Swimmers and a see-through robe aren't appropriate."

"Usually I do get dressed, but this morning Shellie brought breakfast out early, just after I'd finished my swim. I didn't think anyone would mind."

"Well, I mind. What if we had guests? Business people?"

She made a moue and smiled at him. "Maybe you'd cut the deal faster. Most businessmen are susceptible to a pretty woman, you know," she said cheekily.

"Is that how you do your business deals," Les questioned, "in a bikini and robe? No wonder you're so successful."

CJ's frown deepened. "Don't start, you two."

Like Shellie and the considerable complement of staff that made up Murrundi Downs station, CJ was aware of the tension between Les and Natalie. He didn't know the cause or need the aggravation, not after losing Richard.

Somehow, with Richard around to act as a buffer and a natural peacemaker, the two had managed to get on. Both strong personalities, without the gentler influence of his son, their true natures were coming out.

Shellie began to fuss, rattling the plates as she put the used ones back on the tray. "I'll go warm the eggs up."

"Don't bother. I'm not hungry. Fresh toast will do," CJ told her curtly. He gave his sister a sharp look, and wondered if she'd been tippling. It was unusual for her to get stuck into the grog this early in the morning, but having Natalie around tended to make her more nervous than usual. He knew that his sister rarely got drunk, but by midafternoon these days one expected her to have a glow up. She'd never gotten over her husband Peter leaving her for a younger, more beautiful woman, so CJ'd brought her here when Brenda's cancer had got too much to handle and she had stayed on. Though he secretly admitted to a certain fondness for his only sibling, her weakness, as he called it, often made him respond sharply to her.

Dismissing the irritation of his sister from his mind, he clapped his hands for attention. "You know, we've all been in the doldrums since Richard ..." there was no need to finish the sentence. "I've been thinking lately that the property needs sprucing up. We're running out of space here. When Brenda designed the house she didn't allow for entertaining important dignitaries, foreign businessmen or," he glanced at Natalie, "half-a-dozen friends at a time. And, frankly, I'm getting tired of running around to business meetings in Cairns and Brisbane."

"What do you mean? You want to pull the house down and build another?" Les asked. This was the first spark of interest in anything from CJ for weeks. He recognised the particular gleam in his eyes. Thank God, he was coming out of his grief.

"No. I want to do some additions to the main house but I'm thinking of building a mini conference centre here, complete with accommodation. Top inclusions, state of the art electronic technology. That sort of thing. Then I can have interstate and international business people come to me. We've got the Lear jet and the airstrip to fly them in and, after the business is done, we'll show them some outback hospitality. I reckon they'll eat it up and," his features turned crafty, "we'll clinch the business side of things faster."

"Build it. Where?" Natalie asked, her eyebrow arching at what she considered an odd idea. A conference centre at Murrundi Downs. CJ was losing it, for sure.

"We've plenty of land. About two hundred and fifty thousand square kilometres of it." He turned to Les. "When we're in Cairns I want you to check out a few architects there, and Brisbane too. We'll fly them up and they can give us a design and a price."

Les beamed. "I'll get right on it."

Shellie smoothed her lightweight frock over her stomach and didn't say anything, but she thought about her brother's new project. To her all it meant was more work. Jesus Christ, wasn't there a limit?

The man tipped the brim of his hat forward to shield his eyes from the glare of the sun while he waited. A liberal coating of insect repellent on his face and arms kept most of the annoying buggers at bay. Resting on his haunches in the shade afforded by the police department's four-wheel drive, Sergeant Steve Parrish took a notebook out of his shirt pocket. He opened it and read again what had been taken down by Constable Smith on 28 February, 1996, the date of Richard Ambrose's death.

Accidental death had been the coroner's finding but as he read the constable's notes, taken in a rush, his imagination filled in the gaps. Trampled to death. What a bloody awful way to die. God knows, during his time in the force, first in NSW and now in Queensland, he'd seen more variations on ways to die than one would have thought possible. He could even feel a glimmer of pity for CJ Ambrose, but felt far more for his son with whom he'd had a passing acquaintanceship.

Brown eyes studied the harsh country around him. A line of short gums and scrubby bushes grew around the edge of the waterhole and along the flat where the water went underground. He'd heard that if one was desperate one could dig down, maybe a metre or two and find running water. He hoped he'd never have to. When he'd first been appointed to the Mt Isa station, the country and the weather had been difficult to get used to. Policing here was a world removed from the homicide and narcotics squad in Sydney. But the realities – death – were just as harsh.

For the umpteenth time that day his left hand reached into his back pocket for the packet of cigarettes usually there, only to remember that last week he had decided to quit. Damn, he ached for a bloody cigarette, something to do to pass the time. He closed the notebook and put it back in his pocket. Nothing to do but wait.

In the distance a horse and rider approached. Steve glanced down at his watch. Ten to three. Right on time. He shook his head in silent admiration. How did the blacks do it? Billy Wontow said he'd be here at three o'clock and he would be. He figured that the man didn't wear a watch or listen to a radio but he could tell what time it was, with precision, from the movement of the sun across the sky. A neat trick, that was for sure.

"How's it going, Steve?" Billy called as he reined in next to the four-wheel drive.

"Bloody hot, even if it is winter."

Billy grinned at him. "Pretty nice if you ask me." He dismounted, threw the horse's reins loosely over the vehicle's bull bars and rested on his haunches beside the larger man. "Don't like coming to this place no more." Dark eyes studied the waterhole and surrounding land. "Bad spirits here now, since ..."

"I understand, mate. We both know what the coroner's findings were but I just want to go over it again –"

"Did that with Constable Smith. Twice," Billy said matter-of-factly with a shrug of his shoulders.

"I know. I'll feel happier about closing Richard's file if we go over it one last time. Where was the campfire? Could you show me?"

Billy squinted. He stood up and took a good look around. "Not much left to see. Cattle ran over everything. Almost got me too, the buggers." He walked around for a while kicking at stones, moving the earth with his booted foot. "Here," he dropped to one knee. "Charred tree branch. Been moved by the stampede though. Reckon the fire was about here." He moved again, closer to the waterhole and planted the charred stick in the red earth.

Steve Parrish followed him, reading from the notebook. "Richard got on his horse first, right?"

"I didn't have time to saddle mine. Just had the bridle. Got on and took off around the far side of the mob. Might have been able to stop 'em if it wasn't for the third shot. That made 'em all crazy."

"Did you see Richard go down?"

"No. Could hardly see anything for the dust. I knew something bad had happened when there was no sign the cattle had turned away from the water. Had to scramble out of the way, up the rise on the hill, or I'd been a goner too."

Steve Parrish made a note in his own book and then chewed thoughtfully on the end of his pen. Obviously, the catalyst for the stampede had been the rifle shots but exhaustive questioning around town and on adjoining properties had proved fruitless. No-one had seen or heard of any strangers or tourists on hunting trips.

"Can you recall the timing of the shots? How far apart they were?"

"You kidding me, aren't you?" Billy's dark features expressed his derision at the question. "Richard and I were scrambling to turn the mob, then just to stay alive. No bloody way I can remember how far apart the shots came."

Steve smiled. It had been a dumb question but he'd had to ask it in an attempt to satisfy his own curiosity. "Okay. The direction of the shots? North, south, east, west?"

Billy shook his head in exasperation. "Jeez, you're asking a lot of a bloke's memory." Then he went very still. He closed his eyes and his right hand came up to stroke his forehead. For maybe half a minute he stood like a sentinel, unaware of the man near him, oblivious to the insects buzzing around his face. "West. Maybe south-west."

"You sure?"

"As sure as a bloke who was scared shitless could be," he quipped back with a grin. "What you want to know all this for? The young boss is gone, the old boss is getting used to him not being around. You not gonna stir up trouble, are you?"

"Just doing my job, Billy, that's all."

Steve could feel the hairs on the back of his neck rising

and knew it had nothing to do with the weather. Something didn't feel right. He pulled his hat off and ran his fingers through black, neatly cut hair. Was he being overly suspicious for no logical reason? Circumstances and the coroner's report pointed to the stampede and Richard's death being an unfortunate accident. And who – if one took the opposite point of view that it was planned – would want Richard Ambrose dead? As far as he knew the young man hadn't had an enemy in the world.

Steve Parrish had thirteen years police training and experience behind him. Ten years in the NSW Police Service during which time he'd risen to the rank of detective sergeant and served in a variety of squads, including homicide, narcotics, vice and police rescue. He'd transferred to Queensland and had worked for three years at Mt Isa, where he was now one of the station's most senior officers.

"You finished with me, Steve?" Billy shifted uncomfortably from one foot to the other. "Don't like this place."

"Yes. Thanks for your cooperation, Billy." He shook his hand and put his hat back on.

"You going now?"

"Not yet. I'm going to walk up to the top of the western ridge."

"Why you wanta do that?" Billy's curiosity got the better of him.

Steve wasn't sure. "It's the highest place to view the waterhole."

Billy shook his head uncomprehendingly. "Okay, Steve. See you around. Maybe you come out to Murrundi soon."

"Maybe. Thanks, Billy."

He watched the stockman swing into the saddle and ride away then he turned towards the western slope. By the time Steve walked up the incline covered with loose rocks, low growing bluebush and saltbush and the odd termite hill, he regretted his decision to get to the top. Sweat glistened on his forehead below the line of his hat, and damp stains under the armpits of his fawn police shirt had formed. Still, the view was better, in fact, perfect.

Looking down he could see the waterhole, and because there'd been no rain or strong winds to erase anything, a multitude of cattle tracks sparking off in about six directions. How they'd scattered after they'd been spooked could be clearly seen. Yes, all very straightforward.

Curious, he began to wander about, checking the view of the waterhole from several different positions. The ground was dry and hard, with sproutings of acacias and mulga scrub, and the few spindly eucalypts afforded little shade from the sun. His gaze dropped to the earth and in a long dried up puddle he saw the impression of a horseshoe. Interesting. Billy Wontow hadn't ridden in from the west, Murrundi Downs station lay due south. But someone had, and a while ago. And then ... a chance kick of a rock unearthed what he had been subconsciously looking for. Something caught the sunlight and glinted up at him.

He dropped to his haunches and, using a twig, moved three brass casings from their hiding place. Bringing them up close to study, his tanned forehead creased into a frown. Unusual type. He couldn't recognise the type of rifle from which they'd been fired but the fact that there were three put, in his mind, too much strain on coincidence. His gaze scanned the bush around him. Not a lot of cover but probably enough for someone dressed in drab clothing, in the early morning light. He fished a small plastic bag out of his back trouser pocket and placed the shell casings inside. They'd have to go to the ballistics department in Brisbane. A long shot, he knew ... no pun intended, but there just might be fingerprints, or parts of prints on the casings.

He stood up again and whistled softly, a habit he had when he was thinking at top speed. The horseshoe print and the shell casings put a very different connotation on the stampede. Three rifle shots, three casings. Small bore, probably. Coincidence? No! *Deliberate.*

And then, almost casually, his dark eyes came to rest on one of the eucalypts. Part of the trunk had been shattered, unnaturally so. Frowning with curiosity he strode towards it. Trees didn't usually shatter like this, he thought. He pulled out a pocketknife and carefully scraped around the hole. The dead bark and timber came away and something small fell onto the ground. Steve picked the object up and rolled it between his fingers. A bullet.

Suddenly he realised that he had to go carefully with this evidence. There was no point going to his superiors or to CJ Ambrose with half-baked ideas, mere theories. He needed more proof than shell casings and a spent bullet to show there'd been foul play. And if the media or CJ got wind of what he'd found before he could back it up with more evidence, there'd be a bloody circus.

He stopped whistling and began to remember the circus that had occurred on an investigation in Sydney, and had ultimately driven him out of the city he'd been born and raised in.

He stalked back to the four-wheel drive, turned the ignition and the air-conditioning on and stood outside until the cabin's interior cooled down. Finally he slid behind the wheel and gunned the accelerator.

Careful, he knew that's what he'd have to be. Damned careful.

CHAPTER FIVE

The waters of Sydney Harbour shimmered in the morning light as the O'Connors' yacht, *Good Times*, cut white water in the light nor-easterly. They had sailed from the marina at Waverton, gone under the bridge, passed Circular Quay and were gliding towards their destination for the day, Middle Harbour. Brett O'Connor, solid of build and with sandy ginger hair, steered from the stern. Aden, an experienced sailor, so Francey Spinetti had found out on instruction from Brett, attended to the main sail, tacking from starboard to port to catch the prevailing wind.

In the yacht's small cabin Francey and Meredith sat on vinyl cushions watching the men work. Both women knew Brett and Aden didn't consider sailing *work*. To each it was invigorating exercise, fun.

"Nice for a change, isn't it?" Meredith murmured, suppressed laughter in her tone. "Usually I steer while you and Brett work the sails. It's good that Aden knows about sailing, otherwise we'd be taking orders from the 'master' instead of being comfy and in here." Shorter than Francey, Meredith had a freshness to her that was enhanced by styled shoulder-length light-brown hair framing an oval-shaped face. Make-up free she looked younger than her twenty-seven years and into her fifth month of pregnancy she had just begun to show. Under her windcheater she wore a multicoloured long, loose top over black pants to disguise the growing bulge. Meredith's seeming light-heartedness hid a sharp intelligence that had seen her rise – getting a degree part-time and doing a string of courses – to the rank of sergeant in the NSW Police Service faster than most.

With the wind tangling her hair and caressing her face, Francey gazed surreptitiously at Aden, observing how he moved lithely across the deck as if he'd spent half his life on the water. Wearing white jeans, a blue polo-necked sweater and canvas sneakers he looked so fit and tanned that she concluded he must spend a lot of leisure time out of doors. Until today she had only seen him in work clobber: suits and ties. Aden Nicholson in casual clothes, his masculine form subtlely displayed, was a visual delight.

Studying him as he worked the pulleys and manoeuvred the ropes a frisson of excitement coiled around her stomach. It was the same feeling caused by the special way he had looked at her when he'd called for her this morning. On seeing him she had actually gone weak at the knees. But the next instant, in a contrary burst of self-anger, she brushed the confession aside. She was a grown woman for God's sake and it wasn't odd to respond to a very attractive male. She continued to scold herself – she should stop acting like a silly teenager.

"Oh, I'm not sure," Francey broke her reflective thought. "You know Brett's trying to teach me the intricacies of sailing. I could do with the practice. Maybe I should go and help."

"Look at them. They don't need your help," Meredith retorted as she observed Aden moving to the bow to tie the spinnaker down. Her brown eyes twinkled with mischief. "So, give about your boss. Where have you been hiding him for the last three years?"

"I haven't been hiding him anywhere, it's just that ... Well, until now it's been all business." Her friend's half smirk made her add in a rush, "Honest."

"I think he's gorgeous and," Meredith winked, "acceptable. Your dad must be over the moon."

Francey rolled her eyes towards a cloudless sky, relishing the warmth of the winter sun on her face. The O'Connors were well-acquainted with her father's obsession to see his only daughter married. "He is. He met him the night of the awards. Since then Papà quizzes me all the time about him. You know how he nags when he gets his mind on something. But," again her gaze pulled towards Aden who was now with Brett at the yacht's stern, "it's early days yet. Actually, this is our first official date."

"Indeed!" Meredith remarked. "The *Good Times* and the O'Connors consider themselves honoured. What's his background?"

Francey knew that Meredith's curiosity was caused by the detective coming out in her. She had always been a stickybeak, seeking information about almost everyone she came in contact with. "North shore upbringing, private school tie, family well-heeled. He has a younger sister and a brother. Lives alone," her lips twisted in a cheeky grin, "so I'm told, in a luxurious Neutral Bay penthouse. He's been engaged once, so his secretary told me, but it didn't work out. He started his architectural firm from scratch, straight out of uni, and has done amazingly well in ten years. Nowadays, the firm's turnover is several million annually."

"So, he has good prospects?" Meredith stated the obvious as she gave Francey a searching look. "It's about time. You deserve someone nice. That bastard Steinberg did a real job on you. Turned you into a man-hater."

"I don't *hate* men," Francey shot back, "I just find it hard to trust them."

Meredith's words triggered things from the past and, thinking back on it, she admitted that she hadn't had much luck with the opposite sex. First, Mark Rosso. Sexy, Italian, a handsome young man. Mark had been her first experience at falling in love, and theirs had been a brief, passionate affair during her first university year. Mark rented a pokey studio apartment off Missenden Road where they'd met for lover's trysts. Those had been heady days. Freedom from being under the watchful eye of her father, making love with Mark, attending lectures and tutorials, plus the seemingly never-ending round of parties. Not that she'd gone to many. She'd had to work her way through university and study, plus two part-time jobs had left little time for socialising. She and Mark had parted good friends, though he'd dropped out of architecture in the third year. She'd heard that he had married his current girlfriend and they'd moved to Byron Bay where he worked for an architect, drawing up plans.

She felt no rancour or sense of loss when she thought about Mark. With Brian Steinberg the feelings were different. Nothing in her background – growing up in a modest home with loving parents, and a noisy Italian family with cousins and aunts and uncles galore – had prepared her for Bryan. It had all started so innocently ...

"A penny for your thoughts, love?" Meredith clicked her tongue reprovingly. "You're not thinking about *him*, are you?"

Meredith's voice jerked Francey back to the here and now. She blinked and looked around. The yacht was leaning into the wind as it rounded the port side of Middle Head National Park to head west into Middle Harbour. "Yes and no."

"Well, don't. He's not worth it." She hastened to change the subject. "I think the guys could do with a coffee. How about it?"

"Sure." Francey stood, got her balance on the rolling deck then moved forward to the small galley. The burst of activity successfully pigeonholed memories of Bryan Steinberg back into her subconscious.

As she prepared the coffees and opened a packet of biscuits she glanced out the bow and starboard portholes. Of all the harbour's wonderful bays and hideaways they had explored in the past two years since Brett had bought *Good Times*, Middle Harbour remained her favourite. Parks ran along many of the foreshore areas and there was an abundance of beautiful homes which, on some blocks, came down to the water's edge. An architect's delight. One day she imagined herself designing a multistoreyed mansion for a millionaire along one such waterside site.

Brett took the mug of coffee from Francey with a grateful nod of his head. "Want to steer for a while?"

"I'd love to."

Lunch was a gourmet affair served by turning part of the deck into a table top. They all sat cross-legged as they ate, while the yacht, with sails furled, rocked gently in the lessening breeze. Meredith had gone to some trouble with the picnic basket: champagne and beer, pâté and crusty bread, cold meats, two different salads, tabouli and several cheeses because her husband had a weakness for them, and for dessert, strawberries marinated in kirsch and cream.

After they'd eaten, the motion of the yacht, plus a couple of glasses of champagne and a beer for Brett, lulled the O'Connors into a semi stupor. They lay flat out on the deck on towels, using the furled sail for shade as they napped.

"I like your friends," Aden said as he and Francey cleared up the remains of their repast, washing crockery and cutlery in the galley.

"I'm glad. Meredith and I go back a long way – to first grade. She met Brett on a blind date and for them it was the proverbial love at first sight. They've been together for three years and I've never seen a happier couple."

"Brett's in construction, isn't he?"

"Yes. Medium density. He took over his father's company when Fred O'Connor wanted to retire. He's almost doubled the business since then. Meredith reckons he's a workaholic."

"Do you put work his way?"

Francey glanced sideways at him. "Not especially. I let him know if I think there's a project he might want to tender for. That's all. I don't play favourites in business, unlike some of our colleagues. It can lead to problems I'd rather avoid."

"Aahhh, you're a wise woman, Francey Spinetti." He was silent for a moment, then he added, "I think Tony Carlyle might have a project that suits Brett's company's size. I'll talk to Tony on Monday."

"Brett would appreciate that. They're trying to pay as much as they can off their home loan before the baby comes." She smiled her thanks at him. "Every little bit helps." All at once she became aware of how close they were in the confined space of the galley. But, strangely, she didn't feel crowded or threatened as she might with some men. With Aden, she felt ... comfortable.

"I seem to recall you promising to tell me about that long ago relationship. The one," he paused as his finger took hold of her chin to lift it so she had to look him squarely in the eyes, "that hurt you so much."

Francey inhaled deeply, relishing the salty air. She shrugged her shoulders in resignation; he had to know sometime and now was as good a time as any. "Sure, why not. But it's not particularly original or pleasant. I fell in love with my maths lecturer at uni, in my last year of study." The way she said it sounded casual, uncomplicated, but it hadn't ended up that way. "Bryan was thirteen years older than me. He seemed worldly and sophisticated, gentle and caring too." She gave a self-derisive laugh. "Corny, I know, but I thought we had the real thing. He said he lived with his mother, a sickly woman, so we never met at his place. There were other places though. Motels and sympathetic lecturers who loaned him their flat keys on special occasions. Somehow, we managed to see a lot of each other."

She looked away for a moment, a rush of pleasure mingling with the pain. "I was so happy. Not just because my maths improved but because of Bryan. He seemed to be everything I wanted in a man. I saw my future with him. Commitment, family, the whole bit. For six months I walked on a cloud of ... of ... blinkered serenity," she admitted with disarming frankness. Bryan Steinberg had – whether intentionally or not – helped mould Francey into the person she had now become. He had brought out her sense of humour, her warmth, the directness that was her trademark, and he'd given her confidence in her potential to become a talented architect.

"Unfortunately, my ideal of the man – I'd put him on some stupid pedestal – didn't match the reality. As you can imagine, after a while it became impossible for some people not to know about our affair. Someone told his *wife*. I, of course, had no idea he was married until she introduced herself as Cathy Steinberg and confronted me on campus one day. God it was embarrassing! She wanted to know why I was trying to break her and Bryan up." Her tone and expression hardened. "I found out that they'd been married for seven years – they lived at Gosford and Brian commuted each day to university." Her eyebrows lifted meaningfully. "There was no sick mother either. And he had two children, the rat!"

"But didn't he want you rather than his wife?"

Francey shook her head. "Not enough to end his marriage. You see, his wife's family is well off. She's highly strung too. I heard that she had some kind of breakdown after learning of our affair. When her parents die Bryan and his wife will be independently wealthy. Bryan, frankly, inferred that I couldn't compete with that. As well, despite his faults, his weaknesses, I could tell that he really loved his kids." Her long, dark lashes blinked rapidly a couple of times. "I ... my conscience wouldn't allow me to come between him and the children. His wife, foolish woman, still loved him. It was easier," God, *no*, it hadn't been easy – it had been the hardest thing she'd ever done, "to walk away."

"How I got through my studies and passed the finals, I don't remember – it's a blur. I did though, and somehow I survived." Her parents hadn't known what she'd gone through – only the O'Connors – she had managed to keep it secret from everyone else in the family. Just as well, she thought, her protective father may have gone after Bryan with a shotgun.

"Poor Francey." Aden's voice held a wealth of compassion.

"Not poor," she said, and a determined sparkle came into her eyes. "I got wise and I'm getting wiser. I won't allow myself to get hurt that way again."

A passing speedboat's wake caused the yacht to rock crazily in the swell. Aden took the opportunity to lean towards her and touch her cheek with the back of his hand.

"You won't get hurt with me, Francey, that's a promise."

The next instant his lips were pressing against hers. Warm and firm, not dominating, a gentle exploration of hitherto uncharted areas. His arms came around her to draw her close to him and through his thin shirt the heat radiated into her body. They drew back from each other, both breathless, both surprised at the pleasures awakened.

"I'm not sure …"

He cut her off with another quick kiss. "What? Not the boss and the employee thing?"

"Partly." More than that though she wasn't a hundred per cent sure she was ready for the next step. Life was simpler, more peaceful if she kept her heart intact. Besides, she had worked hard to make a niche for herself at Nicholson, Drew and Carlyle; she didn't want to see it come to an end with an ill-timed, perhaps ill-fated relationship. Most of all, and she admitted the truth of it, she didn't want to get hurt again.

"We'll take things slow," he promised, smiling. There had been many women in Aden Nicholson's life. Some light-hearted affairs, others more serious and he'd even wanted to marry one woman. With Francey he already had the feeling that this was it. He knew that because of the past hurt she'd become skittish about romantic involvements and judging by the expression in her eyes as she'd spoken about Bryan, her heart had been badly bruised.

"We'll be discreet. No-one in the firm needs to know we're seeing each other socially. It's none of their business anyway." Out of the corner of his eye Aden saw Brett coming towards the galley. His arms dropped away from her.

"Wind's come up, freshening too," Brett said as he popped his head around the cabin doorway. "Aden, we might as well make the most of it."

"I'd like to help with the sails," Francey said impulsively, smiling at Aden. "Otherwise I'll never learn how to do it properly."

Brett winked at Aden. "We never say no to extra crew, do we, mate?"

"Not when she looks like Francey. I've crewed with some pretty ugly guys over the years. She's a nice change."

Francey's eyebrow rose in question. "I think that's a compliment, but perhaps you should reserve your enthusiasm until you see me work the sails."

"Will do."

Aden Nicholson listened as the man on the other end of the phone line finalised their conversation. Then, replacing the receiver he stared at the blank wall in front of him. Interesting. Damned interesting. Within five minutes his private fax line spewed an official letter confirming what had been discussed. As he read the text he shook his head in wonder at the power of the media. Sue William's article on Francey winning the national body's architectural award had led to her being the cover story in *The Australian* which had created media interest and an interview on the *Today Show* and *A Current Affair*. This was the kind of free publicity some businesspeople would kill for. And yesterday the editor from the *Women's Weekly*, looking for the rags to riches angle, had phoned for an interview. More projects were coming in and the new clients wanted Francey to design for them. As he'd predicted, her award was going to be a financial bonanza for the firm. His expression took on a sardonic twist. He'd probably have to keep a look out for head-hunters trying to poach her away from them too.

The letter trailing in his hand, Aden rose from his desk and made his way to Francey's office.

"It seems that lately I've made a habit of bringing you good news," he said as he entered and took up his usual position on the corner of her desk. "What do you know about CJ Ambrose?" he asked out of the blue.

Francey blinked as her concentration disengaged from the floor plan of the multi-storey office block on which she had been working. She swivelled away from the drawing board to look at him. "Ambrose?" She pursed her lips for maybe ten seconds, thinking. "He's that Queensland man who franchised shoe stores."

Aden grinned and then shook his head. "Not quite. That's R.M. Williams. CJ Ambrose is one of the wealthiest, most influential men in Queensland. Has huge cattle interests and –"

"Oh, yes," the penny dropped. "I remember. He's into all sorts of things. A resort island, condominiums at Surfers Paradise, exports, foreign investments ... Does business from his cattle station somewhere up north. I read about him in a recent edition of *The Bulletin*."

"Good girl!" his grin widened. "I've just talked to his CEO, Les Westcott. CJ wants you to tender a conference centre on his property. Interested?"

Francey blinked again, a habit she had when she was deep in thought and then, having taken it in, her eyes widened with delight. "Of course. Why me in particular?"

"Publicity from the award, I guess. You're the architectural flavour of the month. How are you placed, work-wise?"

Blue-green eyes twinkled at him. "Well, if I work day and night for the next eight days or so I could clear most of my projects. Eddie, in the draughtsman's pool, can do the basic section plans. But," she added with a cheeky smile, "it means cutting out sleeping, eating, dates and all leisure time." The corners of her mouth tucked in to control the smile as she saw his disconcerted expression. "Why? Is the Ambrose project urgent?"

Aden's shrugged his shoulders noncommittally. "As with our Mr Monroe, I've found it a wise policy not to keep excessively wealthy clients waiting. They're used to first-class attention and get impatient if they don't get it." He studied her desk with its mess of rolled up plans, clients' folders and architectural manuals. "Maybe we can lighten your load a bit."

Another multimillionaire. It seemed that the richer they were the more difficult they became. Then a thought came to her. "Where do I have to go?"

"Les Westcott has offered to fly you up in Ambrose's private jet. You'll board at Mascot and be there in a couple of hours. Murrundi Downs station, Ambrose's headquarters, is south-east of Mt Isa."

For a moment she was flattered by the unexpected attention, then she said, "That far! I've never been farther north than Dubbo." She had an uncle, Guiseppe Favorito, on her mother's side, who owned a cafe in the township. Twice a year Carlo and Lucia closed their fruit shop on Sunday and left before dawn to visit him. Guiseppe, a widower, was getting older and all his children had moved to the city and were increasingly busy with their own lives.

Unlike most of her contemporaries, Francey hadn't travelled or holidayed much since finishing university and getting a job with Nicholson, Drew and Carlyle. She had saved every dollar she could put her hands on until she had enough for a deposit on a modest one bedroom unit at Potts Point. Getting ahead career-wise and having the security her parents still strived for as they approached old age, drove her need.

"Okay." Aden handed over the faxed letter. "Read it. It's self-explanatory as to what Ambrose wants. I'll get you a copy of what we have on him in the VIP future customers file – my secretary's brainchild of an idea. Hopefully the more you know about the man, the better you'll deal with him."

"Good idea. Pity it didn't work for Monroe though."

"Yes, well … there are exceptions." He sighed. "It shouldn't take you more than a few days, a week at the most, depending on how finicky Ambrose is." His hand moved to the pile of folders. "Now, which projects can wait till you get back and which ones have to be dealt with expeditiously?" Then, in a softer tone he added, "There's no way you're getting out of tonight's dinner date. Right?"

"You're the boss." As she smiled she couldn't control the touch of colour that warmed her cheeks. They'd been dating twice a week for a month now and it was delightful.

No, Aden was delightful. But she conceded that she was the one continuing to hold back from taking the final step of moving into a full relationship with him. Damn Bryan Steinberg and the memories. When would she be free of him and the pain? She thanked God that Aden was a patient man; he hadn't pressured her to sleep with him but she knew he wanted to, very much. What had her friend Meredith said once? That some women loved too much, and too deeply. She had wondered from time to time over the past few years whether she was such a woman. Contrarily, part of her hoped so, and part of her hoped not.

Grey eyes followed the naked woman's progress as she padded over the tiled floor of the Mirage suite. Of average height, she had a near perfect figure, nipped and curved in all the right places. Shoulder-length brown hair bobbed up and down as she walked, as did her firm up-tilting breasts. Bending and at the same time revealing perfect, round buttocks, the woman picked up a pile of discarded clothes. The response to the view was instantaneous. A heavy throb began low in the stomach and long, tapered fingers twitched in anticipation of caressing the woman's bare skin and bringing her passion to fever pitch.

"You're up early," Natalie said. She stifled a yawn as she plumped herself up on an extra pillow.

"Thought I'd go for a jog, then maybe a swim, before it gets too hot," Trish Pentano replied.

Automatically she folded Natalie's slacks over the chair.

"You and your physical fitness program. You're supposed to be on holiday."

Trish laughed. "I know." She sat on the edge of the bed. "I'm not going to the gym for a two hour work-out, just a jog. For me that's being indecently lazy."

Natalie moved forward and put both hands around Trish's neck. She pulled her forward and kissed her, teasing Trish's mouth with her tongue until she responded. At the same time one hand strayed to her breast to stroke and caress the softness, moulding and working the nipple until it hardened. In a whispering tone, Natalie coaxed, "Stay here. I'll give you an indecent *work-out* and," she laughed throatily, "you'll enjoy it more than a jog around the hotel grounds. I promise."

Smiling at the offer, Trish's hand reached up to trace the contours of Natalie's sharp features and to run her fingers through her platinum hair. She moistened her lips with her tongue, knowing full well that it turned her lover on. "You always keep your promises, don't you, love?"

With surprising strength Natalie pulled an unresisting Trish onto the bed. "You know I do."

Half an hour later and mutually sated, both women lay on their backs, the sheet twisted around their limbs, their fingers lovingly entwined.

In a voice still husky from lovemaking, Trish said, "You never got around to telling me how you went with that builder. Nick Pola ... what's his name?"

"Nick Poladouris."

Yesterday Natalie had spent several hours inspecting the building renovations for her proposed art gallery. The work was going slower than expected, which didn't please her. She wanted it finished so she could cash in on the coming high season. Nick, she'd decided, was on a deliberate go-slow to up the price. Thought he could get away with charging her the earth for materials and labour too. Well, she'd sorted him out.

"We had an enlightening session. Nick gave me the grand tour. He pointed out how expensive everything had got, claimed that there was so much work around the tradesmen were being picky over the best jobs, and that's why costs were escalating. Bastard! Had his greedy Greek eyes all over me too, mentally stripping me." She chuckled. "Nick must have thought he had a chance because as he showed me my office, he went for the grope. Pushed me up against the wall, hands all over me like a bloody octopus. He said he knew I wanted it and maybe we could do a deal on the costs.

"I let him get steamed up then I returned the compliment and grabbed his balls. You should have seen his face." The laugh that erupted from her was tinged with menace. "At first Nicky boy thought all his Christmases had come at once. You know, the man has no finesse – he wanted to do it there on the floor." She watched Trish's eyebrows flutter upwards in distaste. "No bloody way was that pencil dick of his getting anywhere near me. I put the squeeze on him. Literally. Ever seen a Greek tan pale? Little rivers of sweat began to run down his forehead." Enjoying the memory she thought for a moment, "It's interesting how the right kind of pressure on a certain part of a man's anatomy can reduce him to a snivelling wreck. Then I told him what *I* wanted. That he wasn't going to screw me physically or financially and he'd better think twice about the escalating costs."

"How did he take that?"

"Nick wasn't in any position to argue otherwise, believe me. As you know, I have very strong fingers. But, for backup I told him who my stepdaddy was – in case he's the only man in Queensland who doesn't know. I said CJ would be only too happy to send several of his more interesting friends – the type who make the mafia look like wimps – around to visit him." She chuckled as she stroked Trish's hair. "That made Nick go white as a ghost. And then I remembered CJ's advice. I'd heard him once tell Richard that when your opponent's down you don't help him up, you kick him again to let him know who's really the boss. So ... after I kneed Nicky boy in the groin, I walked out." Then she added in a mock solicitous tone, "Must call in today to see how he is, mustn't we?"

"You are deliciously wicked," Trish said with some admiration.

"Thank you. I'm just practising for when I run CJ's empire." Natalie stretched her long limbs and sat up. "I'm starving. Let's drive to Mossman for breakfast. A little café there serves scrumptious apple muffins."

"Okay." Trish sighed. "It's a shame we only have two days here. I could stay a week."

"I agree." Then Natalie had an idea. "Come back to Murrundi with me. CJ won't mind. He likes my friends to visit. Livens the place up."

"Perhaps I could interview him?"

"I don't know," Natalie mused, thinking out loud. "He's a bit journo shy since *The Bulletin* did that job on him. Negative bastards. It took three months, but CJ managed to get the journo who wrote the piece fired."

Trish bit her lower lip. At thirty she was too street-smart to want to get on the wrong side of either Ambrose. "Perhaps not."

"CJ's all enthused about building some cock-a-mammy conference centre at Murrundi. Says big business can come to him for a change. I can't see the sense in the outlay myself but I guess he wants to play the big shot landowner. He's had architects coming and going, one's due up from Sydney. There might be a story in that."

"Maybe. Anyway, I'd love to see Murrundi. I've read about how your mother built and decorated the place."

Natalie quietened for a moment. Mention of Mumsie did that to her even after three years. She blinked back a threatening rush of tears and suddenly her voice took on an artificial brightness. "Good. I'll phone Les. He's taken a few days off to check out the Reef casino. I'll ask him to make space for another passenger on the plane."

CHAPTER SIX

Francey stared at her plate and the huge breakfast her mother had placed before her. "Mamma, I can't eat all this. I'll feel like a stuffed sausage all day."

"Pah, a little stuffing wouldn't do you any harm, you're too skinny by far." Lucia's brown eyes took on a mischievous sheen, "Your boyfriend, Aden, he got to have something to grab onto, hasn't he?"

"He hasn't complained so far," Francey responded with a wink. "Besides, I'll be driving most of the day. A big breakfast will sit like lead in my stomach."

"*Va bene, va bene,*" Lucia gave up. "Eat what you can. Your papà, he will finish the rest."

Carlo paused in his steady munching to look up from his plate. "I don't like the idea that you drive all the way to Mt Isa. Such a long way, it'll take you three to four days. Why you no take the plane like Aden suggested? It's free, it's quick."

"I considered it. Seriously. But then I thought, what an opportunity for me to see some of the country. Why, you and Mamma have seen more of Australia than I have. From Perth to Adelaide, then Melbourne before you settled in Sydney. By comparison I haven't been anywhere. I'll call in on Uncle Guiseppe on the way, and see places I've only read about. Bourke and Charleyville, Longreach and Cloncurry. All that country. Think of the photos I'll be able to take." Her VW beetle was already parked and ready to go at the front of the shop, loaded up with two suitcases, her cameras and film.

"You and your photos. Mamma," Carlo looked across the kitchen table to Lucia, "how did we manage to raise such a strong-willed, independent daughter? She will worry me into my grave."

"Aahh, Carlo, give it up. You know our Francesca will do what she wants, hasn't she always?" She thought fleetingly about her university days and her buying that little flat up near the Cross. Yes, an independent miss was her Francesca. Then she remembered something else and slapped her hands together with glee. "Be happy that she has met a nice young man and that she seems to like him."

"He's nice and he has money," Carlo admitted, then he shook his head, "but he's not Italian."

Francey had been waiting for that remark. "He's part Italian, Papà. He had a maternal grandmother who was half-Italian, half-French. Her maiden name was Simonet."

Mollified by that information, Carlo muttered, "*Sì!* I had my suspicions. Somehow I thought he might be. An Italian can always tell another Italian."

Mother and daughter nodded and exchanged glances but made no further comment.

Carlo cleaned up the food on his plate and took some off Francey's, finishing his meal in silence. After drinking his coffee he heaved himself up from the table and said, "I must open the shop. That Mrs Duchofsky likes to come early. Always she is my first customer." He kissed Francey on the top of her mop of dark curls. "Have a safe journey, *cara*. Don't take any risks on the road. And you show that big man, Mr CJ Ambrose how you can make him a wonderful building. *Magnifico, sì?*"

"I'll give it my best shot, Papà, you can count on it."

The drive would be long but she was looking forward to it. It was her first adventure. And then she recalled that Aden hadn't been impressed when she'd asked for two weeks off, to cover the drive up and back, plus a few days at CJ's property, Murrundi Downs. It meant she'd be away from the office longer than he wanted her to be but she reminded him that she hadn't taken a holiday since starting work and, in her book, she was entitled to a reasonable break. Smiling to herself she recalled his put-out expression. He liked to think of himself as the boss, which he was, but sometimes it felt good to do the unexpected, just to see his reaction. When she had put forward her reason for wanting to drive all the way he'd had no choice but to acquiesce, grudgingly though. She sighed a little sigh. On her return it would be decision time as to which way their relationship went.

The muscles in her body tightened and a warmth stole through her as she remembered last night's passionate kisses. Being celibate for almost four years hadn't bothered her because there hadn't been a man she'd been attracted to. Till now. It was getting harder to say no and she didn't really want to any more, but the fear of being hurt remained too strong to risk it. Yet.

"I've made sandwiches and almond biscuits for you to put in your cooler," Lucia said, bustling around the kitchen tidying things up.

"Thanks, Mamma. I'd best make a start. I'll call you tonight from wherever I'll be staying."

"Stay safe, *cara mia.*"

In the midmorning sunlight Steve Parrish watched waves of heat rise off the bitumen on Camooweal Street, one of the main roads through Mt Isa. Lounging comfortably against an awning upright, the position allowed him to passively patrol a long stretch of the road. A mixture of cars, trucks, utilities and station wagons were parallel parked on either side of the street. Shoppers moved sluggishly, chasing shady awnings, from shop to shop to get their supplies, talking to neighbours or simply walking about minding their own business. A pleasant rural scene. On the surface. But Steve Parrish's eyes, honed by years of detection in the NSW Police Service, knew differently.

It didn't take undue observation on his part to spot the fact that Mrs Hitchener, who ran one of the takeaway shops at the northern end of town, had two black eyes – they showed because the woman refused to wear sunglasses. Which meant Bill Hitchener had visited the Buffalo Club last night and swallowed a gutful. The wife had probably chipped him and he'd laid a couple on her. And over on the other side of the street Sam Bianchini slyly ogled pretty Michelle Mason, the wife of one of the foremen at the Isa mine. Rumour had it that they were in the midst of a red-hot affair. Trouble brewing there – when Mason found out. Three male teenagers, dressed for school, were loitering outside a shop when they should have been in class. Most likely trying to decide whether they were brave enough to do a little shoplifting with him so close. He reckoned they wouldn't. Didn't have the stomach for the consequences, the little pricks. Yes, scratch the surface of any village, town or city anywhere and it was astounding what shone through. He could just about write a book on it.

Sometimes it amazed him that a city boy like him, from the rough streets of Redfern, had slotted so comfortably into country life. Oh, he had to admit that there'd been a few months of strangeness but then he'd settled and it was as if he'd lived for years in the far north. He liked country people, their honesty, the pace, and he loved the stark countryside too, almost as if he'd been born there. His sister and her family in Sydney would have been highly amused at his easy transition to such a different lifestyle.

He spotted a bright yellow VW speeding down the street and his attention diverted from the school boys. The driver jerked to a stop at the red light then, when it turned green, screamed off and flashed past. Braking suddenly, the car began to reverse until it double-parked close to him.

A tall, dark woman dressed in a lightweight white suit, and wearing high heels that put her close to his own height, jumped out of the car and rushed towards him. She was worth looking at. Tanned skin and great legs displayed by the mid-thigh skirt, and in an instant he noted that her lipstick matched the bright pink scarf trailing around her neck. Black curly hair bounced all over the place as she moved gracefully. Foreign-looking too. Was she Italian or Maltese? No, maybe Spanish, or even Greek? He straightened up and waited.

"Oh, Officer, thank goodness," Francey said breathlessly. Then she abruptly stopped. My, he was big. Good country stock, no doubt. But then she remembered her problem and rushed on. "I ... back there ..." Her heart was still pounding fit to burst from fright. "There's been an accident. I ... I hit ... They might be dead."

Steve frowned. He studied the VW's dent on the front passenger side fender; it didn't look serious enough to have caused any deaths. "Miss? You'll have to give me some details."

"Of course." Where were her brains? She took off her sunglasses and looked up into a pair of the darkest brown eyes she had ever seen. Almost black, bottomless. Mesmerising. *Mesmerising?* Yoicks, where had that thought come from? She blinked a couple of times hoping the action would clear her head. "Back that way," she pointed along the road she'd driven through into town. "About four kilometres, I think."

"So, you hit them. A car accident. How many people were involved?" Through his peripheral vision Steve noticed Sam Bianchini crossing the street. The man's curiosity and the possibility of talking to a pretty woman knew no bounds. And she *was* pretty. All that Mediterranean vivaciousness wrapped up in a very appealing physical package. Just passing through, he deduced. He stopped himself, shocked by his level of interest and then disappointment. A faint stirring started inside him and its intensity forced him to sublimate the feelings by adopting a businesslike manner.

"I'm Sergeant Steve Parrish. Your name, miss?"

Francey took a deep breath to steady herself from the fright she'd had and, strangely, from her internal response towards the policeman. Boy, her hormones were really out of whack! "Francesca Spinetti, people call me Francey."

"Where are you from?"

"Sydney."

"Right, there's some urgency here. Now, how many people injured, killed? What kind of a car was involved? I need to inform the ambulance and the hospital. You'd better come with me in my car to the scene of the accident."

"Oh. No!" Francey realised she had misled him. "Not people. I didn't hit any people," and to emphasise the point she shook her head vigorously. "Kangaroos. Two of them. They came out of the scrub, they didn't have a chance. I had no warning. Bang. I hit them. It was awful. I braked and swerved but by the time my car stopped, all I could see was two animals limping off into the bush." She sighed. "Poor things."

Sam Bianchini had come to stand next to Steve. An odd expression crossed his swarthy face as he said, "Kangaroos? You hit a couple of roos?"

"Yes," her blue-green eyes appealed to the officer. "I got such a fright. It was terrible. Please, come with me and try to find them, we have to see if we can help them." During her three days drive north she had photographed many kangaroos: at sunset, grazing by the side of the road, a mother and her joey too. She was appalled that she'd inadvertently injured two of the gentle creatures.

She watched the officer tilt his broad-brimmed hat back on his head and immediately several locks of dark brown hair fell onto his forehead. It struck her that he had an interesting face. Not good-looking, but interesting. A liveliness enhanced his eyes, which was at odds with the firm turn of his mouth and the stubborn squared-off angle of his jaw. It proclaimed that once he had set a course he would not be easily diverted from it. An impulsive thought popped into her head. I'd like to capture that face with my camera lens one day.

"Roos!" Sam repeated, dumbstruck.

Steve tried to hold down the smile that threatened to tug the corners of his mouth upwards. All this fuss over hitting a couple of kangaroos! Definitely a city dweller. Sam would get great pleasure in spreading this tale around town. It wasn't hard to imagine the way he'd start it off. Did you hear the one about the tourist sheila and the kangaroos?

"No one gives a stuff about roos around here, miss," Sam informed Francey. "They're vermin. Eat the grass, cause accidents. No bloody good at all, except for their skins or to eat if you're hard up. You've done the landowners, myself included, a favour if you've knocked a couple off."

Francey looked up at the policeman, a sergeant no less, and saw a similar opinion reflected in his expression. "But I may not have killed them. What if they're injured, in pain? Shouldn't someone investigate?"

"I'm sorry, Miss Spinetti," Steve said slowly, liking the way her name sounded as he said it. "Police here don't have the manpower to do that sort of thing. Besides, they, the roos, have probably bounded off into the bush so we wouldn't find them anyway." He glanced again at the VW. "And by the dent on your fender I'd say they were only dealt a glancing blow."

Francey recognised the suppressed laughter in his voice and her spine straightened. Of course. She should have known. Country folk were used to dealing with this kind of thing. Every day. It wouldn't worry them at all. They saw kangaroos and buffalo and wild pigs as competition for their cattle and sheep grazing. God, she was out of her depth. A city person all at sea in a country situation. They must think her an idiot. From deep within her the control took over again and she became the sophisticated, urbane woman skilled at covering up the odd gaffe.

"I see," she murmured stiffly. At least she had to try to save face. "Thank you for putting me straight," she glanced at Sam Bianchini, "on the roo thing."

"No harm done – except to your fender," Steve stated as he studied her. She was a stylish woman. Citified. He sensed a warmth about her, and he liked the way her cheeks reddened as she realised her complaint sounded foolish. He tried to ease her embarrassment by saying, "Drivers have to be careful in the bush. Roos are impulsive, irrational creatures. I suggest that in future you slow down and sound your horn when you come across them. That usually makes them scatter."

"Yeah," Sam Bianchini agreed, then added, curiously, "Where you headed, love?"

Francey, regaining her equilibrium, remembered the business at hand. "Murrundi Downs station. Is it far from here?"

"About twenty kilometres the other side of town, heading south-east. The turn-off's well signposted," Steve told her. Then it clicked in his detective-trained mind who she was. "You're the architect from Sydney, aren't you?"

Francey's dark eyebrows shot up. "Yes." How did he know? Did she have "architect" stencilled across her forehead or something?

"Bush telegraph," he answered her unasked question. "I believe CJ's expecting you."

"Perhaps you'd like a drink, or a cup of tea? Something before you go on?" Sam asked hopefully, ignoring Steve Parrish's disapproving frown.

Steve wondered what Michelle Mason would think about her lover chatting the Sydney woman up? Not a lot. He watched her smile at Sam and shake her head to his invitation.

"No, thanks. I'd best be on my way." A sudden anxiety to get as far away from these men – but particularly the policeman – consumed her. Why hadn't she thought the situation through before she'd reacted? That was her trouble, her father would tell her, her spontaneous nature. She took things too much to heart, hated injustice and liked to be involved. Too involved perhaps – as had happened with Bryan. But over the years she realised that she couldn't help it, it was her nature to be like that.

All the way back to the car she felt the officer's eyes – twin black beams burning into her. She slammed the car door with a loud bang to rid herself of the jangled emotions which rioted inside, and then she squeezed her eyes shut and tried to conjure up Aden's image. Relief flooded through her as she pictured him, smiling. She sighed. The sooner she did what she had to do here and returned to her own domain, Sydney, and Aden, the better.

It wasn't until Francey had driven ten kilometres out of Mt Isa that her nerves finally calmed down. The countryside looked different once she'd left the perimeter of the large mining town where access to town water meant greenness and flowers. Once she was out in the bush again, the land returned to the familiar reddish-brown colour with old stunted trees and low-growing shrubs of a dullish-green. Giant termite mounds sprang up like strange sentinels of the hot, silent land. The grass, typical of the harsh climate in which it struggled to survive, looked yellow and tired. The sights and places she'd seen on her journey to CJ Ambrose's property had left a lasting impression, and she now had an appreciation for the vastness and toughness of the outback, something she wouldn't have had had she not ventured by road out of Sydney. The people she'd met had been solid country folk. She wished she'd had more time in many of the towns she'd been through to do pictorial studies of the people and the quaint historical buildings.

At precisely twenty kilometres out of town she saw the dirt road turn-off to Murrundi Downs station. Undulating hills almost devoid of trees bordered the western side as she headed south, crossing over several cattle grids along the way. A thin line of shrubs and spindly gum trees marked a water course. As she'd travelled north, she had learnt that's where the creeks lay. Elsewhere, unless she saw bore water windmills, clumps of anything green were rare.

Five kilometres further along Francey came upon the entrance to CJ's vast estate. Two impressively high – maybe three metres – rough-hewn sandstone columns stood on either side of the road and spanning them in black painted wrought iron were the words Murrundi Downs. A wire fence on each side of the pillars ran off into the distance. Three large crows perched passively on the wire, as if watching the car, while overhead a kite floated on the air currents, alert for signs of careless prey. Her welcoming committee, perhaps! The sprinkling of cattle forever munching where they could find feed was evidence of the homestead being close by.

Seeing buildings in the distance as she topped a small rise, she parked and got out of the car for a better look. The red-painted corrugated iron roofed house and a multitude of surrounding buildings sparkled like an oasis amongst the surrounding plains of brownish-yellow, and further back a creek snaked crookedly across the property.

As she approached the homestead a three-tiered water fountain surrounded by a lush green lawn and a formal circular drive of crushed volcanic rock made Francey's eyebrows lift. It seemed incongruous in such a harsh setting. She parked near the front steps of the house which had been built in typical north Queenslander fashion: high off the ground, three metres at least, and on brick piers to increase ventilation. Masses of latticework had become trestles to carry both flowering and green vines, and they disguised the bottom level of the house. Wide sandstone steps proclaimed the entrance and on each side stood terracotta pots from which a profusion of pink, white and red geraniums blossomed. Even in winter the daytime temperature hovered around thirty degrees Celsius; obviously the geraniums had been tricked into not knowing they were flowering out of season.

The main homestead was indeed impressive. The high-pitched roof had several angles to it and ornate, carved timber adorned each apex. A wide screened-in verandah bordered each side of the box-shaped building and had French windows opening onto it. They in turn were bordered by painted louvred doors, showing the proximity of various rooms.

As Francey walked up the steps she straightened her business-suit skirt and took a deep breath to keep the growing nervousness at bay. She was about to meet one of the wealthiest men in the land and that made her mind automatically hark back to what she had read about the famous CJ Ambrose. Aden's comprehensive file, thanks to his secretary, covered much of the private and public life of Queensland's best known businessman. "The man with the golden touch", journalists called CJ – mostly because every venture he involved himself in made him wealthier than he already was.

She'd read about his son's recent death and knew that his wife had died of cancer three years before. He had a stepdaughter, Natalie, and it was assumed that she would one day inherit the Ambrose empire. But what concerned her most in what she had read was the regular reports of CJ's ruthlessness in business.

Success meant everything to the man. Instinctively, that made her wary even though Aden had impressed upon her the importance of this project to the firm. *That* had irked her a little. Aden's firm was doing very well, she knew that from the quarterly balance sheet, so she didn't understand his underlying anxiety for her to do all in her power to get the Ambrose contract. It was pressure she didn't need. She would, of course, do her utmost as a matter of pride. She was as competitive as the next architect and didn't need to be reminded by her boss that if CJ liked what she proposed it could lead to more work for the firm.

Mopping a film of perspiration from her face, she grasped the circular handle of the brass knocker attached to the glass panelled double doors. She struck firmly and waited.

The door was thrust wide open by a woman wearing a white blouse and a navy skirt. "Yes?"

"Good morning." Francey smiled at the middle-aged woman with greying hair. "I'm Francey Spinetti. I have a morning appointment with Mr Ambrose." She fished a business card out of her jacket pocket and handed it to the woman.

Shellie Kirkby studied the card for a few seconds then stared hard at the dark-haired young woman. Something ... As her gaze swept over her features she had the strangest feeling that she had seen or met her before. And her eyes ... they reminded her of someone. After a moment or two she realised she was staring, and she remembered when she'd seen her – the interview on *A Current Affair*. Of course! That's why she seemed familiar. "Sorry, dear, you caught me off-guard. I'm Shellie, CJ's sister. Do come in."

"Thank you." Francey passed over the entrance into the blissful coolness of the air-conditioned interior. "Come into the living room and make yourself comfortable. I don't know where Les is – probably around the property somewhere – and CJ's on an international call. I'll let him know you've arrived."

Left to her own devices, instead of sitting – she'd done nothing but sit for days as she'd travelled north – Francey strolled around the hugely proportioned living area. The floors were polished jarrah and the walls and ceilings were painted white, probably for coolness. Large circular fans rotated to help circulate the already cooled air. Stained timber louvred doors effectively screened off a large formal dining area and most of the furniture, apart from the occasional antique, had a tropical look. Cane had been used extensively and was attractively mixed with brass and glass ornamental tables.

She had read about Brenda deWitt-Ambrose being keen on *objets d'art* and she found ample evidence of this. A set of two Salvador Dali paintings hung on a timber panelled wall, as well there were pieces of Chinese pottery, probably from some rare Ming dynasty, and bronze and marble sculptures. Busts of several famous Roman emperors featured on a wrought iron and glass wall unit.

She walked up to one painting to look at the artist's signature and saw the name, Tom Roberts. Her eyebrows shot up in appreciation and then slowly normalised. Why was she surprised? The late Mrs Ambrose had been able to buy anything she wanted – her husband was a multimillionaire.

"You like Tom Roberts?" came an enquiring male voice from across the room.

Francey pirouetted towards the sound. A tall man, in his thirties, dressed in jeans and a checked shirt had entered the room from a wide hallway. "I do." She smiled at him. "I like Hans Heyson and Streeton too."

"You're a traditionalist then?" Les Westcott asked as he came towards her.

"Definitely."

"You and Brenda would have got along famously. She couldn't stand the Dobells, Whiteleys and Dones of this world." He held out his hand. "I'm Les Westcott, CJ's CEO."

"Pleased to meet you, Mr Westcott."

"We go by first names here. Les and Francey, right?" he grinned at her.

Instantly charmed by his countrified manner and genuine smile, Francey's grin widened. She agreed with a nod of her head. "Even CJ?"

He nodded. "Even CJ."

They moved towards the cane lounge chairs and sat down.

"You had a good trip up?"

"Wonderful. Long of course, but I saw so much." She gave him a droll look. "I'm a confirmed city person – never seen the country at all, well, not beyond Dubbo. It's been a revelation."

The television hadn't done her justice, Les decided as he studied her, noting that she used her hands, her eyes and body language to emphasise points. Very Mediterranean. An observer of people, one of his and Richard's overseas trip destinations had been Italy. They'd taken in the usual tourist things, and he had really enjoyed watching the vivacity of the Italians. They loved to laugh and talk, and to engage in lively fights too. The two-dimensional magazine picture hadn't captured Francey Spinetti's personality he realised, but then how could a camera lens do that? She was quite lovely. As he admitted that his gaze dropped to her hands. No rings. No attachments? Perhaps.

"You should drive back via the coast. There's some spectacular coastlines between here and Sydney."

"I intend to." Ambrose's CEO was easy to talk to, she decided. Though his tone was cultured he espoused no airs and graces and seemed a down to earth type of man. The thought struck her that he was rather like the Mt Isa policeman, Sergeant Parrish. She pulled herself up short. What had made her think about *him*? Determinedly she pushed him to the back of her mind.

"I suppose your workload has increased since the favourable publicity of the award."

Francey gave a mock groan. "Doubled. As soon as I get some firm ideas on what Mr Ambrose, I mean, CJ wants, I'll have to head back to Sydney."

"Really? I think CJ expects you to stay a while. At least a week."

She gasped, and her eyebrows shot upwards. "I couldn't possibly." She remembered the effort it had taken to cajole Aden into giving her two weeks holiday, a *working* holiday she'd reminded him. What would Aden think if she took more time than she had planned? That she was indulging in a real outback holiday. "I'm sure it won't take that long, Les. I have commitments ..."

Les stroked his jaw reflectively. He hoped she would change her mind. "Architects from the two other firms stayed on to get the feel of the place. CJ even set up an office for them. We've a spare room that's used for office supplies, that sort of thing. I brought in the necessary draughtsman's tools and a computer and fitted it out so they could do their preliminary work there. I'm sure he'll expect you to do the same as the others have."

"It's not that I wouldn't like to ..." Francey murmured. CJ's expectations of her were quite unexpected. She didn't want to offend "the man with the golden touch" but she knew Aden wouldn't be pleased, at all.

"No need to decide now. But be warned, Francey, CJ can be pretty persuasive when he wants to be."

"And just what can I be persuasive about?"

Francey turned towards the voice, unaware that she was holding her breath. As CJ Ambrose emerged from the same hallway Les had, she rose to meet him.

There were some men who could emit a defined presence, a kind of charismatic force field that radiated invisibly around them. CJ Ambrose was such a man. And what a weapon it must be during negotiations, Francey thought. He could almost dominate his subjects by the force of his will. She noted that physically he wasn't overly tall, nor overly attractive, but something from within gave him an aura. That and his eyes. He had the brightest, most piercing blue eyes she had ever seen. They seemed as though they'd be able to spear their quarry and hold them enthralled ... or perhaps hold them in fear.

"Mr Ambrose," Francey held out her hand to him, "It's an honour to meet you."

CJ instantly admired her easy grace. "Don't know about honour, Francey." He shot an amused glance at Les, "Some of my competition don't think it's much of an honour – but that's often because they're on the losing end of a business deal."

Trying to contain her awe, she smiled nervously. "Well, I hope I won't fall into that category, Mr Ambrose."

"Don't see why you should. And call me CJ, everyone does."

She didn't feel comfortable calling such an enigma by his first name, but neither did she want to offend. "If you insist." He smiled at her and he didn't look quite so intimidating. She rather hoped CJ Ambrose smiled a lot.

After a moment's silence he said, "I do, Francey Spinetti, I do."

Shellie and another woman bustled in. "What time would you like lunch, CJ?"

"Half an hour." A movement in his peripheral vision caught his attention. "What is it, Lisa? I said I didn't want to be disturbed for the next hour or two," CJ asked the woman standing at Shellie's side.

Francey almost winced at his tone. He was used to giving orders and having them implicitly obeyed. As well, a stab of sympathy raced through her for the woman named Shellie. In his presence CJ's sister appeared to shrink in stature and show signs of agitation, though she tried valiantly to disguise the fact. Could it be that CJ Ambrose was a tyrant in his home? If one judged by Shellie's reactions it was possible. But, she silently avowed, he'd get short shrift if he tried that tone with her, no matter how awesome his reputation. She abhorred rudeness and bad tempers, from anyone – even multimillionaires! Her mother had taught her not to have a bar of such behaviour and she wouldn't, project or no project.

"Lisa Dupre, meet Francey Spinetti. Francey's the architect from Sydney. Lisa's my private secretary," CJ told Francey. "Her office is just down the hallway, the first door on the left. If you need anything, she'll procure it for you. Anything," his blue eyes suddenly twinkled, "within reason, that is."

Lisa Dupre acknowledged Francey with a smile. "Hello." And then she became all business and turned towards her boss. "CJ, Fielding's on the line. I thought you'd want to speak to him."

CJ grunted. "Okay, put the call through to here, will you?"

As Lisa left to switch the call through, Shellie spoke to Francey. "If you'll give me your car keys I'll have someone put your bags in your room and drive your car around the back where there's shade."

Francey appreciated the woman's thoughtfulness and she handed over her keys. "Thank you." Out of the corner of her eye she saw CJ pick up the phone receiver and moved away to afford him some privacy by pretending to study the painting by Tom Roberts.

Les gravitated towards it too. "Every room in the house has paintings, oils, pencil sketches and watercolours," he informed her. "Brenda had a passion for Australian art. CJ reckons the house is a mini art gallery – the huge insurance premium he pays proves it."

"I look forward to seeing them," she said honestly.

"It'll be my pleasure. After lunch CJ usually takes a nap and that's the hottest time of day outside so I thought I'd give you some leisure time so you can unpack. We'll do the grand tour of the place about four o'clock if that's okay with you?"

"Sounds good. But I would like to sit with you and CJ to discuss your needs for the convention centre as soon as possible."

"Of course, not today though. CJ's awfully busy and he just wants you to get settled in. I've scheduled a morning session tomorrow to talk about the new complex, after you've got the lay of the land, so to speak. This afternoon wear something casual and wear sturdy walking shoes, if you have them."

At pains to fit in with the different lifestyle and someone else's timetable Francey agreed with a nod of her head.

"What do you mean? Dammit, Fielding, I told you what to do." CJ's voice, dripping with annoyance, boomed across the spacious room. "I'm paying you good money. Top money. I don't want to hear this shit. You'd bloody well better keep your end up or there'll be consequences."

"Someone's getting a good chewing out," Francey said quietly to Les, trying to hide her discomfort. She didn't enjoy eavesdropping on other people's business but as they were all in the one room it was impossible not to.

CJ paused mid-sentence, only half-listening to Fielding's excuses. His gaze was locked on the young architect, watching her talk animatedly about the painting she and Les were studying. His gaze narrowed as he saw the attention Les was giving her. If Francey Spinetti was half as smart as she was lovely to look at, the next few days could be mighty interesting.

Something Fielding said snapped him back to the crisis at hand. Jesus, that Cooktown land deal had been a foregone conclusion. He had the council in his pocket, the seller wanted the deal and as far as he was concerned, no damned bunch of greenies was going to spoil it. If he had to bring in the heavies, well ... "You've got twenty-four hours to get it under control, Fielding. If you can't I'll send in some people who will. You know what that will do to the tourist business, don't you?"

That sounded suspiciously like a threat, Francey thought as she heard CJ's words. She had read about CJ's bully-boy tactics. Queensland journalists reported that at times he acted as if he was above the law – and he had got away with it. She recalled one article, something about a private road inland to the coast, to one of his properties, being built with local council labour and funds. Probably the man was a law unto himself, with so much wealth at his disposal. Wealth and power. She was wise enough to know they were a dangerous combination.

Lunch turned out to be surprisingly pleasant. Served in a glassed-in conservatory with a terracotta tiled floor and situated next to the kitchen, the furniture was casual, the emphasis on comfort rather than style. Francey loved the room because of the plants. In the air-conditioned atmosphere, with a green shade cloth covering the glass roof, vines and palms and a variety of ferns grew in wild abundance.

"I call this the jungle room," CJ told her, watching Francey's gaze move admiringly around the room. "My late wife holidayed on Norfolk Island once and was invited to Colleen McCullough's for dinner. She came back in raptures over some marvellous room where plants grew everywhere, like a mini rainforest. Insisted we had to have one so I built this for her."

"It's lovely."

"Shellie doesn't think so," Les quipped. "She says it's hard work keeping the plants watered and picking up the dead leaves."

"Yes, I suppose there's that," Francey agreed. "Still, one has an illusion, a feeling of ..." she sought the right words, "tranquillity and coolness."

"It's a good place to come at the height of summer. When it's forty degrees plus outside and there's a wind storm blowing red dust everywhere," said Lisa Dupre, who'd joined them for lunch.

"Do you live at Murrundi, Lisa?" Francey asked as she forked the Caesar salad around her plate.

"No. In the Isa. My husband works at the mine. We've

a small property just off the highway. Pierre is keen to go into business for himself but –"

"The money at the mine's just too good to give up, isn't it?" Les put in succinctly, for Francey's benefit. "It's hard to get out even though the work's dirty and sometimes dangerous. Some say it's the money that keeps most of the miners there."

"I've offered to set Pierre up, Lisa. Whenever he's ready," CJ added.

Lisa smiled at her boss. "Thanks, CJ. But you know Pierre, he's a proud man. Wants to do it on his own."

CJ shrugged. "Well, it's up to him." He turned to Francey and speared her with his incredible, penetrating eyes. "And what about you, Francey? Would you object to a helping hand up the career ladder?"

She thought for a moment. "It depends on whether there were strings attached. Usually there are, which could be related to professional loyalty or business sweeteners later on. Few people actually throw money at you in architecture, the coercion often comes by way of favours, commissions, projects, that sort of thing." She looked CJ squarely in the eyes. "For me it's important to achieve success on my own – without inducements. That way I won't owe anyone anything."

"A person with integrity. How refreshing," CJ softened the sarcasm with a smile. "In all my years of dealing with people I've found that everyone has their price. And, interestingly, it isn't always money. Often it's something more subtle, like success, ego stroking, public acclaim, being put on a pedestal. When I find their weakness, what they want, I give it to them in exchange for what I want." His gaze flicked across to Les and his grin widened. "The system works well, doesn't it, Les?"

"Hasn't failed us yet."

Francey felt a chill run down her back at CJ's frankness and wondered if he would search out her dream, *her* price. Did she have one? She hoped not. But ... everyone had faults and idiosyncrasies, she knew she wasn't immune. Bryan had been an emotional weakness of sorts. Carlo said her weakness was her desire for a career – to be the best at her chosen field, and that it would most likely spoil her chance for happiness. But her dear Papà had a one-track mind. In his language marriage equalled happiness and fulfilment.

"So, that's the secret of your success, CJ?" Francey said lightly.

"Part of it. Damned hard work and having a nose, sensing what's going to work and what isn't, is the rest of the equation. I've been lucky in that regard." He waited a moment then added, "Everyone has their price."

Francey's eyebrows lifted. "Not everyone."

CJ Ambrose loved a challenge. He tapped the top of the table for attention. "All right, Francey Spinetti, let's say for the sake of the exercise that a benefactor came along and offered to set you up in your own architectural firm. He'd carry all the costs – rent, staff, equipment – until you got established and were making a profit. What would you say to that?"

"I'd say tempting, very tempting but ..." and she slowly shook her head.

CJ's eyebrows rose in disbelief. "You'd knock back such a deal?"

Francey's expression turned contemplative. "I'd have problems with it."

"Why?" Les queried as he rested his elbows on the table. She was something, this young architect. It had been years since he'd seen someone display such honesty and lack of awe for CJ's wealth. Naive perhaps but, by jove, he liked it.

"I'd insist on paying the money back, for one thing, and that would take time. And there's the question of loyalty. I was taught that loyalty is an important attribute. As I see it I owe Nicholson, Drew and Carlyle. They've had faith in me, in my talent as an architect. It wouldn't be right to leave them in the lurch to set myself up as a competitor, not yet anyway."

"I'd say with the new business you've already brought to them that you've paid them back tenfold," CJ interposed as he drummed his fingers thoughtfully on the table.

"Maybe," she shrugged her shoulders in acknowledgement. She had. Aden had said so, of late quite often. "Guess I'm just old-fashioned. I'd be uncomfortable accepting patronage from someone else and, as there'd be the likelihood of strings being attached, I wouldn't like that."

CJ laughed loud and long. Then he slapped his hand down hard on the table top, causing the crockery to rattle ominously. "By God, you're not putting me on. I believe you mean every word," he said, his voice tinged with unaccustomed amazement.

Shellie, who'd been standing by the doorway with a tray of mango sorbets, a light dessert to precede the iced coffee or tea, nodded approvingly. "Good for you, Francey." She looked at Les. "Mike Hunter's just called in, he's down by Bindi Creek. One of the stockmen, Fred Muir, has had an accident. They think his leg's broken. Mike said they'll need a four-wheel drive to bring him in."

Les grimaced. "Who's around the place to drive out to them?"

"Billy Wontow. Mike has him doing some fencing around the western dam, where the soil's eroded away."

"All right. Have Billy kit out the vehicle so that Fred can be laid flat in the back. Tell him to take him straight to the Mt Isa hospital." He shook his head, disgusted by the turn of events. They were short-handed and way behind in the winter season's work schedule. Damn it for another piece of bad luck. Bad luck and strange happenings seemed to have dogged Murrundi since Richard's death. "Phone the hospital and tell them he'll be there in a couple of hours."

With an understanding nod, Shellie about-faced to do his bidding.

Les's general grin encompassed Francey in particular. "You might have thought life was peaceful on a cattle station. Not so. If it's not the animals it's the staff. Always some drama happening."

Francey laughed. "So I see."

CJ liked the way she laughed. There was throaty, honest amusement to it, nothing faked. And he could see why Les was drawn to her. She was lovely, in a slightly foreign way. As well, by the way she'd spoken she wasn't overawed by him either. Another unusual occurrence. The other two architects had fallen over themselves with nervousness and a willingness to accede to his every whim. No spines at all, he remembered dismissively. Somehow he didn't think Francey Spinetti would be so accommodating. From the little nuances, the things she said and the way she said them, he deduced that she was an independent, strong-willed woman. His Brenda had been like that and he'd respected her for it, even though they'd had many clashes during their marriage.

It would be interesting to see the kind of design the architect from Nicholson's came up with for the new complex. He had the feeling it would be like her, a little beauty.

Punctually at four o'clock that afternoon, Les knocked on Francey's door for the grand tour, and as suggested she had changed into jeans, a clean T-shirt and Doc Martens. In her right hand she held a broad-brimmed straw hat to keep the sun off her face.

It took an hour and a half to see over the property and its various buildings and places of interest. He took her through the six bedroom house, and showed her where Lisa worked. One bedroom had been converted into an electronic state-of-the-art office with an adjoining door which led to CJ's study. In the roomy, modern kitchen she met Alison Wontow, Billy's wife, and was shown an area off the conservatory which had been made into a spa and sauna – though why they'd need a sauna so far north perplexed her.

Then Les showed her the room CJ had fitted out as a draughtsman's office. Seeing it, Francey began to resign herself to the likelihood of staying at Murrundi until she came up with a design for the new complex. What CJ Ambrose wanted, she thought wryly, it seemed he usually got!

The swimming pool and garden at the side of the homestead were delightful and Les promptly told her that the gardens had been planned by CJ's late wife. Brenda had grown up on the coast and she'd been determined that if they were to live inland permanently, she would recreate some of the flora that abounded around Townsville. No expense had been spared to achieve this. The poolside and the gardens had been professionally landscaped, tonnes of soil had been trucked in and more wells had been bored to obtain a ready supply of water. Water was the necessity which kept everything green and lush in what was undeniably an inhospitable climate.

Francey marvelled at the height and density of the row of conifers that created a protective, living wall around the pool and the artificially grassed tennis court. And then they moved on to the other buildings. There was Les' cottage at the back of the homestead; the station hands bunkhouse and kitchen; a small foreman's cottage; two barns; a stable capable of housing a dozen horses and several outbuildings which housed a myriad of farm machinery. A small generating plant was separated by a high barbed wire fence and beyond that lay two dams still relatively full. Further back were mazes of fenced yards for the stock and way in the distance stood a huge, barn-like structure: a hangar which housed a helicopter and CJ's Learjet. A thin black line lay beyond – the airstrip.

Francey took it all in with a growing respect for CJ's empire. Already getting the feel of the place, she studied the high-standing homestead from a distance, and began to think about the type of design that would best suit the conference complex and where the building should be situated.

As she gazed towards the horizon she noticed something unusual. Out beyond the last building, towards the north, was a hill, no, not exactly a hill, more like a gentle rising slope. Atop the slope stood a large peppercorn tree. A fenced off grassy knoll surrounded the tree. Curiosity made her ask as she pointed, "Les, what's over there?"

"The family cemetery," Les said. "Several of the Ambrose family are buried there. When Brenda passed away, CJ had a plumber put in a water pipe to the area and planted the tree. Looks like a little oasis, doesn't it? It's quite a walk though, so we'll leave that for another time."

As they returned to the homestead via the swimming pool and garden, Natalie and her friend Trish lazed on a couple of loungers after a swim. From the window of his den CJ watched Les introduce the women to Francey. The two had spent the day at Lawn Hill National Park and were animatedly telling Francey that it was a great place to visit. He studied the three women, each of them so different, but his attention returned to the dark-haired Francey Spinetti. She intrigued him, no doubt about it. He frowned, as if annoyed by the thought and with a shrug went back to his desk.

CHAPTER SEVEN

Steve Parrish sat in the wicker chair nursing a beer, oblivious to the condensation that dripped between his fingers then fell in a puddle at his feet. He concentrated on the sun as it set over the western side of Mt Isa; slowly turning the sky a pinkish-orange, then red and finally a mauvish-grey. This was his favourite time of day. He liked to sit here and recap the day's events, going over the ins and outs of life in a big country town where often the worst crime committed that day might be a kid stealing a car and taking it for a joy ride. So different from Sydney.

His lips twitched in a wry grin as he remembered the dark-haired woman and the kangaroo story. Francey Spinetti. He rolled her name around in his head, elongating the syllables, and then his grin widened. She had been the high spot of an otherwise routine day. It was almost as if she had been physically lifted from the streets of Sydney and miraculously deposited on the main street of the Isa. Everything about her screamed *city*, from her lacquered fingernails and perfect make-up job to her power suit and high heels. He closed his eyes and let her image form behind the lids. What a looker! A cosy warmth stole through his body and for once he didn't fight it. Sometimes he did, but now he went with the flow, even though he knew he'd probably suffer later on with a restless night or erotic dreams that stimulated rather than soothed.

Sam Bianchini had said after Francey had marched off in high dudgeon that she was the prettiest sheila he'd seen in a month of Sundays. Not exactly original, but poor old Sam wasn't big on originality. He agreed with him though, which he didn't do often.

Thinking about Francey reminded him of Sydney. Up until three years ago he'd lived there all his life. Without wanting it to happen his thoughts kicked into reverse and took him back in time. Sometimes he missed the big city so much his gut tightened into a hard knot, but at other times he was sure he never wanted to walk down George Street or see the garish neon lights of Kings Cross again.

The best young detective sergeant around, many of his colleagues and superior officers had said of him. He swallowed a mouthful of cool ale, savouring the malty crispness as it trickled down his throat, then he leant back in the chair and closed his eyes. Christ, he had a string of certificates and awards to prove he was good. Not bad for a kid who'd grown up in Redfern and who could have just as easily ended up a crim. But the accolades hadn't done much good the night he'd almost got his partner killed.

His eyes flicked open and in the gathering twilight the expression in his dark depths was bleak. She'd been pretty too! Senior Constable Karrin Brookes of the NSW Police Department's Drug Squad; his partner for six months. He chuckled to himself as he recalled ... half the members of the squad had been running a book on whether they were in the middle of a torrid affair though it wasn't so. Karrin had fallen hard for a guy in the hospitality business and she planned to resign when he got the expected posting to Switzerland.

The drug bust should have been routine.

Steve had been tipped off by a reliable source that a street load of smack was going to be packaged in a semi in Camden Street, Newtown. Routine. Bust them, charge them, write the reports, bloody pages and pages – that was part of the job too, the dead boring part. The raid hadn't gone according to the book though, had it? Shit, no. It had turned into a life and death situation.

Warm, soft rain and a moonless night, deep shadows along corrugated tin fences welcomed Steve and Karrin and two junior police officers that night. From a back lane littered with rubbish they peered into the backyard of the semi through a rusty hole in the fence. As midnight approached most of the houses were in darkness and the area looked and sounded deceptively peaceful.

Silhouetted through the shades of the back window of the semi Steve could make out two people hunched over something. "Looks like the real thing. I'll call for backup," he whispered as he reached for his portable radio.

"Shouldn't we make sure they're actually packing the drugs before we call? The sarge at Newtown station won't be happy if we call a car out on a wild goose chase," Karrin countered.

Steve nodded in agreement as his gaze roved over the tin fence. It might collapse if he tried to climb it, and he'd make the devil of a noise doing it too.

"We could go over the neighbour's side fence, its palings are less than two metres high. Looks sturdy enough," Karrin suggested, reading his mind.

"You're intrepid tonight." He chuckled as he spoke. He

looked at Pete Forrest and Mario d'Agusta. They nodded in agreement. "Okay, let's do it."

Four minutes later the four stood at the rear of the backyard. Placing his finger over his lips, Steve signalled that he'd get close to the window to see what was going on. He carefully threaded his way through the piles of rubbish, tin cans, and old car parts which were strewn across the yard. At the side of the window he edged forward to peep through a tear in the shade. He recognised two men: Lenny Andropoulos, a known drug dealer, and a younger man, Paul Nixon. Both were known to be buddies in the Sydney drug scene. On the table lay a pile of drug making paraphernalia: scales, capsules, paper and plastic envelopes.

Satisfied, he returned to his team. "It's a go," he whispered to Karrin. "Call for backup. No sirens. There's a narrow side passage round to the front, looks relatively unobstructed. Karrin, Pete, make your way out to the street. Mario and I will hold a position here in case they try to flit out the back. When backup arrives, we'll synchronise and go in."

The call to the station made, Karrin gave the thumbs up signal and she and Pete moved off. Steve watched until they were out of sight and then, signalling for Mario to stay put, he edged towards the window.

In hindsight, Steve could never work out what tipped the dealers off. Maybe they'd had a *dog* on lookout. Suddenly the two men jumped up from the table and doused the lights. Steve strained his ear close to the window pane and heard furtive whispering but couldn't get the gist of what was being said.

Then he heard a third voice. A scream. A child's scream. Then silence!

With the traffic situation in King Street Steve knew it would take a police car four to five minutes to get to the address. But now there was a new dimension – a child the crims could use as a hostage, a bargaining point. Damn. Wait, he stifled the urge to react. See what their next move was. His heartbeat began to accelerate, the palms of his hands sweated up. The back door opened a couple of centimetres and the barrel of a revolver peeped out of it.

No time for backup. Maybe they're going to rush out the back, he thought. Could they be bluffed into giving up? He hand-signalled Mario – a probationary constable with about six weeks experience on the job – to take cover. "Andropoulos, Nixon, police. We've got the place surrounded. Come out with your hands up. Now!"

"Bloody pigs. I told you," a voice yelled.

The door slammed shut and Steve heard a bolt being thrown across it.

"We've got a kid in here, pig," one of the men shouted. "Let us out free and clear. She don't get hurt then."

"You're only making it worse for yourself, Andropoulos. We've got you dead to rights. Let the child go, then we can talk about a deal."

"I won't do no deal with no pig. I'm not going back inside again either."

From somewhere within Steve heard a child whimpering. He glanced at his watch. Another three minutes – the longest three minutes of his life. He tried to appeal to the younger man. "Nixon, think about it. The law'll go harder on you if you don't free the kid. What do you want to do? Five years in gaol or would you rather it be ten?"

"Shut up!"

A bullet came through the back door to emphasise the point and then there was silence.

Where the hell was backup? He thought of Karrin and Pete and flicked the portable on. "Take cover. They might rush the front door."

The absolute quiet inside began to worry Steve. He knew this sort of crim – he'd dealt with them for years – they were concocting some harebrained plan, his tightening gut told him that. But what? In his initial reconnoitre he'd seen bars on the side windows which eliminated them as a means of escape. That left the front or the back door. They'd know he would have called for backup, so they had two choices. Make a run for it or try to bargain a deal using the child for leverage. With crims, especially types like Andropoulos, one never knew which way they'd jump.

Another piercing scream from the child galvanised Steve into action. He didn't have time for backup, there had to be action *now*. Checking that Karrin and Pete were in secure cover and signalling for Mario to cover him, he moved forward. It took two blows with his gun butt to smash in the back window and clamber inside. In a brief glance he noted that the drugs were gone and then, flattening himself along the kitchen wall he crept to the doorway which led into a darkened hall. His ears strained to catch any foreign sounds.

With some surprise he realised the heavy breathing belonged to him, and the only other sound was a child's occasional sniffle. He deduced that Andropoulos and Nixon were at the front of the house, planning their move. He used his portable to warn Karrin that they might rush the front door and then he assessed the situation. He thought about going into the hallway but if he did he'd be a sitting duck. His throat dried up with tension so he swallowed hard and took several deep breaths. Maybe another verbal appeal might work ... Shit, didn't they know they were cornered?

The next instant Andropoulos's bulky figure edged around a doorway. The silence was shattered by the explosion of a .38 calibre gun.

"Take that, pig!" The shot was followed by a burst of mad laughter.

The bullet lodged in the plaster wall near Steve's head and in the dimness fine plaster particles sprayed all over him. Close. Too bloody close!

Seconds later, in a flurry of movements, they made their break. One hurled the front door open and half-bent over rushed through it.

The second man began to follow. Steve aimed and fired. A yelp of pain told him he'd hit his mark. The shadowy figure lurched sideways and fell to the floor, howling with pain.

Then, as he moved down the hall, the world went mad.

He heard a hail of bullets. One, two, three ... Steve lost count. Crouching low he crept into the front room and found the child, a street kid of about eleven, cowering in a corner. She looked okay. Several voices yelled, there was a scream, no, two screams after which a rush of blue clad uniformed men stormed the open front door. One officer flicked the hall light on as they entered.

"Parrish," a constable yelled, "they got your partner. It's bad."

Nixon had been wounded in the thigh but Andropoulos, determined not to face more gaol time, had been fatally wounded. Karrin, shot in the neck, stayed on the critical list for three days – the bullet had missed the carotid artery by a mere centimetre. A probationary constable collected a nasty wound, a bullet in the stomach. In the melee the street kid escaped unnoticed.

As soon as Karrin was well enough she resigned from the service. Steve knew she bore him no ill-will but the experience had been too close to live with and her fiancé insisted she leave. There'd been the usual counselling crap, and all the psycho-analysing he could stomach. Plus some he couldn't. Then his superior suggested a move to another section, state licensing, telling him it was better for him to stay off the streets for a while.

The Police Internal Affairs hearing absolved Steve of responsibility over the Smith–Nixon shooting incident. But for Steve, life had gone downhill from there on in. His long-time girlfriend, Tracy, left him to marry another cop. Karrin's fiancé popped him one on the nose for almost getting her killed, and half his mates started to drift away, too busy with their families, they said. And no matter what the internal affairs decision had been, *he* blamed himself, although he couldn't quite put his finger on why things had gotten out of hand.

He knew in his heart, and that others knew too that he was at fault. Rashness or timing or maybe the decision to storm in through the back of the house had pushed the crims into a course of action that could have been avoided if he'd waited for backup and for a hostage negotiator. Whatever the reason, the cumulative effect on him had been profound.

He blinked and stared unseeingly at the front fence which surrounded his neat, fibro cottage. He slowly shook his head. What was the point in going over it again and again?

The whispers had begun after the I.A. finding. Subtle. Sly. "Parrish's lost his nerve." "Parrish can't stand being on the streets any more." They said he was washed up as an effective cop, said all he could ever be was a pencil pusher. His mouth turned down in a grimace as he remembered the digs. He'd never heard anything directly though, just second- and third-hand murmurings.

His mind returned to the present and he saw that it was almost dark. Bugs flew around his head and several mossies were finding him a juicy target. He sighed and pushed the past to the back of his mind, his gaze wandering around the rooftops of the houses on the other side of the street. Mt Isa had been his salvation. The NSW police union had organised a transfer to the Queensland service and he'd asked to be posted to the country – as far away from a major city as he could get.

Steve stood and stretched his one hundred and eighty-five centimetre frame in the darkness, welcoming the cooler night air. Above him millions of stars shone in an ink black sky. He grinned to himself. It had taken him a while to get used to that particular panorama. And then, strangely, his thoughts returned to the dark-haired woman who'd sparked off the memories. Francey ... Why was it so hard to get her out of his head? He tried to think about something else.

The ballistics report should be through any day now. When it arrived he would take a run out to Murrundi and acquaint CJ with the results, confidentially, of course. Quite illogically, the thought of seeing Francey Spinetti again buoyed him immensely, though he knew nothing could come of it. Whistling tunelessly under his breath, he opened the screen door and went inside.

CHAPTER EIGHT

The indulgence of being on holiday evaporated the next morning after breakfast when Francey, CJ and Les had a three hour session on the proposed mini conference centre.

After breakfast Les brought out several folders and a rolled up set of plans, and once the crockery and cutlery had been removed, they got to work. Francey hadn't been idle either. She had compiled a list of items she thought the centre would require and as the hours passed they hammered out what equipment the conference centre would need and just what it was meant to do.

"I see it as having a two-pronged function," CJ decreed. "I want people, they'll be important folks, to feel comfortable. Five star accommodation, and all the facilities one would find in a top hotel which caters for conferences."

"Of course," Francey agreed. She looked down at her list. "A reception and dining area, with bar. A lecture room that houses state-of-the-art electronic equipment, overhead display unit, closed-circuit TV, hi-fi system. I think you'd also want a business room where guests could get onto the Net, send and receive faxes and e-mail, make phone calls and so on. Alternatively, each suite could be equipped with such facilities. Perhaps a leisure room for pool and table tennis, darts, video games. Accommodation would consist of single and twin suite type rooms with private facilities, mini-bars, spa baths, the usual."

"We'd want a kitchen for food preparation and we'll need staff accommodation too because CJ's conferences will be spaced over several days," Les put in. "As well, the facility should be close enough for guests to access the pool and the tennis court."

Francey had already thought of those things but smiled her agreement at him anyway. Looking at CJ she said, "First of all you need to decide where this centre is to be located on the property. Do you have an aerial photograph of Murrundi station?"

"Should be one around somewhere," CJ frowned as he tried to remember where. "Les, go ask Lisa, she'll know where it is."

As Les trotted off to find the photograph, CJ fingered the sets of rolled up plans on the table. "This is what the other architects have come up with. Do you want a peek at their designs?"

Francey shook her head. "I'm already working on a design in my head – I don't want it corrupted by someone else's work." Her expression was disapproving as she added, "Besides, that's not ethical."

CJ shrugged and then decided that he liked her confidence and her frankness. It was also refreshing to find someone with ethics. In that respect she reminded him a little of his son. Richard had been exceedingly honest, a straight upfront kind of man. "You know I expect you to stay until you come up with a complete design?"

"Les mentioned that yesterday. I don't think my boss is going to be too pleased. He expects me back in the office in five days time."

"Don't worry about Nicholson, I'll clear it with him," CJ assured her. He had no doubt that once Nicholson had a whiff of the financial carrot he planned to dangle in front of his nose, he'd be only too pleased to let Francey stay on for as long as was necessary.

"Found it," Les said triumphantly as he returned with a rolled up photo. "It's a couple of years old and we've added two more buildings to the place since then, but it gives a fairly accurate picture of positioning and space." He unfolded the laminated photograph and used a couple of ornaments from the sideboard to hold the curling corners down.

Francey studied the map. How different things looked from the air, she thought. The homestead, the pool and the tennis court stood out quite well, then there was the scattering of other buildings further back from the homestead. She glanced at CJ. "Have you any preferences as to where you want the centre?"

CJ stared at the photo. Twenty-six years ago there had just been land and shrubs and spinifex. He had carved everything with his hands, money and energy, with the belief that one day his would be the finest station in far north Queensland. Now he had achieved all that he'd dreamed. A sudden sadness stabbed at his heart. He had thought, foolishly perhaps, that with all his wealth he could control everything he cared about. Fate had proven him wrong and had brought with it a painful reality. Now he had only Natalie to leave his empire to. A bitter taste rose in his throat and he swallowed hard to rid himself of the unpleasant flavour.

Regathering his thoughts CJ said, "As Les said, it shouldn't be too far from the homestead. How about on the knoll at the left of the main house?"

"Yes, that's where I would suggest," Les concurred.

"Or …" Francey's tone was thoughtful, "the other side of the row of pines?" She tore a sheet of paper off her pad and began to sketch. "You could extend the drive around the back of the tennis courts and behind the conifers and the conference centre could face the pool. If you pulled out two or three conifers you'd have a connecting path from the centre to the pool. That would integrate the conference centre with the homestead quite well, yet still afford the main house reasonable privacy."

"Yes," Les said slowly, "that makes sense. On the knoll, people would have further to walk to get to the pool, the stables and the tennis court. What do you think, CJ?"

"I'm not real good at visualising things" CJ admitted – a strange statement for a man who'd carved a business empire from the ground up. "The idea makes sense." He silently wondered why the two other architects hadn't seen that potential. Both had positioned the proposed conference centre on the knoll without even bothering to discuss it with him.

"Okay. Now what type of accommodation? For how many people?"

"We thought between eight and ten," Les told her, "and in the staffing section allow for up to six. They can have twin or bunk style accommodation equivalent to a three star motel."

Francey could barely suppress her excitement. Her mind was already feverishly working on floor layouts, style and line. Perhaps a courtyard garden of some sort, maybe a large spa. Her fingers itched to get a pencil and ruler into her hand.

After another hour's discussion on details, Francey thought she had enough notes to get on with the job. She rose from the table and began to gather her paperwork. "Well, gentlemen, I think you've given me enough to get started. You've both been very helpful." She looked at her watch. "I'd like to get some preliminary work done before lunch so if you don't mind –"

"What do you work on first, the floor plan or the elevations?" Les asked interestedly.

"The floor plan. Once that's done I concentrate on how the building will look."

"Off you go then," CJ said, with a wave of his hand. "I never try to stop anyone who wants to work. These days so few do."

"I'll show you to your cubbyhole office," Les said, grinning. And then he asked, "You don't suffer from claustrophobia, do you?"

"It's not that small," Francey retorted with a good-natured grin.

CJ's expression was contemplative as they left. The young architect appeared to know her stuff and Les, he grinned and shook his head, could hardly keep his eyes off her. His CEO deserved a good run with a woman for a change, after Nancy, but Francey Spinetti wasn't going to be here long. Yes, he must talk to him, discreetly, of course.

It was always nice to see how the other half lived, Steve Parrish thought as he pulled up around the back of Murrundi's homestead in a space where half-a-dozen vehicles, including CJ's Rolls and a top of the line Range

Rover were housed under a long carport. A crowd of people were lunching on the verandah overlooking the swimming pool and the manicured gardens. He bet they hadn't had a corned beef and pickle sandwich, a tub of yogurt and an apple, as he had. Their table fare would have been more elegant. He felt no sense of rancour at the lifestyle lived by the Ambrose family. That was one of his strengths – a lack of envy, even a lack of plain old ordinary respect for wealth. He knew too that his attitude irked CJ because the older man knew it gave him no power over him.

The whole household, apart from Les Westcott, was there. CJ, Natalie, Lisa Dupre, that friend of Natalie's, Trish something or other whom he'd met in the Isa the other day … and Francey. Even Shellie, who usually ate with Alison in the kitchen, happily sat at the table sucking on a white wine. He'd heard the gossip of her fondness for the grape but in the time he'd known her he'd never seen her under the weather.

"Steve." Shellie Kirkby was the first to see him. "Would you care for some lunch? I can fix you a plate from the kitchen."

Steve shook his head. "Thanks, I've already eaten. I wouldn't say no to a coffee though." He watched her jump up and go to the traymobile to fill his request.

"You know everyone?" CJ asked as he shook the policeman's hand. Though he went through the motions of being polite he was damned if he could take to the transplanted NSW cop. Something about him, a cynicism, a lack of due homage towards him had from the first time they'd met rubbed him the wrong way. He was used to having politicians and public servants in his pocket, so to speak, and that Steve Parrish hadn't come to heel irritated the hell out of him. And yet he grudgingly respected him for it.

"Yeah." Steve nodded generally to everyone but despite himself, his gaze strayed and stayed on Francey a few seconds longer than was necessary.

Natalie patted the empty chair next to her. "Here's a seat, Steve. Come join the party."

"How about a slice of mud cake, Steve? Alison made it fresh this morning," Shellie tried to tempt him as she placed his coffee on the table in front of him.

"Yes, why not?" Natalie encouraged, "Shellie's a firm believer in the old adage that the way to a man's heart is through his stomach." Her grey eyes danced suggestively at him. "Personally, I'd heard it was from a different part of a man's anatomy."

"No. Thanks all the same." In spite of himself Steve chuckled as he spooned sugar into his cup.

"Natalie!" CJ cautioned. He turned to Steve. "Excuse my stepdaughter, she's had one glass too many which sometimes loosens her gutter-type tongue."

"Have not." Natalie argued, pouting first at her stepfather then grinning wickedly at Steve.

"How are the plans going for CJ's Aussie style Taj Mahal," Steve asked Francey.

"Good, thank you." God, was that soft, throaty tone really hers? Francey asked herself as she answered him.

"Do you know what the Taj Mahal is, Sergeant?" Trish Pentano queried with a smile. "It's a mausoleum some Indian shah built to house his dead wife, Mammataz Mahal."

CJ's gaze moved to Francey. "You know I don't want that sort of thing, don't you? I'm not interested in a memorial edifice to me, just a functional conference centre."

"Of course," Francey concurred with a confident smile. "I have a very good understanding of what you and Les want." She stared straight back at Steve. "The plan's half finished." She could feel her cheeks, her whole body in fact, warming under the policeman's constant gaze. But why she had this reaction to him confounded her. Perhaps it was the memory of their first embarrassing meeting or, it could be something else. Whatever, she chose not to put a name to it. "Speaking of which, I'd better get to work on it." She stood and made her excuses. "A great lunch, Shellie, as usual. And now the drawing board calls."

"I'll come with you," said Trish who, on Natalie's suggestion, was doing an interview for a Brisbane paper on Francey's achievements as an architect. "I need to finalise a few points with you." On meeting the architect she had liked the style of the woman and as Natalie didn't appear to be jealous – as she sometimes did – she might as well make her time at Murrundi Downs pay a bill or two. Maybe, having built up some credibility, next time she'd get to CJ himself.

Francey shrugged her acceptance. "Very well, so long as you don't mind me working as we talk."

"Francey," Natalie butted in, "remember, you have to make it a five star conference centre so you-know-who can impress his international business colleagues."

"You've a problem with that?" CJ queried gruffly.

Natalie's hands rose in a mock gesture of self-defence. "Not at all, it's your money, CJ. Besides, I can see how we'll put it to extra use when we have a big party at Murrundi. People can use it as overnight accommodation."

Trish cleared her throat discreetly, "I won't be too long," she promised. "You haven't forgotten that my flight leaves at 2.15 p.m.," she reminded her friend before she followed Francey to her office.

Natalie smiled at Trish. Momentarily she had forgotten she was returning to Brisbane. She would miss her. Damn it, she missed her already. Well, not for long. In a couple of days she would try to con Les into flying her to Brisbane. She sighed silently, she had business to do there too. Last week she'd given Hugh O'Leary, the manager of her art gallery, a free hand with an up and coming exhibition but, really, she should check to see that he was doing a good job.

"You'd better have another coffee then," Shellie said with artificial sweetness as she refilled Natalie's cup. She wished that Natalie was the one flying out. Trish Pentano and Francey were no trouble around the homestead. They kept their rooms neat and organised their own washing, but not her lazy stepniece. Brenda had spoilt her rotten and she'd not had to lift a finger to do anything so, at thirty, she remained as self-centred and self-absorbed as she'd always been. The entire household including Alison, whose exclusive domain was the kitchen, enjoyed the tranquillity when Natalie wasn't around, and that was a fact.

Steve watched Francey and Trish move to the doorway, openly admiring the way the architect's body, encased in blue jeans and a figure hugging T-shirt, swayed with every step she took. He wondered if she had taken an early departure because of his arrival?

"CJ, if you've a few minutes, I'd like to talk to you," Steve said.

"Sure." CJ looked at Lisa. "Hold my calls for the next half-hour."

Steve followed CJ through the homestead's living area, down the hallway and into his study. He deliberately didn't look at the expensive paintings and *objets d'art* or allow himself to be impressed by the extraordinary display of wealth which dripped from every square metre of the place. What good was all the money in the world if it couldn't save your son's life?

"Have a seat," CJ half grunted. He took his usual position at his desk, and waited for Steve to speak.

Steve gave an inward sigh, mentally deliberating on how to tell someone like CJ what the ballistics report had revealed. CJ wasn't going to like it. "I want you to treat what I'm about to tell you as confidential. The details don't go outside this room. Agreed?"

CJ frowned and leant forward on his desk. As his curiosity got the better of him, he nodded in agreement. "I didn't think drama was your thing, what's all the mystery for?"

Steve grinned briefly. "It's about Richard, his death." He watched the older man stiffen and felt a pang of sympathy. People said "the man with the golden touch" was a tough bastard when it came to business but he didn't doubt for a minute that CJ had cared deeply for his only child. "You recall that a couple of weeks ago I met Billy Wontow where the stampede took place. I know the coroner found in favour of accidental death and, really, I was just going over the details for the last time before I closed the file."

CJ looked away. His gaze focused unblinkingly on the last photograph taken of his son. "Do we have to go through this again, Steve? I'm not –"

"Sir, I'm afraid we do. You see I've found possible evidence which leads me to conclude that there may have been foul play." In the silence of the room, Steve listened to the ticking of the grandfather clock in the corner – it seemed inordinately loud. He let CJ digest the first piece of information and from the stunned look on the man's face, decided to give him what facts he had. "After Billy left I went up to the ridge for a look around. I had no expectations of finding anything worthwhile, but I did. I found a horseshoe print in a bit of dried up mud, three bullet casings and a spent bullet which had lodged in a tree."

"Yeah, we know three shots were fired. Billy told us that." CJ's frown deepened. "What are you getting at, Steve?"

"Three random shots from someone moving about, presumably hunting, would have put the casings in three slightly different positions. I found them together, near the horseshoe print. I think it's possible that the shots weren't fired randomly." He paused to check CJ's expression: it was inscrutable. "Let me construct a possible scenario. A rider astride a horse, waiting in the dawn light. He sees the camp stirring and the cattle beginning to move about. Three shots are fired at specific intervals, they create the stampede – the outcome being Richard's death. I think it's possible those shots were deliberate. Someone wanted that stampede to happen and knew that if it did there was a good chance that Richard and Billy might be injured, perhaps fatally."

"Jesus!" CJ's eyebrows lifted. "Who?"

"Indeed. Who would want Billy or Richard dead? That's the puzzle, isn't it?"

CJ tried to grasp Steve's inference. Hell, it was more than an inference. He was talking murder. His son, murdered. A pain stabbed him in the middle of his chest and he grabbed at his shirt and rubbed until it eased. Christ Almighty! It had been hard enough to cope with the fact that Richard had been killed accidentally – but that it could be murder

... Oh, Jesus. The muscle in his jaw spasmed as he tried to keep his emotional reaction in check.

"Those casings could have been on the ground for years," CJ argued.

"I checked that out with ballistics. They did a special test for corrosion and age since discharge. They couldn't give me an actual date but they're positive the casings had been there less than a year. Which fits in with the time frame." He watched CJ nod, absorbing his words then he asked the question he knew he had to. "I have to ask, CJ, did Richard have any enemies? Someone who might have a grudge against him, a score to settle?"

"You seriously believe it's possible, don't you?"

"I do." Thirteen years of policing had given Steve a gut feeling for such things and since the day he'd found the casings he'd started to quietly question people around town as to whether anyone had bad feelings towards Richard Ambrose. He'd found some inbred hostility towards CJ but none towards Richard. To date he hadn't received one clue to back up his scenario of a murder being committed, but still it persisted inside his head.

"If I'd been caught in that stampede, Les and Shellie could have given you half-a-dozen names of people who'd like to see me two metres under, but not Richard. As far as I know my son didn't have an enemy in the world."

CJ's statement gave Steve another line to follow. "Then perhaps whoever did it wanted to hurt you."

"They succeeded in that. But it doesn't make sense." CJ scratched the top of his thinning head of hair. "If someone wanted to use Richard as a bargaining chip, for leverage, why kill him? Why not just threaten to kill him if I didn't accede to the person's demands? And if their grudge was against me, I'm easy enough to get to. There's a security system for the house because of the paintings and antiques but once I'm on the verandah or anywhere else on the property, anyone could take a pot shot at me."

"I know. I'd thought of that too."

"I need a drink. How about you?"

"I'm on duty."

CJ got up and walked over to the small table which held a cut glass whisky decanter and several glasses. He poured a tumbler of Black Douglas Deluxe and drank half in one long swallow. The smooth liquid slid down his throat and almost instantly its warmth began to travel through his limbs, relaxing him marginally. "Have you got anything else?" The question came out of the blue.

"The casings, they're not from the usual hunting rifle. Ballistics in Brisbane have narrowed the bullet casings down to a model that uses 25/25 bullets, probably a Stinger rifle. A smaller bore rifle than usual but not uncommon. Would you happen to know anyone who has such a rifle?" He saw CJ think for a minute then shake his head. "Unfortunately, Queensland doesn't have a register for rifle owners but I'm checking with the importers, hoping they can give me some names to check out. It's a long shot, as they say," he grinned at his own joke, "but it's worth a try."

"Sure as hell is a long shot."

Steve shrugged. "It's an angle to work on. It mightn't lead anywhere but I'm always optimistic."

"Do you know how many men, how many outback families might own a Winchester, probably the Stinger model 'cause it doesn't have too much kick for kids or women? Thousands."

The two men were silent for a moment, CJ sipping at his drink, Steve trying to come up with another line of enquiry. "CJ, inheritance-wise, who would benefit most from Richard's death?"

CJ's answer was prompt. "Natalie. She and Richard knew the contents of my will. Richard would receive the bulk of my estate. Les inherits the resort at Surfers and there are generous bequeathments to Shellie and some others in my employ. Natalie will get a trust fund which will allow her to live comfortably, as well as a parcel of shares." He looked at the policeman. "Of course Natalie's already wealthy, what with her art gallery business. Besides," he shook his head firmly, "I can't see a motive there. Richard and Natalie had a good relationship with each other."

Steve nodded. Natalie deWitt-Ambrose was a strange character. She enjoyed being outrageous just to stir people up but, somehow, he couldn't see her killing her half-brother. Greed, often a compelling motive, didn't seem to apply and he'd racked his brains trying to work up another motive and just couldn't find one. "Could Richard have had a romantic entanglement you didn't know about? A disgruntled lover perhaps or maybe he was involved with someone and there was a third party? The jealousy angle?" Steve knew he was grasping at straws now but it was a remote possibility.

"Not that I'm aware of. Richard had a few flings – there was nothing wrong with him in that department. But nothing serious, I'm sure of it." Then he thought for a moment, "Still, it might be worthwhile checking into. A son doesn't tell his father everything. I know I didn't tell mine all the things I got up to."

"Yes, well, it's a line of enquiry I'll follow up too."

"So, where do you go from here?"

"I'll ask around, discreetly. I'm not expecting to find

any dramatic leads. It could take months to get a clear picture but," he beamed at CJ, "I'm a patient man."

"Good." CJ nodded his head approvingly. Suddenly his earlier opinion of Sergeant Steve Parrish rose a couple of notches. He'd been impressive, this last half-hour. The man appeared to know his stuff. Maybe, just maybe, his original opinion of him had been hastily drawn.

Steve rose from the armchair and moved towards the door. "I'll see myself out. And remember, sir, keep this under wraps, at least until I get more to go on."

"All right." CJ stared thoughtfully at the closing door, his fingers drumming on the desk top. Hell, it wasn't going to be easy to keep this information to himself. And he had trouble coming to terms with the idea that Richard may have been murdered. Such a possibility hadn't occurred to him. So, when Steve found out who did it – and strangely he had faith in the policeman's ability to uncover the mystery – all he wanted was five minutes with the bastard.

Francey dialled the ten digit number and waited. She had just had a wonderful half hour conversation with her mother. Francey knew from her mother's anxious questions that she missed her only child dearly and wanted to know when she was coming back to Sydney. The days were flying by, she realised. She had been away from her Potts Point apartment for almost ten days and so far, she admitted to herself with some surprise, she had been neither homesick nor bored. Although, if she was to be scrupulously honest with herself, she did miss her mother's cooking and even her father's nagging.

"Aden Nicholson."

Francey smiled at the sound of his smooth, cultured tone. "Francey here."

"Aahh, the travelling architect. It's good to hear your voice." Then he added in a huskier tone, "I've missed you. How are things going up there?"

"Everything's fine. The design is coming along, it's almost finished in fact."

"What's it like, rubbing shoulders with the rich and famous? Or should I say in CJ's case, infamous?"

"Interesting." She thought she detected an undertone of envy or impatience, or was she, sensitive creature that she was, just imagining it? "Actually, he's been very nice to me. Everyone has. I've even done a little riding, though ..." she gave a low chuckle at the memory. "I had to sit on a cushion for a day or two till my muscles forgave me."

"So," his tone deepened. "It hasn't quite been all work and no play?"

Again ... what was it? Annoyance? Displeasure? Well, let's get it out in the open. If he had a gripe she might as well hear it. "What's wrong, Aden? You don't sound yourself."

"Don't I?" There was a short pause. "Guess I'm missing my favourite girl. Life's pretty dull around here without a certain sassy-mouthed architect."

Her sigh was audible. "Me too. I'll be home soon."

"Yes, well ..." he said slowly. "You mightn't be home as early as expected, Francey. I've been talking to CJ on the phone, this morning in fact. He has a ... a development he wants you to look at, providing he's pleased with what you draw up for the mini conference centre."

"He hasn't said a word to me."

"He wanted to wait until you'd finished the current project before broaching the matter." Another pause. "It sounds exciting ... and big. He's been negotiating the concept for a resort and golf course development at

Cooktown. He's got a fifty-one per cent interest so he has control, and a Japanese consortium has the rest. The resort's intended mainly for well-heeled Japanese who love to play golf. There'll be condominiums for sale or to rent and two eighteen hole golf courses. Evidently he bought the land ten years ago, for peanuts. It's on the outskirts of town. He reckons the timing's right to develop it."

As Aden spoke something clicked in Francey's head. The conversation CJ had had with a man called Fielding the day she'd arrived. And later she had seen a television news report on a near riot at Cooktown after which three greenies had been hospitalised. That had to be it!

"What about the work piling up in the office? If I stay on I'll be snowed under so deep I'll never get on top of it."

"Don't worry. I've taken some on and have farmed the rest out to Tony. Look, Francey, as I said before you left, CJ may be able to put a lot of work our way. I want you to cultivate this opportunity for all it's worth."

"Even though it means it could be a month, maybe longer before I return?"

She heard his regretful groan through the receiver, but suddenly thought to herself, was it genuine? Disappointment engulfed her like an oncoming tide as she began to sense that as much as she liked Aden Nicholson he was first and foremost a businessman and their personal relationship was secondary to making money. Her mouth twisted in a grimace of a smile as she realised that in some ways Aden and CJ were alike, the probable difference being the degree of ruthlessness each might be capable of.

"I know. I'm not happy about it and I hope you're not happy either but I'm sure you'll agree it's an opportunity we, the firm, shouldn't pass up."

It was her turn to sigh and she did. "I guess." She tried to muster some enthusiasm for the soon to be mentioned project, but couldn't. Deep down a feeling was taking form and growing inside her that she was being manipulated by Aden *and* CJ. She didn't like it, at all!

"Francey, don't mention anything to CJ about the Cooktown thing. Let him bring it up. Okay?"

"Okay." She looked at the half finished left side elevation of the conference centre and said, "Work calls, I've got to go."

"All right. We'll talk again at the end of the week. Bye."

Once she'd replaced the receiver Francey tried to concentrate on the job at hand. Normally she could do site elevations in her sleep, but not at the moment. Something in Aden's manner! She couldn't quite put her finger on it though and then she worried that maybe, with her fertile imagination, she was imagining layers that simply didn't exist.

The lines of the drawing blurred then cleared. Her pencil ran along the ruler automatically, detailing the building line, but her mind was elsewhere. She'd thought, heard, that distance was supposed to make the heart grow fonder, but did it?

Still, she hadn't exactly been pining away for Mr Aden Nicholson. She missed him, missed his pleasant company and his ability to make her laugh, but it wasn't as if she couldn't function without him. She remembered the time Meredith and Brett had been separated for a week. Meredith had been beside herself with loneliness and had driven her crazy with half-a-dozen phone calls every day.

She put too much pressure on the pencil and the point broke. Damn. Deciding on a break she left the cubbyhole office and strolled out onto the screened-in verandah.

Silence, punctuated occasionally by the lowing of a steer, greeted her as she stood at the railing looking down at the pool. So peaceful. She would have appreciated the scene more had her own thoughts been serene. Since her arrival at Murrundi she had made it a habit to walk around the homestead and its environs, not just for exercise but because it helped her get the feel of the place and to visualise better the project on which she was working. Not just the concept of the conference centre but how she could make the building blend with the surroundings rather than stick out unattractively and jar with everything else.

Sometimes she took her camera with her. There were always interesting subjects to photograph, unusual angles, shades of black, white and grey. A couple of stockmen had been shy about having their photo taken and she hadn't pressed them, instead she had photographed other subjects. The disused water tower and the bore water outlet with its trough and half-a-dozen steers drinking from it. The scarecrow in Alison Wontow's vegetable garden against a background of cumulus clouds and, occasionally, she'd catch a stockman on his horse – always a good subject – providing her film was fast enough to catch him in action.

Had she thought to analyse the fact, it would have surprised her how easily she was fitting into life on a cattle station. A natural curiosity made her interested in almost everything that happened. She wanted to know the function of all the pieces of the farm machinery, and what the stockmen did for relaxation. It seemed a lonely life for them but Mike Hunter, the foreman, told her the men were used to it. They made their own amusements. Cards, television, and CJ had a huge library of videos they could borrow. One man was even doing a degree in animal husbandry by correspondence.

"A penny for them?" A voice said from behind.

Francey half turned to see Natalie standing slightly to her left. "Pardon?"

"A penny for your thoughts, as the saying goes. You seemed quite engrossed." Her grey eyes studied the same view. "It's a bit cool for a swim but we could have a game of tennis if you're interested."

Francey smiled. "Thanks, I can't. I was just taking a five minute break from work. Maybe later on, though I warn you I'm not much of a player."

"It doesn't matter. We'll just have a bit of fun."

"I was thinking how fortunate you and Richard were to have grown up with all this," she waved her hand about expansively, "for your backyard."

The comparison made her think of her own childhood playground. A narrow backyard with a tin fence too high for her to peek over into the neighbours backyards. And stacks of fruit boxes from the shop. She remembered that she and Meredith used to make cubbyhouses and play all sorts of games, until her father got cross about it. With passing traffic so heavy the front street was too dangerous to play in, but the back lane, when the weather was right, was perfect for a game of cricket or football with the other kids in the neighbourhood. As she and her friend had grown they had explored to the water's edge of Glebe Point and around Blackwattle Bay watching the rowers from the Glebe Rowing Club practice on the water. Without a doubt she was sure that hers had been a far different childhood to Natalie's privileged one.

"It wasn't always like this," Natalie admitted, her gaze roaming around the cultivated gardens and the blue waters of the pool. "Wait here a minute, I'll get one of the photo albums and show you." Two minutes later she returned with two large albums.

Both women sat on the cane lounge and Natalie opened the first book.

"CJ married Mum in 1971. He'd made a killing on an opal field in South Australia so he paid cash for Murrundi which, at the time, was badly run-down. See," she pointed to a photo of a less than salubrious weatherboard house on brick stilts, the verandah dipping down at a ramshackle angle. "This is where we first lived. Richard was only a baby and back then our backyard was bare earth. No grass or shady trees, no flowers. The first few years money was tight what with CJ trying to build up the herds and purchasing solid breeding stock. It wasn't until Grandfather deWitt died, leaving Mum everything, that things changed for the better.

"Mum believed in CJ's business acumen so she let him handle her estate. All she asked was that he give her enough money to build a decent house." She tapped the wall behind her. "This one. The original homestead was moved and it's now the foreman's cottage. Over a six month period CJ liquidated all her assets and that's what gave him the capital for his initial investments."

"Well, judging from what I've read, CJ's expanded that inheritance quite nicely." More than nicely, Francey thought. CJ's wealth was *conservatively* estimated at over thirty-five million, all of which would be Natalie's one day.

"Right. That's how most people would see it." However, Natalie didn't. As she'd grown up it had rankled that her mother had handed over her entire estate to CJ Ambrose. What if CJ hadn't been successful? He could have lost everything. That he hadn't mollified her somewhat but she remained cross at Mumsie for in her will there had been virtually nothing left to her other than personal jewellery and several of the paintings – which now at least hung in her penthouse apartment in Brisbane. It wasn't fair. In her opinion, by hereditary rights, a third of what CJ had accumulated should be hers now but wouldn't be until he died because of Mumsie. That's why she'd had to go cap in hand to CJ for a loan to start her art gallery business.

Francey turned a couple of pages of the album and saw a young girl with fair plaits dressed in a tennis outfit. "Is that you?"

Natalie laughed. "Yes. Awful, isn't it. I was such a skinny kid. I could play tennis though," she said matter-of-factly and turned a couple more pages. "That was taken after I'd won the under-sixteens' state title."

"Then I'm glad we didn't play tennis. You'd wipe the court with me. My tennis game is of the ping-pong variety."

"I rarely play these days," Natalie said with a nonchalant shrug, "it wouldn't be such an uneven match." Her mother used to love to watch her play tennis. She had rarely missed a match when she'd been young. Brenda had wanted her to try for the professional ranks but she had known she didn't have the determination or the dedication needed to make it at that level. Dear Mumsie. Natalie gazed thoughtfully at a photograph of an impeccably groomed woman with perfectly coiffed auburn hair. Smiling. Mumsie had been her one true confidante. She could and had told her mother everything, sometimes shocking her in the process. Trish had taken over much of that role but she still missed her mother dreadfully.

Francey sighed. "I should get back to work."

"Yes. Can't have CJ saying you're malingering, can we?" Suddenly there was an edge to Natalie's voice. Was the young architect trying to fob her off when she was going out of her way to be friendly? She was very good at sensing such behaviour in people. Too often she'd been hurt when she'd been younger until she'd built a protective wall around her emotions. But she wasn't sure that Francey was being deliberately stand-offish. She'd see ... "There's a new band playing tonight at the Verona Hotel in the Isa. Would you like to come and check out the local talent?"

Francey's frowned unconsciously. She didn't want to appear rude or unfriendly, but something about Natalie deWitt-Ambrose made her feel ... uncomfortable. It wasn't her money or her background. Something else. For the life of her she couldn't put her finger on the reason but it was there, niggling at her. Still, she also realised that Natalie was trying to be friendly so perhaps she should reciprocate.

"I should have checked first. Are you involved with someone back in Sydney?"

Was she? A picture of Aden formed in Francey's head. She was *almost* involved with him, wasn't she? A state of confusion had been brewing within her since talking to him on the phone. She no longer knew if she was or wasn't. "Not full on." Maybe it would be fun to meet some local people, she decided. "Thank you, I'd love to go."

"Good, we'll make a night of it. Go for dinner. I'll tell Alison not to bother preparing anything for us." Natalie smiled, pleased with herself. She enjoyed being at Murrundi, for short stretches, but it didn't compare with the variety of things one could do in a city or coastal resort. Thank goodness she was leaving the day after tomorrow. "We'll go at about six."

Francey stood and stretched. "Fine, that should give me enough time to finish my drawings. See you then."

CHAPTER NINE

Francey reined in her mare Astra, as the creek's bank dropped away. Exhilarated from the ride she glanced back to where the outer homestead buildings were still visible. Les had told her not to let the buildings out of sight as it was easy to get lost on the property if one couldn't recognise the landmarks. She loosened her hold on the reins and let the horse nibble at the moist grass beside the creek which had almost entirely dried up. On the opposite bank gnarled tree roots clung tenuously to the raw, red earth, showing clear signs of erosion. Her head tilted to one side as she surveyed the picture – such a hard, fierce, fascinating land.

As she slipped from the saddle she took her camera with her. About five metres away stood a dead tree, greyish-white in colour with stark, leafless branches pointing skywards. She wanted to photograph it and with the sky a brilliant blue the backdrop would be perfect for the coloured roll of film in the camera.

She walked around studying her subject from different angles, smiling to herself. The plans for the conference centre were finished and tomorrow, when Les flew CJ home from Brisbane, she'd know whether it appealed to him. Oddly, it was important to her that he liked what she had done even if he didn't choose her design. In another burst of reflective thought, as she made ready for the shot, she admitted that over the last week she and CJ had had their moments.

It hadn't taken long for Francey to learn that all the people at Murrundi deferred to CJ's wishes whether he was in the right or otherwise. And it was no wonder Shellie had a drinking problem – the man browbeat her whenever he was in the mood. Nothing she did seemed good enough. Even Natalie refused to push him too far and Les, well, he was too much the suave diplomat to get into a sticky situation with his boss, the man to whom he owed so much.

Her first confrontation had come the day she'd wanted to go into the Isa to get some film processed. Over such a silly thing. Her beloved but worn-out VW had refused to start and the foreman, Mike Hunter, had told her the battery was flat. CJ suggested she drive his Rolls! What a temptation it had been to get behind the wheel of the luxurious vehicle. She almost couldn't resist, but she had, partly because she'd been worried about putting a dent or a scratch on it. When she'd said no thank you CJ had become annoyed and to Francey's astonishment, had stormed off to his study like a spoilt child. Les had whispered to her that she'd probably hurt his feelings – that CJ had his sensitive moments and having his generosity thrown back in his face had most probably offended him. Men! She had shaken her head in consternation. Who would ever understand them?

The second difference of opinion had come about when she had finally stood up to CJ when he'd badgered Shellie about something and reduced her to tears. Through judicious storing of pieces of casual conversation, Francey had learned a little about Shellie's life. A disastrous marriage which ended when her husband left her for another woman. A couple of affairs that had led nowhere and then, when Brenda deWitt-Ambrose's cancer had worsened she had come to Murrundi to care for her and to run the homestead, then stayed on at CJ's request.

One evening Shellie had tippled too much and CJ, who drank rarely, lost his temper and threatened to put her into a detoxification ward. Shellie, befuddled, had been unable to respond coherently. Not Francey. She had jumped unasked into the fray and pointed out that maybe, if someone took the trouble to find out *why* Shellie drank to excess, they would be halfway to solving her problem.

CJ hadn't appreciated her honesty and had told her to mind her own business, that this was a family matter. Les, ever the peacemaker, had seized the moment and escorted Francey from the room and onto the verandah before a full scale row could erupt. For which the volatile Francey had given him a piece of her mind instead and retired, still fuming.

The next morning at breakfast things had been frosty, a situation which had nothing to do with the cooler weather. After lunch CJ had called her into his office and they had debated the matter, sensitively and without anger. To her surprise he'd agreed with her about Shellie. He said she had pointed out something he had overlooked and that as soon as he could he would organise some counselling and treatment for her.

After that, she and CJ had gotten on famously.

Francey lined up her subject, steadied the camera on a fallen log and took three frames.

Having taken the shots she had wanted to she remounted Astra and headed towards the homestead by way of the grassy knoll and the peppercorn tree. She hadn't visited the Ambrose family cemetery and while reading headstones normally wasn't her thing, curiosity made her want to know about the people who rested there.

The small cemetery was lovingly tended. The grass had been freshly mown, though it didn't grow much in the winter, and at the base of each headstone was a bunch of flowers from Murrundi's garden. A one and a half metre high aluminium fence surrounded the plots to keep the hungry cattle out, though the green grass must have been a temptation to them. She tethered her horse and opened the gate. Five headstones. Percy Ambrose, Neville Ambrose, Brenda deWitt-Ambrose, Miles Ambrose and Richard Ambrose. Francey looked at Miles' headstone – the figure of an angel rested atop the marble stone. Reading the inscription she saw that CJ had had a second son who had died at the age of three. She noted the age on Richard's headstone – a year younger than herself. Too young to die and especially so horrifically. She remembered the photo of him in CJ's study. He was a good-looking man with fair hair and green eyes. What a waste.

"This is one place I didn't expect you to be interested in."

Francey recognised Les Westcott's voice before she turned to look at him.

She smiled. "You know me, the perennial stickybeak. Just thought I'd take a look on my way back to the stables." Then she remembered why his appearance had surprised her. "I thought you weren't coming back till tomorrow?"

"Oh, we finished the business early. CJ likes to be home, he's not one for staying in big cities for too long."

She watched Les dismount and in three strides join her beside Richard's grave. She pointed to Miles' headstone. "Tell me about him."

"Shellie knows more about Miles than I do. I wasn't here then. Poor Shellie, she seems to have spent half her life nursing sick people. Guess she had a vocation for it. First there was the grandfather. Percy took sick after they lost their cattle station, Amba Downs. And later on old Neville, CJ and Shellie's father, couldn't work because he'd been kicked in the spine by a horse. Damaged the nerves something awful according to Shellie. He ended up in a wheelchair and she nursed him till he died. Some say that's what destroyed her marriage to Peter Kirkby. Now, Miles, he was four years younger than Richard. Brenda didn't have him immunised and he contracted whooping cough. Shellie and Brenda nursed him around the clock but in the end couldn't save him."

"Poor little thing."

"Yeah. CJ's had his share of family sadness, you know."

"And Richard?"

"That really rocked him, rocked all of us. Richard and I were the best of mates. Everyone loved Richard." He glanced at Francey and wiggled his eyebrows. "He wasn't a lot like CJ, had his mother's nature. You know, more easygoing, and without the ruthless streak that's made CJ a household name in Queensland. Half the people hate 'the man with the golden touch', the other half admire him for what he's achieved. He's found plenty of the population jobs when they didn't have one but that hasn't earned him their gratitude."

"CJ the philanthropist." Francey's smile widened, her blue-green eyes sparkling. "Somehow I've never seen him in that light. Was Richard capable of running CJ's business interests?"

"I think so. He'd have done it differently to the old man. Maybe he wouldn't have made as much money as CJ, but everyone would have loved working for him."

"A nice thing for a boss to aspire to, surely?" Personally, she hoped that one day if she ever had staff under her, that they would think well of her: consider that she was fair and just.

"For some, yes."

Francey studied the headstones again. A whole family, together. It was nice, in a way, sentimental, perhaps to think that they were there, together till the end of time. Fitting, she decided.

"I heard that you finished the conference centre proposal."

"It's on CJ's desk."

"Then you deserve some time off, before you go home. Myself, Hunter and a couple of the boys are doing a muster, moving part of the herd to better grass. We'll be out a couple of days. I thought you might like to come along and see how it's done. There's a lot of riding involved but I think you can handle it."

Francey thought for a moment. Hadn't CJ told Les about the Cooktown project? Or, maybe he'd been told not to mention it. A muster. Could be fun, and think of the story she'd be able to tell her parents and the O'Connors.

"I thought you did that sort of thing with your helicopter."

"Sometimes we do. It's more for large scale mustering where we round up strays over a wide area."

"I'd love to come."

"We'll be roughing it," he warned. "Sleeping out of doors in a sleeping bag. Plain fare food, no showers or toilets."

Francey thought for a moment. "Oh, I think I can handle that for a couple of days, but no more. Especially the toilet facilities part."

"Good. We'll leave at dawn tomorrow."

Together they walked back to their horses and remounted.

"I'll race you to the big barn," Francey challenged and was off.

Les grinned. He didn't care if she beat him though he knew his horse could beat Astra any day of the week. She was coming on the muster. At last he'd have some time with her, alone if he was lucky. Francey Spinetti was one woman he wanted to know a heck of a lot better and by the time they returned, he hoped he would.

No more, Francey groaned to herself. Every muscle and every tissue, including some she didn't know she had, in her body ached. The cattle, creatures she had once thought cute were dirty, smelly, obstinate four-legged beasts and to muster them one needed the patience of a saint. She glanced across at Mike and Les and wondered how they stood, or rather sat, eight to ten hours a day in the saddle. It was torture. And she would kill for a bath, any kind of bath.

The first day out had been enjoyable, seeing the countryside, learning what they did. She hadn't minded the riding, in fact she'd quite enjoyed it, but sleeping on the hard ground in a sleeping bag meant that the next day her muscles hadn't rested properly. Despite that she'd gritted her teeth and vaulted into the saddle. Not for anything would she let these tough, outback guys know that she couldn't hack it. The Spinetti pride was involved and she wouldn't let the family down.

At least they hadn't expected her to go off chasing runaway steers, she just tagged along to oversee what the experienced stockmen were doing. She had taken some great action photos though, which was some consolation.

Les moved his horse over to hers and they rode in perfect harmony.

"Pretty tired, hey?"

"No, I'm fine," she retorted determinedly, gritting her teeth against the truth.

He grinned. Her stubborn streak was as wide as CJ's. "So, you're enjoying it?"

"Yes." Her muscles weren't enjoying it, she silently affirmed, but the rest of her was, and she had learned a lot about the outback country, about what it took to survive here. Les was a good teacher. He'd taken every opportunity possible to instruct her on bush lore, why they did this and why they did that. What they could do if they ran out of water, or if someone got bitten by a poisonous snake. Ugh! She didn't want to think about that.

Mike and the two other men, Lucky and Alan, were good company too, though they didn't talk a lot. She had divined that men in the bush were, to use a cliché, the strong, silent type, mostly content to keep their own counsel. Mike had been a wheat farmer in western NSW but his farm had gone under when the banks raised their interest rate. His wife had left him and now he was alone. But, strangely, he seemed more stoic than bitter.

She had learned some interesting aspects about Les' background too, over long hours on the trail and nights during which the campfire was the only source of light in an otherwise ink-black world. He knew a little about astronomy and had tried to show her where the various star systems were. Stars. She smiled, thinking of the spectacular exhibition of millions of pin points of light in a velvet-black sky. So many of them, and they were so much more vivid in a country sky than in a city where street and house lights and pollution diffused the clarity.

She knew that Les had been orphaned at the age of fourteen and had bummed around from town to town, scratching out an existence until he'd landed on CJ's doorstep. From Shellie she'd learned that CJ had taken him in and given him a chance and had developed him over the years. He had earned two degrees by correspondence, one in animal husbandry and the other in business administration, had a pilot's licence and now he was CJ's right-hand man. The trouble shooter.

Les ran Murrundi Downs, he did all the lead up work when CJ embarked on a new venture, he dealt with the media and the politicians *and* he was the only person who knew all the complexities of the Ambrose empire. That, potentially, made him powerful. And through watching CJ operate, he had built up an impressive portfolio of shares and small properties. Good husband material, her father would have said. She chuckled to herself. She missed him and her mum, missed their laughter and their volatility and their caring.

"We've done well. Picked up over a hundred strays," Les told her. "We'll head back tomorrow and should be at Murrundi by late afternoon. Guess you're anxious to know what CJ thought of your plans?"

"I wouldn't be human if I wasn't," she said tongue-in-cheek. Which was the truth. Secretly she was pleased with the way the plans had worked out. She had taken a great deal of care over the aesthetics, making sure the conference centre's architectural style fitted in with the surrounding landscape. Several visits to two building supply companies in the Isa had shown her what type of materials would work best with the landscape and she was confident, after making sure that the plans complied with the building regulations of the local council, that there wouldn't be any problems in that regard.

She admitted too, deep down, that she would be bitterly disappointed, no matter how fair-minded she tried to be, if CJ didn't choose her design.

That night they camped beside a half dried up billabong located too far inland to attract crocodiles. Much of the surrounding ground was marshy, with thin, tall reeds but there was enough open space near the water to pitch camp. Francey's task was to fetch firewood and while she did this Mike whipped up a damper to go with the plain fare meal of tinned frankfurts, beans and sun-dried tomatoes.

After a long day in the saddle all were hungry enough to scrape their enamel plates clean and drain every drop of coffee from their mugs. Lucky produced a harmonica and began to practise his repertoire of country and western tunes, while Alan and Mike cleared up and set the sleeping bags out around the campfire. Five of them watched a wintry sun set quickly over the western range and then the camp was thrown into almost complete darkness. Within an hour everyone except Les and Francey had retired to their sleeping bags and the sounds of gentle snoring and snuffling mingled with the night noises of the creatures of the marsh: bull frogs, bird calls and the periodic rustling of the reeds as nocturnal creatures sought their evening meals.

Les glanced across at Francey who was poking the fire with a stick and laying a few extra branches on it. The fire light lit up her features, adding extra dimension and depth to the high planes of her cheeks and the luminosity of her eyes. His throat tightened and for the life of him he couldn't think of anything to say. Just being with her, watching her, listening to her talk with the guys and seeing her enjoy the whole experience was enough.

He knew she was unconsciously casting a spell over him, and he treasured the fact that she'd relaxed and told him a few things about herself. About that bastard Bryan, and her embryonic relationship with her boss. He frowned. That could be real competition. A man from her world, the life and things she was used to. But not since Nancy had he felt anything so strong for a woman and so he dismissed the doubts before they overtook him.

Oh, there had been other women. Hookers, high-class callgirls on occasion and in the odd foreign city, but lately he'd been considering a few things. He was getting on. He'd be thirty-seven in six months time. Time to settle down, find a good stepmother for his son. For a while he'd hoped it might have been Natalie. They'd known each other for so long, it would have been a perfect match and gained CJ's approval. But Natalie was a bitch of the first order. She had led him on, let him believe he had a chance and then she'd gone and rubbed his nose in her rejection of him. A muscle at the side of his jaw tightened. Bitch. He'd never forgive her. He didn't care when she'd told him she preferred women, she had deliberately led him on, given him hope ... laughed at him!

Francey Spinetti wasn't like Natalie. As he gazed at her through half hooded lids he had a gut feeling about that. Ambitious though, he admitted, she wanted a career, and that might be a problem. Still, he shrugged his shoulders imperceptibly, he'd attack that problem when he came to it. First things first. Get her *interested* in him, not just as an acquaintance, but as someone she might be attracted to.

Les looked up and saw that a three-quarter moon had come up. Soon it would light up the billabong. He stood and stretched, then casually strolled down to the water's edge. In silence he willed her to follow him, but would she? Minutes later he heard footsteps crunch on the sandy perimeter of the billabong.

Francey took everything in as she joined Les by the water's edge. The moonlight cast a silver beam across the water's surface, the reeds were being rustled by a slight breeze and at the other end of the billabong a mist had begun to rise off the water. It looked primeval yet serene.

"There's a legend about this billabong." He chuckled under his breath. "I reckon there's some kind of story about every billabong in existence." He could see that she was waiting for him to continue. "There were two Aboriginal lovers. Jenna was married to an old man, a tribal elder called Marrani, but she had fallen in love with a young warrior named Yarramong, who came from another tribe. They used to meet at this billabong. One night the old man followed Jenna and found them together. He stabbed the young man to death and threw his body in the water.

"Look," he pointed to the thickening mist, "see how the top layer of the mist has a pinkish tinge to it. That's supposedly his blood. The young wife was distraught and so the story goes, she took her revenge on Marrani by slowly poisoning him."

Francey thought there was probably a scientific explanation for the pink mist but she went along with him. "That's sad." She watched the mist thicken and the pink colour become more noticeable. Suddenly she shivered and wrapped her jacket tighter to her.

Les noticed the gesture and casually draped his arm around her shoulders. "That's not the end of it. You see, Jenna was with child, Yarramong's child. Her tribe thought the son she had was the old man's and welcomed him into the tribe. When he grew up, Pilaroi became the tribe's greatest warrior and a tribal elder. But Jenna, feeling guilty about what she'd done to Marrani confessed to her son and instead of forgiving her he had her shunned – no-one in the tribe was allowed to talk or to help her. Legend has it that she returned to the billabong, where the spirit of Yarramong supposedly lived, and threw herself into the deepest part to be with him.

"None of the Aboriginals swim in this billabong. It's deep in the middle and those who've swum across it, according to the legend, have felt icy fingers trying to pull them down."

Francey looked up and shook her head at him. "That's not a pleasant bedtime story. I'll probably have nightmares about your billabong ghosts."

He swivelled her body around to face him and stepped a little closer. "I can think of something more pleasant for you to dream about." Slowly, so that she knew his intent, his head dipped to kiss her.

Les's action took her by surprise. His kiss was pleasant if not toe curling or shattering but as soon as it ended she diplomatically extricated herself from his embrace.

"No apologies," he said, his voice deeper than usual. "I've wanted to do that for some time."

"Les, I don't want you to get the wrong idea. About us ..."

"So far I haven't got any idea," he countered. "I'm fancy-free and you're not engaged. We're two adults who, I hope, find each other attractive. I'm happy to leave it at that and see where it leads."

"I see." The trouble was, and she didn't quite know how to say it without hurting his feelings, that she wasn't at all attracted to him. But she realised wisely that this wasn't the time to tell him. Better to do it once they were back in the safer precincts of the Murrundi homestead.

They stood together for a few more minutes in compatible silence then Francey yawned. "Well, it's bed for me. Goodnight."

Les watched her walk back to the camp and climb into her sleeping bag. He wanted to chase after her, wanted to talk to her but he had sensed her withdrawal at his embrace and instinctively knew the timing wasn't right. No matter, he was a patient man. He would court her subtly and he began to look forward to trips to Sydney – though he loathed the city – to entrench himself in her heart.

CHAPTER TEN

"It's bloody marvellous. Magnificent! Just what I wanted. Congratulations." CJ's deep voice boomed across the glass walled conservatory to Francey Spinetti. The three sets of plans competing for his proposed conference centre were strewn across the table for all to see. Lisa Dupre and Shellie stood together, with Les and Francey on the other side.

Francey critically appraised the competition. The first competitor had striven for a very different, ultra modern, almost space-age look. The second had gone traditional – not overly imaginative. She studied her own plans and a flush of pride raced through her. They had been worth the extra time she had spent, the long hours worked into the night. Her design harmonised beautifully with the surrounding homestead and buildings of Murrundi Downs.

"Well done, Francey," CJ enthused as he patted her on the back. "As always, it pays to get the best. What do you think, Les?"

Les was still studying the plan, shaking his head in admiration. How had she so cleverly managed to make the planned conference centre look almost like a carbon copy – but not quite – of the homestead itself? The roof line was similar, the building stood up off the ground with steel pillars and had a concrete slab base underneath. There were wide verandahs around the accommodation area, but the master stroke was the inclusion of a glass roofed courtyard garden and spa with several of the function rooms opening onto it. Underneath stood the kitchen and the staff facilities. It all blended well, and the coloured artist's sketch, done by Francey herself, showed a good relationship between the conifers, the pool and the tennis court.

"I agree," Les said in a slow drawl. "I don't know how Francey managed it but it looks fabulous."

"Sure does," Lisa chipped in.

"You'll note that I've stipulated in the specifications that materials used should be of the low maintenance type and that the use of solar panels will help to offset electricity costs," Francey pointed out.

"How long will it take to build?" CJ asked. Full of enthusiasm, he wanted to start straightaway. He'd known instinctively, almost straight after he had met her that she'd come up with the goods. Not only was she a fine-looking woman but she had a good brain too. Soon he would put plan B into action and it helped to know that he had Aden Nicholson's blessing. The man was astute when it came to business dealings. But more importantly, it would allow him to get the best architect – Francey Spinetti – for the job.

"Oh, between six to nine months, maybe longer. It depends on several factors. Weather, readiness of materials, labour. First, you'll need to get a peg out survey and council permission. Then you'll have to advertise for tenders. I suggest you try and get someone local, if you can. That way it should get built quicker."

"Someone with intimate knowledge of building construction should supervise and coordinate the project," Les suggested.

"It might," Lisa ventured, unaware that Les was subtly suggesting Francey, "be something Pierre could do. He worked for a large construction company in Marseilles, before he came here. He knows a lot about building."

"That sounds good, but surely the architect would make the best supervisor," Les stated pointedly.

Francey laughed. "Aren't you jumping the gun a bit? One step at a time. Survey, council approval, tenders. That's usually the order of things."

"Council approval's a matter of form," CJ said confidently. The mayor and half the other councillors owed him big time. "I'd like to think we could get a good deal of the project under way before the wet."

"Which usually starts in November, right?"

"It starts when it starts," Shellie advised cryptically. She liked this young architect and not just because she'd stood up for her against CJ. She could talk to Francey and had often bent her ear for half an hour or so while she'd worked away at her drawings. She also knew that Les liked her, a lot. That was interesting. Somehow she didn't think Francey was Les' type but time would tell. And she had, almost miraculously, mellowed her brother. CJ seemed more affable and less cantankerous and impatient when young Francey was around. He sought her out too, to ask her opinion on the odd business matter, even though she had little experience in business. Funny, she had never seen him do that before, not with Richard or Natalie or herself. Somehow Francey seemed to have won a special respect and affection from him and she knew that CJ was a hard man who gave little of either lightly.

CJ gestured and Shellie poured champagne into the five glasses and handed them around. He held up his flute and made a toast. "To Francey. Congratulations. Your company has won the project design hands down. I hope your boss intends to give you a nice bonus for this."

"Thank you," Francey replied. She smiled modestly at CJ's praise, then followed up with, "He'd better if he knows what's good for him."

"I suppose this means you'll be heading back to Sydney soon?" Lisa said.

"'Fraid so. I'm running out of excuses to stay on." She looked at CJ. "I'd like to take this opportunity to thank you, CJ, in fact all of you for your hospitality. I have enjoyed my time at Murrundi and will treasure the memories." She meant it. The weeks here had been enjoyable. It had not only widened her business horizons but allowed her to see a different way of life other than what she had experienced. Meredith and her mum, as well as her cousins Rosa and Daniella would stare goggle-eyed when she told them about roughing it on a muster and the other bits of exploring she had done.

CJ drained his glass. "Not so fast, my girl. You won't be packing your bags yet. I want you to look something over at Cooktown. Come into the study and we'll talk about it."

So ... Cooktown *was* on the agenda. Les smiled, satisfied as he watched CJ and Francey head off down the hallway to his study. Good. Very good.

Trish Pentano watched Natalie replace the phone receiver with a resounding bang. Her dark eyebrows lifted in apprehension as she followed the tall woman's long, angry strides to the picture window from which an unparalleled view of the Brisbane River could be seen. While she contemplated whether to risk asking what was up, her gaze roamed about the luxurious penthouse apartment.

Off-white thick pile carpet, a sea-green leather lounge in a futuristic modern style, two white lacquered wall units and strategically placed ceramics, paintings and lithographs adorned the walls. It was like a miniature version of Natalie's art galleries. She thought of her own modest one bedroom unit – even though she spent more time here – with a touch of envy. The best of everything was Natalie's motto. She had it all.

"What's wrong?" Trish asked finally, as she was meant to. She joined Natalie by the window. "More trouble with your builder mate, Nick?" Natalie had told her that Nick had behaved like a lamb ever since their confrontation and that the new gallery at Port Douglas was almost finished. What else could it be?

Natalie remained silent but inside she was fuming. Myriad doubts and confusion bombarded her brain and her senses which caused her stomach to tighten up until it almost cramped. And she could feel another tension headache coming on. Something strange was going on at Murrundi Downs, she felt it deep within her and it had the potential to affect her personally.

"What is it?" Trish encouraged. Running her arm across her lover's shoulders she gave her a hug. "Tell mamma, hey?"

Grey eyes that had darkened to slate turned on Trish. "*You* are not my mother," she spat. She ran her right hand agitatedly through her short hair as she tried to control the black mood which threatened to engulf her. These moods were becoming more frequent of late, clouding her reason, altering her disposition. She had to fight hard to keep the darkness at bay. Stay calm. Think, Natalie, think. Breathe. The darkness began to lighten, the racing of her pulse eased and her breathing relaxed.

Seeing that Trish had moved away to regard her pensively, she pirouetted about and chameleon-like, gave her a brilliant smile. "Sorry, love, didn't mean to snap." She shook her head and her features lost their bleak, angry expression. Softened. "Sometimes ... I ..."

This wasn't the first time Trish had witnessed Natalie's mercurial mood changes. One minute light-hearted and laughing, the next, contorted with an unreasoning and unreasonable anger. "It's all right, forget it. I've got to go down to the *Courier Mail* to pick up a cheque. We're still on for the theatre tonight, aren't we?"

Natalie looked at her blankly. "The theatre?" Then she remembered. "Yes, of course."

"Good." Trish picked up her jacket and headed for the door.

"I'll be going back to Murrundi tomorrow. First flight to the Isa if I can get a seat."

Astonished, Trish turned. "But the Whiteley exhibition. The Lord Mayor's opening it tomorrow night. Surely you want to be there?"

Natalie shrugged as if it wasn't important. "Hugh can manage, I'm sure. There's something's going on at Murrundi and I have to find out what it is."

"What do you mean?"

"Francey Spinetti, the architect, she's still there. The woman should have gone back to Sydney a week ago. I think something funny's going on." Seeing Trish's uncomprehending look, she added with a meaningful lift of an eyebrow, "Between CJ and Francey. She's pretty, in a foreign sort of way, and intelligent. CJ's filthy rich and hasn't looked at a woman since Mumsie died. He likes her. I've seen how he looks at her, how Les looks at her too," she ran her tongue around her lips, "as if he could eat her right up. So, do you get my drift?"

"CJ and Francey!" Trish's eyebrows lifted in turn. *An item.* She laughed nervously, then realised she shouldn't. Oh God, Natalie in a black mood wasn't to be underestimated or trifled with. She had seen her flashes of rage and cruelty first-hand, even been on the receiving end once or twice and had the scars to prove it. "There's such an age difference, I can't believe it."

"I'm going to check things out. I'll put an end to it if they're having an affair."

"Why not just let things run their course?"

Suddenly Natalie's features twisted. "You fool!" she screamed, "what if he wants to marry her? Where does that leave me? On the outer, that's where." Stalking from the window to the lounge, she chewed furiously on her lower lip as her mind conjured up all types of scenarios. Francey walking down the aisle in white, maybe another child, *a new heir.* "I won't allow it to happen, I ... I won't. I can't." She stared wild-eyed, almost trance-like at the other woman. "The Ambrose inheritance belongs to me. Me."

Seeing that her lover was working herself into a frenzy again, Trish tried to calm her down. "Get a grip, love. What you have is a severe case of fertile imagination. Maybe Francey's doing more work on the conference project, who knows? I'm sure your suspicions are unfounded."

This time Natalie managed to get the panic under control and held the demons at bay. "Yes," she said tight-lipped, "you're probably right. Still, I'm going home to Murrundi to check the situation out, first thing tomorrow."

Trish saw that it was useless to try and deal with her in this mood. "Okay, fine. I'll see you tonight." Shaking her head she reached for the door knob and exited the apartment.

Natalie barely registered that Trish had gone.

What could she do if it were so, if Francey and CJ were romantically involved? Her gaze narrowed on a ceramic vase displayed on a marble column. Her hands balled into fists and she forcibly uncoiled them, bringing them to rest on the back of the lounge. If her suspicions were found to be true the situation would have to be handled carefully. She didn't want to get CJ offside. But there were ways.

A sly, contemplative smile spread across her face. She would concentrate on Francey, make it clear to her that she wasn't wanted at Murrundi. She knew her type; warm-hearted, sensitive. Weak. Yes, she was sure she could convince Francey Spinetti that Sydney was a much happier, healthier place to be.

As he arrived at the Murrundi homestead Steve Parrish saw two bulldozers pushing mounds of earth on the other side of the row of conifers, levelling a huge area. CJ didn't believe in wasting time. Typical of the man. Once he had something in his line of vision, whether it be the acquisition of a company, a new project or the destruction of someone's hard-earned reputation, he went straight for it – like a killer shark.

And *she* was still here. That was good news as far as he was concerned. He'd talked to Lisa Dupre the other day in town and learned that Francey was staying on to draw up a preliminary design for some newfangled resort project at Cooktown. He didn't care what kept her here – he'd stopped pretending indifference – so long as he got to see her on whatever pretext he could think up.

As he got out of the police four-wheel drive he squinted against the morning sun. There she was, coming out of the stables. Dressed in faded blue jeans that clung almost indecently to her long, long legs, and a red figure-hugging skivvy, it covered her upper body but gave scant protection against the cool morning. She looked bloody marvellous.

"Good morning," he tipped his hat to her.

Francey recognised the sergeant the moment she exited the barn. There was no way she could avoid him as she walked towards the homestead. But ... why should she try to? If she could only understand why he made her feel uneasy and protected at the same time. Perhaps it was the job thing, or could it be the sheer, intimidating size of him? Or, if she were totally honest with herself, was it because she found him strangely attractive? more so than Les, more so than Aden. Though why that should faze her now that she was almost over Bryan confounded her too.

"Hi, Sergeant. Lovely day."

"Bit cool, Francey. Nice for a change. Grapevine told me that CJ chose your design. Congratulations."

"Thanks." She groaned mentally as the telltale flush of pleasure spread through her cheeks and continued on through her body all the way down to her toes.

Steve laboured desperately to keep the conversation going. "You're staying on, I believe. Doing another project for CJ. You must have an easygoing boss."

Francey found herself laughing. "Gee, it's hard to keep a secret around here."

Steve seized on that. "Where exactly is back home?"

"I live at Potts Point now but I grew up in Glebe. The place had a real village, small town atmosphere to it, kind of like the Isa."

"We were practically neighbours. I was raised in Redfern."

"Then the Isa must have been something of a culture shock for you?"

"Not for long," Steve admitted. "I amazed myself and the locals with how quickly I fitted into the place. It probably helped having the odd holiday on my uncle's farm down at Braidwood when I was a teenager."

"I'd heard you'd come up from the NSW police. You might know a friend of mine, Meredith O'Connor?"

He nodded. "Never met her but I know the name. Has a reputation for being a top officer."

"That's Meredith," Francey said with a grin.

They followed the path around the back of the homestead and went up one of the side verandah's set of steps.

"Well, now that you're here for a while, I might see you in town more often. I'd enjoy buying you a coffee or a wine at one of the pubs. If I'm off-duty, of course."

Was this the backhanded way policemen or perhaps country people suggested a date? Her lips twitched with the effort of not smiling. She'd keep her options open. "Maybe," she said enigmatically as she opened the French door into the living room. "I presume you're looking for CJ?"

"I am."

"He's in his study. I think you know where it is." Then, as he turned away she had a thought. "Steve, perhaps you could do me a favour. I have some film I want processed. Would you mind …?"

"Of course not. No trouble at all."

"Come into my office and I'll get it for you."

She beckoned for him to follow her out through the kitchen to a small room, hardly bigger than a broom cupboard. While she rummaged around for the film rolls he took a peek at what she had on the drawing board. Having worked as a carpenter's assistant on a couple of Sydney projects before he'd joined the service, he could read building plans. Impressive. She was halfway through drawing a rough layout of what appeared to be a hotel complex, complete with pool, courts and golf course. He read "Stage One" centred at the top of the page. On a pad beside the drawing were rough sketches, a lot of calculations, loads, weights, room dimensions, that sort of thing. Yes, indeed, Francey Spinetti knew her stuff.

She turned back to him, noticed but ignored his interest in the plan and said, "Three rolls. Tell the chemist, the one in the mall, that I'll pick them up at the end of the week. And thanks."

Her smile, which showed a set of perfect white teeth and a perfectly curved, generous mouth, made Steve go all tense.

"Oh, Steve, what are you doing here?"

Steve turned around to answer Les Westcott's question and glimpsed the put-out expression before he masked it. Interesting! "Just doing an errand for Francey," he answered truthfully as he shouldered his way out of the small room. "I'll take care of these for you," he promised as he put the rolls into his breast pocket. "Now, I really should see CJ."

Les's gaze was as cool as his tone. "You know where his study is."

Pleased with himself, Steve whistled tunelessly as he made his way to CJ's study and knocked on the door.

"Come in, Steve. What news have you for me?" Steve closed the door behind him before he started to speak.

Ten minutes later, after Steve Parrish had left his study, CJ sat motionless in the chair, deep in thought. The plot thickens, as the saying went ... The policeman's information had been succinct, to say the least. He had tracked down a girlfriend of Richard's, a young school teacher by the name of Penny Ormond. Their relationship hadn't been serious but the fact that Penny had broken up with her former boyfriend, Paul Andronicus, to date Richard, could be significant. Steve had ferreted out that Paul, a carpenter by trade, had been quite upset and had once threatened – in front of witnesses – to get Penny back.

Exhaustive checking through the considerable township of Mt Isa had drawn a blank. Andronicus had disappeared, moved on to places unknown shortly after Richard's death. Steve said that a statewide police bulletin was going out to all stations about Andronicus, that he was wanted for questioning, and Steve was confident that this was a good lead, the best so far. But with regard to the ownership of the rifle that had fired the bullets, he had no information whatsoever.

CJ grunted and then shook his head. Parrish was doing a sterling job, no doubt about it, and, no matter that he'd said to keep things quiet, maybe it was time to let the family know that Richard's death had been no accident. Maybe someone at Murrundi knew something or had information that might help Steve's case and perhaps didn't realise it.

Yes. Tomorrow he would assemble all the staff and tell them the situation in the hope that it might jog someone's memory.

*

Francey swished her body this way and that, checking how her long skirt clung to her in all the right places. The gold thread lurex long-sleeved top, together with a long strand gold chain and matching earrings proclaimed a touch of elegance for the party she'd been invited to: Pierre Dupre's fortieth at their home in town. CJ, Les, Natalie and Shellie had also been invited and she was going with CJ in his Rolls while the others travelled in the homestead's Range Rover.

Nothing like a bit of class for the migrant's daughter from Glebe, she thought as she applied a final sheen to her lips. She remembered being in Aden's BMW – it seemed so long ago. Their fragile, emotional involvement seemed a distant memory too and lately she was finding it difficult to recall his features and the thrill of being with him. When had her feelings towards Aden started to cool? Had it happened because she was out of the office? Was it the phone call, during which he'd made it obvious that their relationship came second to business? Somehow, she couldn't imagine Brett O'Connor putting business before Meredith ... but maybe she shouldn't use the O'Connors as a yardstick to compare relationships.

Still, she consoled herself with the thought that even if she and Aden weren't meant for each other, and she was pretty sure now that they weren't, he had freed her from the tyranny of her memories of Bryan Steinberg. She had come through stronger, more complete, confident. Aden had helped to make her heart whole again and brought her out of her self-imposed shell. For that she would always be grateful to him.

The Dupre house, a sprawling ranch-style weather-board set in a refreshingly leafy garden was ablaze with coloured lights and party noises as CJ parked the Rolls. Loud jukebox music could be heard coming from the backyard and already a throng of people were spilling out onto the front verandah, chatting, laughing and enjoying each other's company.

CJ kept Francey's arm tucked in his as they made their way through the house to the rear patio. After a while Francey's head spun with all the names of people CJ insisted on introducing her to. The mayor, the superintendent at the hospital, several doctors and numerous executives connected with the mine.

Her blue-green gaze eventually lighted on Sergeant Parrish who stood on the fringe of the crowd. With his height and breadth he was hard to miss, and she noted that he looked smart, rather "un-copperish", in his casual clothes. Black slacks and boots, a long sleeved collared shirt and a multipatterned vest. Kind of laid-back, dressy country and western, she guessed.

"CJ, let the girl go," Lisa admonished her boss for his proprietorial air towards Francey. "I want her to meet some regular folk," she added, raising her eyebrows at the types Francey had been introduced to: the upper eschalon of the Isa, people CJ knew and dealt with.

"Thanks," Francey whispered gratefully as the two women made their getaway, giggling. Suddenly what she wanted to do was to talk to Steve Parrish, despite her earlier apprehension towards him. But it wasn't to be. She found herself drawn into a new group of people and after what seemed like hours later, looking up as someone touched her arm, she recognised the man she had met the first day in town standing at her elbow.

"Hello, architect lady. Sam Bianchini, remember me?"

She laughed and shook her head, her ebony tresses swaying to and fro. "I'd rather forget, not you in particular, but the way we met."

"Bumped into any roos lately?" Sam teased and when queried by one of the women, with Francey's tacit approval, told them the story of Francey's encounter with the kangaroos.

"You wanna dance?" Sam asked.

"Gee Sam, if Michelle catches you you'll be in trouble," one of the women said in a half whisper.

Sam shrugged his shoulders but his gaze roved furtively over the crowd looking for the woman with whom he was supposedly having an affair. Deciding it was safe he led Francey onto the covered patio, where a temporary timber floor had been laid, and began to twirl her about.

Francey soon found out that country people were very hospitable, especially the men, many of whom couldn't wait to dance with her. But when a rather large hand took her by the arm and twirled her off the floor, and she saw that it belonged to Steve Parrish, she smiled with gratitude. They moved to the edge of the noisy throng and Steve slipped away for a moment or two to get them fresh drinks, giving Francey time to catch her breath.

"Looks like you're having a good time,' he said as he handed her a glass of white wine.

"I think Sam, Tim and Dimitri intend to wear me out on the dance floor."

"Yes. Around here it's called 'get the girl exhausted and wear down her resistance' – much as they do when they're roping a steer – so they can have their wicked way with her," he replied, a mischievous twinkle in his eye.

Francey's eyebrows rose sharply. "I don't think I care for the analogy between women and cattle. Besides, how do you know about such ruses? Practiced them yourself, hey?"

"I'm a cop. It's my job to know about everything."

"And do you," she queried, intrigued by his confidence, "know about everything?"

He thought for a while, his dark eyes sparkling in the play of lights above them. "Not everything, perhaps, but most of what's important around here." He elaborated, "Like your partner, Dimitri. I can tell you that he has a wife and two children at home and he's always out for a good time. Sam's all right but he's having it off with Michelle Mason, the wife of one of the mine's foremen. Tim's a good bloke. He works on a station north of here, he's footloose and fancy-free."

"What about you?" she asked pertinently.

"Me?" His features assumed a thoughtful expression. "I'm like Tim. A good bloke." He paused for a moment then added, "and available."

"That's good to know." Francey realised that they were verbally fencing with each other, and that both were very much aware of the undercurrent of attraction between them. It was exciting, and exhilarating. Apart from Aden she hadn't even remotely flirted with any male since Bryan. And then, as she looked up into his hard, hewn features her initial awkwardness, of feeling left-footed around him for no apparent reason fell away.

"Dance?"

Francey glanced at the crowd of jumping, gyrating party animals squashed into the dance area and shook her head. Had it been a slow dance she might have said yes. "It's not worth it, the bruises, I mean."

He grinned in understanding and marvelled as they began to talk naturally and easily, expanding on what they knew about each other. It was as if the slate of their previous meetings, where there had been tension and some awkwardness, had been wiped clean. Of course, he realised that he'd be just as happy to look at her, without too much talking, but Francey, he soon learned, was a woman who liked to talk. Not useless, frothy chitchat though, she had a keen brain and an interest in many things and when she became passionate about something, he sensed that she was the type who wouldn't be easily dissuaded from her beliefs.

"CJ told us about your investigation into Richard Ambrose's death. Everyone at Murrundi can't believe you think he may have been murdered. They all spoke so fondly of him. I wish I'd had the opportunity to meet him." From what she had heard about Richard from Shellie and Natalie, and from Les and Billy Wontow, she was sure she would have liked the man.

A muscle twitched in Steve's jaw. CJ had done what he'd asked him not to do. He should have known the old man wouldn't keep the information to himself indefinitely. CJ was the sort who had his own agenda on everything that concerned him. Christ, imagine if a journalist picked up the story? Then Andronicus would go to ground and he'd have Buckley's of finding him. He expelled his breath noisily, trying to hide his irritation. "Well, the investigation's in its early days. Clues are few and far between. Frankly, I don't know how far I'll be able to go with it, without a clear motive or a definite suspect or suspects."

Francey remembered how Shellie and Natalie had cried when CJ relayed the information to those assembled by the swimming pool. She'd seen that Les had been shocked by the news too. That a person could deliberately plot and execute a stampede to get rid of a rival, or for revenge, or even for financial gain, proved to her that violence knew no boundaries; it was as much alive and well in the bush as in the city.

"But you'll do your best? I know CJ would appreciate it."

"Rest assured, Francey, I'll follow up every lead I can ferret out." He looked down at her. "I liked Richard Ambrose, he was an okay guy."

Francey smiled, reassured by the tone of his voice and the determination in his eyes. She believed Steve Parrish wasn't the type of man to promise something he couldn't deliver.

"So, how's your latest project going?" he asked, wanting to get off the gloomy subject of Richard's death.

"It's the biggest thing I've tackled in my architectural career. Quite a challenge, I can tell you. To get a comparison with what's already been built, next week Les is flying me to Cairns. We're going to inspect some resort complexes along the coastline, and we're going down to Surfers as well."

"Sounds tough," his sarcasm had a soft edge to it. "You're going to be spoilt with all this jetsetting around and living the lifestyle of a millionaire. The adjustment will be hard when you return to everyday life, like the rest of us."

"Don't worry, I've plenty of friends in Sydney, and my parents, who'll bring me back to reality soon enough." She looked up at him. "Do you ever get down to Sydney?"

"Not a lot, but who knows ..." He shrugged enigmatically. Then his ears picked up the change in the music as it slowed to half its frenetic pace. "Come on, let's dance." He took her by the hand and half dragged her towards the dance floor.

Strong, yet gentle, Francey thought as Steve's arms closed around her and pulled her close. And light on his feet, considering his size. She felt enveloped yet not smothered. Safe, she felt safe. She laughed to herself. Why wouldn't she feel safe? He was a policeman, for God's sake. But deep down she knew it was more than that. There was something genuine about Sergeant Parrish, he had a no-nonsense belief in himself, a no-frills kind of guy. What one saw was what one got. And so far, as her gaze subtlely explored the breadth of his shoulders, the expanse of his chest, the ruggedness of his features, she liked what she saw and felt. More than she knew it was wise to.

Elsewhere, above the noise and high spirits, three other pairs of eyes took note of Steve and Francey dancing together.

Les Westcott could barely suppress the scowl as he made polite conversation with Pierre Dupre, the birthday boy. Hell, what did she see in that lummox-headed cop? The same cop that CJ had recently begun to have time for. He controlled the urge to sneer as he replied to some inane remark. Parrish was a nothing, a non-achiever. He'd chickened out of the Sydney police scene when it had got too hot for him and had come, tail between his legs, to the Isa to drone the rest of his life away. Did Francey know about his past? Probably not. He'd make sure she found out, not through him, of course, but via someone else. Maybe Shellie. CJ's sister enjoyed a gossip, but then she liked Steve and probably wouldn't bad-mouth him. His gaze moved to Sam Bianchini who looked as if he was arguing with Michelle Mason. Maybe Sam. He owed him a favour or two. A hunch told him he could be encouraged to give Francey the dirt on Parrish. He began to weave his way through the crowd of people towards his target.

CJ Ambrose, deep in political manoeuvrings with the mayor, Darren Turk, fixed his gaze on Francey and Parrish for a moment or two before looking away. They made a nice couple. He frowned at the thought. Mismatched, he changed his view. Young Francey had too much ambition for Parrish, even though he'd been forced to rethink his opinion of him since Parrish had started to investigate Richard's death. He didn't often make mistakes in gauging a man's character – it was too important in business dealings to underestimate a man – but in Parrish's case he had. The man was a quiet one, the low-key type who just went and got things done. Solid, and he reckoned he could be depended upon in a fight. A man to have on your side rather than against you.

"CJ, when are you gonna put your money where your mouth is and build that art museum you've been talking about for years?" Darren Turk challenged as he sipped his scotch and soda.

CJ's gaze returned momentarily to Francey, noting that she was smiling up at her dancing partner as if she hadn't a care in the world. "Sooner than you think, Darren. You know I've owned that parcel of land near the river for years. Now that I've found a top rate architect, if I can twist her arm a little, she might come up with an acceptable plan."

Darren Turk followed CJ's gaze. "You appear to have a lot of faith in that young woman." He nudged CJ in the ribs. "Is it all business between you two?"

"We're just good friends, as the saying goes," CJ answered, being deliberately obtuse. Then he laughed heartily. Like most of the folks here Turk would believe what he wanted to believe.

Standing on the fringe of the conversation between CJ and Turk, Natalie stiffened as she heard her stepfather's deliberate innuendo. CJ liked to play games and enjoyed baiting Darren, politically and personally. But, was "just good friends" an accurate description of his relationship with the architect? Since her return to Murrundi she had made a point of observing CJ and Francey together, and she honestly hadn't seen anything to indicate that they were having an affair. However, that didn't mean that they weren't. They might be being extraordinarily discreet.

The irksome thing was that Francey was still at Murrundi when she shouldn't be. She should be back where she belonged, in Sydney. She guessed that the architect could just as easily work on the plans for Cooktown in her office, as at Murrundi. So why wasn't she? What was the big attraction to staying with CJ? Was she trying to slowly worm her way into his confidence? Did she want to make herself indispensable to him? God, that had been done before, countless times by women throughout the ages. Well, she didn't intend to sit around and watch that situation eventuate. There was too much at stake.

"Would you like to dance, Natalie?"

Natalie blinked twice to clear her thoughts. Mike Hunter was standing right in front of her and she hadn't even noticed him. "Dance? Oh, yes, Mike, that would be nice." As they approached the dancing crowd she saw Sam Bianchini cut in on Steve and then whirl Francey away to the other side of the dance floor.

It shouldn't be too hard to think of a way to get rid of Francey Spinetti. Maybe she could discredit her in CJ's eyes. That would be best, but it might also be difficult to achieve, and she couldn't risk getting her stepfather offside. Still, there were other methods, ideas and ... she smiled broadly at Mike and he smiled back, thinking she was enjoying being with him. A plan began to form in her devious mind.

CJ heard Francey's sigh as they sped towards Murrundi in the Rolls in the early hours of the morning. He grinned in the darkness. "You seemed to have a good time tonight. Plenty of male attention."

"I did. I thought country men were laid back and shy. I didn't find too many of those guys at Pierre's party."

"Some are, particularly if they're from remote stations and don't get to talk to a pretty girl too often. You might find it hard to believe, but when I was a youngster, I used to be painfully shy of talking to women."

She stole a look at his profile. "I do find that hard to believe."

He chuckled at her dry response. "I had a female teacher, her name was Belinda Marshall. We had composite classes in the country back then, in a small tin-pot kind of school. I thought Miss Marshall was beautiful. My first crush, I guess. I loved to bring her things. Wildflowers, an apple, even little poems that I'd written. Made a real fool of myself over her, for a couple of weeks."

"A couple of weeks! What happened?"

"I thought she'd wait a few years, ten or twelve, until I grew up." He chuckled. "You see, I was only eight at the time. But then her husband came to join her and I realised it was a lost cause."

"Poor CJ," she said, laughing with mock sympathy. Her thoughts harked back to the party, to those she'd met, but mostly back to her time with Steve. Safe in the car's darkened interior, she allowed herself a dreamy smile, and let the wave of warmth course through her for several minutes. But all too soon came reality. Nothing could come of it, more the pity. She wasn't going to be at Murrundi long enough for a relationship to develop. Still, she told herself as she sighed again, it was nice to dream.

"You know," CJ said out of the blue, "the Isa's a growing township, what with the mining and cattle. The mine's the largest producer of silver and lead in the world, and amongst the top ten producers of copper and zinc. Over twenty-four thousand people live there. It's thriving and growing, the mayor reckons the town could double in population in the next twenty years. An architect could make herself or himself a comfortable living up here." He let her digest that. "There'd be commercial projects and home building, and even graziers need new buildings from time to time."

"Are you suggesting that Nicholson, Drew and Carlyle open an office in the Isa?"

"I'm not. All I'm saying is that an enterprising architect could do well here if he or she wanted to grab the opportunity."

"That's food for thought," she answered enigmatically. It was. And she had thought of it, fleetingly, casually. One day as she'd sat at the drawing board looking out on the expanse of countryside through the window it came to her that she had fallen in love with the land, with its harshness, its vast empty spaces. Almost as if it drew her magnetically to it in some inexplicable way. She had told Alison Wontow and Shellie and they had nodded in understanding, as if the same thing had happened to them many years ago.

The outback, wresting a living, making a home with its blatant inhospitability was a challenge that strangely aroused an emotional response in her. A fact all the more startling because it was unexpected. She knew that this land was unforgiving and unfeeling – it didn't play favourites or care about the survival of individuals – yet she found its very intractability appealing although she didn't quite understand why. It came from some feeling deep inside her, for which she had no explanation.

But should she contemplate such a radical change? Leave Sydney, for good? The muscles around her heart tightened at the thought of it. Her parents and her lovable, noisy bunch of relatives, the friends she'd have to leave behind, could she bear to?

Francey stared at the bedside clock. Three a.m. Sleep eluded her. Her mind was too worked up, over the party, over Steve, over CJ's tantalising suggestion about going it alone as an architect in the Isa. Oh that CJ, he was a cunning character. He had deliberately put the provoking thought in her head, knowing she couldn't resist analysing the pros and cons of it. The man was getting to know her too well. She yawned and stretched, rolled over and closed her eyes tightly.

Ten minutes later she sat up in bed. Damn. Maybe a glass of warm milk would settle her.

Putting on her robe she padded barefoot through the homestead to the kitchen and flicked on the light. Alison kept a shipshape kitchen, everything sparklingly clean and in its rightful place. She poured a little milk into a cup and placed it in the microwave.

She looked up as a noise at the back door caught her attention. Les was punching in the security code to open the back door. Looking the worse for wear he came into the kitchen. He held a bottle of whisky in his left hand and a glass in the other.

"Aahh, the party girl," he said in a slurred tone as he wobbled towards her.

"Hi, do you want some milk?" she asked though she knew he wouldn't and that it would probably curdle in his alcohol-soaked stomach. She watched him shake his head vigorously then stop. He put a hand to his forehead and rubbed it hard, as if something hurt. She was sure something did!

"D'ja hav' a good time?"

"Yes. The party was very nice."

"Saw ya dancin' with lotsa men."

"Not lots," she corrected, "three or four maybe."

Les moved closer, listing slightly to the left. He put the bottle down noisily on the counter top. "Spent a lot of time with Parrish, didn't ya?"

She shrugged but didn't answer. Her gaze moved to the microwave, willing it to hurry up. It did. She took the cup out and added a teaspoon of sugar, then she stirred the contents noisily. "Goodnight, Les, see you in the morning."

"Don't go." He put his hand on her arm as she turned away. "Wanna talk ta ya."

"We both need to get some sleep. We'll talk tomorrow."

"No. Wanna talk now!"

His hold on her arm tightened. A niggle of alarm spread through her. Alcohol did strange things to some men: some reverted to real pussycats, others became belligerent and aggressive. It wasn't difficult to work out which way Les went when he had a few under his belt.

"Ya shouldn't waste yer time on Parrish. He's a loser, a quitter."

"Because he left Sydney over a certain situation? I don't think that makes him a loser," she was stung enough to defend. "Sometimes making a fresh start is the only sensible thing to do."

"I'm more your type, Francey. We're two of a ... a kind," he said with a grin that was more of a leer. "We're smart, ambitious. I've got plans. In another couple of years I'll have enough money to do great things by myself. I'll not have to be CJ's lap-dog then."

"That's nice," she said, trying to extricate herself from his hold. "I wish you every success."

Getting impatient, he shook her a little. "Don't ya get what I'm trying to say?" He shook his head as if to clear the fogginess inside it. "You and me, together. Give *us* a chance, Francey. Please." He drained the remainder of the amber fluid in his glass and plonked the vessel so hard on the counter top it cracked.

"Look, I don't think –"

Before she could finish he pulled her into his arms and began to rain kisses on her forehead, her cheeks, her chin, desperately seeking her mouth, which she wouldn't allow. She twisted her head away both from the reek of him and his unwelcome attention.

"You know," he whispered thickly, close to her ear. "If ya didn't want a bloke ta get the wrong idea ya shouldn't traipse aroun' in see-through gear. Turns a bloke on, it does."

"You're drunk. Let me go, Les."

She hadn't realised how strong he was. His arms were like bands of steel and she could feel the evidence of his arousal as he ground his groin against her stomach. One hand moved to the knot of her robe, trying to loosen it. A wave of disgust and then anger rushed through her. Who the hell did he think he was? She hadn't asked for this or encouraged him at all. She wasn't going to take it.

Remembering the training she'd taken in self-defence – to please her father – she thought she wasn't in a good position for an effective response, but she had to do something. She wriggled her arm free and it came up in a flash. She struck him hard across the side of his head, hoping the shock of the blow would knock some sense into him. His hold loosened, enough for her to bring the flat of her hands down hard on his wrists and break the hold.

"Ya hit me!" His hand went to the side of his face, rubbing the imprint of her blow. "All I wanted was a little kiss and cuddle, ta tell ya how I feel," he slurred the words reproachfully, "ya didn't hafta hit me."

Francey retreated, putting a few paces between them. There was little point trying to talk sense to him when he was this drunk. "Look, we'd better call it a night."

"Oh." A voice came from the kitchen doorway. "I wondered who was making all the noise," Shellie said as she bustled into the kitchen.

From the look in her eyes, Francey saw her instant assessment of the situation. She gave her a relieved smile. "I was warming some milk to help me sleep."

"So I see. What are you doing here, Les Westcott? You look a disgrace." Her gaze took in his mussed up hair, his shirt half hanging out of his trousers, and the red welt across his cheek, which she ignored. "Go on, off you go to bed."

"What a good idea," Francey said and with a wink at Shellie made a quick getaway, leaving the older woman to attend to Les.

Minutes later, sitting up in bed as she sipped her milk, she was surprised by the gentle tap on the door.

Shellie poked her head around. "You okay, Francey?" Seeing that the young woman wasn't too sleepy she came in and sat at the end of the bed. She prefaced her words with a shake of her head. "He didn't mean any harm, you know. Les is a good man. Sometimes though, when he's had a few too many he goes off the rails, or when Natalie baits him he can lose his temper." She patted Francey's feet under the blanket. "He's fond of you, you know, so don't be too hard on him."

"It's all right, Shellie. Les isn't the first man to make a pass at me and wear my mark as a result."

Shellie nodded. "Yes, I saw that you could defend yourself. He was quite hurt that you'd slapped him, though no doubt he deserved it. You'll see," she gave a gentle chuckle, "tomorrow, when he's over his hangover, he'll be most apologetic. He was like that with his wife. Always apologising after a row no matter who was at fault. Not that it did him much good in the end." She got up and retraced her steps to the door. "So long as you're not too upset by his bad behaviour, that's the main thing."

"I'm fine," Francey assured her as she left. But was she? she asked herself as she looked at the closed door. Les' behaviour had been unexpected. It would be hard to look him in the eye and act as if nothing had happened. Tomorrow they needed to sort things out, for both their sakes. Especially as they'd be spending quite a lot of time together over the next week.

CHAPTER ELEVEN

Francey eased back in the leather chair, the whistling hum of the jet barely audible, and closed her eyes. What a week it had been.

The first time she had sat in this seat in CJ's Learjet she had secretly admitted to being nervous, for more than one reason. There had been a noticeable tension between her and Les since the incident in the kitchen, even though he had come to her the next day and apologised abjectly as Shellie'd said he would. But where once she had been relaxed with him, now a wariness prevailed and she knew it would take time for that to settle down, if it ever did. At least she knew that alcohol plus Les equalled a combustible situation and as they jetted around, checking out the resorts on CJ's list, she would be cautious of him.

She had also been apprehensive about flying. After all, she had never flown before and here she was strapped into a super-expensive private jet, with Les at the controls, about to fly to their first port of call, Cairns. She had hoped she wouldn't embarrass herself by being airsick. She hadn't. In fact she had enjoyed every second of the flight and when Les put the engine on autopilot and beckoned her up to the cockpit to show her how the plane worked and for a better view, she reverted to being an adventurous kid, wanting to know about everything.

Her parents said she had been born with a wide streak of curiosity which had got her into a few scrapes when she'd been young. Like when she'd wanted to see the view from the roof of a boatshed down by the harbour's edge. She and Meredith had clambered to the top, skinning their knees and elbows, and then sat on the painted galvanised tin with their sweaters underneath them so the tin wouldn't burn their backsides. They'd enjoyed the spectacle of various crafts plying their way up and down the waterway, but when it came to climbing the eight or ten metres back to the ground, their adventurous nature had deserted them.

Eventually one of the workers in the boatshed had to call the fire brigade to get them down. Recalling it all, she smiled to herself. They'd only been eleven and she still remembered the sore bottom – her father had been very angry with her for causing such a fuss – she'd had for several days because of that escapade. When they'd arrived in Cairns the sultry tropical climate had almost taken her breath away, as had the white, chauffeured limousine that met and took them to the Hilton Hotel. Over the next three days the limousine drove them around several exclusive resorts and up the coast to Port Douglas and back.

Francey was definitely stretching the description to call it all *work*! Drinks by the pool late in the afternoon after being shown around the resort complexes by deferential managers, a pleasant dinner either at the hotel or one of the many restaurants where Les was well-known. Real tough! And Les. He'd been such a gentleman, not a word or a glance out of place.

If only her parents could see her. The greengrocer's daughter from Glebe enjoying the pampering, the mild bowing and scraping because they were in CJ's employ. How easy it would be to become seduced by the good life. But, she'd kept her perspective, and resisted the thought of being over-impressed. Lucia Spinetti had instilled that down-to-earth trait in her and it prevailed, though for a short while she had enjoyed the game of pretending she was someone important.

Then the same procedure had been repeated in Surfers Paradise. When they wound up their tour of inspection on the Gold Coast, the limousine took them to Coolangatta airport, the best surprise had come. After take off and levelling out at six thousand metres, Les said there'd been a change of plans. CJ had radioed that they were to fly to Sydney, where they had overnight accommodation booked at the Regent Hotel. This was so Francey could visit her parents, check her apartment and get more clothes if she wanted to. A nice gesture.

She hadn't expected CJ to be so thoughtful. And ... she did miss her parents a little. Regular phone calls home made it less lonely, but sometimes she just wanted to see them, talk to them, tell them what she'd experienced and what she was doing. And intimate that her life and expectations were changing – the change so subtle that some of the time even Francey herself was unaware of it.

Her parents had been surprised and delighted to see her. Lucia had fussed far too much, tut-tutted that she'd lost more weight – which she hadn't – and both wanted to know everything about CJ, the multimillionaire. Even her father's eyes had widened impressively when she'd described the home and the extent of the Ambrose empire. But she'd scowled when she had seen the gleam in his eye and teasingly said that CJ was much too old for her. They shared a wonderful four hours together before she'd gone off to stay overnight at the Regent.

The next morning she fitted in a two hour session with Aden Nicholson, to bring him up to speed on the Cooktown development. She shifted restlessly in the seat, hearing the leather squeak against her back as she remembered the time in his office. The staff at Nicholson, Drew and Carlyle had been delighted to see her. Aden had given her a bear hug welcome. Then it was down to business! He'd wanted to know about the development of the mini conference centre and, more importantly, how the plans were coming along for the multimillion dollar project at Cooktown.

With a sinking heart she realised that whatever her feelings and expectations of Aden had been in absentia, they had shrivelled up and died. She thought that he knew it too but tried to avoid any mention of their personal relationship. What, she wondered as she sat opposite him, had she seen in him? A surface handsomeness, intelligence, sophistication. Why hadn't she noticed his hard, business edge? How had he disguised it and taken her in? The reality of seeing him differently made her experience a sense of loss for what might have been, yet, in another way, it made her feel completely free.

Quite illogically, by the time she'd left Aden, she was angry and disappointed more with herself than with him. She had foolishly and romantically embellished Aden with attributes he didn't possess. And then, without conscious volition, her thoughts had turned to Steve Parrish. She'd smiled as she remembered how well they were getting along now. Steve was real. Genuine.

Later, the taxi had deposited her outside Meredith O'Connor's modest home at Bronte for a brief visit before she met Les at Mascot airport. Her friend had squealed with delight at the surprise visit. They had talked non-stop – she'd even told her about Steve, and how the romance with Aden hadn't worked out. Meredith, now almost eight months gone and with a protruding stomach that could barely fit behind the driver's seat, had insisted on driving her to the airport.

Francey's eyelids opened and she ran the fingers of her right hand through her black hair, untangling the curls. With a stab of surprise she realised that she was looking forward to getting back. To Murrundi. To the harsh plains, the low hills, the rugged lonely land.

She shook her head and smiled in wonder. Who would believe it? She, a devout city dweller who loved the salty sea breeze on her face and in her hair; who artistically admired the angular shapes and forms of city buildings; enjoyed the jostling, crowded streets and accepted the noises of thousands of people as background music as they scurried about their business was falling in love. With the outback, with the freedom, the starkness and the determination of the people who survived and tried to bend it to their will.

Pharaoh's sleek coat glistened with sweat from the hard ride Natalie had given the stallion as she reined in near the stable door late in the afternoon.

Almost as if he'd been waiting, Mike Hunter came out from the dimness of the stalls and held the bridle as she slid from the huge horse. Natalie took off her leather gloves and ran her hand through her sweat-streaked blonde hair, making it stand up crazily, yet attractively about her longish face.

"Thanks, Mike," she said airily as she threw him the reins.

"Didja have a good ride?"

"Wonderful. The recent rain has put some water in a few of the creeks and the waterholes. I rode towards the western boundary. I think l gave Pharaoh a work out he'll appreciate. That horse needs to be ridden hard." Pharaoh was the fastest of all the horses at Murrundi and everyone knew it.

"See any feral pigs? Lucky said he saw a pack out that way last week. We don't want them hanging around with spring only six weeks off. They could have a go during the calving."

She thought for a moment, well aware that Mike was hanging on every word. He amused her. She didn't quite lead him on, but she'd smile and use enough body language to make him think he had an outside chance with her. Hah. Fat chance any man had with her. "No ..." She pursed her lips provocatively. "I didn't see anything other than cattle and a few emus."

"CJ called a while ago. He and Les are off to Canberra to see some minister, for the environment, I think. About the Cooktown project. They'll be away for a couple more days."

"Right, thanks for that." She patted Pharaoh's neck affectionately. "Time to give you a rubdown, boy, you've earned it." The foreman and stockmen had been told that she wasn't to be waited on hand and foot. That if she rode Pharaoh she was responsible for watering, feeding and grooming him. Damn CJ and his old-fashioned ideas. When this was all hers, her grey eyes encompassed the sheds, the barns, the back of the homestead, she wouldn't lift a finger if she didn't want to.

"No problem, I'll do it," Mike offered. He began to lead the horse around, letting him cool down before he took him to the trough.

Smiling her thanks she walked away. Men were so predictable. They spent most of their waking hours thinking with their dicks. Even Les, who had a good brain, was clearly besotted with Francey Spinetti. Oh, she'd heard the gossip. Aunt Shellie couldn't keep a secret if her life depended on it. She knew about the little altercation between them in the kitchen after Dupre's party. And then there was CJ, the way he acted around her; attentive, smiling, putting on his well-known charm. It was sickening. The "Spinetti syndrome" as she'd dubbed it, was becoming near endemic amongst the more interesting men. Why, even Steve Parrish, whom she genuinely liked, rather than pretended to like, seemed more then casually interested. What did they see in her? She'd be damned if she could fathom it out.

That was men for you. A woman, on the other hand, was more sensitive to your moods, knew how to get you worked up better than a man too, knew all those little secret places you longed to be touched in – the places *men* never thought of. And women could satisfy you just as well. Her train of thoughts made her think of Trish, made her feel suddenly horny then lonely. Trish had become the only person she could talk to, really talk to, these days. She missed her, even missed the reproachful, confused looks she got from her when she had a problem or was in one of her black moods.

Her eyebrows lifted as she spied the earlier subject of her thoughts. Francey sat on the top rail of the breaking-in yard's fence, taking photos of Billy as he worked on breaking in a three-year-old gelding. Almost noiselessly, Natalie climbed the fence and her quarry, intent on the hullabaloo within – the bucking, snorting, near uncontrollable horse and Billy, who hung on one handed, shouting and whistling – didn't even notice until she spoke.

"Hi there."

Francey jumped with fright and grabbed the railing beside her for support.

"I didn't mean to frighten you."

Francey grinned. "My own fault. Guess I got caught up in what Billy's doing."

"He's one of the best breakers around," Natalie told her proudly.

"How long does it take, I mean, to break a horse in?"

"Depends on the horse. It could take a week, maybe three, maybe longer. Billy's good because he's patient and he doesn't hurt them like some breakers do. Some think fear will do the trick, but Billy uses kindness and he talks soft and low to them most of the time."

A couple of stockmen were sitting on the fence on the other side of the yard. Another sat astride a horse inside the yard, ready to help if Billy got thrown or wanted to get off in a hurry. Dust boles from the horse's hoofs kicked up in the air mingling with angry neighing and snorting as the gelding pitted its will against that of the man, desperately trying to avoid the inevitable: that the man – inferior in strength but superior in intellect – would master him.

"I'm glad I brought my camera. I think I got a couple of good shots."

"You're right into photography, aren't you?"

"It's more of a hobby, really. Therapeutic. In the past I've used it when my brain overloads with work or if I have a mental block with a design. Time out with my camera gets rid of the junk inside and brings back the perspective."

"Have you considered exhibiting?"

"I'm not sure I'm good enough for that."

"Perhaps you'll show me your portfolio one day. I could tell you their worth," Natalie offered.

"That's nice of you. Perhaps. One day."

"Well," Natalie sensed Francey's uncertainty and honed in on what was perhaps her weakness, "if you'd like to photograph something really special I could show you some wonderful Aboriginal paintings."

Francey's eyes widened. "That would be great." Alison Wontow had told her about the Aboriginals in the area, about their beliefs and how they made use of the land. To photograph something so ancient and rare was something she had never expected to be able to do.

Natalie smiled sweetly. The bitch had taken the bait. "Well, whenever you've got a couple of spare hours. It's a bit of a ride but nothing you can't handle considering you've been on a muster." She pretended to think for a moment. "Why not tomorrow afternoon, if you can spare the time."

Francey thought. The plans for Cooktown were going well. Ahead of schedule, really, and CJ wouldn't be back for another day or two to see the progress. "Yes, that would be perfect."

No-one saw them leave the stables the next afternoon. Natalie, slightly in the lead, with Francey following, rode south, off the property of Murrundi Downs station and onto the free range. The late winter's day was cool, the sky a clear azure except for a patch of white clouds hanging on the western horizon. Francey's mount, Astra, carried a saddlebag containing two cameras and a tripod plus several rolls of film. Pharaoh carried Natalie, water canteens plus a canvas bag with afternoon tea packed by Alison.

Francey marvelled at the land as they travelled, the aridity of the foothills, the soil and the sparse vegetation even after recent rains. The vastness of the plains that ran as far as one's visibility went was awe-inspiring, as was the remoteness and ... the silence. Not a bird nor the sound of any animal other than the horses' hoofs, intruded upon a quiet so intense one could almost hear one's own heartbeat. The rich, bold colours of the land and the sky fascinated the aesthete within her. The true deep-blue, the rusty-red of the earth, sometimes reminded her of dried-up blood. She suddenly shivered at the thought, wondering where on earth it had come from. She squinted in the sunlight, knowing that one had to have stamina to survive out here – be mentally and physically strong to withstand the unrelenting land. What was it about the outback that got under one's skin and into one's heart? She pondered the question as they trotted then cantered for a while before easing to a more relaxed pace.

"Let's give the horses a bit of a run," Natalie called out.

"Okay."

Francey pushed her borrowed hat down hard on her head, dug her heels into Astra's flanks and urged her forward as Natalie took off. Clods of earth flew up towards her as the horse broke into a full gallop. She had never seen Pharaoh go flat out before and, God, could the horse run!

Natalie flattened out over the horse's neck, she and Pharaoh becoming one as the pace picked up and, to encourage more speed, she flicked the whip against the stallion's rump. The distance between the two horses grew until Pharaoh was almost out of sight. Glancing back, Natalie saw the gap and slowed her mount. Her smile was triumphant as she waited for Francey to catch up.

"That wasn't much of a contest," Francey complained tongue-in-cheek as she reined in.

"I guess not. It was more for Pharaoh's benefit than for ours. He loves to stretch out." Natalie patted his mane. "Don't you, boy?" Then she swivelled about in the saddle and looked to the east. "We're following the old creek bed," she pointed out a row of spindly eucalypts that denoted water was near, "to a kind of ravine, it's like a small canyon and is about five kilometres from here. The Aboriginals who lived there about four thousand years ago were called Kalkadoons. They used to hunt and gather in and around the ravine where it was cooler and because a supply of water could usually be found all year round, although the creek bed's dry now and has been for years. That's where the Aboriginal paintings are."

"You know the place well, then?"

"Like the back of my hand. Richard and I used to ride there a lot when we were growing up. He was keen on Aboriginal stuff, he even pestered Billy into teaching him how to play the didgeridoo."

"Did Richard play it well, the didgeridoo?"

"No," Natalie laughed, "he was awful. Mum hated the sound of it so he had to practise out back near the stockmen's quarters. They didn't think much of it either."

They ambled along, sometimes in companionable silence, sometimes talking casually about the land and its first inhabitants. The topography changed gradually as the afternoon wore on. The foothills became a little higher, the vegetation thicker and Francey began to notice outcrops of huge boulders on either side of the track they followed.

"We're coming to the canyon now," Natalie said. "We've time for a good look at the paintings, and for you to take photos. Then we'll have afternoon tea and head back. Don't want to be caught away from the homestead after dark. It's dangerous for the horses and us, what with some of the rough terrain and the wild pigs."

It was cooler in the ravine, with the high earth and boulder hills angling narrowly down. A strong breeze blew then eddied, making whistling sounds amongst the trees and rocks. They left their mounts after tying the reins around a stringy bark tree and with Francey toting her photographic equipment, headed up along a narrow track sprinkled with boulders. A rocky overhang jutted out like a protecting umbrella, with the ground slanting up towards the back.

"This is one of the Kalkadoon's campsites. See the ash marks in the rock from their fires? Go to the back of the cave. You'll have to bend over a bit because you're tall. That's where you'll see the paintings. Have fun."

"You're not coming?"

"I've seen them before, lots of times. I'll make a fire to boil the billy. By the time you're through the tea should be ready."

Francey did as Natalie had instructed and, bent over almost double, she half walked, half crawled to the back of the overhang, where anyone sheltering would have had the most protection. The paintings were there. Almost a hundred random drawings, some etched into the sandstone like an engraving, others painted on with varying shades of ochre and clay which, over time, had begun to fade.

Francey set the tripod up, wishing she'd brought a portable set of lights with her. She'd have to fiddle with the aperture and the timing mechanism to do these subjects justice. She spent a good three-quarters of an hour filming studies of hoop cranes, skeletonised fish, a flock of emus, a kangaroo in full flight and several stick figures. Representations of humans perhaps, she thought, maybe even an ancient family.

What she photographed had great meaning for her. This was history. The ancient artists, primitive and simple in their style, may have passed into history but they had left something that endured through time to let those who followed know they'd once been here. She shivered at the symbolism of it all and was more than a little moved. Somehow, the paintings struck an emotional chord within her and she knew this wasn't the first time she had experienced such unexpected depth of feeling here at Murrundi Downs. Even though she remained at a loss to explain it.

She stayed until the light began to fade and all the jiggling with the camera settings wouldn't result in a half-decent shot. Packing up, she made her way down the rocky slope to where Natalie had a rug set out. Plates of cakes and biscuits and two enamel mugs of billy tea steamed invitingly.

"How did it go?"

"Wonderful," Francey said, smiling. "Thank you for bringing me here."

Natalie smiled back. "My pleasure. You must be hungry after all that activity." She pointed to the cakes and the tea. "Tuck in, they're good." Then, raising her face to the sky she gauged how much daylight was left. "We'll have to do some hard riding on the way back to beat the dark."

Francey nodded in agreement as she enjoyed two cup cakes and dunked a biscuit in her tea, relishing every morsel.

Afterwards they repacked their horses and Natalie mounted first. She looked down at the remains of the fire and said, "Francey, kick sand over that, will you. There's not much chance of causing a fire here, but one should do the right thing."

Francey did so and then, as she looked up Natalie's horse suddenly reared, then sprang forward and bolted down the ravine in the opposite direction to which they'd come. The reins were hanging loose and Natalie lurched forward to grab the horse's mane. Pharaoh was out of control!

"Natalie!" Francey screamed after her.

Forgetting the fire, she put her foot in the stirrup and made to mount but to her frustration, the saddle slipped off and fell in a heap beside Astra. Damn. Who had loosened the saddle's girth? She glanced up again to see Natalie disappearing around the bend in the ravine, holding on for dear life. With a grunt she picked the saddle up and put it on the patient Astra.

Worried about Natalie she mounted quickly and gave chase. As she emerged from the ravine she fully expected to see Natalie and Pharaoh somewhere in the distance. She saw nothing and no-one. She stood up in the stirrups to get a better view. Nothing! She shook her head in disbelief. It was as if the earth had opened up and swallowed Natalie and Pharaoh.

Where could they have got to? Had Pharaoh thrown Natalie? If so, surely she would see some evidence, the horse ... a figure on the ground. She scanned the surrounding area, straining her eyes for a glimpse of some movement, some form of life. Nothing remotely human. Then she studied the ground trying to find a trail, hoof prints, anything, but the ground was too rocky. No evidence existed that a horse had passed this way.

An awareness of the terrible stillness descended on her. She licked her dry lips and frowned. Natalie was an expert horsewoman, she would soon get Pharaoh under control again, and then she'd come back for her. Of course she would. Her blue-green eyes surveyed all she could see. Empty undulating plains, hillocks, straggly gums and spinifex.

She frowned. Which way was Murrundi?

What should she do? Don't panic, was the thought that immediately came to mind.

Should she wait here or return to the campfire, where Natalie would expect to find her? She looked at her watch. An hour to sunset. Perhaps she should ride out the other end of the ravine and try to work her way back but, which way was back? She didn't have a clue. She hadn't paid enough attention to landmarks or anything because Natalie had been her guide. Besides to her, a novice, they all looked pretty much the same. What was it Les had said to her, more then once? That if someone got lost in the bush or became disorientated, they should stay put. That was safer than moving around and perhaps becoming more lost, though she wasn't sure how she could be more lost than ordinary *lost*!

She looked around her, at the stark countryside, willing Natalie to appear. She didn't. Finally, sighing, she turned Astra around and retraced her steps to the campfire which had stopped smouldering. Darkening shadows were climbing down the ravine arm in arm with an accompanying chill. Stay calm, she told herself but already her pulse had started to race and apprehension was stiffening her spine.

Now, with only half an hour of daylight left, Francey was forced to reassess her situation. It seemed clear that for whatever reason, Natalie wasn't going to or couldn't return. Dear God, she hoped she was all right. So, what were the alternatives? She sighed again, it looked like a night in the ravine. How bad could that be? She dismounted and scrambled towards the fire, poking about with a stick. Maybe she could get it going again. After several frustrating minutes she stopped. No such luck!

Okay, plan B. What did she have with her? No lighting, no food or water but at a pinch she could use Astra's saddle blanket for warmth, though her nose wrinkled up at the thought of the smell. Oh, well, she said to herself stoically, she would just have to make the best of it … until morning.

She removed the saddle and blanket, led Astra to a clump of yellow grass so she could feed and dragged the saddle up under the overhang just as sunset extinguished all light.

When darkness fell, it enveloped everything. It was blacker than anything she had experienced. Blacker than when she had been on the muster where they'd taken care to keep the fire banked all night. And the wind had dropped, causing an eerie stillness. It was going to be a long, uncomfortable night but she took heart in the fact that at first light the Murrundi people would send out a search party. Natalie had probably told Alison Wontow where they were going, so all she had to do was get through the night and everything would be fine. By tomorrow evening she'd be laughing about the escapade.

But despite all the mental bolstering up, tentacles of fear began to nibble at the edges of her mind, drawing power from the darkness and her own insecurity. What if Natalie couldn't get back to Murrundi? What if she hadn't told anyone where they were going? What if …?

The blackness pressed in on her and she wrapped her arms around her torso, hugging and rocking herself, trying to dredge up some inner strength. The darkness was so thick she couldn't see her hand in front of her face. She closed her eyes and the blackness became softer, more reasonable, less threatening.

But try as she might she couldn't stop the voice that repeated in her head until the trembling began in her arms and legs and finally overcame her. You're alone ... alone ... *alone.*

CHAPTER TWELVE

As a small child, Francey had been afraid of the dark. Afraid of sounds she couldn't recognise and shadows that seemed unnatural and threatening. Now, as the blackness enclosed her, those childhood fears resurfaced. It was like being in a void, a terrible nothingness.

She could hear her heart beating, the pace increasing as fear won over reason and the blood began to course heavily through her veins. Even her breathing sounded different, laboured. Her nerve ends tingled for no reason. Everything had become highly accentuated because of the dark.

Her hearing was twice as acute, and tuned in to the night sounds. She could hear Astra's bridle clinking, and her occasional neigh or hoof stomp. The sound of the breeze which had died before sunset returned to stir the shrubs and trees. Branches scraped against rock, leaves rustled, and the cold intensified, working its way through her clothes, her skin, to her very bones until she began to shiver.

Sitting on the hard rock beneath the overhang Francey tried to roll herself into a tight ball. She drew her knees up towards her chest, clasped her arms about them to hold them there, and let her head fall forward onto her knees. She wrapped the horsy smelling blanket tight around her shoulders, vainly trying to find a modicum of warmth but she knew this was as comfortable as she'd get. Now, if only she could fall sleep!

She couldn't. Never had she felt so wide awake and so alone. She tried to pep her courage up with the reminder that this was only one night. With mock bravado she convinced herself that she could get through this, and when she was back at Murrundi, she'd laugh about the experience with CJ and the others.

She wondered if Natalie was all right, or was she stuck somewhere in the bush like her, alone? And then she mentally replayed the events from the time she'd kicked sand onto the fire. She shook her mop of black hair in consternation at what had happened. *Nothing* should have happened. For the life of her she didn't know what had made Pharaoh bolt. He was a frisky horse, but she'd watched Natalie handle him with ease all afternoon. So her sudden inability to control him was puzzling, in the extreme.

Scrunched up defensively against the blackness she tried to remember what Les and Alison and Shellie had said about being in the bush, about surviving. Already her mouth felt dry and it was becoming hard to salivate. By tomorrow morning she would be really thirsty. Dehydration. Les said that became the real danger for anyone lost in the bush without water. In the summer, because of the temperature, one could expect to last only a day or two in such conditions. But this was August, one didn't sweat or need as much water, she reassured herself. Besides, by midmorning she'd be found and on her way back to Murrundi.

The wind strengthened, whistling under the overhang, buffeting her as she sat there. The rock beneath her was stone cold and the chill evening began to make her shiver. She yawned. God, she was tired but the cold, the darkness, the wind, *her fear*, stopped her from relaxing enough to fall asleep.

What a stupid damned thing to have happened. She yawned again and closed her eyes, trying every trick she could think of to fall asleep. Counting sheep, saying the rosary, singing songs to herself, nothing worked. For Francey sleep became as elusive as warmth on this cold winter's night.

As the first grey light of dawn peeped over the top of the ravine an exhausted sleep finally settled over her. She had shivered most of the night, cramped as the cold seeped into all her muscles, and had ached from the effort of trying to mentally keep the chill at bay.

The cloudy sky obscured the sun and stopped any morning warmth from seeping into the depth of the ravine. She shivered in her sleep. Her body now on its side, she used the saddle for a pillow and had the old musty blanket draped over her torso. Her knees were drawn up and her hands lay pressed between them, subconsciously seeking whatever warmth she could.

Francey woke with a start. A noise. A rock from the back of the overhang had come loose. With one eye open she watched the fist-sized rock roll down the slope onto the ravine floor. Daylight. Thank God.

Unkinking her slender frame she sat up, stretched and moaned at the stiffness of her body – she ached from head to toe. She blinked a couple of times against the light and then focused on her watch. Eleven fifteen. Midmorning!

She should have felt refreshed but she didn't. As her brain became truly awake she did a mental calculation. They, someone, should have reached her by now.

She tried to swallow but there was no saliva in her mouth. She coughed and then moaned as her stiff muscles objected to the activity. Why weren't they here? What could be keeping them? Aahhh, they might be looking for Natalie too, so it could take longer. God, how much longer? She looked down into the ravine for Astra. The horse was nowhere in sight. Standing up, she then scrambled down the slope, almost slipping to the ravine floor. No sign of the horse.

Now she was truly alone. No company, not even of the four-legged variety, and no means of getting out of the ravine, even if she decided to. Stuck.

Don't panic!

She panicked. She began to walk back and forth, five steps one way, turn, five steps the other. Walking helped her to think. She forgot that she was wasting precious energy, drying herself out a little more with every step, every turn. Think. Up till now she had been able to tell herself that everything would be all right. That it was only a matter of time before someone found her. Doubts crept in, multiplied, tripled. What if Natalie had been found unconscious and couldn't tell them where she was? They'd have no idea of where to look. In her mind's eye she remembered the plains, the never-ending stretch of land that went in all directions. How could anyone find a single person without a clue or two? It would be impossible.

This is no good, she told herself. Get a grip, for God's sake. Show some intestinal fortitude. Her body came to an abrupt halt. Oh, yes, that would get her a long way, she derided. She wasn't stupid. She was stranded. No water and no transport and for all she knew, no-one knew where she was.

She slowly sank to her knees, closed her eyes and bowed her head.

Sergeant Steve Parrish enjoyed fossicking despite the fact that most of the people in the Isa had told him there were few precious gems to be found loose on the ground. The experts hadn't been one hundred per cent right, experts rarely were, he'd found. He had discovered traces of ribbon stone and jasper and a shard or two of crystalline quartz. Besides, since the day he'd found some fine specimens which had checked out to be trilobite fossils his primary interest had become fossilised rocks. Specimens were in demand at tourist shops along the Queensland coastline. A nice sideline hobby for him too.

However, when he went out he didn't really care whether he found anything or not. His main enjoyment came from the activity of stuffing his saddlebags with supplies and taking off on his horse for a few days camping, something he only did in winter because it wasn't too hot. Curiously, he had never gone camping when he'd lived in Sydney but up here he loved it and had been doing so on his days off ever since he'd come to the Isa. His sister would have laughed herself silly at him, "the scourge of Redfern" as he'd been known as a teenager, enjoying such mundane tasks. He had a map of the district which he'd divided into grids and he was systematically camping in each one, spending a few days looking around and then moving onto another grid the next trip.

Yesterday he had camped beside a shallow creek that had a few millimetres of water flowing in it, enough for cooking and washing. After breakfast he'd struck off to the east, pottering about in his usual fashion. Steve acknowledged that some folks thought it a strange hobby for a copper. He didn't give a damn what they thought. One day, he'd bring Francey out, if she'd come with him. Thinking about her he smiled as he ambled along, kicking over stones, sometimes dropping to his haunches to turn one over and dig with his small pick amongst the debris.

Much later in the day he turned back towards the creek, deciding to follow its trail back to camp. Creek beds were often a good place to find fossilised stones, if one had the patience to dig for them. Today hadn't been a good day though and his specimen bag was empty. As he returned to camp something caught his eye. His eyebrows shot up in amazement as he looked up from the creek's bank to find, not only his own horse hobbled so it wouldn't stray, but a second, saddleless horse with the reins trailing on the ground.

Vaulting up the bank he then slowed his approach so he wouldn't spook the other horse. He picked up the reins and his hands moved towards the bridle, looking for some mark of ownership. On the metal part of the bridle was the word "Astra". And sure enough, on the mare's left rump was the brand MD. Murrundi Downs. Bloody odd! Clicking his tongue, he led the horse to the creek and let it drink its fill, all the while studying it.

"You're a long way from home, girl," he said as he patted her muzzle. She nickered in agreement and nuzzled his hand. He'd better find out what she was doing wandering so far from the station. Maybe one of the stockmen had had an accident.

He took his mobile phone out of his supply bag and patched a call through to the Isa police station, got Murrundi's number and dialled again.

"Shellie?"

"Who's that?"

"Steve Parrish. I'm out in the bush, camped on Browns Creek. I've come across a Murrundi horse, no saddle. Anyone missing?"

"Oh, Steve, thank God. That must be Astra. Things are in a mess here. Mike and the boys are out looking for Francey."

Steve straightened. "Francey. Shellie, you'd better explain."

"She and Natalie went for a ride yesterday afternoon, off the property down south-west. Natalie's horse bolted and by the time she'd got Pharaoh under control and returned to where Francey was, there was no trace of her. They've been looking for her since first light."

Steve stroked his chin. "You said south-west?"

"Natalie said they went south-west."

"Have you got the helicopter out looking?"

"Can't. Les and CJ are away. I've spoken to them and they're on their way back now. Les won't be able to get the helicopter up until mid to late afternoon."

"Okay. Look, I'll start a search in this area. Keep me posted through the police station, will you?"

"Of course. As soon as we find anything, I mean, Francey, we'll let you know."

His brown eyes looked at the foothills around him, the red earth, the odd grouping of spindly gums and bluebush. Damn. Francey lost, out here. Jesus Christ. This was killer country. His jawbone tightened until it ached. He remembered one of the first cases he'd been on after arriving in the Isa. There had been an all-out search for a woman lost in the bush. Her off-road vehicle had run out of petrol but she hadn't stayed with it. She'd thought she could walk and find someone. They had found her two days later, dead from heat exhaustion.

Unbidden into his thoughts came the image of Francey lying face down on the red earth, not breathing. A wave of fear such as he'd never known before surged through him. Francey wasn't used to the bush, she wouldn't know how to survive out here ...

Steve knew he was no tracker, not like Billy Wontow, but because there'd been recent rain the ground might be soft enough for him to find and follow Astra's trail. Without further ado and with an economy of movements he packed up. Five minutes later, repacked, his horse saddled and Astra's reins tied to his saddlebag, he was ready to go.

Astra's trail led to the east, slightly south. Walking for twenty to thirty metres he found Astra's track. Mounting his horse and with eyes peeled on the trail he moved forward through the yellow grass and mulga. As Steve continued to follow Astra's trail he saw that the horse, probably thirsty, had followed the smell of water to the creek. Ahead, in the distance, he saw that he was heading towards an area known to have a small, narrow ravine and it was definitely east. Definitely.

CHAPTER THIRTEEN

How long Francey sat in a depressed state she declined to put into a time frame. As the sun warmed her head and the top of her shoulders she looked up. Clouds were splitting to allow the sun and a bright blue sky to show through. Somehow, beginning to feel warm made things better, and with it came a wellspring of hope.

She couldn't just sit idle and wait. She had to do something, anything.

A fire.

The hope grew as she thought the possibility through. Smoke from a fire would be visible many kilometres away, and the fire would warm her and keep the fear away. But she had no matches! She sighed pensively but her mind was set, focused. She glanced around the floor of the ravine and saw plenty of fallen twigs and tree branches, dried grass and dead leaves. All the necessary components for a fire except that she needed a match to ignite them. She walked back up the rise to where the saddle and saddlebags sat. For two minutes she rummaged through the bags, hopeful of finding a box of matches. No such luck. Her eyes came to rest on one of her cameras. Lenses.

Glass. Magnified light equals a spark equals ignition! Concentrated heat from the sun on a certain spot could make a spark and start a fire. Yes! She grinned. Her shoulders squared confidently. She could do it. In movies it happened often enough and didn't the actor always make it look simple?

But she was no girl scout. The grin spread a little wider across her face, her first smile since sunset yesterday. She would give it a damned good try.

It took an hour to gather materials and arrange the signal fire on the site where Natalie had boiled the billy. Once she had done that, she put dried gum leaves with pieces of dried grass on top of a wide branch as she remembered seeing done in the movie *Quest for Fire*, but instead of using friction – her hands and a pointed stick to create the spark – the camera lens would be her medium. However she wasn't sure whether the sun was strong enough yet to create sufficient heat to strike a spark, and after half an hour her arms and shoulders ached from holding the lens tautly in position.

Nothing happened. No spark, no puff of smoke and then *voilà,* fire.

Patience had never been Francey's strong point – she was too active a person. But after her sorties to find wood, and building the fire up, the lack of water and food had begun to weaken her constitution. And perversely, all she could think of as she waited was liquid. Various types of liquid. Ice cold water, ice blocks. White wine with the condensation dripping down the outside of the glass; thin soup; Coca Cola. Images of CJ's pool, the spa and the Pacific Ocean floated before her glazed eyes to add to her torment.

Her throat was parched and felt raw. Swallowing had become painful. She had no spittle, not a drop of moisture inside her mouth. Fatalistically, she knew that if she had to spend another day without liquid she'd probably lapse into delirium. Then it wouldn't matter about the fire. It wouldn't matter about anything.

Her eyelids drooped, then closed and her thoughts drifted to Steve. They had a date this Friday night. It would be a relief to cry but even her tear ducts had dried up. She missed him. And she wanted him. Yes, she could admit it, now. *She wanted him* – the sudden depth of her feeling in this regard left her breathless. Then, curiously, as she hovered in a semiconscious state, a line of people marched before her closed lids. Her parents, Meredith, whose baby was almost due. CJ and the people at Murrundi. She'd come to think of them as her friends. And there were the things she'd never get to do ... buildings she wouldn't design.

Her eyelids flickered and opened and she stared at the camera lens. Light, damn you! Anger and frustration welled up inside her. She bent close to the grass and saw the barest wisp of smoke. Her hand shook and a frown wrinkled her brow. Had she wanted to see it so much that she'd imagined it? Maybe she had. Her heartbeat quickened. She blew gently on the grass. A puff of smoke rose timidly, and finally a single spark. She fed more grass, continuing to blow until the first flame caught and she heard a faint fizzling.

She nurtured the embryonic flame as if it were a precious, mysterious deity, willing it to grow into a signal fire.

The silence from his mobile phone attached to his belt gave Steve an ominous feeling as he followed Astra's trail. No phone call meant Francey hadn't been found, yet. The trail headed south-east from the creek and though the horse had rambled, grazing at night as it made its way towards water, the general direction was clear. South-east, not west. In Steve's opinion, it was little wonder he hadn't heard from Murrundi, they were searching in the wrong quadrant. Another half an hour and he'd call in, let them know the direction of the horse's trail and his position.

Ahead of him stood low foothills and the rocky outcrop simply known as the ravine. He had heard stories in town that a tribe of Aboriginals once lived there, and he knew about the cave paintings too, but hadn't been inclined to visit the place. That's where Astra's trail was leading.

As he rode his thoughts took him back to the first time he'd ventured out in the bush alone. He'd been nervous, he remembered that. After all it was an alien environment to a city person, even one who'd had a passing acquaintance with country life. Christ, Francey would be scared witless by now.

A couple of kilometres closer he thought he saw something. Squinting, then staring hard he made out a wisp of smoke rising out of the ravine, clearly visible against the blue sky. He dug his heels into his horses flanks and urged it into a full gallop.

Have to find more wood for the fire. Francey looked at the pile of branches she'd gathered. She blinked back the weariness and shook her head. It wasn't enough to last all night. She rubbed her lips together, praying for a little moisture. None. A wave of dizziness worked its way down her body, through muscles that sagged with fatigue. She dropped the branch haphazardly onto the pile and jerked upwards. Can't stop, got to find more, she thought.

Steve saw her before she saw him. He reined in, bringing his horse and Astra to a steady lope. And for the first time in his life he said a prayer of thanks to a God he'd never had much time for. A lump formed in his throat and he swallowed it. Francey was alive.

He took the scene in. She had managed to get a fire going! A trail of smoke rose steadily towards the sky. She was gathering more supplies but the effort of doing so had cost her. He watched her stagger as she turned away from the fire to search for more fuel. Her beige sweater and her jeans were streaked with dirt, and her dark hair was in a tangle. A lopsided smile wreathed his angular features. She was the most beautiful thing he'd ever seen.

Seeing her struggling to stay on her feet clarified a lot for him, both in his mind and more importantly in his heart. As he'd followed Astra's trail across the plain his one all-encompassing thought had been of Francey and how when he found her he wouldn't let her go. Despite his earlier reservations he now believed she was his present and his future. He loved her, he decided. It was as simple as that.

"Francey."

Her slender length jerked upright and a frown crept across her forehead marring its smoothness. She ran a dry tongue around even drier lips and tried to concentrate but for hours all her energies had been trained on one task, finding more fuel to burn. She had to. But now ... Her head tilted to one side, listening. Had she heard a voice? Slowly, hardly daring to hope and trying to control the sudden trembling, she twisted around.

The smoke from the fire partially obscured what she was trying to see but she thought she could make out a horse and rider standing about two metres away. She pressed her fingers against her eyes and looked again. Still there. Maybe it was ... "Natalie"? she croaked, her throat so dry she could barely articulate the word.

Unlooping the water canteen from around the pommel of his saddle, Steve slid from the horse and ran towards her. He saw her eyes open wide in amazement as she recognised him and then, in an instant, the remaining strength went out of her. She began to slip towards the ground but he managed to catch her as her knees made contact with the earth.

"Steve ..." she whispered, "I ..."

"Don't try to talk." Easing her onto the ground he knelt back, placing her head on his thighs as a pillow. He wanted to kiss her but he contented himself with stroking her cheek and pushing the dark tendrils of hair back off her face. "Drink." He put the canteen to her lips. "Just a little."

Francey tried not to gulp down the life-giving liquid. Never had water tasted so good! It dribbled down her chin onto her throat, onto her sweater – she didn't care. She coughed and gagged as she swallowed too much at once.

"Slow, now. There's plenty. Too much too quickly and you'll make yourself sick."

Francey nodded, understanding, as she stared up at him. She almost had to pinch herself to be sure she wasn't hallucinating. Steve. Her Steve. Rescuing her. Her lips moved in a tremulous smile. Then, shakily, one of her hands rose to touch his face. Warm, a bit sweaty, a day's growth of whiskers. Real. If she was dreaming she didn't want to wake up. She wanted to ask so many questions. How had he known? Why had it taken so long to find her? Was Natalie all right?

Steve saw the lines of exhaustion around her mouth and eyes. Even her breathing seemed shallow but he was sure she would be all right. He'd seen cases of dehydration before and thankfully hers didn't appear severe. His gaze scouted the ravine, noting its high, sharp walls and lack of protection. Another day out here and ... He clamped the thought down, cutting it off. He didn't want to think about that. Looking up at the sky again he tried to calculate how much daylight remained. Maybe ninety minutes. He studied her again. Her hands held the canteen feebly and her eyes were opening and closing as she fought the exhaustion.

There was no way she'd be able to ride back to Murrundi in this condition. Not today. Unless Les got the station's helicopter here quickly. He had to let them know she'd been found. He frowned, puzzled. Something didn't make sense and it niggled at the back of his mind. Why had Natalie said they'd been south-west when they'd clearly gone south-east? He pushed the question to the back of his mind, he'd deal with it later. First he'd make camp and get Francey settled. What she needed was liquid and rest, then something light to eat.

"We're going to have to stay here overnight," he said. Her eyes opened and he saw the fear in them. He stroked her cheek. "It'll be all right, we'll be quite cosy."

"Wasn't cosy last night. C-cold ... The wind came up ..." she managed, croakily.

"Trust me," he soothed. "It'll be fine."

He zipped himself out of his leather jacket, folded it up and put it under her head. "Have some more water, Francey, then you should sleep while I set up camp. Okay?"

She nodded, eyelids already closing.

After twenty minutes of furious work they were set up for the night. He laid a groundsheet and the sleeping bag and lifted Francey into it without waking her. To keep the dew off and the cold at bay he'd stretched a nylon tarp over the bedding and anchored it around a spindly shrub and a large rock. Those tasks accomplished, he remounted and rode out of the ravine to make the call on his mobile.

"I've found Francey and she's okay," he told Shellie.

"Where?"

"In the ravine where the cave paintings are. South-east of Browns Creek. Is Les back?"

Shellie looked out the kitchen window to see the Learjet taxiing down the airstrip towards the hangar. "As we speak."

"If he can get the helicopter up straightaway, tell him to do so. If I don't hear it coming I'll assume there's a problem. I've made camp. We'll stay here overnight and Les can pick us up in the morning."

"CJ's very upset about all this. I ..." she faltered, "I've never heard him in such a rage. He'll want to talk to you, I'm sure."

"No can do in the ravine. The mobile won't work there because of the height of the walls."

"But, Steve –"

"Got to go, Shellie. I don't want to leave Francey alone for too long. If she wakes up and I'm not there she might become frightened. I'll call you at first light. Promise."

Lengthening shadows were creeping across the ravine's floor as Steve made his way back to the camp. Francey hadn't moved a muscle, she was really out to it. Good, that gave him time to prepare something to eat. No haute cuisine, that's for sure. He went over to his bag of supplies and tipped everything out. Coffee, sugar and powdered milk. Dried vegetables, Spam, two onions, oil, a tin of tomatoes, chicken noodle soup, half a loaf of stale bread and a packet of one minute noodles. Yes, he could make *something* with that.

"What do you mean, you can't get the helicopter going?" CJ raged through the phone's receiver at Les. "I want her back tonight. Yes, I know Steve said she was okay but she's probably dehydrated. I want her back so a doctor can check her out." His temper was out of control and he thumped his fist down on the top of his desk for extra emphasis.

Natalie, creeping down the hallway, stopped near the partly open doorway of CJ's study. A wave of disappointment rushed through her as she realised that Francey had been found, safe and well. Flattening her body against the wall, staying in the shadows, she listened.

"Something in the fuel! Bloody hell, what's going on here?"

She smiled to herself, imagining Les' colourful reply. He wouldn't be bashful about stating his opinion. She had thought it a masterstroke to add water to the helicopter's fuel tank and leave the top half open to make it look as if rainwater had got in. She knew just enough about helicopters to know that they would have to siphon all the fuel out and then refill it, which would take hours. She'd covered that angle in case Les got back in time to go searching today. Maybe she should have put sand in, but that would have looked deliberate and she'd been at pains to avoid suspicion of anything other than natural causes.

But, she sighed with pure frustration, all her efforts to put a fear of the outback, of staying on at Murrundi into Francey's head may have been wasted. She had ridden hell for leather out of the ravine, then had doubled back and hidden in a small cave she knew of. She had watched Francey peer about looking for her and had been hard-pressed not to laugh out loud. Then, evidently, Steve Parrish had come along and found Francey. She ground her teeth and her hands clenched into fists at her sides, the long fingernails digging into her palms in anger. She'd come so close to achieving her goal. Still, she tried to rationalise the situation, maybe what she had done was enough. She had given Francey one hell of a scare and that would possibly be sufficient to send her on her way ... permanently.

Damn Steve Parrish, damn the man to hell. After another warm day out in the ravine Francey would have been ... well ... a lot worse off, maybe too far gone to save.

"All right," CJ thundered, "I don't care how long it takes to get it right, make sure you're up at first light. I want her back for breakfast."

Natalie did a smart about-turn and returned to her bedroom. She closed the door and leant against it, thinking. Tomorrow there would be questions from Les and CJ and probably Steve Parrish. She had to make sure she had the story down pat.

She had stumbled across desert plains where the earth had long ago cracked for want of water. So weak, she had been reduced to crawling centimetres at a time, until a tropical rainforest emerged out of nowhere – straight in front of her. With all that greenness there had to be water, and she desperately needed water. She cocked her head to one side and heard its lyrical liquid sound running over time-smoothed stones and submerged logs.

Using a precious ounce of energy she ran her hand over her cracked lips and tried to swallow, but there was nothing to swallow. She crawled some more and stopped, panting, her heartbeat racing. She waited for the exhaustion which made her weakened muscles tremble to subside. The thought and sound of the water urged her on.

Her hands were bleeding from small crisscross cuts from the rough ground but she had gone almost beyond feeling the pain. She just had a terrible need to drink and to replace the fluids the sun and wind and time had drained from her body.

She raised her head, now she could *see* the waterfall. The body of water thundered a good fifty metres to the lake below and a spray, like a fine mist, hovered continuously about half a metre above the level of the water. She began to crawl towards it and seemed to make progress, but no matter how diligently she moved along the ground Francey couldn't reach the life-giving liquid. It began to rain. She heard and saw fat raindrops fall on the leaves, on the ferns and through the high canopy of the trees, but none fell on her.

To be so close to relief – to that which would prolong her life – but for it to remain out of reach so as to torture her. Always out of reach … And then she heard a woman laughing, the sound was maniacal and malicious and recognisable. Natalie!

She woke with a start, her body jumping, her eyes popping open. Darkness surrounded her except for the steady glow of light somewhere close by. Disorientated she tried to remember where she was. Oh! She looked at the rocks around her, at the expanse of black sky with its stars winking knowingly and remembered. The ravine.

"Well, Sleeping Beauty awakes."

Francey started at the sound of a male voice. She looked up and saw Steve Parrish studying her from his position on a nearby rock and remembered everything. Natalie's horse bolting, being alone, scared, being so thirsty she thought she would die, and then Steve finding her. And, thank God, she didn't feel thirsty any more.

"Drink?" He handed her a mug. "It's chicken noodle soup. Should warm you up."

She wriggled into a sitting position under the sleeping bag and took the mug. "Thank you." She sipped slowly because it was hot and as she did so, another of her senses awoke. A delicious smell wafted across the air towards her. She realised how hungry she was and so did her empty stomach because it began a distinctive rumbling. She tried to ignore it. "I ... I didn't thank you ... for finding me," her tone was halting. "How did you?"

"I was out camping, fossicking." He grinned at her. "Your horse found me. I called Murrundi and they said you were missing. I followed Astra's trail which led here."

She gave a hoarse laugh. "You make it sound so simple."

He shrugged. "Do you want to talk about what happened?" Secretly he wanted to know whether her account would match up with the story Shellie had given him.

Her stomach continued to grumble and she up-ended the mug and drained it. Her mouth watered and her nostrils dilated at the aroma coming from the fire. "I'm starving, could we eat first?"

"Sure, I've been waiting for you to wake up." He moved down to the fire and began ladling his stewed concoction onto a plate. "Only have one plate," he apologised as he handed it to her with a spoon. "I'll eat my share out of the saucepan. Would you like coffee now or later?"

"Later." Francey looked at the plate. In a moment she would drool, which would be just too embarrassing. "Smells delicious." She took a mouthful. "Tastes delicious."

He laughed. "You'd think anything was delicious after not having eaten for nearly thirty hours."

She shook her head. "No I wouldn't, I'm fussy. My mamma taught me to appreciate good food from an early age, we Italians are like that."

After the ordeal she'd gone through Steve couldn't believe her jocularity. She had been stranded, scared, thirsty and God knows what else, yet she'd bounced back as if what had happened to her was nothing out of the ordinary. Perhaps, he thought, she didn't realise how close she'd come to becoming a statistic. One more day and she might have been just that. The thought scared him. He'd come close to losing her before he had the chance to tell her how he felt. Of course now wasn't the appropriate time but he would later, when she got over this experience. Well, that would be another matter.

"So, what's in this marvellous concoction?"

He lifted an eyebrow. "Do you really want to know?" She nodded. "Okay. When I go camping, just for a couple of days, I travel light so as not to weigh my horse down with supplies. The stew's got onions and noodles, vegetables and Spam." His eyes twinkled mischievously. "I'm saving the bread and beans for tomorrow's breakfast." His tone became serious, "The most important item to carry is water, enough for me and my horse, or to at least know where water can be found." He looked up at the ravine walls. "Do you know there are probably pockets of water up there in rock pools from the last rain?"

"I didn't know that. You mean I could have climbed around and found water?"

"The Aboriginals would know where to find it. You might have too but you might not. Especially if you didn't know where to look. You could have fallen and hurt yourself as well."

"I'm glad you found me," she said simply and sincerely.

He reached across and touched her cheek. "Me too." The temptation to take her in his arms and kiss away the fear and the bad memories was almost irresistible. She might look dishevelled and fatigued, but he'd never desired a woman more. And from the occasional thoughtful way she looked at him he sensed she was aware of something special blossoming between them. God, he hoped so.

"I ... I don't think I would have survived another night out here alone."

He shook his head. "You would have." He studied her as she ate. "One thing's got me curious though. How on earth did you get that fire started without matches?" She told him and he whistled in admiration. "For a city slicker that's not bad. Makes you a survivor in my book. I bet CJ will be impressed, you know he appreciates inventive people."

As they sipped the coffee he'd made she told him everything that had happened since she had ridden into the ravine to photograph the cave paintings. She paused for a moment then asked, "So what happened to Natalie? She just disappeared. It was eerie."

"All I know is what Shellie told me. Her horse bolted, she got it under control and when she came back to look for you you'd gone."

Francey blinked. She couldn't have heard right, could she? She stared across the top of the steaming mug at him, her expression puzzled. "Gone? I didn't go anywhere. When I couldn't see her I remembered what Les said about staying put and came back to where we'd boiled the billy." She pointed at the fire. "Here." She frowned and then shook her head. "I don't understand, I was here all the time."

Steve looked thoughtful. He smelled a rat, a tall, grey-eyed, platinum blonde rat. But why? What was her motive in leaving Francey alone in the bush? It didn't make sense. However, he wasn't going to say anything at this point in time. Natalie was CJ's stepdaughter and he'd need to be sure of his facts before he came out and accused the woman of arranging this situation. "I'm sure we'll get to the bottom of it when we get back to Murrundi," was all he said.

Francey yawned and stretched her arms above her head as the feeling of exhaustion began to overtake her again. She had to sleep. She wanted to talk to Steve too but that would have to wait. There would be time tomorrow, the rest of her life even, she hoped.

"Why don't you settle down," Steve suggested. "Dehydration takes the energy out of a person. You need rest and liquids, in that order I think, though I'm no doctor." He tucked the sleeping bag around her more tightly, and as desperately as he wanted to he resisted the urge to kiss her.

She yawned again and forgot to cover her mouth. "Steve, you've been wonderful. But ..." through her sluggishly functioning brain, she thought then asked, "where are you going to sleep?" She had the groundsheet plus the sleeping bag which was draped over and under her.

"Don't worry about me. I've roughed it before." He grinned at her. "On stake-outs, in observation cars, behind clumps of bushes. I'll bed down close to the fire and be quite warm, I assure you." He knew that wouldn't be so, and he'd be lucky to get a wink of sleep, but that didn't matter. Francey being comfortable mattered more.

"Oh, good ..."

Sleep enveloped her in a matter of seconds, and he sat there watching her. The fire played shadows and light on her face, allowing him to study each feature. The slant of her brows, the free spirited hair that framed her face in wild waves, the straight nose that snubbed up at the tip and the delectable curve of her mouth. Especially her mouth. He felt himself getting all hot and bothered just thinking about what he'd like to do with that mouth, with all of her. He growled low in his throat. Maybe he'd better put some more wood on the fire and check the horses.

The night wind rattling the tarp stirred Francey from a deep sleep. As consciousness roused her she shivered, feeling the chill air settling around her neck. The fire's embers glowed bright enough but she thought she should bank it up so it didn't go out. She made to rise and shivered again with the cold. What a strange land. Steaming hot, flooding, dry as an oven in summer and chillingly cold in winter. One certainty was that one couldn't get bored with the sameness of the weather.

"What's wrong?"

She answered the muffled question. "The fire."

"I'll attend to it." In the near total blackness she sensed rather than saw Steve's huddled figure reach across and work two more branches into the embers. She watched until they caught and the flames began to burn brightly again. Steve. What would she have done without him? Perished? Possibly. The thought of what might have happened filled her first of all with a confused sense of sadness and then with a rush of joy. She was alive, because of him. And from deep inside her came the need to express, to share that joy with him.

"Steve?"

"Yes?"

"I ... I'm cold." She heard him move close to her and said, "You must be even colder, you've no warmth, no blanket."

"I'm okay. Give me your hands."

She did and he began to chafe them briskly. She decided that wasn't what she wanted. "I'm still cold. Perhaps you should come under the sleeping bag too. Don't the experts say something about two bodies being able to radiate more body heat than one."

"I'm not sure ..."

"Please."

A current of cold air wafted around her as he disturbed the edges of the sleeping bag and crept close to her. His arms came around her to pull her against his chest. She heard him sigh and could barely see his face, just the outline of his head. A smile played around her lips in the darkness and she became aware of the accelerated beat of her heart and a singing in her veins. Better, but not perfect. She knew of another way to radiate heat. Amazed at her boldness but compelled by feelings she had repressed for so long, she inched her face up to his and kissed him. She heard his surprised gasp but then he kissed her back, quite deliciously. She wriggled closer. Her hands crept under his leather jacket and worked their way up his chest.

"What are you doing?"

Francey chuckled low in her throat. "Trying to get warm. What do you think I'm doing?" She kissed him again.

He took the initiative and deepened the kiss, his tongue playing with hers, probing, merging in a mutual dance with her sweetness while, ostensibly to warm her, his free hand caressed her back and her behind. He manoeuvred her onto her back and she twined her legs around him. Groaning, he found her lips again and they were warm and willing. God, how much could a man take without losing control?

Eventually he drew away from her. "This isn't a good idea."

She touched his face with her hand and traced his features, her fingertip tingling at the touch. She wanted him so much and she thought he wanted her too, he'd shown his feelings towards her in many little ways. The sly glances, the odd touch, the husky inflection in his voice. But maybe she'd misinterpreted them. Could she have mistaken compassion in his eyes for desire? Should she back off and keep her pride intact? Then he spoke and his whispering tone dismantled all her doubts.

"Oh, Francey." His arms tightened noticeably about her. "I've dreamed so many times of us being like this. Together. From the first moment I saw you in the Isa I wanted you." She had haunted his dreams ever since that first meeting. "My darling, I want it to be perfect between us when ... You're tired, you've been through an awful ordeal. When you're stronger ..." his voice trailed away into nothingness but hinted at a promise of future joy together.

A shiver of emotion shafted through her. He felt the same way she did! She took hold of his hand and placed it over her left breast. "Feel my heart beating beneath your hand. It's not tired, it's lonely." There was a catch in her voice. "I've been lonely for so long Steve, I don't want to be any more. Make love to me now. Please."

"But –"

"No buts." She was silent for a minute, then she laughed incredulously. "The stories Meredith's told me about policemen's exploits – I didn't think you were such shy creatures."

"Shy! I'll give you shy." His hands began to caress her, and then sought and found the buttons to her shirt and deftly undid them, then they moved again to the zipper on her jeans.

"Promise?" she whispered.

"You bet," he replied enthusiastically.

In the hazy afterglow of their lovemaking, lying naked and entwined and delightfully warm beneath the sleeping bag, Francey smiled a satisfied smile against Steve's moderately hairy chest. The rhythmic rise and fall told her he had drifted into an exhausted sleep. They had made love twice. The first time had been an urgent coupling to slake their pent-up passion for each other. The second time had been slow, tender, rapturous. Her impulsive nature made her want to tell him that she loved him but it was too soon. Their relationship was as yet too new, too precious for words. With a little, impatient movement of her head, she remembered ... Years ago Bryan had ignited her passionate nature and he had also almost destroyed it. Steve had renewed her capacity to love. Her lips moved against his warm skin to kiss it softly.

Francey let her hands run over him. It was wonderful to explore his body, feel the contours of his hard muscles, the fitness of him while he wasn't aware of it. Her hand moved greedily and lower, to the thick, arrowing curls below his navel. She sighed. Touching him awoke a need and she could feel herself pulsing inside with longing and, she chuckled to herself, she had been on a self-imposed starvation diet for years, too many years. She should let him sleep. But ... Her hand moved lower to enclose him and stroke and caress until, even in sleep, he hardened.

Gently she rolled on top of him and began to kiss him into wakefulness.

A pre-dawn stillness lay over the land as Steve opened his eyes to greet the morning. Beside him Francey slumbered, cuddled into his chest. He smiled crookedly as memories of last night overtook him.

He'd been right about her. She sure had a passionate nature and that he'd been the recipient of all that stored-up emotion made him a very happy man.

He knew now that he'd wanted her from the moment he'd set eyes on her but had subjugated the desire because he didn't think he had a chance. No wonder she'd dominated his thoughts and his dreams for weeks. It was a brand new day and he had a brand new relationship, one which he hoped would last forever.

Then he remembered his promise to call Murrundi. Gently, so as not to disturb her he disengaged himself, dressed and, shivered against the chill of the cold winter's morning. Taking his mobile, he swung bareback onto his horse and cantered off out of the ravine to make the call.

CHAPTER FOURTEEN

CJ, Natalie, Steve, Les, Shellie, Mike and Lucky sat around the mahogany dinner table post-morteming the event of Francey being stranded in the bush. Just after first light Les had picked up Francey and Steve in the helicopter and left Billy Wontow to bring the two horses back. On their return Francey, though protesting she was fine, had been put to bed to await a visit from a Mt Isa doctor.

"What's this I'm hearing?" CJ growled at Natalie. "You claim you said you and Francey'd gone south-east. Mike and Lucky are pretty sure you told them south-west. Damn it, someone's stretching the truth here."

"I'm positive I said south-east," Natalie confirmed, her grey eyes widening innocently at her stepfather, a ruse she'd tried on him from an early age when it was necessary to get out of a scrape. "I'd been through a harrowing ride and though I was exhausted I don't think I'd get east and west mixed up." She fixed her startling, near hypnotic gaze on Mike and batted her eyelids. "Someone got confused, that's all. It was an innocent mistake, CJ."

"Which could have cost Francey her life!" Les pointed out. "It may have if Steve hadn't stumbled upon her," he added with a grudging nod of approval at the policeman. Inside though, he seethed with jealousy that Steve had come out the hero in this fiasco. Moving his gaze he observed Natalie and noted the pink flush on her neck, a sure sign that she'd orchestrated the situation. He'd grown up with her and knew her moods, her highs and lows, when she was being truthful and when she was lying her head off. Without exposing his opinion by look or expression he couldn't help but wonder what stupid kind of game she was playing. But then he should be used to it. She was notorious for playing games to suit her own purpose.

He recalled the last time she had taken a dislike to someone: CJ's secretary before Lisa. She had hounded the woman and made her life such a misery she'd simply packed her bags and walked away. Now, it seemed, her bitchiness, if one could call it that, was active again. The derisive thought came to him that the heir to CJ's fortune was becoming weirder and weirder.

Mike Hunter scratched his head and flushed. He moved restlessly in the chair, as if he longed to be somewhere else, *anywhere else*. He played with the Swiss army knife he always carried, twirling it on the table top as he spoke. "Well, CJ, I guess it is possible I didn't hear right. We were all kind of upset at the time."

"Bloody stupid." CJ stared at Mike until his gaze shifted. "I should damned well hand you your walking papers."

"CJ, don't," Natalie appealed, draping her hand over his forearm. "Mike said it was an honest mistake. Everyone makes mistakes." Her eyebrows rose meaningfully. "Everyone," she repeated, implying that even he wasn't infallible. She smiled sweetly at Mike which, from the way he shifted again, added to his sense of embarrassment.

Steve Parrish hadn't spoken during the discussion and seemed content to just take it all in. As a cop he had a nose for guilty parties and he certainly had his suspicions about Natalie. But, ironically, he admired her ability to worm her way out of it. For her own strange reasons she appeared to have planned the operation, he was sure of it. He thought Les held the same opinion, and that Mike Hunter, who obviously had a crush on the blonde, was prepared to take the blame to get her off the hook with CJ. Fool!

Jesus, what a family. CJ with his bombastic arrogance, Shellie with her drinking problem and Natalie who, in Steve's opinion, was beginning to appear seriously dysfunctional. When everything had settled down he'd try and talk Francey into moving into town, away from all these peculiar influences.

"Where's the bloody doctor? Didn't you tell him it was urgent?" CJ yelled at Shellie, who started in response.

"I did. He's on his way. His surgery said fifteen to twenty minutes." Of their own volition her hands came up to fiddle with the buttons of her blouse and then her hair. She stopped suddenly, knowing it annoyed CJ, who at present was annoyed enough for everyone. She hadn't seen him this put out since Richard's death. After living under the same roof as him for years she knew that he liked things to run smoothly, and that such a thing could happen – Francey's life being put in jeopardy – made him very angry. He'd come down with another of his headaches if he wasn't careful, she thought dismally. God, she hoped not. Then she'd have to nurse and fuss over him until it went away.

An agitation began in her stomach and spread throughout her entire body. She ran her tongue tentatively around the inside of her mouth; it was as dry as the weather. Oh, what she wouldn't do for a quick nip, for her nerves of course. She glanced slyly at the kitchen doorway. Maybe she could sneak out without anyone noticing. Alison knew she kept whisky in the pantry, in the soy sauce bottle, but she didn't nag her about it.

"Humphh." CJ stared Mike and Lucky down, his displeasure showing loud and clear. "Okay you two, back to work. We've got a station to run here."

For big men the two scuttled out of the dining room with extraordinary speed.

Then CJ turned his attention to Natalie. "And you, miss. Let me say this, I'm very disappointed in you. In future, you and Francey don't go riding again together unless there's a third party present and a mobile phone in the saddle bags. Understand?"

Disguising her chagrin at his accusatory tone, and sensing that he hadn't been taken in by her story nor Mike covering for her, her reply was meek. "Yes, CJ, whatever you say." Then, studiously ignoring everyone else's gaze she rose from the table and left the room.

CJ had never really liked her. She blinked a rebellious tear back as she went to her room. Even when Richard had been alive he'd favoured his son over her. And CJ was the one who'd insisted she go to boarding school when Richard hadn't. Oh, yes, CJ had always made his preferences clear, she remembered. And now he was doing it with Francey, the bitch. Well, she still had another card or two to play ...

CJ's sigh sounded more like a growl. He sat back in the chair and stared disconsolately at Steve Parrish. "I don't know how to thank you, Steve. You've done me and Murrundi a great service. I won't forget it."

"No need, sir. It's my job. The main thing is that Francey's okay." He looked the older man squarely in the eyes. "That's one hell of a woman. She's got more guts than some men I know."

The front doorbell rang and Shellie jumped up and murmured the obvious, "That must be the doctor. I'll take him straight through to Francey."

On opening the front door of the homestead Shellie got the surprise of her life. She had been expecting Doctor Benjamin Passfield, their usual medico, but instead a familiar and smiling face greeted her. "Barry!" she exclaimed.

"Shellie. Hello. Mabs in the surgery told me you were here."

Doctor Barry Ryan. Shellie stood rooted to the spot, unable to move, unable to breathe. In front of her stood the man she had fallen in love with so many years ago in Townsville. She could feel her heart racing, her cheeks warming at his inquisitive, friendly gaze. He'd loved her too, so he'd said back then, but he had had an invalid wife and couldn't leave her. After their affair had been in full bloom for a year she had done the right thing and had left and come to Murrundi. So many thoughts and memories crowded into her head she could hardly think straight.

"Are you going to ask me in?" his smile was genial, his voice gentle.

Somehow she pulled herself together. "Of course, silly me. Do come in, Barry. The patient's right this way." He hasn't changed at all, she thought as she led him to Francey's room. Same pepper and salt hair, same kindly hazel eyes. The fluttering in her chest spread to her arms and her fingertips. Seeing him again after so long felt strange yet wonderful. Until she remembered Kate. She must ask about his wife, once she plucked up the necessary courage.

Francey was sitting up in bed pretending to read a magazine.

"Here's the patient."

Barry beamed at the young woman. "What's the problem?"

Shellie, trying to hide her nervousness and a peculiar sense of shyness because she was still out of step, filled him in on what had happened.

"How do you feel now, Francey?"

"Fine." Her eyes challenged him. "I'm only staying here until you go then I'm getting up. There's nothing wrong with me."

Barry smiled then performed a routine examination: took her temperature, her pulse, her blood pressure and sounded her chest.

"I think you're right. You seem well enough to me. Slight case of dehydration, that's all. Lucky you're so healthy." He turned to Shellie. "Make sure Francey has plenty of fluids, maybe some Gatorade if you have any around, and Francey," he turned back to his patient, "you may have periods of fatigue over the next couple of days. So plenty of rest, preferably in bed. Will you do that?"

"Yes, doctor. Of course," Francey promised, smiling.

"You'll come and meet CJ, won't you?" Shellie asked Barry. "He's been quite anxious about Francey."

"Certainly. Lead the way."

A huge sense of relief washed over CJ when Doctor Ryan pronounced Francey fit enough to work if she wanted to. It wasn't her getting back to work that concerned him, he'd scarcely slept a wink last night agonising over what she may have gone through in the ravine. He was genuinely concerned that her ordeal might have had a detrimental, longer lasting effect on her. That Murrundi had been the cause of it filled him with an overwhelming mixture of anger and frustration. He'd never have forgiven himself or others if something dire had happened to her. And he also wasn't a hundred per cent satisfied about Hunter taking the blame. He sensed that his stepdaughter had organised the situation – and for the life of him he couldn't understand why – however proving it would be impossible. Still, he knew she knew he wasn't pleased and that he held her responsible.

"She's a healthy young woman," Barry pronounced. "I don't think she's been overly traumatised although there could be some after-effects. She seems to have a level head on her shoulders and I don't think there'll be too many post-trauma symptoms. Encourage her to talk about it as much as she wants to, that in itself may be sufficient therapy to stop any mental trauma."

"Thank God for that," CJ rumbled in his hoarse voice. Then something occurred to him. "You're new, aren't you?"

"Doctor Passfield's retiring at Christmas, I'm taking over his practice. My daughter's husband recently got a job with the Isa mine so it's worked out well. It will be nice to be close to her, now that I'm a widower."

"I didn't know. I'm sorry about Kate," Shellie murmured, and then subsided guiltily at CJ's questioning glare.

"I appreciate you coming out," CJ said gruffly as he shook the doctor's hand. "I guess we'll be seeing more of you from time to time, seeing you're taking over from Ben."

"Most likely," Barry agreed. "I'm sorry, must go. I have other calls to make."

"I'll see Barry, I mean, Doctor Ryan out," Shellie offered.

As soon as the doctor had left CJ turned to Steve and Les. "Francey's okay and that's the main thing. Thanks Steve," he slapped the younger man heartily on the shoulder. "God knows what condition Francey'd be in if you hadn't happened to be out that way."

"Perhaps it's best not to think of that," Steve put in. He had been quietly observing CJ, noting the play of different emotions on his usual poker face. Anger and then relief had consecutively graced his features. It clarified something he had thought for quite a while. The old man had, for once, let his guard down and become genuinely fond of Francey Spinetti. Perhaps, he frowned to himself, more than just fond.

"I was glad to help out," Steve said. "Billy should be back by now with the horses, so I'd better make tracks. I'm back on duty this afternoon. I'll just go and say goodbye to Francey."

CJ's forehead beetled in a frown as he watched Steve walk towards Francey's room. Damned familiar! He didn't like the fact that Steve assumed a familiarity beyond that which his job called for. Steve and Francey. He recalled how cosy they'd been the night of Pierre's party. Odd, but the thought disgruntled him more than he felt comfortable with. She was too good for the likes of a common policeman. Too good, indeed.

Without further ado Steve walked down the hallway which led to the bedrooms. He already knew which one was Francey's because he'd insisted on carrying her there from the helicopter. He caught her in the process of throwing back the covers to get out of bed.

"You sure the doctor said you could do that?"

"Not you too," she arched an eyebrow at him as she rose from the bed. "I'm not an invalid." She smiled. "I really do feel fine."

For a moment or two they stood looking at each other, remembering all that had happened in the ravine. Then Steve reached for her and gathered her close. It seemed the most natural place to be and she knew he could feel her tremble through the thin cotton nightie but she didn't care. Slanting her head back to receive his kiss, her arms slid up around his neck to pull him close to her. Fingers twined through his dark hair and she savoured the thick texture, the warmth of him, the fact that he seemed as emotionally involved as she was.

Eventually Steve pulled back. "I've got to go, but I'll call you tonight, promise."

She stroked his jawline. "I'll be waiting."

Shellie walked all the way with Barry to his four-wheel drive, curiously tongue-tied when there was so much she wanted to say to him. How long had it been since they had seen each other? Almost ten years, but the feelings inside her were still strong and had never died as feelings sometimes did. She couldn't tell him that, of course. She had no idea how he felt ... or whether there was someone else in his life.

"I am so sorry about Kate," she said eventually. "When? How?" she stumbled over the awkwardness of the question.

"About eleven months ago, her heart. She didn't suffer too much, thank God. She'd suffered enough over the years as it was."

"Yes." Shellie remembered the slight, attractive,

wheelchair-bound Kate. The woman had been crippled with rheumatoid arthritis and a weak heart, but had always managed to maintain a brave face in public despite her medical problems. Shellie's affair with Barry had begun several months after she had taken the receptionist's job in his surgery. Starved of affection for years, falling in love with Barry Ryan had been easy. He'd been kind, considerate and interested. All the things her faithless husband, Peter, had never been. They had been discreet for Kate's sake, and Barry had been honest with her right from the start, saying it couldn't lead anywhere – that he'd not leave his wife. Eventually the strain had become too much and Shellie had been the one to leave town. Oh, how many years ago? Seven or was it eight?

"Jodie and her husband Ken have settled into the Isa. They've been here for three months. Actually, Jodie told me about Ben's practice being up for sale." He looked at her with those kind, puppy dog eyes of his and smiled. "Funny how things work out, isn't it?" She nodded wordlessly, barely able to believe that they were here like this, talking as if they'd last met yesterday. Well, he was doing most of the talking, she was just looking and listening, taking it all in, absorbing the wondrous feeling of being with him once more.

"Look, why don't you have dinner with us one night. Meet Jodie and her husband. Would you?"

"I'd love to," she said, smiling cautiously at him.

He opened the car door and slid behind the wheel. "How about Thursday night? We'll go Chinese. That used to be your favourite if I remember correctly."

Her smile widened with pleasure because he'd remembered. "Yes. That's fine. I'll meet you at the surgery, about seven o'clock."

He turned the ignition on. "I'm looking forward to it already." He reached out through the open window and touched her cheek for the briefest moment. "I've missed you ..." and before she could answer he gunned the accelerator and moved off down the drive.

Shellie watched the vehicle until it went up over the rise and out of sight then turned and walked up the steps to the homestead, the widest smile engraved on her face.

In her bedroom, Natalie deWitt-Ambrose paced the floor barefoot, alternatively biting her nails in agitation and finger-combing her platinum short locks in a gesture of anger and frustration. She'd made a serious slip up and she knew it. The Francey thing – her jealousy and anxiety over the architect's relationship with CJ – had sent her into a mental tail spin. She'd overreacted. But, she reasoned, it had been a good plan to strand her nemesis in the ravine. With Les and CJ absent she'd have gotten away with it if Steve Parrish hadn't stumbled upon her before mother nature had done her work. Shit! Of all the bad luck. And now she'd alienated herself from CJ and Les.

Oh, yes. She had seen the way Les looked at her. He could barely conceal his dislike for her. She would have to watch *him*. Les had a vindictive, sly streak to him, she knew that from years past, *and* he thought he had a score to settle with her. And CJ, her mouth pouted petulantly, he'd never liked her. Only her mother's constant intervention on her behalf had, over the years, made CJ treat her with a modicum of outward affection and respect. She sighed. Mumsie wasn't around to act as go-between any more and since Richard's death her relationship with CJ had deteriorated because of that damned architect, Francey, CJ's pet.

Tossing her head back, her grey eyes narrowed as she looked about the room. So what! She didn't need CJ or for that matter, any man. She had money and she was a successful businesswoman in her own right who didn't have to ask him for anything. But, and she admitted it even though it hurt, she had always craved his sincere affection and knew she would never have it. Her thin lips curled in a menacing sneer as she repeated the words in her head over and over again. Patience, patience … All she had to do was to wait. When CJ died everything would be hers to do with as she pleased. That, she decided, would be the most perfect revenge on her stepfather for his lack of love. And top of her hit list would be the dismissal of Les Westcott. Oh, what pleasure she'd get from that.

But what to do about Francey Spinetti? She had failed to scare her off and no doubt she'd continue to worm her way into CJ's good graces – the woman could do no wrong as far as he was concerned. She needed time to regroup her thoughts and plan a new course of action. She'd go to Port Douglas, maybe have Trish fly up to be with her, and work on a foolproof way of getting rid of Francey. Maybe Trish could help her plan something.

Buoyed by the thought of being with Trish and having a new scheme in the works, Natalie's dark mood lifted. She took an overnight bag out of the wardrobe and began to pack.

In the early hours of the morning, coming home from a date with Steve, Francey came upon CJ and Les discussing business in the spacious living room. Papers were spread all over the coffee table, together with coffee cups and a half empty brandy snifter glass which she guessed belonged to Les.

"A bit late, isn't it?" CJ greeted her with a scowl. Been with Parrish, no doubt. His stomach turned at the thought of the two of them together. Damned if he knew what she saw in the man.

"I am over twenty-one, you know," she teased, ignoring his annoyed stare. During her months at Murrundi she had come to realise that CJ was possessive, not only of what he owned and controlled but also of those who worked for him. That was too bad – she had no intention of allowing him to rule the roost when it came to her personal life. She and Steve had had a wonderful night together and she wasn't going to let CJ's grumpiness spoil it.

"I see that you two believe in burning the midnight oil. Some international crisis?" Francey said, pointing at the paperwork.

CJ put his empty coffee cup down and shook his head. "The opposite. I've got a fifty-five per cent interest in a small company called North West Abattoirs near Cloncurry and they're in financial trouble. It's been running in the red for two years now. Les thinks we should sell my share for whatever we can get, and frankly, I don't see that I have another choice."

Francey hid her surprise that he was speaking of his business interests so openly with her until she remembered that he had done it before, on several occasions, but more in passing conversation than serious discussion. She recalled the town of Cloncurry; she'd stopped there for lunch and a walk on her way to Mt Isa. A picture of a pleasant country town, typically Australian, danced before her open eyes. A town whose life blood, she suspected, depended to some extent on the abattoir plant. Despite her tiredness she was curious and sat on the sofa beside Les. "Why isn't it making a profit?"

Les allowed himself a few seconds to savour the aroma of her perfume and her closeness ... their thighs were almost touching on the sofa. A growing feeling of frustration took hold of him until, with difficulty, he brought it under control. "Competition," he informed her. "A Japanese firm has opened a state-of-the-art abattoir at Normanton and sells meat direct to the Japanese market. Our plant is sixty-five years old. We need to upgrade but I can't see that it's worth the effort or the financial cost."

Francey thought again about the small town and the people who lived there. "If you made the effort could North West compete in the market place?"

"Of course. There's a the rail link planned for Mt Isa and Cloncurry, and we've an established domestic market. The Japanese mob have to freight some of their product to Karumba for live export overseas."

"How many jobs are involved?" she asked.

"Over a hundred, not including some seasonal positions. It's a tough decision for the staff but most of them would get a fair redundancy payout."

"What good will that be if they can't find another job? I'm sure you realise that even a hundred people out of work could drastically affect the economy of a small town," she argued passionately.

"We know, but there doesn't appear to be another choice," CJ said. "I can't continue to pour money in without getting a return, my accountant in Brisbane's told me that several times. It's just not good business."

"But what about the old Aussie saying, give a bloke – or in this case a battling Aussie company – a fair go? Australia can't keep selling off its own or soon there won't be anything left." She looked speculatively at CJ. The man had millions, he could probably afford to prop the abattoir up indefinitely, if he chose to. But she knew his reputation as a hard businessman and a good profit margin was undoubtedly of paramount importance to him. Still, a certain appeal glistened in her eyes as she said, "Surely there must be something you can do."

"It's not that I don't want to," he admitted. "I've held the controlling interest in North West for twelve years. The Murrundi stock go there for slaughtering. I believe it's still a viable business if ..."

"If what?"

"I just can't justify the outlay of more than half a million dollars to refit, not with the profit and loss statement being what it is. We need to alter the labour structure too." Suddenly he had an idea. He smiled across at her. "Tell you what, how about Les gives you the file to go through. Maybe," he glanced at Les, seeking his agreement, "you can find something we've missed. A way to keep the company going."

"I'm not a businesswoman," she said with a shake of her head. But even as she said so she knew that she would find something. The thought of so many people, their families, the business folk in the town, suddenly having their livelihood cut off and with no other way of replacing it, was causing her to go into a mild depression on their behalf.

"That's a good idea," Les agreed. "However, we can't put off the decision for too long. Thirty-six hours at the most."

"Why?"

"We've got a prospective buyer."

"If North West's doing so badly, why does someone want to buy it?"

CJ answered. "Les thinks the buyer represents other

interests. Possibly the Japanese company. They'll absorb the competition and then close the place down."

Francey hated the idea of that happening. Not the fact that the Japanese were making what was probably an astute business move, she just didn't want to see people and families out of work. Too much of it was happening all over Australia. "Okay," she accepted the challenge. "I'll look over the paperwork." She flashed them both a wide smile, "I can't imagine I'll find something you two professionals have missed though."

"Good girl," said CJ and grinned. He was inordinately pleased with himself for no logical reason. He too doubted she would come up with any kind of escape plan, but that she wanted to try – even though it was out of her field of expertise – impressed him.

"Well, I'm for bed. Goodnight gentlemen."

"Goodnight," Les echoed. "I'll drop the file into your office in the morning."

CJ sat at his desk staring at Francey's neat handwriting, several pages of it. Within twenty-four hours she had come up with a plan for North West Abattoirs which just might work.

She'd related their problem to something she had read years ago in a newspaper about a fruit processing company being in financial trouble and threatening closure. The unions hadn't been pleased but the workers had gone ahead and invested all their savings in the company and become shareholders, and therefore were very keen to keep the company solvent. There was no reason why the employees at North West couldn't do the same. She doubted whether they'd come up with more than a hundred thousand dollars but that would give them enough equity to borrow the remaining amount necessary to refit the plant.

She had suggested too that all workers agree to a ten per cent pay cut until the company broke even again, and, on a rotation basis, each employee would work half a day gratis. That would cut the labour costs and pull them into the black quicker.

Damned innovative, he reckoned, though he doubted that the unions would think so. Chuckling under his breath he reached for the phone to ring Les. His CEO would be impressed and what's more, if he could swing it and she agreed, Les could fly her down to North West so she could present the proposal to them in person.

Yes, Francy Spinetti was coming along just fine. The woman had more business acumen than she realised. He grinned to himself. She was surprising him all the time.

Francey had made the cubbyhole office she worked in her own during her time at Murrundi. Working on the preliminary design for the Cooktown project she had several enlarged photos of the site plus an aerial view pinned up on one wall where she could easily see it. There were rolls and rolls of prepared drawings standing upright in a corner and a conglomeration of other materials, computer, books, files and vinyl folders, all neatly marked, spread over the tiny desk.

She hummed as she worked on a detailed section of the plan: the foyer and mezzanine floor, and was thrilled because she had just learned that Meredith had given birth to a baby boy, Mitchell Adam. Mother and baby were doing well, according to Brett, who'd been so excited he'd hardly been able to get the words out. Perhaps, if CJ agreed, she'd take some time off and go down to Sydney to visit her ... and her family, of course.

Mamma and Papà were getting used to her not being around and she'd even bravely broached the possibility of settling in Mt Isa. She'd also hinted that she'd met someone. Her father had plied her with questions as usual, and yes, she'd said it was serious and he had been delighted about that but not too thrilled about the possibility of her being so far away from them permanently. Oh well, it was hard, no, impossible to please everyone.

Looking up and out the window, to get the kink out of her neck, she could partially see the progress of the mini conference centre. The ground level cement slab had been poured, the steel strengthened vertical columns which would hold the first floor level had been bricked and the formwork for the first level was almost complete. She shook her head, silently marvelling at how quickly the construction was going ahead. The local council had rubber-stamped the project, just as CJ had said they would. Pierre had organised a crack team of sub-contractors and the project was ahead of schedule thanks to him. Pierre knew his stuff, which was a great relief. She could trust him and knew that if there were problems he would come directly to her.

Her gaze moved to the swimming pool and the garden in the foreground. Spring was evident in the new sprouting of leaves on many of the perennials, the jasmine which trailed around one of the side verandahs was in full bloom and its heady scent permeated the air once one stepped beyond the homestead.

"How's it going?" CJ's gruff voice asked from the doorway.

"Come see."

She showed him what she'd been doing and the pile of finished drawings. "Another week should see it done."

"Great. Right on time. I'll be meeting the Yakismoto consortium in Cooktown in two weeks to finalise details. I'd like you to sit in on it, maybe answer any questions from the design point of view."

"Of course."

"I was just going over to the building site. Want to stretch your legs for twenty minutes?"

"Sure." Francey slid off her stool and picked up the hard hat sitting on the corner of the desk.

As they walked down the back verandah steps CJ threaded Francey's arm proprietorially through his own. She smiled. Of late, CJ showed signs of being quite possessive of her. He often sought her out to ask questions, not only about business, but about her past, her parents, what she'd done as a child. It was as if he was extraordinarily curious about such things. His attention was sweet and surprising because she hadn't expected him to be interested in her on a personal level, but then she put it down to his nature; he was voraciously inquisitive about everything.

At the site, they peered at the ground level where brickies were working on the kitchen and staff accommodation rooms. "There's so much to think of in building this, building anything, I guess. Didn't realise, up until now," CJ stated.

"You're right. It's critical not to forget anything important otherwise it can cost a fortune to rectify."

"Francey." One of the workers came up to her. Bill Davis was the master plumber sub-contracted to the site. His team had been working for days, putting in trenches, pipes and preliminary plumbing.

"Hi, Bill, got a problem?"

"Maybe. I don't think enough allowance has been made for floodwater run off."

"Flooding!" Francey's blue-green eyes glanced around the homestead and the stockyards. "Here?"

"It's been known to happen," CJ put in. "I know we're a good way from the creek but at times, when the plains flood down from the Leichhardt River, the water can come up to the stockyards."

"What do you suggest Bill?"

"It's gonna add to the cost, but twice as much piping and a larger diameter runoff pipe downhill and away from the swimming pool area could stop water from seeping into the homestead's recreation area."

"Could we put in holding tanks? You know, those cement tanks I see all over the place," Francey suggested. "The tanks, together with pumps, could then be used for watering either the gardens or stock."

"That might work," Bill agreed, nodding. "We could dig in three or four tanks on the downhill slope and divert run off pipes into them."

"What do you think, CJ?"

"Sounds good. One has to plan for all sorts of contingencies out here," he said to Francey. "We haven't seen a flood for eight or nine years, so according to Murphy's Law, we could expect one in the next three to four years."

She looked at Bill. "Want me to amend your drawings?"

Bill shook his head. "I'll rough the changes in and you can initial them. That'd save time."

"Have you seen Pierre around, Bill?" CJ asked.

"He's up top helping the guys put down the formwork for the next slab."

Francey led the way up the ladder to the formwork level. A mass of timber and steel lengths wired and fixed into place showed the overall floor size of the building. Plumbing connections and electrical wiring conduits stuck out like strange apparitions and at least nine men scrambled over various points, working on the formwork. Francey spied Pierre down the other end manoeuvring a plank into position. Waving to him, and with CJ following, she began to move along a series of boards that zigzagged across the top for the men to walk on.

Almost in slow motion, it happened ...

Pierre, standing on the edge of the formwork, overbalanced and lost his footing. In a split second Francey saw him, arms and legs akimbo, toppling over the side of the formwork and the protective railing, his hands scrabbling in mid-air to find something solid to grab onto. Then, above the regular site noises came an awful thud as he hit the ground.

"Oh, God!" she half screamed and turning around by-passed CJ on the way back to the ladder. By the time she and CJ got to where Pierre lay they saw that he'd fallen across a stack of timber. Half-a-dozen men, strangely silent, surrounded Pierre, while one knelt beside him, tentatively checking him over.

"Looks like his leg's broken," one said. Which was obvious from the unnatural positioning of the limb.

Senses on full alert, heart beating overtime, Francey stared at a prostrate Pierre Dupre. He had been knocked unconscious by the fall and there could be a skull fracture. "Someone go tell Lisa and call an ambulance."

"Wouldn't it be quicker to get Les to helicopter him to the hospital?" CJ queried.

Francey had done first-aid training and she verbalised

her doubts. "CJ, he's unconscious so we can't tell if he has internal injuries. Moving him could be fatal."

CJ nodded gravely. "You're right." He barked an order at one man. "On the double, over to the homestead. Let them know what's happened. We want an ambulance and a doctor here in twenty minutes."

Francey and another man, Hans, the designated safety officer for the building site were kneeling by Pierre, checking his breathing.

"All right," Francey, despite the shock she felt inside, made her tone confident and decisive. "The best we can do is make Pierre comfortable." She glanced around at the concerned faces. "There's nothing you can do. Some of you go have a smoko, the rest, back to work." She glanced at Alan Trent, the assistant foreman. "Take your orders from Alan until further notice."

She stared at Pierre again noting that he'd landed with the top half of his body on his side. His airways were probably okay but she didn't like the fact that he hadn't come round. Hans had put smelling salts under his nose but the odour had no effect. "Could someone find a blanket? he'll be going into shock. Try the stockmen's bunkhouse."

Lisa Dupre was remarkably calm when she saw what had happened to her husband. She came and sat beside him, held his hand and stroked his head until the ambulance arrived. Five minutes later both Lisa and Pierre were on their way to hospital.

"Here, drink this," CJ handed her a small glass.

"What is it?" Francey asked.

They had stayed at the building site long enough to confirm that Alan Trent should act as temporary supervisor then returned to the homestead. Both sat on the part of the verandah that overlooked the pool.

"Brandy. You need it," he said gruffly. "That was nasty, what happened to Pierre. Poor bloke."

Francey nodded. "Accidents happen on building sites all the time. I've seen a few. Supervising architects are required to inspect sites on a regular basis."

"You handled it well, but it's still a shock. Drink up now, sip it if you want to. That's an order, Francey."

At any other time Francey may have taken offence at his authoritative tone but not now. She was upset. She'd come to know Lisa well and Pierre too, to a certain degree, and liked them both. Wrinkling her nose at the odour she took a couple of small swallows and coughed. "Ugh, I don't like this stuff."

"It's only Napoleon, the best money can buy, and the woman doesn't like it," CJ commented to no-one in particular.

Francey persevered with the alcohol, feeling it warm her insides, slowly doing its work and calming her.

"Pierre's accident could slow the building down a lot," CJ muttered. "With him controlling the tradesmen I'd hoped to get the building to lock up stage in case the wet comes our way."

"We'll find someone else. We'll just have to look a little further afield." The brandy was taking effect, mellowing her, easing the internal distress she felt. She knew an efficient work site needed a sound project supervisor who could organise the diversity of skills that were needed on the site. Pierre had been good at his job and finding an equally good replacement wouldn't be easy.

"Hmmm, that'll take time." CJ stroked his jaw

thoughtfully, the germ of an idea sprouting inside his head. "Of course, there is someone ..."

Quirking an eyebrow up at him, she asked. "Who?"

"Someone who knows the site intimately, has one hundred per cent understanding of the design and who lives practically on site."

She frowned, and then it hit her. "Me!"

"Yes. You."

"But I'm ... an architect, I'm still working on the Cooktown plans. I –"

"Which, according to you, are almost finished," he put in succinctly. "Why not, Francey? You could do it, I know you could. Or," he paused, "would you be nervous about being on a work site with a bunch of guys? Perhaps you don't think you could control them?"

She looked directly at him. "There are lots of reasons. It's not my field of expertise, but of course I could control them. I get along with men, tradesmen, very well. It's just, mostly a conflict of interests ..."

"Explain that?"

"Aden Nicholson pays my salary. I don't think he'd take too kindly to paying my wages and me working for you."

The phone on the glass-topped coffee table rang and Francey leant across to answer it. "Yes, Lisa, how ..."

CJ watched her expressive face as Lisa Dupre brought her up-to-date on Pierre's condition. So much vivacity and a quick intellect too. He found their verbal battling, on the odd occasion, quite stimulating. She had breathed new life into Murrundi, and him.

"Yes, all right. I'll tell CJ straightaway," and then she replaced the receiver.

"Well?"

"Poor Pierre. A broken femur, two cracked ribs and a fractured skull. They're going to airlift him to Cairns hospital – it's closest – so a neurologist can look at him. Lisa said they're a little worried about the skull fracture, something about compression."

"I see. Lisa's going with them?"

"Of course. She'll call from Cairns when she knows more."

"Now, we were saying, as to your conflict of interests," he gave her a conspiratorial grin, "that's easily fixed. Come work for me. Leave Nicholson, Drew and Carlyle. I think you've just about outgrown them anyhow."

CHAPTER FIFTEEN

Francey's eyes widened. "Are you serious?"

A bushy eyebrow rose. "I'm always serious when I offer someone a job."

"But ..." She stopped, thinking. CJ was right. She had outgrown Aden and his architectural firm. Her life had begun to head along a different path, partially due to CJ and the things she'd learned through him, and partially due to Steve and the changes that had been wrought within herself since she had come to Mt Isa. But then she recalled what she'd said about loyalty the day she'd met him. Did she still owe Aden? The answer came quickly, no! He'd got a nice fat fee for her designing the mini conference centre and he'd get another for the Cooktown project. She was doing the work and he and his partners were raking in the profits. Funny, she'd never seen it that way before. If she worked for CJ she'd be better off financially and probably better off career-wise too. Who knew where it could eventually lead?

"Sleep on the offer. Just remember it's a serious one."

"What would I do after the mini conference centre's finished?"

"You know me, Francey, I've always got something on the boil." He appeared to contemplate for a minute. "Such as you designing an art museum for Mt Isa. The mayor, Darren Turk, cornered me at Pierre's party and got me to agree to doing it. I've been promising to for years, ever since Brenda died. Have no fear, my dear, you'll earn your salary, which will be a damned sight more generous than what Nicholson paid you." He wrote a figure on a piece of paper and handed it to her. "This is for starters and I'll make allowances for you to see your family. I know you're close to them. How about, say, five to six all expenses paid visits to Sydney per year to see them?"

Oh, it was tempting. Very. "All right, CJ, I'll think about it."

CJ had said to sleep on the idea but that was exactly what Francey didn't do. If she accepted his offer her life would change, really change. Up until now she had thought of her time at Murrundi Downs station as an extended working holiday, one that would end in the not too distant future. She had been able to put off making any career decisions until then. But now, with Pierre's accident, decision time was being thrust upon her.

There were pluses about staying around the Isa. She loved the country, the people and she was deeply in love with Steve Parrish. Her lips curved in a smile as she remembered the last time they'd made love. It had been extraordinary. She even thought that she had come to understand "the man with the golden touch" pretty well. He wasn't the monster most people thought him to be – granted though he was difficult to handle, but he certainly wasn't impossible. Working for him in a variety of capacities would be a challenge. How he ran his empire, how he thought and operated. She immediately thought of the things she could learn and the structures she would design.

But there were minuses. Not seeing her parents very often, or her friends – Brett and Meredith and baby Mitchell – in particular. And ... the problem with Natalie. For no good reason she appeared to dislike her intensely. Why else had she planned that stunt in the ravine? Oh, yes, she had worked out that her being stranded had been a deliberate act on Natalie's part.

She turned on her side and plumped up the pillow. Perhaps she should talk it over with Steve. No. The decision had to be hers and by morning she knew her answer would be yes.

Trish Pentano jogged along Four Mile Beach at Port Douglas towards the small village. The weather hadn't heated up yet, the humidity was still low, but that would soon change as the monsoon period approached in at the end of the year. She changed direction and trotted away from the beach and along the back streets heading in the direction of Natalie's art gallery, where a shower and a change of clothes would be waiting prior to them strolling down to one of the sidewalk cafes for brunch.

She loved the laid-back lifestyle of this resort village and wished she could afford to live here permanently and somehow make a living. Turning into MacCrossan Street she had a thought – perhaps she should offer to run Natalie's business interests here. Since she and Natalie had been together she had gleaned considerable knowledge about the art world, artists and selling works to tourists, enough to do as good a job as the next person. She could supplement the wage with the occasional tourist or environmental article and manage quite nicely.

The gallery didn't open till 10 a.m. so she jogged around to the back door and let herself in.

"Natalie, I'm back," she called out as she went into the amenities room which held the shower, toilet, several lockers and a couple of storage crates. On a bench seat stood her blue vinyl bag with a change of clothes: underwear, sandals, shorts and singlet top of course, it was too hot for anything more.

She shrugged her shoulders when she failed to hear a response and went into the shower cubicle and stripped off. Thank God, old Nick the perve wasn't around any more – he'd been doing the occasional touch-up job for weeks – otherwise Natalie would have had to stand guard at the door. Men, they were pathetic really, the way just about all of them thought women couldn't resist them.

Eight minutes later, smiling at her squeaky clean reflection in the mirror, Trish ran a brush through her hair, applied a bright pink lipstick and went to find Natalie. She wasn't in the showroom checking out the latest wares: colourful, predominantly tropical paintings set against stark white walls with overhead spotlights. Neither was she in the storage room where paintings were kept until they could be shown or crated up after they'd been sold. She headed for the office.

Natalie sat behind her free-form, glass-topped desk, staring right through her. No smile of recognition, no flicker of the eyelids. It was as if she were in some kind of trance. The occasional twitch of a muscle in her left cheek was the only sign of life. Trish's heart sank. Another mood. She sighed and came into the room, her steps tentative. What was the matter with her friend and lover? Over the last two to three months Natalie had moved through one excessive mood to another. It had become wearying, to say the least.

Ignoring the depressed state Natalie allowed herself to sink into might work. "Hi," Trish said brightly as she sat in the chair opposite. "Natalie, I'm starving after my run, are you ready for brunch?"

No response. No acknowledgement that she'd spoken. Jesus, she was getting creepy.

"Natalie." Louder this time. "Come on, hon, snap out of it."

Nothing.

Trish looked at the desk, perhaps she would find a clue there. Natalie's talon-like fingers lay flat on the glass, half covering a fax. She slipped the paper out from under her fingers and read the brief message.

Thought you'd like to know. CJ's offered Francey a permanent job, designing for him and assisting him in his business interests. She's accepted. Les.

Oh! That's why the mood was upon her. Francey again. Natalie had become obsessed with the woman. Trish was no psychiatrist but from a layman's point of view, Natalie appeared to be exhibiting signs of paranoia regarding the young architect. She personally thought that Francey was a likeable, respectable woman and was undeserving of her lover's scheming and condemnation. But Trish was far too street-wise to voice such an opinion because she knew what would result. A temper tantrum of gigantic proportions.

"Les, the bastard." Natalie's head jerked backwards and she spoke with obvious venom. "Rubbing my nose in Francey's popularity with CJ. Well, it won't last." The fingertips of her right hand began to drum against the glass-topped desk creating a tinging staccato type sound. "She's city through and through. In a couple of months she'll get bored with the place, particularly when the wet hits."

"Of course she will," Trish soothed, trying to talk her through and out of the mood. "Be patient, love. Don't fuss with schemes and things trying to get rid of her. You'll see, it will happen quite naturally. She'll long for the city, for her friends, for the beach and decent weather and she'll be off." Natalie's unhealthy preoccupation with Francey Spinetti was beginning to concern her and make her lover difficult to live with.

"What if she doesn't? What if she's able to wrap CJ around her little finger and get him to propose to her? What then?"

Trish thought for a moment. "Well, if that happens and, mind you, I don't think it will, but if it does, *then* you move and go all out to get rid of her."

"Will you help? Maybe you can dig up some dirt on her. I just know she's not as pure and wholesome as she makes out."

Trish forced a smile. The idea of trying to hurt Francey didn't appeal because she believed that the problem was all in Natalie's head. But she'd try anything to placate her. "I'll see what I can find out."

Natalie thought about what Trish had said for a good moment or two, the corner of her mouth twitching. "You're right. I'll ignore her whenever I'm at Murrundi and if we have to find a way to get rid of her then we'll do it together."

"Right." Trish began to relax. Natalie was coming out of her mood. "Now, how about we go get something to eat?"

CJ finished reading the proposal from North West Abattoirs. They had bought the deal thanks to Francey's sincerity in delivering both the truth and a workable solution. Les had reported that she had done a fine job down there. She had come over as sincere and the workers – some of them pretty hard cases – had responded to her straightaway. He nodded approvingly, he'd known they would.

He kept her busy these days, what with supervising the building site, preparing a report for the Yakismoto people and doing preliminary work-up drawings for the Brenda deWitt-Ambrose Art Museum planned for Mt Isa. She had also taken over helping out in the office. While Lisa supervised Pierre's convalescence she had put on a temporary replacement, Kim Najin. Kim was nice enough but she needed direction and CJ had confidence that Francey could give it to her.

Francey was like him in that she liked to keep busy. It hadn't escaped his notice either that Les was pleased she'd come on board because it meant he'd be able to spend more time with her. So, as soon as she had settled in he'd have Les begin to instruct her on the ins and outs of his business empire. If she was going to be a part of the operation she might as well know how all of it ran.

He grunted smugly to himself as he got up to walk to the window and look out across the verandah at what he could see of the mini conference building site. The concrete for the first level was still curing but carpenters were busy assembling the frame on the ground. Funny, he'd never been so interested in seeing a project go up as he was with this one. Francey was brimful of enthusiasm and it was catching.

CJ's thoughts turned suddenly to his stepdaughter. Natalie had shown no interest in the conference centre. Come to think of it she hadn't been overly inclined to learn the extent of his business interests either. When she'd been younger all she had cared about was having enough money to do what she wanted to do. Brenda, he realised, had spoiled her dreadfully. In hindsight he should have done something about it but it was too late now. Natalie was thirty and her character, questionable at times, was already set.

While standing there he suddenly became aware of a tingling sensation in the thumb and the first finger of his right hand. Damn, it was cramping up, losing the feeling. Not surprising, really, after the many rough years he'd lived in his youth. In the bush, in Coober Pedy, building up Murrundi. Little wonder his body was starting to act its age. He was getting old, that's all. He shook the hand vigorously but the tingling ran up his arm and into the back of his neck. Then in the next instant the whole arm went numb.

Jesus, what was going on?

A searing pain grabbed behind his neck and ringed around his head. Sharp. Throbbing. *Intense.* The breath whooshed out of his lungs, and it felt like someone had thrust a red-hot poker through his skull. He groaned as the pain tore into him. He couldn't stand. It knocked him to his knees. His left hand moved to his head, rubbing, trying to stop the intense pain. Stressed by it, the room began to spin, revolving slowly, then the revolutions became faster, faster. His breath came in short gasps and a bubble of bile travelled up his throat, almost choking him. He gagged, then vomited on the timber floor.

His head felt as if it would burst and the pain was so bad he didn't care about anything, so long as it went away. Still on his knees and with sweat pouring out of him, he was immobilised by the intensity of what was occurring, unable to think, unable to pray, unable to even call out for help.

How long he remained that way, he didn't know or care. But ever so slowly the throbbing in his head began to ease. Jesus Christ, he felt awful. Getting to his feet, his right hand still numb, he staggered out of his study to his bedroom and collapsed on the wide bed.

He felt drained, and his clothes were soaked with his own sweat. What had happened to him? He never got sick, other than the occasional dose of flu. As his brain began to function again he tried to make sense of it. Was it some kind of food poisoning? He'd had oysters for lunch. That could be it. Relief flooded through him. Oysters were renowned for making people sick if one got a crook one. And he'd been bloody crook, indeed!

Exhausted by the experience, his limbs still trembling with weakness, but satisfied that he'd identified the cause, CJ closed his eyes and drifted into a dreamless sleep.

CHAPTER SIXTEEN

Francey knocked on the front door of Steve's modest bungalow and while she waited she looked about her. The sun's final rays were sputtering over the horizon and a crispness was invading the late spring evening. It was hard to believe that she'd been up north for nearly five months. There had been so many changes in her life in such a short space of time. Breaking away from Aden, working full-time for CJ ... and Steve. Just saying his name to herself made her smile on the inside. She hadn't seen him for several days and the very thought of him prompted a coil of excitement to tighten low in her stomach as she anticipated seeing him.

The door opened wide and Steve stood there, grinning. Wearing a black, rollneck sweater and faun slacks, he looked marvellous and handsome and virile. He swept her into his open arms.

"I've been waiting all day for this," he said softly as his lips found hers.

They clung to each other. Fused, hearts beating in tune, little moans escaped from their throats as the heat of their bodies penetrated the other's clothes. Her hands crept around his neck, the length of her straining against him as if she couldn't get close enough.

"Mmm, that was good. Dessert before dinner." There was laughter in her voice as they eased back from each other.

He nodded his agreement. "I was just about to put the steaks on," he told her and took the bottle of wine from her.

"Not so fast," she said. "How about a tour first?" She hadn't been to his house before and was curious as to how the man she loved would decorate his home.

His eyebrows rose. "It's not like CJ's station, a tour of my place will take about five minutes tops." She gave him a certain look and he shrugged his shoulders. "Okay."

They walked down a short, tiled hall to the combined living-dining room which was furnished simply with a three-piece black leather lounge and a pine wall unit which held the stereo and TV and an assortment of books and bric-a-brac. Three huge prints of dolphins frolicking in the water dominated one length of wall and along another were several shelves which held his collection of semiprecious stones. The galley style kitchen was modern and functional: white cupboards with granite-style formica tops. Francey, ever the architect, noted that the entire floor area was covered with ceramic tiles for coolness and that the drapes in each room were lined to keep out the heat. Vents in the ceiling evidenced air-conditioning, a must for pleasant living in this hot, arid part of the country.

"Here's the bathroom," he opened the door wide for her. "I haven't got around to renovating it yet but it's on the agenda for next year. And down the hall there's three bedrooms, each with built-ins."

Francey saw that the two smaller bedrooms were empty but the main bedroom, which was of good proportions, had a king-size bed, side tables and a tallboy chest of drawers with an oval mirror. Everything was neat and shipshape, which impressed her – Steve appeared to be a tidy housekeeper.

"What's the mattress like?" she asked as she sat on the edge of the bed and tried to bounce. "Hard. Oh, I do like a hard ..." she gave him a studied, seductive glance, "mattress."

He came and sat beside her on the bed. His arm went round her shoulder so he could draw her up against the side of his body. He said in his stern, policeman tone, "You, miss, are asking for trouble."

She laughed throatily as her hands came up to capture his face. Her blue-green eyes stared longingly into his brown ones, the flutter of her heartbeat increasing as she looked into those dark, impenetrable depths. "Oh, yes. Please."

With a mock growl he eased her back down on the bed and ... laughing, kissing, touching, they undressed each other, then Steve drew Francey hard up against him. By now he knew where to caress and fondle to bring her to a high state of arousal. And he loved to watch the way growing passion darkened her eyes to sea-green, and how her lips heated and softened under his constant assault. She drove him wild too, with the sensual movements of her body, writhing beneath him, encouraging him. God, how empty his life had been before her, but as he kissed and suckled her nipples until they hardened he realised it wasn't empty any more.

Breathless from his kisses and from the bold straying of hands through her dark curls to the most intimate, sensitive part of her body, she could feel the heat building within her, especially when the tip of his hard penis teased her there. He was driving her wild with wanting him and he knew it. Suddenly she wriggled down in the bed and forced him partially inside her.

"What do you want?" he whispered.

"You." As if he didn't know. She was trembling with pent-up longing for the ecstasy he could bestow upon her.

"Where?" he teased, his own voice husky with passion.

So tense that her nerve endings felt extraordinarily sensitised, she pleaded. "Inside me. Deep." She sighed. "As far as you can go."

He plunged into her then, just once, then stilled. "Like this?"

She couldn't control her gasp of delight or her body's shuddering response. "Oh, yes. Yes." She kissed him, deeply, thrusting her tongue into his mouth in a replica of what she wanted his penis to do to her.

Steve almost lost control. She was the sexiest, most giving woman. He began their dance of love and she matched his ardour with that of her own ...

Sated, Francey snuggled into him, her hand playing up and down his chest. "I think I'd like to stay here, like this, forever."

"Me too."

"But I'm starting to get hungry ..."

He kissed the tip of her nose. "I'm beginning to see that you're a very demanding woman. I get the message."

Francey didn't leave a morsel on her plate. "Steve, you're a great cook," she complimented him sincerely as they began to stack the dishes.

"I like to cook."

"Good, you can do it all the time when we ..." He stared down at her and lifted an eyebrow. "When we what?"

Oh! What? *When we what?* Move in and set up house together? Get married? They hadn't talked about commitment, they had skirted around the subject a couple of times but hadn't there been some unspoken understanding that their relationship was leading up to that? Yet nothing had been said or confirmed. "I mean, I, not we ... when *I* come here again," she finished lamely, her cheeks flaming with embarrassment. They had been seeing each other for a month. Was that long enough to contemplate a more serious, more defined relationship? Her desires were equally divided. Half of her wanted to take the next step while the other half felt it would be wise not to rush into things. As well, she didn't want to put Steve on the spot. She loved him and she thought she'd heard him say that he cared too, in the throes of passion, but both seemed reluctant to talk their feelings through. It was too soon. Yes, better not to rush things, their future happiness was too important.

She decided to change the subject, before she put her foot in her mouth again. "CJ's asked me to accompany him and Les when they go overseas in February. They're going to Singapore, Hong Kong and London." She tried not to let the excitement show in her voice. "CJ's signing the official partnership papers with the Yakismoto Consortium for the Cooktown project. Then they're going to Hong Kong to check his investments – an advertising company and a few blocks of home units. He wants to see how things are because China will be taking over in July. There are rumblings, rumours, that everything might be nationalised, which would lead to a shift, a downturn in the city's economy. After that they're off to London for bank meetings and then some rest and relaxation at some country estate. CJ has friends he likes to visit at that time of the year."

"Sounds real tough," Steve said tongue-in-cheek, then he remembered her project. "What's going to happen to the mini conference centre while you're away? Is Pierre fit enough to supervise it?"

"Not yet. CJ says the work will stop if the wet gets bad here. That's why he and Les are going overseas to do business. To get away from the rain, I guess."

"It'll be a great experience for you, I'm sure."

Francey detected a note of something, was it envy? Steve was the least envious person she knew, but she'd picked up on something. Maybe he didn't want her to go. She hoped that was it.

"How long will you be away?"

"I'm not sure. Maybe a month."

She saw his frown and the tightening of his mouth and said straight out, "You don't want me to go."

"Hell, no. It's your job, you work for CJ now. You'll have a grand time seeing all those wonderful places. It's just ..."

"Just what?"

"That I'll miss you like crazy, that's what."

Smiling with relief she came and sat on his lap. The index finger of her right hand traced the contours of his face as she said, "I'll miss you too. Every hour of every day."

He gathered her close to him, his lips nuzzling her throat. God, no woman had ever done what Francey Spinetti did to him. She tied him in knots, made it hard, no, impossible for him to think straight when she was this close. He wanted her so much. Wanted to see her beside him when he woke in the morning and the last thing before he went to sleep at night. He wanted to see her across the kitchen table, he wanted to see her hanging out their clothes on the clothesline and help her with the shopping. He wanted to plan the rest of his life around her, with her.

"You know, I think we should keep you, us ... quiet. Be discreet for a while," Steve said. "The Isa's a small town and people here love to gossip. I'd rather they didn't do it, didn't speculate about us until we're ... until ..."

"We're more comfortable with each other," she finished for him.

"Yes. Okay?"

"Okay."

He kissed her warm, willing lips and tightened his hold on her. So far they were good together in every possible way, but something about her trip niggled at him. Les Westcott and CJ. He didn't enjoy the idea of her being almost constantly in their company for a month or more. He wasn't sure about CJ, the man was old enough to be her father and Westcott, well, he couldn't blame the man if he was attracted to her. He'd seen the way Les looked at her, sizing her up, speculating. Waiting, watching like a bird of prey. Westcott was sophisticated, a man of the world and Steve'd made enquires and knew he was wealthy in his own right. Years of working for CJ had made him so.

Damn it, he was jealous of him being close to Francey for a prolonged period of time. The thought amazed him and at the same time depressed him as he compared himself to his competition. What did he have to offer Francey? A policeman's income wasn't great but he got by okay, but would "okay" be enough for her? He didn't know. He snatched a sly glance at her profile, loving the way her nose tilted up at the tip, the strong line of her jaw, her crazily independent head of hair. God he loved her, but he wouldn't tell her yet. He wanted to further nuture their closeness. When she came back from her overseas jaunt and if it was still the same between them, then ...

"I'm going to Sydney to see my parents for Christmas," Francey said as she nibbled his ear lobe. "Would you, if you could get some time off, like to meet them? On Christmas Day we have a big party at my aunt's home at Abbotsford. All the family comes: uncles, aunts, cousins, grandkids. It's noisy and exhausting and they feed you till you burst." She kissed him. "I'd love you to come."

A blank expression masked Steve's reaction to her offer. He hadn't been to Sydney since ... He didn't know whether he could face the city and the reminders of his shortcomings. He'd done so well here the last few years, putting it all behind him. Did he want to stir the memories up again? "I'd like to, very much. But it might be difficult. I'm a single guy so I'll probably be rostered on Christmas Day."

"Couldn't you pull a few strings?" She wanted him to meet her parents, get their approval. She'd like to show him off to all her relatives and friends too but most of all, the thought of being away from him over the festive season made her usual sunny nature spin into a mild depression.

"Are you trying to coerce the law, Miss Spinetti?"

She pressed her body hard against him. "Not the law in toto, just one particular lawman."

"I'll see what I can organise." He kissed her thoroughly, breathlessly, his hands moving over her torso, cupping her breasts, wandering over her round buttocks and kneading them to let her know the state of his arousal.

Responding to his touch, the urgency of his demands, she whispered half-heartedly, "We haven't finished cleaning up."

"It can wait," he said and plunged his tongue into her mouth, swirling, delving, dominating her with the rise of passion, "but this can't."

Steve sat at the desk in his pokey office in the police station, sorting through the pile of reports from last night's watch. Two burglaries, an assault outside the Outback Motor Inn, three cars stolen and an attempted sexual assault on an Aboriginal woman behind the fire station. The usual.

From his top drawer he took out a folder marked "Ambrose, Richard," and slowly leafed through the contents.

He hated to admit it but he had come to a stalemate on Richard's murder. Exhaustive checking through the township and the outlying stations had come up with only thirteen rifles that took .25 cartridges. All thirteen rifle owners had alibis for the time of the stampede, so that line of enquiry had reached a dead end. He rummaged through more paperwork and found a three week old report on Paul Andronicus. The carpenter had been sighted at Charters Towers but when two policeman had closed in to question him, he'd slipped through their net and escaped. Unfortunate. If the guy had half a brain he'd deduce that the Queensland police had an APB out on him and he'd either lie low or disappear interstate.

Steve clicked his tongue in disgust. The trail was going cold and he knew it. CJ was disappointed. Damn it, he was disappointed. He wanted to find the person or persons responsible for Richard Ambrose's death badly, the senselessness of the killing outraged him. His fingers drummed on the desk top, a habit he had when he was thinking. Find a new trail, a new line of enquiry, experience told him, but what? where?

He stared at the paperwork, hoping some inspiration would pop out at him. Billy Wontow. He wasn't a suspect, he'd almost been killed along with Richard. But maybe he should have another talk to him. He took a deep breath. Maybe ... he should interview everyone at Murrundi, see if any minute clue had been overlooked.

His fingers stopped drumming, and he grinned. What did he have to lose other than a couple of hours of police time?

The week in Sydney before Christmas was a bittersweet time for Francey. Seeing old friends and braving a visit to Nicholson, Drew and Carlyle's Christmas party, which she'd done mostly to convince herself that no residue of affection remained for Aden. None did. Being the centre of attention at her parent's home where she was staying until the new year because she had sublet the apartment at Potts Point had had its good and bad points. Mamma fussing, Papà disappointed that things hadn't worked out with Aden and that she was working so far away from them. She weathered it all as best she could.

And after so many months up north she could see it all from a surprisingly new perspective. The hustle and bustle of city streets was overwhelming. She almost choked on petrol fumes as she waited to cross at the corner of Market and George Streets, and while she loved the salty smell of the sea she also began to long for the faint odour of eucalypts and the wide open spaces of the Isa.

CJ had given her a special, secret task of which even Les was unaware. He'd been thinking of having a base in Sydney to extend his interests in the largest capital city in Australia and had asked her if she wouldn't mind looking at some Sydney real estate on his behalf. He wasn't fussed whether she checked out an established house or found a decent block of land where she could design a suitable residence. The only stipulation had been that it had to be on the harbour with a jetty. So, between chasing real estate agents, buying clothes for the forthcoming overseas trip, seeing to a passport and to CJ's request, she was one busy woman.

When she had time to think about it she found the revelatory change within her curious, but she had changed, markedly, in less than six months. The city in which she'd been bred was just another city – it would always be her favourite city – but the centre of her universe had shifted north, to Murrundi and to Steve. A wave of loneliness ran through her as she put the finishing touches to her mother's Christmas tree, placing the angel at the apex of the pine needles. Steve had told her he couldn't get leave for the holidays so they wouldn't be together. However she'd convinced herself that there would be other Christmases together, dozens and dozens of them, she hoped.

"Looks wonderful, *cara*." Lucia stopped to view the tree on her way through to the kitchen from which mouthwatering aromas wafted through to the living room. "It's good to have you home, if only for a little while."

Francey detected the reproach in her voice and said brightly to ward off a possible outbreak of tears. "You should be happy for me, Mamma. I'm doing what I want to do. Look at the projects I've designed. I'm learning so much from CJ and Les, and seeing so much."

"*Capisco bene.* All that is fine but I wish you were closer to home, to us."

Francey sighed. They had had this conversation before. "Mamma, I'm going to be twenty-seven in a few months time. Many women my age have been up and far away from home for quite a few years."

Lucia wrung her hands together then spread them wide. "I know, I know. I am being selfish. Carlo said that you had your life to live, as we had ours, and you must live it the way that is right for you."

"Oh, Mamma," Francey moved close to her mother and put her arm around her. "This will always be my first home, no matter where I live. The memories here will last me a lifetime."

"*Sì.* Of course." Lucia wiped a suspicious wetness from her eyes. "You are going to see your friends the O'Connors after dinner?"

"Yes. I've only seen them once since I've been here, I've been so busy. I'll be back in time for midnight mass, I promise."

Lucia nodded on her way through to the kitchen. Her little girl had changed since she'd been away. More independent, if that was possible. But there was something else. A glow about her. She was in love, she was sure of it. Francey had hinted as much, if only to keep Carlo from nagging her about settling down, but she hadn't said with whom. Aahh, life had been so much easier when she was a youngster Lucia thought as she stirred the bolognese sauce. Then I had some control over what she did, where she went. Now that she's an adult I have none and it is hard to let go. Now I have to wait and hope that she will not forget me. Aahh, as my Carlo would say, that's life, so I must not worry. She disguised a sniff and blew her nose with her handkerchief.

"Francey, tell your Papà to shut the shop or dinner will be overcooked."

"Yes, Mamma." Francey smiled as she went to do her mother's bidding, as she had done so many times over the years, knowing it was useless. If her father had last minute customers he would not shoo them out without attending to them. She knew what he'd say when Lucia tried to scold him. "Wife, a sale is a sale. If I do not make the customer happy he will go elsewhere for his produce. That is not good business."

Her father's simple business creed was a good one, she thought, a pity more businesspeople didn't feel the same way. She must remember to mention it to CJ.

Steve Parrish stood indecisively at the front gate of the two-storey blonde brick Abbotsford home on Christmas Day. He had interfered and reorganised the rosters at the police station to get two precious days off, time to spend with Francey in the city he'd once sworn never to set eyes on again.

Music and conversation noise, laughter and children squealing could be heard coming from the rear of the house. He grinned. This must be the place – Francey had described it to a T. He walked up the tiled path to the front door and pushed the button. Eventually someone came, a middle-aged woman with grey hair and wearing a lime green slacks suit.

"I'm looking for Francey Spinetti." He tried to ignore his discomfort at the way the woman stared at him. Sharp black eyes gave him a swift, thorough once-over, assessing him, though for what he wasn't sure.

Then she smiled and gestured effusively with her hands. "Come in, come in. I'm Francey's Aunt Josephine, people call me Josie. You're just in time for lunch. And *Buon Natale!*"

She led him down a wide, tiled hall, across a large living room furnished with dark-timbered pieces of furniture, through the kitchen and out to the backyard. The backyard was long and wide and led down to Hen and Chicken Bay and further along, the Parramatta River. A swimming pool was getting plenty of use and the huge quarry-tiled patio had a pergola overhead. Laden with grape vines it offered shade from the sun. A long table covered in a white tablecloth almost groaned with the weight of the food on coloured plates and platters.

Steve's eyebrows lifted as his gaze moved to the crowd of people standing and sitting around in groups. There were adults and teenagers and children running, laughing and playing with their new Christmas toys. Nostalgia overcame him for a moment as he remembered the Christmases of his own childhood. Family and friends crowded into their small semi in Redfern, hot turkey and roast pork dinners, plum pudding and Christmas cake.

"Steve!"

Francey saw him and almost dropped the small child she'd been nursing on her hip. She hastily gave the toddler to her mother and rushed over to him.

"I can't believe you're here." She gave him a spontaneous hug, no matter who saw or who raised their eyebrows. All morning she had been trying to contain her depression because she wouldn't see him on this very special day and here he was. She shook her head in disbelief, glad that her prayers had been answered.

"I can't believe it either." He laughed and swung her around, her happiness was contagious. "God, it's good to see you."

She smiled up at him. "I want you to meet everyone. Come on, we'd better start with my parents."

Lucia was impressed with Steve's height and natural manner, and instinctively knew he was a strong man who would be a good match for her independent daughter. Carlo decided instantaneously that somewhere in Steve's genes he had Italian forebears and he liked the policeman's straight, up-front personality. Aunt Josie, Daniella's mother, whispered to Francey that he was a "hunk", and one of her cousins, Rocco Biviano, gave him an approving nod as they talked about, of all things, fishing. She watched Steve enthusiastically munch his way through servings of prawns and calamari, pasta, plates of cold meat and salads washed down with glasses of Frascati, and then he polished off several slices of *panettone* before he admitted to being – in his words – stuffed.

"Don't you have relatives to visit?" Francey asked quietly as she handed him a cup of coffee. She looked around the backyard and saw that the children had quietened down, the first excitement of Christmas day over, and some of the men were lying on the lawn, snoozing in the shade. The women, cousins and second cousins, aunts and great-aunts, were talking animatedly in small groups.

"I have a sister, Michelle, she lives in Randwick. She and her husband, Mike, and their three boys have gone away for the holidays."

"Where are you staying?"

"I managed to get a room at the Cross, the Boulevarde Hotel."

"When do you have to go back?" It was a question she hated to ask but she wanted to know.

"The twenty-seventh, 6.30 a.m. flight," he told her with a grimace.

As soon as they could decently get away, without raising too many eyebrows, they did. Francey insisted that they were going to visit Meredith, Mitchell and Brett – which they would, on Boxing Day – but in reality they wanted to be alone. Steve's room at the Boulevarde was perfect.

CJ stood by the window of the dining room looking out beyond the verandah and the pool where a heat haze shimmered and blurred the angles of the half finished mini conference centre. In the background, Shellie and Barry were playing a Christmas carol CD with songs about white Christmases, snow and more snow – completely out of place in an outback Christmas.

If he concentrated, which he didn't care to do, he could hear the conversation at the table. Natalie and Trish were debating some political matter with Les who was vigorously arguing the government's case. On the table lay the remains of their sumptuous cold Christmas dinner.

Something was missing. More than one something, two.

It was their first Christmas without Richard. He swallowed the lump in his throat as he thought of his son. Richard had dearly loved the feel and the celebration of Christmas time. His eyes would light up like a child when he knew it was close and he always decorated the tree and house with streamers and tinsel. He gave out the presents from under the tree, he even played appropriate songs on his guitar, not very well, but no-one cared. Thinking, remembering, CJ lifted the champagne glass to his lips and after a silent salute to Richard's memory took a long swallow.

It hurt, remembering. Remembering what had been and what could never be the same again.

And he missed *her*. Francey. The realisation came as no surprise. Her zest for life and her infectious brightness had lifted the household out of the doldrums since Richard's passing. She was a true breath of fresh air. Suddenly, and the thought took him by surprise, he couldn't imagine her not being a part of life at Murrundi.

Shellie came up and stood beside him. "Are you all right?"

No, he wasn't all right. He felt miserable. He very nearly said so in his gruff way but stopped himself. It wasn't his sister's fault that this melancholy had overtaken him. Damn it, he should appreciate her more. And he would. He'd make it a New Year's resolution, be kind to old Shell. After all, she'd turned the corner with her drinking problem and even a blind man could see what she thought of her doctor. And another thing was true: Shellie was the glue that bound Murrundi together. Funny that. It was usually the outback women who did it better than the men. The man went out and wrestled with the land, tried to bend it to his will, but the woman somehow and often quite miraculously kept everything at home running smoothly.

"Yes, I'm fine," he lied stoically.

Shellie heard the words, the forced inflection. She knew CJ too well and knew when he was telling the truth and otherwise. Richard. She brushed back a tear. She missed him too.

CHAPTER SEVENTEEN

Francey and Meredith O'Connor sat on outdoor plastic chairs on the back verandah of the O'Connors' Bronte home while Meredith breastfed baby Mitchell, who was almost four months old.

"Well, at least I had the chance to meet your man," Meredith said. "I liked Steve. Brett liked him too, I could tell."

"He's a man's man but he socialises well. We're very *simpatici*."

Meredith's eyebrow lifted as she stared at her friend. Wearing cut-off blue jeans and a red singlet Francey looked relaxed and happy. "So, it's the real thing? The ghosts from the past have gone?"

"You bet," Francey said with a grin, using the phrase Steve was fond of. The two days of Steve's leave in Sydney had passed in a whirl. They'd spent as much time as they could together. Played tourist, gone to the beach, and he'd even come home for dinner the night before he left, much to the raised eyebrows of her mother and the delight of her father. Carlo had shamelessly sounded him out on his prospects, his assets and if he liked children.

Remembering, her cheeks warmed becomingly. Later, Steve had laughed at her embarrassment, accepting it all in good grace. Parting at the airport the next morning had been a real wrench for both of them. It would be several weeks before she returned to Murrundi because CJ had sent a fax asking her to choose his Sydney property. She expected to do lots of hoofing around before she found suitable real estate. That he was showing sufficient trust in her to handle such an important and expensive transaction boosted her confidence enormously.

Francey studied Mitchell's fair hair, inherited from his father, and his dark blue eyes which came from Meredith's side of the family. For a moment she tried to imagine herself with a baby of her own, but couldn't. She wasn't ready yet, and wouldn't be for a few more years. There remained buildings to design, and CJ's business to learn properly.

"I'll put this little man down then we'll have a cup of tea," Meredith promised as she took a sleepy Mitchell to his room.

Left alone, Francey's thoughts returned to Steve. She hadn't believed she would meet someone she would be so compatible with, not after Bryan, but she had. One thing niggled at her consciousness though, she knew that he kept a part of himself to himself. She was sure it had something to do with what had happened during his time in the NSW Police Service. She knew about the bungled drug raid and how his partner had almost been killed. Sam Bianchini had gone to great lengths to tell her the tale at Pierre's birthday party. But she sensed that wasn't all. Perhaps Meredith knew more, but would she tell her?

Meredith wheeled the tea trolley out, complete with an array of iced cakes arranged on a china plate, and broke her train of thoughts. "Motherhood suits you," Francey complimented as she watched her friend pour two cups of tea.

"That's what everyone says. Even the guys from my section can't believe how maternal I've become. They rib me unmercifully, of course. I love it though, being with him, watching him grow and learn to do new things every day. Going back to work in a couple of months will be hard, but it's a financial necessity."

"Brett's finding it tough? Not much work around?"

Meredith's shoulders shrugged. "Doubtless you know the building trade's tight at the moment. We're getting by, but with the mortgage, I don't have the luxury of choosing to stay at home. Hopefully it'll be just for a few years."

Francey nodded in sympathy. She was no stranger to life's struggles. She'd watched her parents labour for years to pay off their mortgage and while they had, they still worked long hours to bring in a reasonable income. "Now that I'm working for CJ I might be able to push some work Brett's way – if he comes in with the right price. CJ's asked me to look at some Sydney real estate while I'm here, with a view to either building or renovating a home somewhere on the harbour. He wants a mooring too, naturally. I'm not quite sure why he wants a Sydney home when he spends about eighty per cent of his time at Murrundi, but who am I to argue with the boss? I've looked around a bit already and it's interesting, seeing the market place from a different angle, a purchaser rather than an architect."

"So that's why you've been running all over the place. Seen anything you like?"

Francey laughed. "Plenty. I've been in and out of so many mansions my head's spinning. I've found two pieces of real estate that could suit. One at Kirribilli, near

Careening Bay. The other's at Point Piper, a stone's throw from Felix Bay. Both properties are old, they need a lot of work, so perhaps it'd be better to bulldoze and start from scratch. The potential's there, with million dollar views to boot."

"And you'll do the design, of course."

"Of course. CJ will have to give final approval and he'll decide which property and whether it's to be renovated or totally rebuilt." She grinned. "You know, I've always wanted to design a mansion on the harbour."

"CJ Ambrose keeps you busy. How do you find time for Steve?"

"Oh, we manage. I don't mean to make CJ sound like a slavedriver, he isn't. If you do what he wants when he wants you to do it he doesn't interfere with your social life. If he did I'd have something to say about it."

It was Meredith's turn to grin. "I imagine you would." Her friend had never been backward about laying her cards on the table, or righting a wrong when she'd perceived one had been done.

"Meredith …" she began tentatively, the need to know had been building inside her since they'd had their first cup of tea. "Tell me about Steve. You know about him, don't you? The real reason he left Sydney."

Meredith stared at her friend, seeming to deliberate for a long moment. Finally she nodded, "If you want me to. You know, I'm sure a lot of what happened has been blown out of proportion. Cops are the worst or the best gossips in the world and keeping a secret if you're in the job is impossible. As it was told to me, Steve was knocked about emotionally by what happened to his partner, or rather nearly happened to her. And you probably know that his superior put him into another section. Time passed and he seemed to settle, though, reputedly, he hated shuffling papers.

"One night, he was off-duty but still had his gun on under his jacket. The story goes that he went into a local bottle shop to buy a carton of beer and got caught up in a robbery in progress. Apparently he froze, couldn't respond, and he did nothing because both crims had guns. He was, according to some, in a position where he could have drawn his gun and taken control. He didn't. Theoretically, and the opinion's divided, he did the right thing by playing it safe and not putting the shopkeeper in danger. The shopkeeper could have been hit if shots were exchanged, but the other school of thought, from the gung ho brigade, was that he should have taken more positive action but chickened out."

"Did he get into trouble with, what do you call it, internal affairs?"

"There was the inevitable inquiry." Meredith's eyebrows rose. "Steve was unofficially reprimanded for not taking the initiative, mostly because the crims got away and haven't been caught. He had another psychological evaluation which decided that he was fit for duty and was moved to yet another department." Meredith thought for a moment. "I guess those in command were making it clear to Steve that he'd let the force down."

Francey looked at her friend. "How do you know all this? I mean, you're in forensics, it's not your field at all."

"I checked a few things out myself. I had to know because I wanted to make sure my friend wasn't getting tied up with someone who, maybe, had some unresolved problems."

"Do you think he has problems?"

Meredith's expression remained thoughtful. "I think he *had* problems, but after meeting him and from what you've told me about how he handles his work in Mt Isa, how he rescued you and everything, I'd say his problems are in the past." She didn't add, but couldn't deny the thought ... Providing he didn't become involved in any life and death situations in which guns played a part. That could prove stressful to him.

Meredith saw that Francey needed more convincing. "Look, Steve's an okay guy and a good cop. Policing is tough these days with so many crazies around and the politics of it all. Everyone's under pressure, especially cops in the front line. Sometimes, it all becomes too much and when it does one never knows how one's going to react. What happened to Steve could happen to anyone."

"You could say the same for most professions today, there's pressure everywhere."

"Right," Meredith agreed.

"You know," Francey decided it was time to change the subject, "I might get Brett to come with me and look at those houses on the harbour. I'd value his opinion."

"I'm sure he'd love to. Over the Christmas and New Year break there's not much work being done." Francey stayed on for dinner and didn't leave until well after 10 p.m., but she returned to her parents home in Glebe with a lighter heart. She had gleaned more information about Steve, what made him tick, what made him tense. She understood why he hadn't wanted to tell her what had happened. He had his pride which had been dented by the experience of learning that he was fallible. Knowing about it would help her in her relationship with him, she was sure of it.

*

Francey stood in the conservatory looking out as the rain sheeted down, obliterating everything beyond three metres from view. She had never seen rain like it. It went on and on, relentlessly. Day and night. Occasionally it stopped, which lulled her into a false sense of hope that it was over, but then more dark clouds would roll in and down it came again. Les had said they got such weather every few years and often it went on for weeks. Unbelievable.

Thank goodness the mini conference centre had the roof and walls up, which meant some tradesmen could do internal work under Pierre's supervision. Pierre had to use a cane to support his still weak leg, but at least he was back on the job and so was Lisa. Her efficiency at running the day-to-day affairs of CJ's business had been sorely missed.

She was glad they were leaving on a commercial flight tomorrow for Singapore. She enjoyed the light, the sun, the warmth. Days and days of rain and mud and slush had caused her personality to wallow, making her understand the meaning of the phrase, "gone troppo"!

She went into her cubbyhole office to survey the half finished building plans for CJ's art museum. Goodness knows when she would get the opportunity to finish them, especially now that CJ had exchanged contracts on the Kirribilli property and wanted the house torn down and a new, illustrious mansion designed and built by the end of the year.

On one of her brief visits Natalie had expressed amusement and some derision that CJ was building another *something* – but not something he could make money from, snidely implying that he was doing it just to keep Francey in work. CJ's stepdaughter had snubbed her time and time again during her two days at Murrundi, making it clear that she couldn't stand the sight of her.

What was the woman's problem? she wondered. She appeared to be, ridiculous as it seemed, jealous of her relationship with CJ, which didn't make any sense to her. Francey chewed her lip thoughtfully as she studied the plan on the drawing board, making some pencil notes on the side of the paper. She wasn't too cut up about Natalie's behaviour; she hadn't been overly taken with the self-indulgent woman, her dislike was something she could live with. As long as they weren't in close proximity to each other very often.

Her thoughts turned to something more pleasurable: the forthcoming trip. A shiver of childlike excitement raced through her, she was looking forward to seeing new places and meeting new people. Oh, she knew it would be a working holiday but she was equally sure that there would be compensations along the way.

Singapore lived up to Francey's expectation of being all and more than she had hoped it would be. The sights, the sounds and even the smell and bustle of the place enthralled her.

They were ensconced in the luxurious penthouse suite of the Meridian Mandarin hotel, which had a panoramic view of Singapore's busy harbour and parts of the highrise buildings surrounding the city.

In the afternoon, Les, who'd visited the city many times, took her on a personal tour of the more popular places: the zoo and the botanical gardens. That night they dined at one of CJ's favourite haunts then nightclub-hopped until the wee hours. Tomorrow, though, would be all business: a day-long meeting with the Yakismoto consortium to thrash out final details and then sign the contract for the Cooktown development.

Francey studied the small conference room assigned to them by the hotel's management. Ash panelled walls, a long teak-topped conference table, leather chairs, panoramic views of the harbour from the floor to ceiling windows, several tastefully subdued watercolours on the walls and a beverage making facility in a timber panelled alcove completed the picture. All very pleasant and efficient. She was very nervous but very excited also.

She would be addressing four topnotch wealthy businessmen led by Nikko Yakismoto, a renowned Japanese industrialist, on the design aspects and building schedule of the Cooktown project. She had given presentations before, some to illustrious Sydney clients, but this would be her most important presentation. And in a way it didn't help that CJ had absolute confidence in her. She wished he didn't, for if she fouled up, he would be all the more disappointed and, strangely, she didn't want to disappoint him.

Les came into the room with a sheaf of documents, portfolios and a set of rolled up plans under his arm. He glanced at the presentation clip-board and the overhead projector, saw they were ready, then nodded at Francey.

"They're on their way up, CJ has just met them in the foyer."

Francey nodded.

"Nervous?"

"You bet!"

"Don't be, you'll be great." He came up to her and took both of her hands in his. "The consortium wants this project to go ahead, they know it's an excellent financial deal for them, otherwise they'd be investing their money elsewhere. We're doing all the hard work and they're just putting in a chunk of the capital. Out of all of them," he confided, "Nikko is the one to watch. He's sharp and he's known to be hard-headed. He was educated in England so he's fluent in English, the others only have a smattering so they'll have an interpreter in tow. Oh, yes, remember to allow extra time for that during your presentation."

The door opened and several men, including CJ, filed in. Immediately, one of them caught Francey's attention. Immaculately dressed in a white shirt and patterned tie and a beige lightweight suit for the tropics, the man exuded an air of self-confidence and importance. He was about Francey's height, with black, short-cropped hair flecked with grey at the temples. Very distinguished. She looked from him to CJ and back again. Two strong-willed, successful men. It would be interesting to see who would eventually gain the upper hand.

CJ made the introductions. "Francey, I'd like you to meet Nikko Yakismoto, and his associates Ti Masuku, Oke Narishima and Edmund Kope. Mr Chee, on your left, will translate as necessary."

Each man bowed slightly in turn to Francey.

"I am delighted to meet you, Miss Spinetti," Nikko took over the conversation as he shook her hand in western tradition, "I have been most impressed with your design work." He studied her features openly then turned to CJ, "You are most fortunate to have such an attractive as well as clever assistant."

"Thank you," Francey said as a matter of form, and despite her inclination to make spot decisions on people, reserved her opinion of Nikko Yakismoto. She had caught something in the way he looked from CJ to her and back again. As if he wanted to say more but Japanese politeness forbade it. With her curious nature she longed to know the relevance behind the look.

"Well, gentlemen, we've a lot to get through. If you don't care for refreshments I suggest we get started," CJ said authoritatively. He wasn't going to relinquish the head position to Nikko. What's more he didn't particularly like his sly glance at Francey. Nikko was known to like the ladies, even though he was, supposedly, a happily married man. He'd bear watching during the negotiations. "I'll hand things over to Francey Spinetti. She's going to go through the design with you and explain the building schedule." CJ grinned as he gestured with his right hand for Francey to take the podium.

"Thanks, CJ." She waited for everyone to be seated then she began. "You each have portfolios in front of you with scaled down drawings of the project site which includes sketches of the first golf course, the accommodation complex and the five star hotel. I know you're familiar with the plans but there are several additional changes I should point out.

"Stage two will consist of a second golf course and the third stage will be another group of condominiums close to the hotel complex which will form a triangular arrangement of rented apartments, privately owned condominiums and the hotel itself. The details are marked as stage three."

"If I may enquire, Miss Spinetti, what is the overall building time for the complete complex?"

"That's covered in the appendix to the specifications, Mr Yakismoto. The estimate is five years." She noted a low murmur from the Yakismoto team.

Nikko frowned. "That is a long time. My colleagues and I were hoping that –"

"Keep your shirt on, Nikko. The reason it's being spread over five years is explained in detail. We want to minimise capital outlay by building the first golf course, the condominiums and the hotel. The hotel should, on expected use, pay for itself in five years. We'll sell the condominiums off the plan and as they're built they'll pay for that part of the project and the golf course." Frowning, he took a breath. "Later, we'll borrow capital for the second golf course and the third stage will, when it's sold off, pay for stages two and three. I think five years for all stages is a reasonable time frame."

"Yes, admirable, CJ." Nikko paused, his gaze still focused on Francey. "My colleagues and I believe the demand for such condominiums will be great in my country. We believe we could sell all the condominiums, stages one and three, at the one time which would repay the loan and pay for the golf course and the hotel. Then we could borrow to build the second golf course and use profits from the hotel to pay off the second loan. All this could take place, we believe, over a period of three and a half years, four at the most, rather than five."

"Mr Yakismoto, if I may," Francey regained control. "One reason why it's proposed to take the five years is that this is a project of considerable size. Labour, freight and supply of building materials, council permission and the weather itself – for several months of the year Cooktown is unseasonably hot and there's the monsoon period as well – will slow the project's progress."

"I understand, Miss Spinetti, but surely all this is debatable, a matter of how we prioritise the building of the complex?" Nikko queried.

"Of course, of course," CJ replied with some impatience. Nikko either had some bee in his bonnet or he was trying to take control of the project for himself. Well, he'd see about that. "That's what we're here for, to iron out any last minute problems or glitches. Les, what do you think about Nikko's shorter time frame?"

The discussion between what was optimally desirable and not possible due to the siting of the complex raged on for the next two hours, with Francey doing on the spot rough calculations on re-costing the project the way Nikko's consortium had suggested. She could tell from CJ's tight expression that he wanted things his way, though Nikko's plan had merits. Unfortunately Nikko hadn't taken into consideration the difficulties of the site and the weather. She could also see that both men were rapidly reaching an impasse and by lunchtime negotiations had all but ground to a halt.

Over lunch, CJ growled to Francey and Les, "Well, what do you two think? Can we get it all together within a three and a half year time frame?"

"No way," Les shook his head.

"If you can compromise to four, it might be possible, and in a way Nikko's plan has several good points. The return on the investment would come in earlier, which would lessen our borrowing costs," Francey offered.

"Damn Nikko, always wanting things his way. There are other backers I could approach ..." CJ muttered, thoroughly disgruntled.

"Why?" Francey queried, "You've put the hard yards in with Yakismoto. I don't think he's being unreasonable. Let me have twenty minutes before we reconvene to do some more calculations."

"Okay, go for it, girl."

*

Francey let the hot shower wash the travails of the day away. It had taken until 6 p.m. that day to finalise the building schedule, get the contract signed and confirm borrowing details and an approximate starting date, depending on council approval and environmental studies being satisfactorily completed.

She smiled as she towelled herself dry. Goodness knows what the outcome might have been had she not been there. CJ had been his usual hard-headed self, wanting his own way, initially unwilling to see the positive side of Yakismoto's plan. Her and Les' commonsense approach and preparedness to compromise had saved the day, and possibly the project.

She had watched CJ's rage bubble and boil within as Nikko tried to exert control over the proceedings, which made her wonder why CJ bothered to do business with someone who obviously irked him. She knew her employer had enough business clout to attract any number of investors to such a project. In the end she guessed CJ chose Nikko despite the negatives between them because of his extraordinary financial *and* political connections in Japan.

Nikko had wanted her to be the project manager but thankfully CJ had stood firm on that and had said no. The thought of being based in Cooktown for several years, or having to commute regularly backwards and forwards from there to Mt Isa, and being away from Steve, had not been a pleasant one.

Once again she grinned, this time with self-satisfaction. Her baptism of fire, her first dealing in the exalted business world to which CJ belonged had gone exceedingly well. She was pleased with herself and she sensed that CJ and Les had been pleased with the way she had operated.

Opening the wardrobe door she peered at the contents. Tonight CJ said they'd celebrate a successful deal so, which outfit would she choose?

Billy Wontow casually mounted the steps of the Mt Isa police station and went up to the front desk.

"Hello, Neil," he said to the station's senior constable. "Is Steve in?"

Neil Smith, a nuggetty, ruddy-faced man of about thirty with a thatch of ginger hair and a face covered in freckles shook his head negatively. "You've missed him by half an hour, he'll be away for the rest of the day. Is it important, Billy? Can I help you?"

Billy shrugged. "Maybe." He lifted what had been trailing in his right hand, carefully placing a long thin item wrapped in a sugar bag on the counter top. "When I was doin' a bit of a clean up I found this behind a box in the tack room attached to Murrundi's stables. It could have somethin' to do with Richard Ambrose's death. Might be what Steve's been lookin' for."

"A rifle?"

"Yep. A Stinger. Dunno how it came to be in the tack room or who it belongs to though. All the rifles are kept locked up at the homestead, except for one Mike Hunter has, and he keeps his under lock and key. I reckoned Steve might wanta take a look at this."

"Did you handle it, Billy?"

Billy looked askance at the senior constable. "'Course not, I know about fingerprints and all that stuff. Soon as I recognised it I bundled it into the sack and brought it straight in. Didn't even tell CJ about it."

"Good man."

"Reckon I'll leave it and you can pass it on to Steve."

Neil Smith nodded approvingly. "Will do, Billy. As soon as Steve returns."

With an upward flick of his finger, denoting the conversation was over, the laconic Billy left the station.

"Comfortable?" Les asked.

"Mmm, and exhausted," Francey replied as she sank deeper into the first class seat on Qantas flight Q212 returning to Sydney.

"It has been hectic," Les agreed. "Trips with CJ are like that. The man doesn't know the meaning of the phrase, 'take the time to smell the roses'."

Francey chuckled. "You're right."

"You handled it all well, you know, considering …"

Francey managed to disguise the yawn with her hand. "You think so? I'm glad." She pressed a button and the seat reclined. "Wake me when we reach Sydney, but not before, for anything. Okay?"

"Okay." Les' head turned to look down at her. With her eyes closed he had the luxury of being able to study her without impunity. Miss Francey Spinetti, daughter of Italian migrants had been a hit wherever they'd gone. In Singapore her commonsense and CJ's respect for her intellect had helped secure the Cooktown project without a toe-to-toe fight with Nikko Yakismoto and it had been named the Jasmine International Condominium and Hotel Resort. Then, in Hong Kong, she had sat for hours and absorbed details of CJ's investments there and accompanied them on all the inspection tours.

In London, CJ had given her some time off to explore the sights and architectural delights. She'd been off at first light till late in the afternoon, independently finding her way around one of the largest cities in the world, absorbing it all and coming back to the hotel with enthusiastic accounts of where she'd been and what she'd seen. They'd gone out every night for dinner and to a show or nightclub. She'd been delighted by the opera *La Boheme* at Covent Garden and the live theatre show of Sir Andrew Lloyd Webber's *Sunset Boulevarde* – for which he'd managed to get seats at an obscene price. And she had of course loved the several cocktail parties they'd attended at the residences of businesspeople who lived in Belgrave Square and Knightsbridge.

He had enjoyed watching her. She was like a big kid, her enthusiasm for new experiences knew no bounds and he soon realised that CJ was getting as big a kick out of her enjoying herself as she was. Not for the first time Les wondered whether the old man was falling in love with the lovely Australian-Italian woman. He knew CJ had been angered by Yakismoto's attentions towards Francey and since they'd departed Sydney he had pondered the question about CJ's depth of interest in her without securing a satisfactory answer.

Then there'd been more rounds of business in London, and Francey had had to go and buy warm clothes to survive the cool English spring. After a week at the Ritz they'd gone to visit CJ's friends, Freddie and Marcia Beauvois, The Earl and Countess of Rankilawr, who had a rambling but well-preserved manor house in Kent.

For him that had been the most enjoyable time. For a while he had had Francey all to himself. They'd explored hedged narrow country lanes together, lunched in quiet, picturesque pubs, rode across the English countryside on horses from the earl's stables and visited the odd castle or two. He recalled how she'd been taken with the old moated keep of Bodiam Castle. And later, her blue-green eyes had sparkled with pleasure when they'd had afternoon tea with the Duke and Duchess of Norfolk who at the time happened to be in residence at Arundel Castle.

Les continued to study her features in repose. The mass of curls, the lips, full and kissable, the steady rise and fall of her chest as she slept convinced him that she was the woman he wanted to spend the rest of his life with. He believed that he could make her happy, given the chance ... if Parrish wasn't around. His eyes narrowed as he thought of the policeman, his *competition*. Was there a way to take him out of the picture? In business he was good at removing obstacles which stood in the way of success – CJ had taught him well. Removing Parrish, the obstacle, from the scene could be regarded in much the same way. He knew the Queensland police minister personally so maybe he could arrange a transfer for Parrish and, once out of sight and out of mind, he'd have a better chance of wooing this interesting, independent woman beside him.

He relaxed back in the seat and closed his eyes. Not to sleep, but to think and to scheme ...

CHAPTER EIGHTEEN

C J watched the expressions as Shellie, Doctor Barry
Ryan, Natalie and her friend Trish, the Dupres and
Mt Isa's mayor, Darren Turk, were given the grand tour of
the now finished mini conference centre by Francey and
Les.

He especially noted his sister's reaction, not to the
building, but to her doctor friend. Shellie had always
shown her feelings – as opposed to him being the other
way inclined – and it was obvious that she was in love
with the quietly spoken medical man. He could foresee no
problems with that because Barry clearly reciprocated, and
he silently agreed that she deserved some happiness in her
life. At fifty-five, it was overdue, and remarkably, her new
found happiness had effected a turnaround in her drinking
habits; she didn't need the crutch of alcohol any more and
he was glad.

As Natalie moved about the mini conference centre,
mentally noting the attention to detail, the quality of
workmanship and the innovative yet functional design, her
hatred for Francey rose to new heights. Like it or not
Francey was good, better than good, a very talented

architect. She had never been a reverent person but over the last few months she had prayed in her own peculiar way that CJ's pet would fall flat on her face on this project and in turn CJ would become disenchanted and send her packing. That hadn't happened and didn't show signs of happening. The woman was slowly but surely worming her way deep into CJ's business structure and his trust. Suddenly, her resolve hardened. She had to get rid of her. Permanently.

"Francey, I like the way you've done this garden," Trish commented innocently, unaware of her lover's ire. Perhaps she could organise some type of article in an architectural magazine. She would ask CJ before the day was out.

Francey studied the courtyard garden of tranquillity which stood as a centrepiece inside the complex. Subtle landscaping, a Japanese style trickling pool and stream, weathered stones and a variety of ferns and rainforest plants gave an aura of lushness to the space. "Thanks, I thought it would enhance the guest's enjoyment of the centre."

"I'm sure it will, but ..." Natalie quipped as she threaded an arm through Trish's. "I don't know how CJ's going to make effective use of this place." Grudgingly she complimented the person she saw as her rival for CJ's attention. "It looks great and I bet it cost a bundle, but from my point of view return on those dollars could be relatively slim."

"I disagree," Les, who'd overheard Natalie's criticisms, put in smoothly. "This complex will show investors we mean business, that we have what it takes to pull off any type of commercial development anywhere in Australia or, for that matter anywhere in the world. Also, after the formal opening ceremony next week, which will be conducted by the state's attorney-general, we've scheduled our first conference for the following week and will have another two over the next two months." He looked at the mayor. "Mr Turk, Darren, is keen to use the place for select business investment seminars directed at Mt Isa, and will pay a handsome rental fee for the privilege. Right, mayor?"

Darren Turk agreed with a nod of his head. "My only regret is that the centre wasn't built in the township, but I understand and commend CJ's reasons for it becoming a part of Murrundi."

Pouting, Natalie turned away. Clearly everyone was against her. Hadn't it always been so? From a young age she'd sensed that people didn't like her or find her attractive. But she had got even as she'd grown up. She smiled a little smile to herself, remembering. Everyone who'd hurt or slighted her had eventually paid the price. But, the cliché came to her, she would have the last laugh, by God she would.

Quietly observing the exchange, CJ was hard-pressed controling the urge to smile as he saw his stepdaughter's petulance. Her behaviour made him frown. What was the matter with Natalie? She had been irritable and irrational for months now. Each time she returned to Murrundi she had a chip on her shoulder. Why? Her moodiness wasn't caused by business worries. They shared the same accountancy firm and he had it on good authority that business-wise, Natalie was doing very well indeed. So what continued to upset her? She had been a difficult teenager, having temper tantrums that only Brenda could control but by now she should have outgrown them.

The next instant he dismissed Natalie's grumpy behaviour from his mind. Regrettably, but he couldn't help it, he had little fondness for his stepdaughter. Something about her, whether it be her manner or her personality, had precluded real affection ever growing. "Let's adjourn to the homestead," he bellowed paternally, "Alison has prepared a superb lunch for us all."

Steve Parrish read the Brisbane's ballistics department's report on the Stinger rifle Billy Wontow had left at the station. He growled deep in his throat with frustration and then threw the single sheet of paper back onto the desk. The rifle didn't match the bullet he'd found near the stampede site. He'd hoped, been so sure ... The trail of finding Richard Ambrose's killer had been stone-dead for a good month or two and his hopes had risen when the rifle was handed in. He stroked his jaw reflectively as he rethought what he'd been doing. Every avenue of investigation, the minutest detail, had been checked and rechecked. Nothing. His only human lead, Paul Andronicus, had disappeared into thin air and so it seemed, had the offending rifle.

He shrugged his shoulders as he put the report inside the Ambrose file. This didn't mean he was giving up but he'd run out of places and people to talk to. He studied the rifle resting atop his in-tray. It should be returned to Murrundi. A slow smile creased his serious features. At least while he was there he'd have the opportunity to see Francey for a few minutes. Old CJ sure kept her busy these days and with him working shifts, they had precious little time together.

Francey looked over the crowd of people standing in the reception foyer of the mini conference centre partaking of hors d'oeuvres, pâté and top-dollar French champagne. Her gaze caught CJ's. He winked and gave her a triumphant smile. Then he raised his glass to her in a silent salute.

She smiled back. Their first conference had been a resounding success. The delegates – business investors who'd come from Indonesia, Hawaii and Hong Kong – had been impressed with their three day stay at Murrundi. They had listened to a range of projects on offer: the development of a cattle station on the Gulf for the Middle East trade and two resort projects. One was near Katoomba in the Blue Mountains of NSW, the other was planned for the outskirts of Byron Bay, also in NSW. The next step was to take the proposals back to their relevant home offices and discuss them further with a view to investing, initially, in the resort project near Byron Bay.

Always honest with herself, she admitted that her head was in something of a whirl at just how successful the three days had been. The centre's accommodation and facilities had been a real hit. Lisa Dupre had done a marvellous job organising the catering and staff and she was sure each investment company delegate would take a very positive message back home.

Tomorrow afternoon she was booked on a commercial flight to Sydney to check up on how CJ's Kirribilli mansion was shaping up. Council approval of her building plan had been received so now Brett could organise the demolition of the original building prior to a concrete slab for the new house being poured. Her pulse rose a notch or two at the thought of seeing Steve. Just a lightning visit before she caught her flight. In Sydney there'd be time to catch up with her parents and friends – as CJ had promised her in his job offer. Hectic was how she described her life at the moment. CJ was involved in so many things. He even wanted her to learn to fly the Learjet so she could get to and from places quicker but she had vetoed that plan for the present. It would be fun to learn how to fly but only when she had the time for flying lessons!

Les sidled up to her and said quietly, "The delegates are in raptures about this place. They've never had such a good time, privately as well as business-wise, and they've enjoyed seeing the ins and outs of a working cattle station."

Francey nodded. "That's the message I'm getting too."

"You're going to be in Sydney for a week, aren't you?"

"That's the plan. Why?"

"Oh, no reason other than I'll be away for a couple of days myself. Mike Hunter's doing a muster of the north-west plateau and I thought I'd give him a hand using the helicopter to herd the strays."

A glow of admiration warmed CJ's insides as he watched Les talking animatedly with Francey. She had come up trumps, this little architect, *his* little architect. He sure knew how to pick a winner. He took a sip from his champagne flute then looked towards Francey again.

Without warning his vision blurred, then doubled. He gave his head a slight shake and he could see properly again. He quickly shrugged the sensation off. Must be tired, all this pushing himself to reel in the deals and the dollars. Jesus Christ, it wasn't as if he needed the money, he had enough to last several lifetimes. Sometimes he wondered why he had this drive inside him. Why didn't he start taking things easy, let Les run the show? His protégé was itching to. And now, between Les and Francey he knew they'd do an excellent job running his business interests.

But he couldn't settle back and relax, retire, and he knew it. He couldn't stop because doing deals and making money was as natural to him as breathing.

Darren Turk patted CJ on the shoulder. "Congratulations, old son. Another success."

"Thanks, Darren." He tried to ignore the growing, curious numbness that had crept into the fingers of his right hand but his glass slipped out of his grasp and smashed on the marble tiled floor. Within seconds a waiter was at his side sweeping up the shards. CJ tried to flex his fingers but could feel nothing. He hastily hid his hand in his trouser pocket.

"That's a waste of good champagne," Darren joked. "I'll get you another."

"No, I've had enough," CJ replied and forced a grin to hide the fact that suddenly he didn't feel great. "Obviously."

"I'd like to have a word with you about that art museum, CJ. The Chamber of Commerce wants to put on an arts and cultural festival next year, between May and July. If the museum was finished … it'd be a great drawcard."

CJ stared at the mayor. "I'll say this for you, Turk, when you get onto a pet project you're like a dog with a bone." He thought for a moment. "I believe Francey has some more work to do on the plans but I can't see any reason why it shouldn't be up and running by the time of your festival."

Darren Turk beamed. "That is good news."

CJ barely heard the man's reply, he was trying desperately to get some feeling back into the useless hand resting inside his pocket. He wanted to flex the fingers but the message wasn't getting from his brain to the extremities. Hell, what was the matter with him? He had to get away from Turk, away from everyone who might cotton onto this new weakness. "Yes, well. Excuse me, I'd better do some mingling."

*

Mike Hunter finished giving his instructions to the five station hands who were going to take part in the muster starting at first light tomorrow. He then went up to CJ and Les, who'd been sitting in on the meeting, to make sure everything was satisfactory.

"You'd better keep an eye on that new man, Finch," Les said to Mike, "I reckon he hasn't got as much experience as he says he has."

"I'm aware of it," Mike agreed, twirling his Swiss army knife between his fingers as he spoke. "The muster and the boys will soon sort him out."

"Wish I was going myself." There was a note of wistfulness in CJ's voice. "Been years since I've done a bit of hard riding."

Les chuckled as he glanced at CJ. Wearing grey moleskins and a green and yellow striped shirt, at fifty-nine he looked fit enough to go mustering, that was for sure. "You've done your share over the years. Why don't you come in the 'copter? Francey's away but Lisa can take care of the business for a couple of days."

CJ didn't need to take long to think about that suggestion. "No thanks, helicopters and me don't mix. Can't stand all that swaying and dipping about. Enough to make a man chunder all over the place."

The two men grinned at each other, neither believing the enigmatic CJ capable of such ordinary, lowly things such as being physically ill. CJ had the reputation of being as strong as a mallee bull.

"We're planning on bringing four hundred head in," Mike said, "then we'll drive them to the abattoir at Cloncurry. Should be away a week, maybe ten days, if everything goes to plan."

CJ studied the foreman. "Make sure that it does. Timing's important. North West Abattoirs are waiting on those animals, they've orders to fill."

They talked for a few more minutes about the details then Les and CJ left the bunkhouse to return to the homestead. Outside, dusk was falling and a burnt sienna haziness lay over the stockyards and the outer buildings.

"Did Francey get a chance to tell you before she left?" Les said. "The Cooktown project's been approved by the EIS."

The pain hit him without warning. It started at the back of his head and was breathtakingly sharp. Cruel. CJ gasped from the force of it and came to a dead stop, his hands scrabbling to his head as if touching it would somehow contain the pain. Then in the next instant his left leg gave way under him. He crumpled forward onto the red earth and rolled onto his side.

"Gron ... web'll ..." CJ tried to speak but what came out was garbled and unintelligible.

"Jesus, CJ, what's the matter?" Les dropped to his knees beside him, trying to turn him onto his back. He saw the fingers of CJ's hand gripping his head, as if trying to protect something. He saw too that he'd turned very pale and was trying to talk but couldn't. Beads of sweat glistened on his forehead. "I'll get help."

Les rushed back to the bunkhouse and yelled at the top of his lungs. "Something's happened to CJ. Mike, come with me. Lucky, ring the house, tell Shellie to get onto the doctor. You two," he pointed to two men playing cards, "grab a couple of blankets for a stretcher. Come on, hurry it up. Now!"

"What do you reckon it is?" Mike asked as they rolled CJ onto the blanket.

"God, I don't know. Could be a fit. No, maybe a stroke." He gestured to the men to grab an end of the blanket. "Come on now, lift."

The pain edged out all awareness of his surroundings and of what Les and the men were doing for him. He didn't react when they placed him on his bed, didn't even notice they'd done so. His eyes were shut tight, trying to screw out such agony as he'd never before experienced. Tears formed at the corners of his eyelids and squeezed out and down his cheeks. He prayed for oblivion to release him from his suffering. His prayers went unanswered. He became aware of a woman's voice. Brenda? No. Stupid. A guttural moan escaped from his throat. The pain was stopping him from thinking straight. Brenda was dead. *Shellie.*

"He's had bad headaches before, but never like this," Shellie told the two men.

"How long before Barry gets here?"

Shellie glanced at her watch. "Ten minutes. He dropped everything as soon as I called." She looked down at CJ. His face had turned whitish-grey, his clothes were soaked with sweat but his hands had stopped clutching his head. They now lay limply at his sides, as if holding them up took too much effort. He moaned again, like a wounded animal and then his body went limp.

"Jesus," Mike whispered, "he's unconsious."

"Yes, but his breathing's okay. Let's try to make him more comfortable," Les suggested.

The two men stripped CJ down to his underwear and gently rolled him under the bed covers. They had just finished their task when Doctor Ryan arrived.

Shellie shooed the other men out and watched from her position at the foot of the bed while Barry gave CJ a thorough examination. It was like old times, almost, watching the man she loved work on a patient but this time the meaning was especially important for her because the patient was her brother, her only close living relative.

As Barry removed his stethoscope and put it into his black bag, she tried to keep her voice calm. "Is he going to be all right? What's the matter with him?"

Barry looked at her, his eyes locking with hers. "I wish I could give you a clear-cut answer, Shellie. I need to ask CJ certain questions regarding the symptoms and until he regains consciousness I can't do that."

"He could be unconscious for hours."

"I know, but I don't think he will be."

"All right. I'll make some coffee and we'll wait together."

His smile was tinged with gratitude and compassion. "That's a grand idea. I'll ring my surgery," he took out his mobile phone, "and ask them to get Doctor Wilson to fill in for me."

Pasty-faced, CJ sat up in bed with three pillows under and around him to keep him upright. The nauseous feeling was abating and at least he hadn't been sick like before. Some of the feeling had come back into his hand though it still felt incredibly weak. It was time for serious questions and he'd never shirked a tough one in his life.

"You're the doctor, what's the problem?"

"Well," Barry spoke slowly, consideringly, "I think you realise it's more serious than just bad headaches. You need to have some tests done to pinpoint the medical problem. A CAT scan to identify where and what the difficulty is and an MRI, a slightly different scan which we use to define whether the problem's benign or malignant."

CJ's gaze narrowed. "You know what it is, don't you?"

"I've my suspicions, but it wouldn't be professional of me to offer a diagnosis without the results of those tests."

CJ snorted and thumped the bed cover with his fist, "Jesus, Barry, you sound like a politician. Can't you give me a straight answer, mate?"

Barry shook his head. "What I can do, and what I've already organised while you were unconscious, is to have those tests done at the earliest possible time. Tomorrow, in Brisbane, if you're up to it."

CJ blinked then looked at him hard and long. "That serious, hey?"

The doctor's expression was sober. "I think so."

CHAPTER NINETEEN

In the specialist rooms of neurosurgeon Doctor Jack English, Doctor Barry Ryan and English studied the test results on the X-ray illuminator.

"A classic textbook case," Jack English said as he studied the foreign mass, a mass that shouldn't rightly be there, but was and showed a light-grey on the scan. The earlier EEG had also confirmed its presence. "Glioblastoma, one of the most aggressive types of brain tumours."

Barry took off his glasses to pinch the bridge of his nose before he spoke and when he did his tone was thick with emotion. "Yes, I'm afraid so." Kept to himself though was his compassion for the patient and an even deeper feeling for the woman he loved. She would be devastated by this news.

"Look how it's growing. Could operate to slow its growth but it wouldn't reduce it for long, and it's in a delicate position. The operation might kill the patient rather than the growth."

"What about radiotherapy?"

"Purely palliative. Might give the patient more time, if he wants it."

Jack English looked at his colleague, they'd been friends since medical school. "Hmmm. What are you going to tell him?"

Barry shook his head, the expression in his eyes sad. "CJ isn't the kind of man you fob off with half-truths. He deserves to know, no doubt he'll need time to make," he paused, thinking for a moment of the times Shellie had tried to explain her brother's vast financial empire, "arrangements."

Jack nodded. "Poor bastard."

CJ's legs were rubbery, his stomach was churning and he noticed that his fingers shook as he used the security card to let himself into the luxurious suite of the Hilton Hotel.

He had insisted on going to the specialist by himself, gruffly telling Les he didn't need to be mollycoddled. In hindsight that hadn't been smart. Shock was beginning to set in ... He moved to the hospitality bar and poured a whisky, a generous one. He downed it in two gulps. Without waiting for the alcohol to take effect, he poured another and took it with him and literally fell into a chair. As he settled he gulped down half the glass' contents and only then did he begin to relax as the smooth Johnny Walker began to warm his insides.

Suddenly memories of past close encounters with near death situations overwhelmed him. He'd looked death once or twice in the face before and survived against the odds, but this! His hand rubbed his skull where Barry had said the tumour was growing, putting pressure on areas that affected his eyesight and his motor skills. Eventually it would stop him from functioning all together.

Just what had Barry said to him? He was more than a little confused. The two doctors had talked a lot, given him details, options. What he could expect by way of symptoms, about radiotherapy, about how much time he probably had left. Christ. He began to sweat. He touched his arm, the skin was cold and clammy. Months, not years!

Anger welled inside him and he gripped the glass so hard he cracked it. He let it fall to the floor, uncaring of the mess. *Months*. Maybe a year if he was lucky. Shit. Lucky! Doctors sure had a funny way of phrasing things. He thought of Francey, seeing in his mind's eye her slender figure and her lovely features. A wave of intense pain gripped his heart. Why now? And then a gurgling kind of a chuckle rumbled through his chest. A stillness came over him as, with a sense of fatalism he didn't know he was capable of, he mentally and emotionally accepted the doctors' diagnosis. After all, he'd always been a realist. But God, what bloody rotten timing.

He rested his head back on the chair and closed his eyes. Tiredness sapped the energy from every muscle and he sagged into the thickly padded chair, not resisting the weakness. The news sapped the strength from him but even as he sat in repose he knew that he couldn't give in to the feeling. There was too much to do in too short a time. Things to organise. What to tell people? A frown creased his forehead. The truth. Yes. Les would have to be told, he'd need him to take care of the many things which had to be set in order. The others, of course they had to know too, but at a time of his choosing. No point in worrying those close to him unduly.

And he had to decide whether he agreed to an operation and radiotherapy. English had said a clinic in Switzerland was the best and the operation would give him some extra time, but at what cost? Both men said the treatment would make him ill and listless. They'd been honest, telling him that there was no cure and at best it might extend his life by a few months, if he was lucky. That word again. He grimaced. Lucky!

His uneasy gaze scanned the suite. He scarcely registered the French provincial reproduction furniture or the view from the top floor of the city and the Brisbane River.

How often had he said the words during his life? He'd been a lucky bastard. He had won that mine and found opals in Coober, and he'd been lucky to have had Brenda for a wife, she'd been good for him. Lucky too to have made the right decisions business-wise and amassed a fortune. Then Francey had come along, and he'd been lucky there too ... But now his luck was running out and his millions weren't one bit of help. How ironic, the thought came out of nowhere, he had all the money in the world to get the best doctors and medical treatment but it was too late to do any good.

On reflection he had a few regrets about his life but then who didn't. Mary. Yes, he'd been very wrong to let the affair with Mary end as it had. Selfish bastard. Yes, he admitted it. He'd only cared about himself and how he could set himself up on the road to success. He should never have let her get into a difficult situation – pregnant and without support. Especially since Richard's death he'd thought of her a good deal, and had suffered many sleepless guilt-ridden nights wishing that he'd handled things differently.

He also regretted some of his business deals. How often had he been too determined to get his own way no matter who got hurt? Francey, with her principles and high morals had shown him an alternative way to do business in the short time she'd been at Murrundi. What was it he'd thought about her when they'd first met? That she had too many scruples to be a successful businesswoman. He'd been wrong. Week after week she was proving that she could be successful without resorting to underhanded methods. He admired that in her.

Uninvited a blurriness formed in his eyes and tears began to run down his cheeks. Tears of regret, frustration and the luxury of something he had never allowed himself before, a characteristic he derided in others – self-pity.

The door clicked as the knob turned and he straightened up in the chair and rubbed the wetness off his cheeks. He recognised the rustle of parcels being laid on the buffet and Les' lithe stride as he approached.

"You're back," Les said superfluously. "How did it go?"

As he came face to face with the man who'd been his boss for almost twenty years, one look gave him the answer. CJ's pasty face and the slight tremor of his hand as he brushed his forehead telegraphed the fact that the situation wasn't good.

"You'd better pour yourself a stiff one," CJ said, "and get me another."

Les poured the required drinks, handed CJ his and sat opposite him. In a tentative tone he asked, "So?"

Ten minutes later Les' lean features had taken on the same ashen hue as CJ's. It couldn't be true. Not "the man with the golden touch". CJ Ambrose was, had always been indestructible. A tumour. Terminal. His brain couldn't, it refused to accept the truth. He had fashioned his ideas, his business skills, his attitude to life on that of the man he respected above all others. He'd never thought about it much but he did now. He loved him like the father he'd never really known. Loved his gruffness, his tough attitude to business and his sense of fair play, unless he was closing a business deal, when all that mattered was to win. He tried to imagine a world without CJ. He couldn't.

"You'll get a second opinion?"

CJ nodded. "Of course. Barry told me to and I've more appointments tomorrow but, really, they showed me the scan's results. There's this mass in my brain and it's almost the size of a small egg. It's been suggested that they take out what they can then hit me with a course of radiotherapy. Barry says it's not a cure, that the damned thing will grow again but it should at least buy me some time. They reckon up to thirty-seven months if I'm lucky." He looked at Les. "I don't expect another specialist to tell me any different to what I've learned today, however I'll go through the motions."

"I'll come with you."

"No, there are things I want you to do."

"But CJ, I want to ..."

CJ smiled at the younger man, instinctively knowing that he was churned up about the development in his health. "I know, and I appreciate the thought but, lots of things have to be done, Les, before ..." he paused. "I need you to help me do them."

"What sort of things?"

"I've got to get down to Sydney, see how everything is progressing on the house that O'Connor fella's building for me. And I have to meet a couple of people. I want you to set up the meeting for me. It's a delicate one and will need your diplomatic skills. Then, when we come back, I've got to put all the businesses in order. That's going to take a while."

Les's frown was one of curiosity. "Who do you need to meet in Sydney?"

CJ smiled and held his glass out to him. "Here, get me another drink and I'll tell you a story, a true story. You're going to be amazed at its conclusion."

Two hours later Les Westcott lay fully clothed on his bed in the hotel suite staring up at the ceiling. He'd just put a very drunk CJ to bed – he was none too sober himself – but he had retained enough presence of mind to be able to go over, once again, the amazing truths CJ had just told him. Fate. It was bloody amazing how things worked out.

In the semi-darkness of the room he allowed himself a predatory, satisfied smile. The proverbial shit would hit the fan when Natalie learnt what was on CJ's mind. Serve the bitch right. After what she'd done to him over the last few years, led him on then laughed in his face ... she deserved all she was, or wasn't, going to get ...

Brett, Meredith and young Mitchell O'Connor stood beside Francey admiring the view across the harbour to the city from the Kirribilli building site.

On one side of the wedge-shaped block stood several neat piles of bricks, left over from the demolition of the previous home. A bulldozer had levelled the block last week and tip trucks had taken away the excess soil. Already the proposed swimming pool had been excavated and its boundaries pegged out. The mammothly proportioned concrete slab for the main structure, with plumbing and electrical outlets sticking out garishly, had been poured yesterday and would take a month to cure – if the good weather held.

"The view's magnificent," Meredith said in between trying to stop Mitchell from scrambling down to the ground to explore the earth and a few puddles left by last night's shower.

"Nothing but the best for our Queensland multimillionaire," Brett quipped. "Meredith, you should see the plans, talk about a mansion. It'll rival some of the estates around Vaucluse and Elizabeth Bay."

Meredith winked at her friend, "Perhaps you'll win another award for the design."

"Don't bank on it. Back then I had Aden pushing my talents for his own advantage." She had eventually come to the conclusion that Aden Nicholson must have lobbied hard to put her in contention for the national award. Still, she thought with a secret smile, look where it had got her! "I think I've got past the stage of needing that kind of acclamation."

Meredith nodded her agreement. "Your life has changed dramatically since you went up to Queensland."

Francey noted the glint in Meredith's eyes and knew she wasn't talking solely about her business life. Steve Parrish had also been a dramatic change for her. There'd been a time when she had thought she would never be able to love again but Steve had changed all that, forever. Just thinking about him made her go all warm inside and wish he was here. For some reason, possibly a little vanity, she wanted him to see what she had accomplished. Perhaps he could fly down later, when the house was finished so she could give him the grand tour.

"I wonder why Mr Ambrose wanted to build here, at this particular time?" Meredith asked, her curiosity aroused.

"I'm not sure, maybe he's thinking of taking up some Sydney business ventures, or maybe he sees it as a good investment. I mean, one can't lose with this type of real estate."

Oddly, Francey wasn't privy to CJ's real reasons for wanting a house in Sydney particularly when he seemed happy enough at Murrundi. She believed he was going to begin an assault on the Sydney development market, that's why he wanted a possible base from which to work while in Sydney. Since she had learned about the diversity of his business portfolio and the schemes that took his fancy, he was capable of expanding anywhere. If so, that probably meant she'd be spending more time here which she knew would please her parents.

She had enjoyed the experience of hunting and securing suitable harbourside real estate and then designing a home to reflect his wealth but she'd made sure, right down to the indoor/outdoor swimming pool, the tennis court and the new jetty and boathouse, that the emphasis would be more on comfort than a "show" home which would take maximum advantage of the view. He'd given her *carte blanche* as to size and design, hardly bothering to glance at the finished plans before they'd been submitted to council. That he had that much faith in her ability certainly boosted her self-confidence a notch or two.

For fifteen minutes they tramped around the site. Francey took half a reel of film to show the site's progress to CJ, and shots of the views, from every possible angle. Meredith had given up on Mitchell, resigned that he would get filthy as he crawled towards the biggest pile of earth he could find.

"This job will put us solidly in the black," Meredith whispered to Francey. "Brett's been doing it tough for months, the economy's tight."

"I'm glad. Not that he got the job because of favouritism. His tender came in the lowest."

Meredith winked. "Brett made sure of that. Once this place is built it should act as a drawcard for more work for him."

"I'm sure it will, he's a fine builder. Have you organised a baby-sitter so you can join me and my parents for dinner tonight?" Francey asked Meredith.

"Sure have, especially as you're shouting."

"We can meet at the Hyatt for drinks then wander up to Spellson's about eight. I've managed to twist Mamma and Papà's arm. They're coming too."

"Good, I'm fond of your parents, especially your mum. I like the way she roasts your dad."

"Yes," Francey grinned. "She doesn't let him get away with too much, that's for sure."

Brett, who'd been wandering around the perimeter of the slab, checking the formwork, came over to them with his mobile in his hand. "Just got a call to do a quote at Mosman." He looked at Francey. "Could you give Meredith a lift back to Bronte? Would you mind?"

"Of course not. Off you go. Good luck, I hope you get it."

The expected third degree about her love life occurred as soon as Francey picked her parents up in the hire car and headed back towards the quay.

"You still seein' that fella Steve?" her father asked as he seated himself next to her.

"Yes, Papà. We see each other a lot, whenever work and his shifts permit." Which wasn't often enough as far as she was concerned.

"So? It's serious. When you gonna get engaged? He'd better do the right thing by you or, cop or no cop, or he'll have me to answer to."

"Oh, Carlo, let her be. Our Francey's a big girl now. A woman. She's in charge of her own life," Lucia defended, clucking her tongue in disgust.

"I'm her papà, I have a right to know what's happening in my daughter's life."

No you don't. Francey almost said the words out loud. "Look, Papà, I love Steve and I think he loves me. We're very happy together but neither of us are talking marriage yet. Maybe in a little while."

Carlo cleared his throat unhappily. "You know your cousin Daniella's having another baby?" he prodded, his tone implying that it was about time Francey did the same.

"That's nice. I'm happy for her." She sighed with relief as the parking lane of the Hyatt came into view. Meredith and Brett would be waiting for them in the bar. They'd act as a buffer to her father's dogmatic insistence in wanting to know the ins and outs of her love life. She realised then, for the first time, how she had unintentionally distanced herself from them. Her life was different now. She was different. The sad thing was, her father couldn't or didn't want to see it.

CHAPTER TWENTY

With eyes half-closed Francey watched the sun peep through breaks in the vertical shades hanging across Steve's bedroom window. The early morning temperature was cool enough to make her snuggle back under the doona, her body automatically seeking the warmth of the man who lay beside her. She smiled and gave a languorous cat-like stretch. At this very instant life was good. They had two whole days to spend together.

Life was good in other ways too. Career-wise, she felt fulfilled. She studied Steve's inert form and decided that she couldn't be happier emotionally as well. Her smile widened. Slowly, their relationship was deepening. They were becoming more committed to each other but as she'd told her father several times during phone conversations, neither were in a hurry to tie the knot. Both wanted to be sure of their feelings and when they were they'd quietly get engaged and take things from there. Poor Carlo, the perennial nagger, would have to be satisfied with that.

Steve yawned and opened his eyes, blinking several times as he became accustomed to the light. Twin pools, almost black, stared at her and then the edges around his eyes crinkled, fanning wrinkles diagonally out as he grinned sleepily. "Good morning."

"It is. And I think it's your turn to make breakfast," she said, reaching forward to kiss the tip of his nose.

His hands moved under the covers finding her body and pulling her to him. "You're a hard woman, Francey Spinetti," he complained as he rubbed his whiskery growth against her cheek while his hands were busy reacquainting themselves with her curves.

She giggled suddenly as their bodies touched. "And *you're* a hard man, Sergeant," she said provocatively as she arched against him. "I like that in a man."

"You are definitely becoming oversexed," he muttered in a half-growling tone as he began to kiss and caress her.

She laughed throatily. "And you object to that!"

Half an hour later, their bodies still entwined, Steve voiced something that had been in and out of his thoughts for a while. "I wonder what CJ thinks of our relationship? If he approves?"

"Why should he approve or disapprove?" Francey asked with a querulous stare. "What I do on my own time is my business, not his. Actually, we've talked about lots of things. My family about whom he seemed quite curious, and his family. World politics, the lot. But we *don't* discuss my personal life."

"Mmmm, I would have thought he'd show some interest. He's the kind of person who likes to keep a finger on the pulse, know what everyone in his sphere of power is doing."

"Les is the one who disapproves," Francey admitted. "I think he's got a yen for me himself." She moved back several centimetres to study him and her lips twitched. "He's intimated that he doesn't understand what I see in you."

A frown creased Steve's forehead. "Is that so! Westcott. I knew I disliked something about him. More than one thing, really. Can't put my finger on what it is but I sense a kind of passive-aggressive quality to him. Like he's a primed powder-keg just waiting for someone to light the fuse."

Francey laughed at Steve's fanciful description. "Oh, Les is all right, providing you know how to handle him. He's helped me a great deal."

Steve's left eyebrow lifted. "Has he now?"

She gave an impatient sigh. "In a business sense. Explained how CJ's empire works, the extent of it. Taught me some things about the cattle business too, though it'll take years to get a proper handle on all of it."

"Well, I guess it's in his interests to do so. You're lightening his workload, I imagine."

"True. Still, some people would get defensive. Les hasn't, he isn't possessive in that respect. He's happy, or at least he seems happy to share his knowledge with me."

"Probably CJ's told him to."

"Probably." She was silent for a moment and then she prefaced her words with a sigh. "There's something else too. CJ's got this bee in his bonnet about wanting to give me a party for my twenty-seventh birthday. I said I didn't want one, but he's insisting." Her eyebrows widened meaningfully, "I mean, really insisting. You know what he's like once he does that – the order's practically carved in stone."

"Maybe he's trying to make you feel more like one of the family. What's the harm in a smallish party?"

"He doesn't want a smallish party. He wants to invite just about all the neighbours in the region, businesspeople in the Isa and certain politicians who owe him a favour, I think. Maybe he has some secret agenda, I don't know. It's getting out of hand. The numbers are now up around one hundred. There seems to be no stopping him without having a rip roaring row."

"Methinks you've never walked away from a row if you thought one was warranted." He ducked quickly to ward off a playful blow to his jaw.

She gave him a warning glare. "Don't think I haven't thought of it but ..." her voice faded away and her blue-green eyes took on a far away softness tinged with noticeable anxiety.

"But what?"

She shrugged, unsure of how to articulate what she was thinking. "I don't know. He seems, he's ... I don't think he's well, though naturally he does his best to hide it. Of late he's been getting debilitating headaches. Ever since he went to Brisbane and had those tests Les told me about when I came back from Sydney. The tests revealed some kind of tumour, an operable one. Next week he's flying off to a clinic in Geneva in Switzerland, with Shellie, for specialist treatment. I don't like to make a fuss when he's not himself, especially when I know he's trying to be kind."

CJ, kind? He'd never heard the multimillionaire described as kind before. "I didn't know old CJ was sick," Steve's tone was thoughtful. "It's benign? That means it's treatable, doesn't it?"

"Of course it does," she retorted quickly.

He put his index finger under her chin and lifted her head up so she had to look him in the eyes. "Stop worrying." He smiled at her, a quizzical, boyish grin, as if he had just had a revelation. "You're pretty fond of the old guy, aren't you?"

"I guess I am." Her answer held a note of surprise in it.

"Well, I suggest you give in gracefully. Let him give you a party if he wants to, where's the harm in it?"

She pondered over that suggestion for several minutes and then sighed. "I guess you're right."

Feeling as if he'd won a small victory, he grinned and asked, "Now, what would you like for breakfast?"

Natalie's art gallery, situated in a renovated bond store on the bank of the Brisbane River, was a hive of activity. Under Hugh O'Leary's artistic direction teams of tradesmen were working on everything from new lighting displays to arranging bales of hay. Sheets of half rusted corrugated iron and old fence palings were also placed in such a way as to enhance the theme of the exhibition – "Country art from all over Australia".

The place looked a shambles, with crated paintings carefully stacked away from the activity. But Trish, now an old hand at seeing how Natalie's exhibitions came together, knew everything would be picture perfect for the six thirty opening by the premier.

She watched the general hullabaloo with a dispassionate eye as she waited for Natalie to arrive. Her Sydney flight had been delayed twenty minutes and she had a good idea what mood she'd be in by the time the taxi deposited her at the front door. Natalie's moods weren't getting any better, and she was becoming quite worried about her. There were times when she questioned why she stuck around, bearing the brunt of her bad temper. But ... she was genuinely fond of her, and she understood the source of her anger even if she didn't agree with it.

Francey, quite innocently she thought, was the cause of her lover's escalating moodiness. Natalie had mentally blown the "architect thing" out of all proportion and it was rare for a day to go by without her venting her spleen about Francey in some way or another. She knew about Natalie's attempt to frighten her off by leaving her out in the scrub. Also that she'd tried on more than one occasion to insinuate to her stepfather that the architect could be spying on his business interests for a competitor, to gain some advantage over him. Ridiculous, CJ had told her bluntly, but that hadn't put an end to Natalie's suspicions. She was paranoid about being short-changed of what she considered her rightful inheritance.

The bizarre thing was that Natalie had plenty of money of her own. Recently she had inherited a healthy trust fund left to her by her grandfather, Miles deWitt. Then there had been her mother's inheritance, half of Brenda deWitt-Ambrose's personal estate. That combined with the increasing success of her art galleries meant that Natalie hadn't a financial worry in the world.

No, it wasn't the money, Trish was sure of it. The problem was that Natalie considered CJ's fortune to be her birthright, the birthright Brenda deWitt-Ambrose had let CJ pry out of her control. That rankled Natalie and was probably the base cause of her lover's problem. And now that Richard was gone and she could be considered the sole heir, she wanted it all.

She saw Natalie walk up the front steps, stand at the entrance with her hands on her hips, yell a couple of orders at Hugh, then turn on her heel and head for her office. Stifling a sigh, Trish followed. Slowly.

"Hello, love. Have a good flight up?" Trish went up to Natalie and gave her a hug. She kissed her on the mouth and as her arms went around her she felt the tension emanating from every pore of Natalie's body. She was so uptight, one day she would snap.

Natalie absorbed the warmth of Trish's comforting softness, saw the affection in her eyes and began to relax. Her hand caressed Trish's cheek and then her fingers tangled in the brown curly hair. "I missed you. Next time I have to go to Sydney, you're coming with me." She watched Trish lick her lower lip, an unconscious gesture which always turned Natalie on. Her hands began to rove over her lover's body, seeking the curves, finding the little spots where Trish liked to be touched. "God, I've really missed you," her voice deepened, husky with need.

"Me too." Trish murmured as she traced the outline of Natalie's lips. Natalie caught the finger and drew it into her mouth sucking it in deeply, swirling her tongue around it. She stared deeply into Trish's hazel eyes and started to unbutton her blouse.

Trish's eyebrow rose. "Here?"

"I can't wait, I want you now …"

They were both half undressed, panting slightly with the urgency of their need, when a loud knock on the office door brought their mutual caressing to a stop.

"Go away!" Natalie shouted. She winked wickedly at Trish. "I'm busy."

"The Tom Roberts paintings have arrived, love," Hugh's unfazed voice was muffled by the thickness of the door. "We both have to check them for damage – it's a clause in the insurance contract, remember?"

"Shit!" Natalie didn't hide her displeasure. She looked down at Trish's bare breasts and repeated, softly this time, "*Shit.*" With difficulty she brought her raging passion and need for fulfilment under control. "We'll have to take a raincheck, darling. But don't run off, I want to talk to you about something important." She grinned mirthlessly. "It looks like talk is all we'll be getting to do today." She remembered Hugh at the door. "I'll be out in a minute."

An hour and a half later Natalie reappeared in the office doorway. "Things are getting hectic here, love. There's not much point in you hanging around."

"Okay, I've got some research to do on an article anyway."

"Before you take off, I want to run something by you," Natalie said. "Look upon it as a story idea, if you like."

Intrigued, Trish waited.

"I want you to go to Sydney to see if you can dig up some dirt on Francey Spinetti, the bitch."

Trish tried not to let her disappointment and her reluctance show. She'd been dreading this yet unconsciously expecting it sooner or later. "But why? I thought we'd agreed to adopt a wait and see attitude."

"There must be something in her past, something I can use to drive a wedge between her and CJ."

"What if there isn't?" Something deep within Trish rebelled at the thought of checking into Francey's past. She honestly liked and respected the woman and it didn't seem smart to try to crucify someone that CJ seemed to admire so much. But to say so to Natalie at this point in the conversation would start a full on rage.

"Use your imagination. Make something up. I don't know," Natalie said angrily. "Few people have led perfect lives, nuns and priests included. There's often something in their past they'd rather keep hidden. Dig deep, find it. Maybe her parents even. I don't care what it is, just find something I can use. CJ's flying off to Europe soon and when he comes back he's going to throw a big birthday party for her. If I could have it by then ..." Her eyes narrowed thoughtfully. "You don't sound very enthusiastic about the idea." Then the tone changed, became plaintive, almost childlike. "You promised you'd help me, remember?"

Trish felt trapped. Her conscience longed to say no but the appeal and the hint of desperation in Natalie's eyes made her want to agree, if only to keep the peace between them. Deep down she knew she was being manipulated by a master manipulator and she also knew that there was little she could do about it.

"All right. When do you want me to go?" Perhaps it would be good to get away from Natalie for a while ... and she'd always liked Sydney.

Natalie smiled. She'd won. Trish and her scruples could be such a nuisance sometimes. "The day after tomorrow. All expenses paid of course."

Having said what she wanted to say she turned and disappeared back into the gallery.

Trish shook her head, her shoulders drooping as she stared reflectively at Natalie's retreating figure.

CJ stood near the airport window watching several aircraft taxi towards the arrivals section. He didn't want to think about what lay ahead but he had to. Funny, on reflection he'd found that he wasn't afraid of the thought of surgery, the radiotherapy or even of dying. He'd thought he might be, but he wasn't. He'd lived on the land too long, knew the cycle of life: birth, growth, death. Sometimes surprises but no escapes. And, the thought came to him, with what the doctors said he could expect over the coming months dying would be a relief, a release from the pain.

Barry had explained about the radiotherapy and what it would do to him. Nausea, extreme tiredness, his hair would probably fall out. But if the treatment worked and shrank the tumour, then he'd gain the most precious commodity he could think of – time.

He saw Shellie coming towards him loaded up with magazines and a couple of books to read during the long flight to Geneva. He felt guilty because he hadn't told her the truth yet. No-one but Barry and Les knew. She'd be angry with him when he finally did. He had made the decision that the fewer people who knew for the present, the better – until he set in motion the plans he had to.

There was still so much he wanted to do but he knew he had to prioritise everything and concentrate on the most important things. This treatment should give him time. He grimaced with self-derision: time not money was now his most precious commodity.

The interrogation room of Cairns police station had a strange smell to it even though it was air-conditioned: cheap air deodoriser, cigarette smoke, stale coffee.

As he waited for the prisoner to be brought in, Steve Parrish thanked his tendency towards persistence. The luck had finally turned his way. His one lead for Richard Ambrose's suspected murder, Paul Andronicus, had been arrested for drink driving. The Mt Isa police station had been faxed and he'd grabbed a flight to Cairns the next day because the offender could only be held for twenty-four hours by law.

The door opened and a police constable led the prisoner in. Steve motioned Andronicus to sit at the table and as he did so the constable moved to sit on the chair near the door.

Steve double-checked the charge sheet. "Paul Andronicus?" His quarry looked the worse for wear. Still hungover with a five-o'clock shadow across his jawline, the swarthily built man dressed in dirty blue jeans, black T-shirt and elasticised boots looked him squarely in the eyes.

"Yeah. So?"

"I'm here to ask you a few questions. My name's Sergeant Steve Parrish from Mt Isa."

Andronicus straightened up in the chair. Suddenly alert, he eyed Steve with a modicum of respect. "I didn't do anything illegal in the Isa mate, someone's given you a bum steer."

"That so? We'll see. I'm going to ask you some questions. You are not obliged to say anything unless you wish to do so. But whatever you do say may later be used in evidence. Do you understand that?"

"Yes."

"Where have you been, Paul? I've been trying to find you for over seven months. You left the Isa in a bit of a rush, didn't you?"

"Yeah, I did. That's not a crime, is it?" Andronicus replied with a touch of bravado.

Steve allowed a grin to flash across his face. "Not yet. So, what have you been up to?"

"Nothing illegal. I'm a carpenter, mate, I go wherever there's work. I've been to Charters Towers and down to Townsville then up here to Cairns. Lots of projects going on here."

"You were in the Isa when Richard Ambrose died, weren't you?"

Andronicus' forehead screwed up in a frown. "Reckon I was. Bad luck for the bloke, that stampede. Lousy way to die."

Steve offered him a cigarette which he refused. The ploy was to try to be his buddy, get his confidence up a bit. "It was. The corpse was barely recognisable. Had to be identified by his dental records."

"Yeah …" Andronicus gave him a strange look. "Well, what's that got to do with me? I'm in the can here for drinking too much and having a car accident. What've you come all the way from the Isa to question me about? I paid all my bills, I swear I did."

"You and Penny Ormond were something of an item until Richard Ambrose started to take an interest in her. Is that correct?"

The eyes narrowed, the tone became defensive. "We might have been. So what?"

"I've spoken to several people back in the Isa. They say you were really cut up about Penny Ormond dumping you for Ambrose. That you threatened," he paused to take a black book out of his shirt's breast pocket, flip it open and read a direct quote, "'to teach Ambrose a lesson he'd never forget'. Several people at the Irish Club have given me sworn statements to the effect that you threatened Richard Ambrose's life."

"Now wait a minute." Andronicus held up both hands, palms forward. "How do you expect me to remember something I said almost a year ago? Even if I did say it I was probably pissed at the time. Jeez, what are you trying to pin on me?"

Steve reckoned it was time to get formal. "I feel it fair to warn you, Paul Andronicus, I have evidence that Richard Ambrose may have been murdered. I am reminding you that what you say here," he pointed to the video camera at the end of the room, "is being recorded and may be used in a court of law against you."

"Shit, mate," beads of sweat began to form on the carpenter's forehead. "I didn't touch Ambrose, I swear it."

"You'll have to do better than that, Paul. Unless you can give me an alibi which can be corroborated, you're the best suspect I've got."

"What? So CJ's put you up to this? The old bastard wants his pound of flesh. An eye for an eye stuff ... He lost his bloody son and heir so someone has to pay."

Steve shook his head. "This has nothing to do with Mr Ambrose. I'm a police officer carrying out an investigation into Richard Ambrose's death. I found evidence that shows the stampede may have been deliberately started. Someone wanted to hurt Richard Ambrose, maybe the intention was to give him a scare, but the scenario backfired and Richard was trampled to death. That makes his death manslaughter, or murder, depending on how the prosecutor views the evidence. On whether he thinks he can make murder stick. *Murder,* Paul, think about it."

"I didn't do it. Honest. It wasn't me. Give me a lie detector test or something, whatever it is you blokes do. I'm innocent, I swear it."

"We don't do lie detector tests, that's done in the USA."

Steve watched Paul Andronicus cover his face with his hands. All aggression was gone now and fear emanated from the suspect.

"So far all I can see is that you had a motive. Jealousy. If you didn't do it you need to come up with an alibi, old son. Where were you on the night the stampede took place?" He looked at his notebook again. "That was Thursday, 28 February, 1996."

"Jesus Christ, how the hell do I know where I was that long ago? I can't damned well remember what I did last week." Paul ran a hand through his unruly dark hair.

"Well, I'm going to give you some time to see if you can dig something out of your memories. Maybe it'll come to you. Otherwise you're coming back to the Isa with me for further questioning."

"Do you want a tea or coffee?" the young constable asked the now distraught Andronicus.

"What? Yeah. Yeah. Black coffee with two sugars. Thanks."

The two policemen left the room, leaving Paul Andronicus with his thoughts.

Outside the young constable asked Steve, "Do you think he did it?"

"Hard to tell. He's sweating like a guilty man, but I don't know." Steve paused for a moment's reflection. "It would be neat for me if he was. I could close the file. We'll give him half an hour, that's enough time for him to sweat."

"Right."

"How long have you been in the job?" Steve asked the young constable.

"Six weeks. Does it show?" The younger man grinned nervously at the more experienced policeman.

Steve smiled sympathetically. "Not much."

Steve let Paul Andronicus stew in the interrogation room for forty-five minutes before returning to him, by which time the guy's tan had faded markedly. He noticed that the offender's hands were trembling and that he laced them together so it was less obvious.

"Okay, you've had plenty of time to reflect. Care to make a statement?"

Andronicus nodded his head. "I didn't do it. I've been trying to think of where I might have been that night. It's bloody hard trying to remember that far back. Somehow, I think I was either at one of two places. Playing snooker or at the Burke and Wills Isa Resort in a back room playing cards."

"I'll need names so I can have your story verified." Steve's optimism plummeted. What if his story checked out? If Andronicus could corroborate his whereabouts that night?

"You see, it came back to me when I got to think about it. On Thursday nights in the Isa, if I wasn't on a date, I'd play snooker or cards. You can check with Remy Schneider on the snooker and, let me think. If it was cards I'd have been with Sam Bianchini, Jerry Duvall and Alby Watts. We had a regular foursome."

"You're sure?" Steve asked as he wrote the details down on a pad.

"As sure as I can be with my memory."

Steve looked at the constable. "Take him back to the cells while I check his alibi. It will take several hours."

"You see, Sergeant," Andronicus said as he went out, "I really didn't do it. I just hope you catch the bastard that did."

It took four hours for the Mt Isa police to track down those named by Andronicus. His alibi checked out.

Damn it, back to square one again. Steve's expression was bleak as he left the police station. He'd been fairly certain that Andronicus had been involved. He wandered along the park which bordered the shoreline. The tide was out and sepia-coloured mud flats stretched almost a hundred metres out to sea. He scarcely noticed them. His thoughts centred on the Ambrose investigation. Where could it go from here? He'd better come up with something. His boss, Inspector Reg Clarke, had made several dire mutterings that an officer with his experience should be working in Brisbane where his expertise could be put to better use.

Steve frowned as he walked along, kicking a stone into the mud as he went. Where had his boss got such an idea? Had someone put it into his head, he wondered?

"Natalie deWitt-Ambrose speaking."

"Hi, love, it's Trish. I've got something for you." God, she wished she hadn't but she had dug deep and found something unsavoury on Francey Spinetti.

"On Francey?"

"Yes. Her old boss, Aden Nicholson, gave me a clue or two. He's still liverish that she dumped him, business-wise. She was a real dollar earner for his company, you know."

"Really." Natalie's tone betrayed her impatience. She didn't want to hear plaudits about Francey Spinetti. She was up to her eyeballs in that kind of information. "What did he say?"

"She had an affair at university with her tutor, a professor called Bryan Steinberg."

"Jesus! What's radical about that? Probably half the students at Sydney uni have had it off with their lecturers or tutors. It's one way of getting a passing grade, I guess." Her long, tapered fingers began to drum rhythmically on the desk top. What was Trish doing? Having a nice holiday in Sydney at her expense. She'd better not be. This wasn't what she wanted. It had to be something with more oomph than an affair.

Trish added hastily, "There's more. Steinberg was married with two kids. Nicholson said Francey didn't know that at the time of the affair, but we've only her word for that. She told him that she found out he was a family man when the wife fronted her and asked her to leave her husband, Bryan, alone."

"That's interesting …" Natalie said slowly, fingers drumming, "but …"

"Here's the best bit. I'm not sure even Francey knows. Aden did a little digging himself, he's a nosy bastard. He learned that Steinberg's wife, she's supposedly a touch nervy, had a stroke because of the trauma caused by her husband's affair. She was totally devoted to him. Poor woman's confined to a wheelchair, I checked that out and it's true."

Trish took a deep breath and in doing so smothered what remained of her conscience. She might as well get it over with. "Natalie, picture the headline: *Brilliant architect ruins marriage and disables innocent wife.* Should do well in one of the women's rags, don't you think?"

"Bloody beautiful!" Natalie's blue eyes glinted maliciously. She had her! The feeling was sweet, as sweet as good sex. Mmmm … Which reminded her. "When are you coming home?"

After a pause, Trish replied, "Tonight. See you then, lover."

CHAPTER TWENTY-ONE

Francey checked and then rechecked her reflection in the mirror, smoothing down the skirt, fiddling with the shoestring straps, realigning the pearl pendant around her neck and the drop earrings. She had chosen the black sheath gown she'd worn the night she had won the architectural award in Sydney because CJ had waggled a finger at her and said that she had to look her glamorous best. As her gaze ran over the gown's close-fitting form she reflected that this was the most sophisticated outfit she owned.

God, she was nervous. She wasn't used to being made a public fuss of. Her parents had never had the wherewithal to do so. The thought came to her that maybe she had erred in telling CJ that one day when they'd been chatting. The wretch had remembered and somehow got it into his head that she'd been deprived and secretly wanted a big bash, even though she'd told him, pointedly and repeatedly, that she didn't. Aarghh! There were times when she could cheerfully throttle CJ, no matter how well meant the gesture was.

She could hear people arriving, they were coming from everywhere. Flying in from surrounding cattle stations as far away as Normanton to the north and Charters Towers to the east. And there'd be a generous sprinkling of the top echelon of businesspeople in and around Mt Isa. The CEO of the mine, just about everyone on the Chamber of Commerce, and as if that wasn't bad enough several politicians, long time cronies of CJ were expected. Of course there'd be plenty of friends too. She'd made quite a few since coming to the Isa.

She sat on the backless dressing table stool to do her hair. Up tonight, she decided. A French roll with a couple of loose curls hanging down near the temples. Steve liked it that way. Usually she left her hair loose because it was so untameable but tonight called for an air of sophistication so she decided her hair should look special too. Pleased with the result, she stood up and took several deep breaths. Time to mingle …

The staff at Murrundi, including Shellie, Lisa, Alison and the stockmen, had gone all-out for Francey's party.

Fairy lights were strung in the pine trees bordering the pool, coloured lanterns hung on ropes around the garden and the canvas sails which normally shaded the pool in summer had been erected to keep any evening dew at bay. In autumn the mornings and nights were generally cooler, but not cold enough to force people indoors. Casual furniture and extra tables and chairs were scattered around the lawn and several waiters bustled about the outdoor bar preparing the glasses and beverages. Tuning up for the evening was a five-piece band on a makeshift stage at the other end of the pool. The overall effect was one of festivity.

Francey stood on the verandah watching. She blinked a couple of times and shook her head in amazement. All this fuss for her! Beyond the pool she could see the lights of the mini conference centre glowing through the pines. The rooms were being put to good use to accommodate overnight guests and the kitchen was busy preparing supper. Two spits were already turning with sides of beef and lamb and along the verandah were long trestle tables covered in table cloths on which supper would later be served.

"What are you doing? Hiding?" CJ came up and put his arm around her shoulders. "You're the star attraction. Come on," he took hold of her hand. "There's some people, neighbours from up Camooweal way I'd like you to meet. They were very impressed with the way you got the workers at the Cloncurry abattoirs on side."

Francey turned to look at him and, as she did, it was hard not to show her surprise at his changed appearance. The operation and treatment in Geneva had cost him. There was the scar, of course and most of his hair had fallen out. He'd lost close to ten kilos in weight, which made him look trimmer and, thank goodness, his colour had returned. He was so different to how he'd been when he'd first got back – a pale and exhausted old man. Tonight, in his dinner suit, he looked almost like the CJ of old and she was glad.

"Something the matter?" he asked.

She smiled and improvised. "I didn't expect you to be wearing a dinner suit. Very impressive."

"Couldn't fit into it before but now I've lost some weight, I thought I'd give it an airing."

"You look splendid."

"As do you, my dear," he said gallantly, smiling at her lie. "Shall we?"

The party was in full swing by the time Natalie and Trish made their appearance. For most of the afternoon Natalie had threatened to boycott the event, and had planned to claim she had a dreadful headache. Only Trish's skilful diplomacy had turned her around. She'd said that it was poor tactics to be seen to be hurt by the way CJ was spoiling Francey and that it wouldn't be wise to let people assume that she was jealous of the *birthday girl*. Nor would it be smart to let CJ sense it. Now more than ever he seemed inclined to make the occasional comparison between Francey and Natalie in which his stepdaughter usually came off second-best.

Natalie, standing on the fringe of the crowd and exquisitely outfitted in an ice blue short skirt cocktail frock of pure silk with a matching stole, displayed the elegance of the wealthy woman she was. Trish, too, looked stunning in a pink shot satin number that Natalie'd bought for her.

Les Westcott, who mostly gave Natalie a wide berth, was inordinately attentive. He organised their drinks and their hors d'oeuvre and made polite chitchat. When the conversation dropped to a lull, their gazes became jointly glued on the tableau of Steve Parrish and Francey dancing together.

"Make a nice couple, don't they?" Natalie said to Les with tongue-in-cheek sweetness. Instinct told her he wanted Francey Spinetti for himself. She saw a naked hunger glint in his eyes every time he glanced Francey's way. He could hide it from most but not from her, she knew him too well. He'd looked the same when he'd fancied her. Poor old Les, he tended to let his feelings show too much which made it easy to hurt him. Child's play, really. She went on. "They're very *familiar* with each other, aren't they? Like lovers."

"How would you know? Your experience in a heterosexual relationship is zero, isn't it?" he countered.

"Who was *your* first? That half-caste Aboriginal girl, Sally? Or was it Louise McReady from your boarding school?"

Natalie, pleased that she'd hit him where it hurt, refused to rise to the bait. She pouted. "Now, now, don't be a bad sport. That's discriminatory, you know." Silently though she answered him. Both, Les dear, *both*. First Louise. They'd discovered each other when they were in the school infirmary suffering from influenza – they'd been isolated so the germs wouldn't spread through the entire dormitory. The house mistress used to check on them every few hours. Remembering made her go all shivery inside. She and Louise had had a wonderful time discovering each other's bodies for the first time. Then, while on school holidays in Murrundi's hay loft one drizzly afternoon she had shown Sally what extracurricular activities she had learnt.

"What's discriminatory?" Shellie asked as she and Barry joined the group.

"Oh, nothing that would interest you, dear," Trish rushed in. "Just talking politics. Boring stuff."

"Have you met the Minister for Primary Industry?" Shellie asked Trish. "He's an interesting man. There might be an article about country life in it for you."

"No. I …"

Shellie threaded her arm through Trish's. "Come on, I'll introduce you."

Natalie smiled indulgently as the two women and the doctor walked away. Her Aunt Shellie sure was a try-hard. Then her sharp gaze noticed a man she didn't readily recognise. Curiosity got the better of her. "Who's that?" she asked Les, pointing discreetly towards the stranger.

"That's Roy Preston. A journalist. One of CJ's acquaintances."

"I haven't seen him at Murrundi before." Over the years she had met most of CJ's friends and business colleagues but not the tall, spare man, probably in his early sixties and dressed in a grey lounge suit. She wondered if Trish knew him and stored the query away in her mind to ask later on.

"They go back a long way, to when CJ first bought this place. Roy knew your mother. Was an old flame, in fact."

"Really! Fascinating. You must introduce me."

Les gave her a strange, almost secretive look. "I'd be glad to, a bit later on if it's all right with you. There's something pressing I have to do for CJ." And with that he turned on his heel and walked away. All the way around the pool he felt her indignant stare follow him and he smiled as if he were privy to some huge joke. Soon, Natalie, soon.

About nine thirty, after the band had finished a set and were taking a ten minute break, CJ stepped up on the makeshift stage and commandeered the microphone. He saw before him a sea of faces, some still clustered around the flagstone patio where they'd been dancing, others in small groups, laughing and talking. Francey, he noted, was talking to Lisa Dupre and her husband Pierre.

"Ladies and gentlemen. Welcome to Murrundi. I hope you're all enjoying yourselves. Tonight is a very special night. We're celebrating the birthday of the newest member of my team, the architect who designs all my new projects. Where are you, Francey? Come up on stage and take a bow."

Reluctantly Francey moved towards the stage and did just that, speaking quietly into the microphone. "Thank you all for coming and sharing this night with me but especially, thanks to my boss, CJ, who's so generously organised tonight. Enjoy!" She jumped down from the stage as quickly as she could and made her way over to where Steve was talking to Mike Hunter and Lucky Pajello.

Steve took her hand and squeezed it. "You were great. See, I told you it wouldn't be too difficult."

"Folks," CJ went on. "There's a twofold reason for me inviting you here tonight. You just heard one reason, now it's time for the other. Bear with me, 'cause it's going to take some getting out.

"Most of you have known me since I bought Murrundi. A few of you knew me before that, when I was a bum out of my pants jackeroo scratching around for a living. None of you," and he looked briefly at his sister, "know about a certain episode in my life which started me on the road to success in one way, and damned me in another. I'm talking about the time I spent in Coober Pedy, nearly twenty-nine years ago.

"I scored big in an opal mine. That's public knowledge and it gave me the grub stake to get this place." He waved his free hand around expansively to encompass the property. "What no-one knows is the secret I've kept all these years because I've not been proud of it. Now I feel compelled to tell you, to tell the world, in fact."

Trish and Natalie, standing side by side, their arms touching, glanced enquiringly at each other. "This might be a scoop. You'd better listen up. I'm just praying he's not going to announce his engagement to the bitch," Natalie hissed.

Trish doubted that very much but she refrained from saying so. "Do you have any idea?"

"None whatsoever," Natalie replied with a forced chuckle. What was he up to? she wondered. She knew him.

When he performed these type of theatrics it was usually to announce the completion of a big deal. Maybe that was it, but what on earth did it have to do with his time in Coober Pedy? She remembered that he'd rarely spoken about that episode in his life and she had always assumed it was because he'd been broken up about his partner Mickey Edgar's death. But … maybe there was more to it.

"I've only ever loved two women in my life," CJ went on, his sentences quickening as he strove to get through it. "Brenda, my late wife, was one such love and there was another. Way back in those Coober Pedy days I met a young woman, she was much younger than myself. Her name was Mary Williams. She was like an oasis in a desert – and if you've ever worked Coober you'll understand what I mean. We fell in love and had an affair. Mary Williams was too good for me, 'cause back then all I thought about was making money and of getting a stake to set myself up in Queensland. I wasn't prepared to make the kind of commitment Mary expected. Well, I found my stake in the bounty of opals and I decided to leave – yes – leave. Leave Mary, sell the mine lease. I had what I wanted and, at the time I also had a fiancée, Brenda, waiting for me in Townsville. Brenda fitted into my future plans and I knew she'd be an asset as a wife.

"Bear with me, folks, this prelude is important. You'll see why in a couple of minutes." He paused to wipe a layer of perspiration from his forehead. Damn it, saying the words was hard, but not as hard as what he was about to say. "Then Mary told me she was pregnant."

A shiver ran through Natalie's body accompanied by a sense of foreboding. God, she had this awful feeling … Unconsciously she pressed closer to the one person who truly understood her, silently communicating her affection.

"He got a woman pregnant," Trish whispered. "What's so rare about that?"

"Shut up," Natalie spat at her. Her concentration was focused on the man on the stage. The man she'd always been in awe of, was afraid of and had never been close to or won his affection, though in her own odd way she believed she had tried.

"I was angry with her but please, understand, I did love her. You all know what a ruthless bastard I am." He paused to hear the ripple of agreement from the crowd. "Mary didn't fit into my dreams or my future plans. No sir. I had it all mapped out. Marry Brenda deWitt, buy a property, amass a fortune. Mary was so young. Guileless, unsophisticated, and a kid hanging about my legs would have only held me back."

CJ heard another low murmur from the hundred or so people staring at him attentively and, needing to finish, he rushed on. "I wanted her to get an abortion but she refused. We fought over it and then I left Coober Pedy for good. But I sent her enough money to see her through comfortably. Why am I telling you all this, baring my soul, you might ask. When my son was killed last year, for the first time in many years I thought about Mary and the child. *Our child.* I wondered what he or she was like. Got a huge case of the guilts, I guess. I wanted to find them and try to right the wrong I'd done both of them so long ago. I didn't want anyone to know so I asked a friend of mine, Roy Preston, to make discreet enquires. Roy, perhaps you'll come up and tell the folks what happened."

Roy Preston made his way to the front of the crowd and then stepped up on the stage. He cleared his throat nervously before he spoke into the microphone. "My friend, CJ, loves to give me the easy jobs." He paused while some of the crowd gave a short laugh of appreciation. "Tracking Mary Williams and her child back to 1970 was an investigative nightmare. The task took many weeks. I learnt that she'd moved to Adelaide, where she worked in a shop but made few friends. When her child was born, a little girl named Jennifer, Mary was already a sick woman. She had leukaemia and she passed away within three months of Jennifer's birth. The child was adopted by a couple who couldn't have children of their own." He paused to let that sink in. "Then the trail went cold. The couple seemed to disappear into God knows where. But, finally, after some persistent digging, I traced them to Melbourne and to Geelong and finally to Sydney, where they still live." As an aside, he added, "I've all the documentation – birth certificate, adoption letters, everything legally needed to prove that Jennifer is CJ's natural child, should anyone want to peruse them later on."

Impatient, CJ took the microphone back. "I was excited by Roy's news. I'd found out I had a daughter. I wanted to get to know her – and I did. I guess, in a way, I hoped she'd replace the son I'd lost. I've always believed that blood's thicker than water." A twinkle came into his light-blue eyes as he milked the audience's air of expectancy. "I guess you're all wondering who she is. *She* doesn't know yet and I hope it's not going to be too much of a shock to find she's related to an old reprobate like me ..."

"For Christ's sake, tell us ..." Natalie hissed in Trish's ear. Her heart was pounding, the colour had drained from her face. Her *beloved* stepfather hadn't said a word about his other daughter, it was as if she didn't exist. Bastard. At that moment she hated him more than she believed she could hate anyone. He was going to install this ... bastard child of his. Give her status over herself. Well, she'd see about that.

She turned her head slightly and saw that Les' gaze was fixed intently upon her. He knew. He was watching her, waiting for her reaction, trying to gauge her feelings as CJ dropped "the bombshell". She knew he was enjoying this. Bastard too. She added his name to her hate list.

"Without further ado," CJ said theatrically, "friends, neighbours, I'd like all of you to meet my natural daughter …"

CHAPTER TWENTY-TWO

"Jennifer Williams." His gaze roamed from Shellie to Lisa, rested briefly on Natalie and Trish then moved to where Francey and Steve stood side by side. "Jennifer's name was changed. Her adoptive parents christened her Francesca Lucia Spinetti, she's known as Francey. Yes, ladies and gentlemen, my architectural designer, Francey Spinetti is my daughter. Will you join your old man on the stage, Francey?"

"*What?*" Francey stared at Steve then at Les, who grinned hugely and nodded confirmingly at her. Her legs went weak and her head began to spin. CJ's daughter. Her! What was he talking about? What kind of ruse was he trying to put over? Her mouth tightened. She wasn't amused. People began pushing her good-naturedly towards the stage.

She tried to think. No! She was Carlo and Lucia Spinetti's child, daughter of Italian migrants and she had a horde of noisy Italian relatives to prove it. His claim was crazy ... she couldn't be CJ Ambrose's love child. Her father was Carlo, her mother, Lucia. For a moment she stood rooted to the spot, the colour having drained from her face. She was embarrassed, mortified and finally after several seconds during which people around her began to cheer and clap madly, a slow, combustible anger began to spread through her. What kind of ploy was this? Being CJ's daughter made no sense, at all!

She looked for Steve but he had disappeared and accidentally her gaze landed on Natalie who was staring at her malevolently. Natalie disliked her, over the months she had made that clear enough, but if CJ's claim was true — she still couldn't believe it – she had made a deadly enemy. Oh, God, how had she got herself into this madness? For that's what she believed it was, total, absolute madness.

CJ called to her above all the cheers and handclaps. "Come on, Francey. I know it's a shock, love, and I'm sorry for the surprise disclosure but I thought this the best way to tell you. An announcement to the world. It is true as Roy said, and to prove it absolutely, let me introduce two special guests who've come from Sydney to share this night with us. Lucia and Carlo Spinetti, Francey's adoptive parents."

Francey stared at CJ through a haze of confusion as his words sank in. Mamma and Papà. Here. Then ... then ... just maybe all of it – God, no, she couldn't grasp the concept, but it might be true.

"Are you all right?" Trish whispered to Natalie, her hand on her arm.

"Oh, yeah," Natalie quipped bitterly, "the news couldn't be better. At least he's not going to marry her." She'd been wrong there. All those months thinking CJ was falling in love with Francey. It was worse than that, much worse. The bitch was his daughter. And ... now he had an heir again and where did that leave her? Out in the cold.

"Damn the lot of them. Come on. I can't stand any more, let's get out of here."

Trish sensed her lover's anger in the tight lines around her mouth and the look in her eyes. A shiver ran down her spine. Natalie aroused by passion was magnificent, aroused in anger she could be fearsome. And lately, the frequency of her mood swings led Trish to believe she was capable of anything, even burning Murrundi down if the thought appealed to her.

"Ummm, shouldn't you stick around and tough it out? People will talk if we just disappear."

"Stuff them. Let them talk their bloody heads off. They're all a bunch of inbreds and wankers anyway." Natalie stopped for a moment to take a deep breath, then she whispered, "If I don't get away from here I'll be sick."

"Okay, let's go." Taking her by the hand she led Natalie through the party goers, and out towards Murrundi's homestead.

As Steve Parrish made his way to the back of the crowd he heard the comments.

"Who'd have thought it …"

"Bloody wonderful. Like a miracle."

"Jesus, she's going to be worth millions."

"So, that's why old CJ got her up here to work, so he could check her out. See whether she had the right stuff. Cunning bastard."

"She has, old son. Intellect, looks and now, or when CJ kicks off, truckloads of lovely money."

"I could help her spend it."

By the time he got to the fringe a trough of depression blanketed him. Francey Spinetti – CJ Ambrose's daughter! It sounded unbelievable but he didn't doubt that it was true. CJ was too careful, too astute to contrive such a falsehood. Even so, he couldn't grasp it no matter how hard he tried. CJ and Francey *related*. Francey. Potentially wealthy beyond anyone's wildest dreams.

She's out of your league now, an inner voice taunted him.

Francey the architect was one thing. Eminently suitable. He'd thought they'd make a good team. The architect and the cop. But Francey the millionaire's daughter and the cop? No. His jaw flexed. He couldn't see that. CJ, the cunning old so-and-so had known it for almost a year and kept it under wraps while he'd assessed her, became fond of her and seen that the fondness was reciprocated. He'd lost his son and found a daughter whom he was tutoring to eventually step into his shoes as Richard would have done had he lived. He really was the man with the golden touch. Suddenly he thought of what might have been. His plans, his and Francey's plans. He thrust his hands disconsolately into his trouser pockets. Damn CJ to hell.

At the bar he picked up a glass of whisky and downed it in one gulp. Then, as he made his way up to the verandah of the homestead he almost collided with Natalie and Trish as they hurried inside. He was enough of a humanitarian to spare CJ's stepdaughter a compassionate thought or two. She looked devastated. Fair enough. Natalie had thought she was the only apple on the tree, the heir apparent. Now she had a rival that CJ was obviously fond of.

Standing on the higher vantage point, carefully watching the people mill around the stage shouting congratulations, he saw his future *with* Francey going down the tube. His fingers closed around the small box in his left-hand trouser pocket. Tonight he'd been going to ask her to marry him, had thought it appropriate on her birthday. He couldn't now. Wouldn't. She had moved beyond his reach. The picture had changed, irrevocably. He, a forty thousand plus a year cop could never fit into her elite world, a world she had settled into with remarkable ease, he'd noted, as if she'd been born to it.

He ran a hand distractedly through his hair and let the sadness flow through him for what couldn't be. Even if she still thought she wanted him, he'd have to be strong for both of them. It would never work – the differences were too great. They had truly moved into different worlds.

His sighed loudly. Maybe the next time Inspector Clarke talked about him transferring to Brisbane, he'd give it serious thought.

Steve turned on his heel and walked away from the party.

"I knew there was something," Shellie was saying to Les and anyone else within earshot. "From the moment I greeted her at Murrundi's front door I felt something. It was her expression, I think. I know now that it reminded me of Richard. Then later, when she and CJ would row, they were so alike. I don't know why I didn't cotton on sooner. It all makes sense now. The rage he got into when Francey was lost in the bush. Why he was so fond of her and trying to train her in all the aspects of his business world." CJ had a daughter. She smiled … and she had a niece. "Francey's got the business brains too, just like him." She looked enquiringly at Les. "You knew, didn't you?"

Les shook his head. "Not until CJ told me. Then, like you, lots of things clicked into place." He smiled. "It's wonderful, isn't it? I mean, we're all fond of her, thought of her as part of the family and now, well, she really is."

"Yes, it's given CJ a lift. God knows he needed it after Richard, and that tumour scare."

"I notice Natalie hasn't come over to congratulate her," Les put in maliciously.

"Oh, that one," Shellie muttered, "probably sulking. She'll have her nose out of joint for a while. Expected to get the lot after Richard's death."

"I guess she did," Les said quietly, and was unable to wipe the pleased smile off his face, though he knew he should. Tonight Natalie deWitt-Ambrose had got her comeuppance and been delivered a substantial hiding. He'd like to be somewhere close enough to hear what she thought of tonight's happenings but she and Trish had slunk off to console each other. Oh, well, he was patient, men on the land had to be. He could wait.

He also noted Steve Parrish's absence. Good. He prided himself on being able to read people's character and if he'd read Parrish right, with Francey now being CJ's main heir, the cop would consider her differently. That suited his plans perfectly. Everything was falling into place. Francey'd be unhappy for a while about Steve's disaffection but *he'd* be there to console her and to make her see that they were better suited. Soon Francey would inherit most of CJ's estate and together they'd rule the roost. Yes, he intended to put all his energies into making sure that came to pass.

CJ looked at Francey and a frown formed across his forehead. He tried to second-guess what she was thinking, feeling, but couldn't. Shock. Disbelief. He'd expected that but he saw more. He knew her. She was angry with him. Bloody angry. Angrier than he'd ever seen her. He hadn't expected that. He sensed there were questions she wanted to ask. She'd want more detailed explanations too – she deserved them and he'd provide them.

He watched as she hugged her parents and saw each of them shed a few tears. Joining them, he said quietly, "I'm sure we'd all feel more comfortable in my study. There's lots to go over. Francey, I suppose you have a million questions."

She couldn't bear to look at him. Even though, presumably, he was her own flesh and blood. She was furious at what he'd done. He shouldn't have made his announcement the way he had. He should have told her privately, given her time to adjust to the change before he'd bellowed it to the world in that typical CJ Ambrose grandstanding way. "All right. I'll lead the way."

Carlo whispered to CJ as they walked in unison. "I know that look, my friend. You probably do too. She's about to erupt like a mini Mount Vesuvius."

"I'd better make sure we have some wine, maybe that'll dampen her down." CJ beckoned a passing waiter. "Bring a bottle of white wine to the study, will you?"

Once the four were ensconced in CJ's spacious study, Francey wasted no time in venting her feelings.

"How could you?" She stared at CJ, hands on hips, her blue-green eyes blazing. "Assuming your's and Roy's story is accurate how could you tell all those people, make a public announcement without telling me first? You should have granted me the courtesy of telling me in private. I felt foolish, ill-prepared ..."

"I can see that you're angry. I didn't –"

"I'm not angry, I'm furious! I was embarrassed. People congratulating me for turning out to be –" she almost choked on the words, "your daughter. Falling for it hook, line and sinker. Well, I'm not so easily convinced. You'll have to prove it to me and it'll take more than a few official documents to do that."

Lucia spoke then, comforting her with a gentle pat on the hand. "Francey, *cara*. I feel your pain, your anger."

"No, Mamma, I don't think you do. It was ..." She found her feelings incredibly hard to put into words. "My whole life's suddenly been turned upside down. One minute I knew who I was, where I'd come from, the next I'm hearing something different. I can't explain it well, but it's not a pleasant feeling."

Lucia went on. "Perhaps CJ should have informed you first. But, darling, it is true what CJ said. You are his and Mary Williams' child, not ours. If you blame CJ then you must also blame Carlo and I. You should have been told the truth long ago. We were cowards. We were afraid you mightn't love us any more if you knew we weren't your real parents. *Capisci*?"

She had heard if from her mother's mouth, it seemed that he was her biological father but it took more than that to be a real parent. "Mamma, that's silly. You and Papà will always be my parents. I couldn't love anyone more than I love the both of you. You raised me, saw me through all my childhood scrapes and illnesses. Fed me, clothed me, educated me. Did the best for me with what you had." And she meant it. She turned an angry gaze on CJ. "CJ was never there for me as a child or as an adult. Now he wants to take over the role of father."

"Francey, I want you to understand, and Carlo and Lucia, too. It's not my goal to cause a rift between the three of you. I think what you have together is wonderful. In fact, I'm envious of it. No-one could have done a better job bringing Francey up," CJ admitted. "But now we all know the truth about your parentage, we're all linked by the fact." His penetrating gaze forced Francey to look at him. "I want to be allowed to be a part of your life and I hope and pray you will want to be a part of mine."

Francey began to tremble. She couldn't deal with all the ramifications now. CJ Ambrose, "the man with the golden touch" – her father. God, it meant so many things, conflicting things. Values, memories altered. Oh, there were too many for her to think clearly about. All at once her anger abated as quickly as it had been aroused. "Please, CJ, I need time to think. I want to talk to my, to Mamma and Papà."

Nodding, CJ stood up. He hid the hurt well. She hadn't exactly rejected him but he knew that he had to play it carefully now and give her time to come to terms with everything. He didn't blame her for her confusion, her anger. Francey was so much like him, she just didn't know it yet. "I understand. I'll get back to the guests. Mingle. Get Shellie to organise supper. You will come out to cut the birthday cake, won't you?" He watched her mute nod and had to be satisfied with that. He quietly let himself out of the room.

When they were alone, Francey turned to her parents and asked the first question. "How long have you known?"

"About five weeks," Carlo told her. "CJ flew down to Sydney with his offsider, Les. They came to see us and told us what he wanted to do. Swore us to secrecy. Of course, we didn't know either until then. The name on your birth certificate, where it says who the father was, were just initials. CJA. We hadn't looked at it for years, didn't put it together until CJ talked about Mary, described the kind of person she was. Then we knew it to be the truth."

"Mary ..." A lump lodged in her throat as Francey spoke her birth mother's name for the first time. "I need to know so much. About her, how it all happened, how you came to adopt me. There's so much to absorb." She made a funny, half strangled sound. "I feel like I've been hit by a runaway road train." Momentarily she thought about Steve, wondered at his reaction to the announcement. Would he be pleased for her? Was she pleased for herself? In all honesty she wasn't sure. It changed how she felt about so many things, past, present and future.

Lucia took a sip of her wine and said, "I will tell you all that we know. Carlo and I had just come from Perth to Adelaide. We'd leased a fruit shop and milk bar in Glenelg, near the beach. One day a young woman, she was only a little pregnant then, came into the shop answering our advertisement for a room we had to let. It was Mary. She took the room, and as the months passed we got to know her well. She didn't seem to mind my broken English," Lucia added with a self-conscious laugh.

"Mary was so looking forward to your birth, making matinee jackets, bootees, bonnets. On Saturday's she helped us serve in the shop – it was our busiest day – and then she would have dinner with us that night and attend mass with us on Sundays. Sometimes she talked about CJ, telling us that she cared for him but that he was a *brutto*, selfish man. Then as her time got close I could see that she wasn't well. It was a blood problem. Later we found out that she had a type of leukaemia, one that develops rapidly. Several times we had to get the doctor to her …"

Carlo took over the story. "Her determination kept her going, you know. She had to stay strong for your birth, but the labour was long and it tired her more than we or the doctor's realised. She never really recovered her strength and slowly, she just faded away. The illness does that to pregnant women, so the doctors said.

"She died peacefully in her sleep when you were almost three months old." Carlo sniffed back a tear. "We didn't know what to do, *cara*. We had come to love you as our own, as we had come to care for Mary as a very dear friend. We spoke to our parish priest. He knew we wanted *bambini* of our own but after seven years God had not blessed us. Father suggested that we adopt you and bring you up as our own daughter." He gave her a gloriously happy smile. "And we did."

"*Cara*, Mary, your mother would have been so proud of you, of how smart you are. I am sure that somewhere she is looking down on you, caring for you, watching over you."

"Oh, Mamma." And then the tears began to flow. From all of them. Carlo and Lucia for their memories. Francey, for the discovery of her past, how it had all begun.

"Here." She handed Francey a black velour box. "We have been keeping this for you since Mary's death. The time never seemed right to give it to you," said Lucia, "but I think now, at this very moment, it is appropriate." Francey opened the lid and stared through a veil of mistiness at a magnificent opal pendant. The spectrum of colours, their diversity and their depth, fascinated her.

"It is a harlequin opal which belonged to your mother," Carlo explained. "CJ gave it to her because it was one of the first opals he found in his mine, so she told us. Mary would want you to have it *and*, Francey," he paused to wangle a finger at her, "Lucia and I know you and your stubborn ways. You must try not to think too harshly of your father. CJ did wrong, he has admitted that to everyone tonight and I have no doubt that he has suffered great mental anguish for what he did. He loves you like a daughter, we can see that. Like I love you. Remember that when you judge him."

She looked down at her hands, suddenly aware of the colour, the brownness. CJ wasn't olive-skinned, but she was, like Carlo and Lucia. *Strange.* "I don't even know what she, what my real mother looked like," Francey said quietly, her emotions and curiosity at a peak. She should hate CJ for stirring up this mess, making her question, doubt, wonder. But she knew that she couldn't, even though at this precise moment she didn't *like* him very much.

"Here. We only have the one photo – I believe CJ has a couple of others. It was taken outside our fruit shop by a customer," Lucia said as she handed the photo to Francey.

Francey studied the black and white photograph showing a young, slim woman with dark, slightly wild curly hair, obviously in the first stages of pregnancy. She was simply dressed in a pale, patterned sun frock and white sandals. Her eyes suddenly widened and then she understood about the colour, and so much more. Her mother was part Aboriginal.

CHAPTER TWENTY-THREE

Francey was kept busy until the early hours of the morning answering people's questions, smiling at their congratulations and outwardly appearing to enjoy herself. Internally though, she was in turmoil.

She was concerned by Steve's absence and needed his strength and commonsense to help her through this. Someone told her he had left shortly after CJ's speech. She wanted to talk to him and pour out all her feelings, but that would have to wait.

Her parents had been wonderful. Lucia, so understanding, gentle, trying to tell her in a few hours the many things she wanted to know about Mary. CJ kept his distance, as if sensing that she needed time to adjust to the changes his *little* speech had wrought. Les Westcott was a tower of strength and stayed by her side when he thought he was needed, fending off the overly curious and smoothing her transition from respected architectural designer for CJ Ambrose, to the lofty status of daughter.

As the party began to wind down Francey saw her parents to one of the suites in the mini conference centre.

"*Che bella*," Lucia exclaimed as she walked around the suite, admiring the luxurious decor. She had never stayed in such opulence before and was in awe.

"You did all this, *cara*?" Carlo asked as his large hands waved effusively about the room.

Francey explained. "Not the actual work, but the planning, down to the last detail." Her smile widened. "That's what an architect does, you know."

He nodded his head thoughtfully, as if finally understanding exactly what she did for a living. His dark-eyed gaze roamed about the room, taking it all in. "*Sì, capisco*. You are very good at what you do," he pronounced.

"Of course she is," Lucia fussed, then she asked. "Do you think anyone would mind if I used the spa? I've never had a spa bath before."

"Mamma, use whatever you like. That's what it's here for."

"Tomorrow Les promised to take us up in the helicopter for a tour of the property. Isn't that kind of him?" Carlo informed.

"You'll enjoy that. Murrundi is a big place."

"He's going to show us where you got lost in the bush." Lucia's eyes narrowed. "That woman, Natalie, I would like to have her alone in a room for two minutes. To give her a piece of my mind."

"Mamma, don't. That's all over, long ago." Francey thought for a moment and then she confided in her parents. "That episode is the least of Natalie's problems at the moment. I'm sure that tonight's news, about my relationship to CJ, has shocked and surprised Natalie, as it has most people. I think CJ was remiss in not, somehow, including her in the whole event. She must be feeling a little left out of things." It was odd in a way but despite Natalie's nastiness and rudeness to her she did feel that CJ was treating her harshly.

"Ahh! There you go, being kind again, *cara*," Carlo said. "It is a good trait, my child, but I would not spend too much time worrying about that Natalie. From what I saw of her she looks able to look after herself. A tough little number, in fact."

"I agree," said Lucia with a dismissive sniff. Francey stifled a yawn. "It's getting late. I'll let

you two get to bed. Breakfast will be late tomorrow. Come over when you feel like it."

"*Buona notte, cara*, sleep well."

Should he try to talk to Francey? He wanted to. CJ paced the bedroom floor, hands behind his back, striding out. Seven paces to the right, turn, six paces to the left.

Commonsense told him he should allow things to settle, let Francey become accustomed to her new station in life in her own good time. But then, he grimaced to himself, time was a luxury he simply didn't have. He had gained a little time by going to Geneva. The headaches and many of the other symptoms had receded to a bearable level. But for how long?

After watching her surreptitiously for most of the evening, he had kept his distance even though what he wanted to do more than anything else was to hug her to him and be able to call her "daughter", *his* daughter. He smiled widely and, despite his anxieties was pleased with himself. Francey was all and more than he had hoped for in a child. She showed such promise and in many ways they were so alike. But she also had a lot of her mother in her ... the good traits. Gentleness. Understanding. The capacity for love. She would make a great successor when his race was run.

His thoughts were interrupted by a knock on the door. He glanced at the clock on the bedside table 3 a.m. Maybe it was Francey!

"Come in."

Natalie thrust the door open wide and stepped inside.

"You bastard. How could you?"

She came and stood in front of him. She was tall enough for their eyes to be level with each other. Her hands drew up to her hips and her legs were thrust wide apart in an aggressive stance. "How could you entertain the idea of your little bastard being welcomed with open arms into this house, this community? Where's your sense of propriety, CJ? I always admired your thoughts on propriety."

"You're drunk."

"Damned right I am," she mumbled, her voice moving up half an octave. "I reckon I've a bloody right to be after tonight's performance. So Francey's your *love child*." Her glance swept over him. "You dirty old man. No, sorry, you were a young man then. When you were engaged to my mother, penning her loving letters from your bloody cave in Coober, you were screwing a half-caste bitch. Oh, yes, I found out she was part Aboriginal, Les obligingly told me."

CJ's hand rose to strike her but stopped centimetres from contact with her cheek. "Drunk or not I'll not have you talk about Francey, or Mary, like that. Mary was a fine young woman whose life was tragically cut short." His lip curled in derision as he made the observation. "You always did have a dirty tongue and a dirty mind."

Natalie, who'd flinched as his large hand had come towards her, took a backwards step. Her grey eyes blazed with all the repressed anger she'd bottled inside her for months. "Since Richard's death I've been the rightful heir, everyone says so. You're going to give her what's rightfully mine. Do you think mother would approve of that? I'm damn sure she wouldn't. You wouldn't be where you are today without the deWitt money. *She* doesn't deserve any of it. Shit, you think I should be pleased about that possibility?"

CJ's eyes narrowed on her disdainfully. "Don't presume to think you know what I plan to do and ..." he added forcefully, "whether you approve or not, Murrundi and my fortune belong to me, to do with as I please. You have no control over it, understand?"

"Is everything all right?" came a voice from the doorway. Francey, barefoot and in her bathrobe, stood in the open doorway.

On recognising the voice, Natalie spun about, wobbling unsteadily. "Right? No, you bastard, everything's not right. You're not right. You shouldn't be here ... you ... shit-faced usurper. Why don't you go back to Sydney where you belong."

"Take no notice of her, she's drunk," CJ said, his tone dark with disapproval. "I suggest," but it was more of an order, "Natalie, that you return to your room and sleep it off. We'll talk about rights, your rights as you perceive them, in the morning."

But Natalie was too drunk to recognise the steel in her stepfather's tone. Her chin pointed upwards stubbornly as she jabbed his chest with a finger. "Damn you, CJ, I'm sick of you always calling the shots. I want to talk about it *now*."

"Well, I don't," he said coldly. "The matter's closed till the morning."

"Natalie," Francey tried to intervene. She could see the coldness in CJ's eyes and knew that if Natalie pushed him too far she'd later regret it. She half turned to see Les and Shellie coming down the hall, disturbed by the commotion and moved forward to take Natalie by the arm. "Come out to the kitchen, Natalie, I'll make us a cup of coffee."

"Don't touch me you bitch. Everything was fine until you came along!" Natalie yelled and lunged at Francey, catching her off-guard and tangling her left hand in her dark curls. The other hand dealt her a stinging blow to the side of her face. Francey's head rocked sideways and her eyes watered.

Before she could land another blow CJ grabbed Natalie by her forearms and roughly pushed her past Francey and out the doorway towards Shellie. He saw the red welt on Francey's face and it took all his self-control not to retaliate. Barely controlling his anger, he shouted, "Get her out of my sight before I do something I'll regret!"

It took both Les and Shellie to lead a disturbed, still angry Natalie who was yelling incoherently at CJ, back to her room.

CJ, embarrassed, looked at Francey. "Are you all right?" He watched her nod mutely. "I'm sorry you had to experience that. Do you want to come in and talk?"

She shook her head as she gently massaged the mark on her cheek. "It's late. I think we'd both better try and get some sleep. Your house guests will be up and about for breakfast by around 9 a.m."

"All right. We'll talk in the morning." As he watched her turn away and return to her room his gaze remained thoughtful. She was having difficulty adjusting to all she'd learned tonight. That was to be expected. Having her parents here would help her through it, he hoped. Just now there'd been a look in her eyes that told him as eloquently as words could to give her some space. He would.

By 6 a.m. Francey gave up the idea of getting any useful rest. She had tried, but as soon as her head hit the pillow the memories of the evening's events, the words, everything flooded through her mind. *She was CJ Ambrose's love child.* Incredible. And he'd probably known it from the moment he'd laid eyes on her. Sneaky so-and-so. He'd been watching, judging and testing her from day one. Unbelievable ... but true. Her parents had said so, and after talking privately to Roy Preston the evidence was irrefutable.

That CJ Ambrose was her father was harder to accept than the fact that she was part Aboriginal. She didn't mind that at all. It explained some things that had puzzled her for several months. Her almost instant love of the land, the real feeling she had for it, for being a part of it. As well as how she loved to listen to Alison and Billy Wontow tell stories about their tribe and their customs. Some inner part of her had unconsciously responded to it all.

But deep inside her resided a sadness for never having known the woman who had given her life. Lucia had spoken of Mary Williams so fondly, and even CJ ... Her gaze hardened. What a selfish, ruthless individual. Callously walking away all those years ago. She hoped he'd suffered feelings of remorse. A lot. He had a great deal to answer for. He'd destroyed Mary's life, turned her own upside down and had even wrought havoc on her adoptive parents lives. Anger bubbled up inside her again. Why had he done this? So he could get what he wanted, whatever that was!

Giving up the idea of sleeping, she got up and dressed. Jeans, sweater, denim jacket; late autumn mornings were cool on Murrundi. She went out to the stables and saddled Astra. A brisk, morning ride would clear the cobwebs and, hopefully, settle her inner turmoil.

She rode north, keeping the distant line of trees that marked the creek in view. By now she was familiar with the landscape around Murrundi but as her horse picked its way along she unconsciously found herself heading towards the homestead's cemetery.

Inside, an extreme restlessness had taken control, thoughts pulling her this way and that. She reined in near the aluminium fence and dismounted. Dew was still on the grass but she didn't care. She went and sat beside Richard Ambrose's grave and, reading the words inscribed on the headstone she slowly let out a heartfelt sigh. Then her gaze moved to the one for young Miles. Her half-brothers. She had never had the opportunity to know them, or they her. Would they have liked each other, she wondered? Her gaze returned to Richard's grave. If he were still alive, she thought with a wry twist to her mouth, she wouldn't be sitting here. None of last night's revelations would have occurred and she'd probably still be working for Aden. Richard's death had been the catalyst that had spurred CJ into seeking out the past and all that followed.

Why had CJ revealed his parentage to her, to anyone? She stared hard at her half-brother's headstone, mulling it over. Why? And then it came to her and the sudden knowledge knocked the breath from her lungs. Why hadn't she seen it sooner? Of course. CJ was grooming her to take over his empire when he … *He had no other blood heir*. Shellie had no children, Les, his right hand-man wasn't blood related and neither was Natalie.

Her hands began to tremble and a shudder ran through her body at the enormity of the thought, and worse, the reality. Oh, God. That's why Natalie had made that scene – she'd seen her inheritance as sole heir slipping through her fingers. She covered her face with her hands, pressing her fingers against her forehead. Suddenly the responsibility of it, of what it meant to be CJ Ambrose's only living child, hit her. She couldn't do it. No way! Working as his architectual designer, learning the ropes was one thing, but running the whole show? Her head began to swim as she thought of the ramifications, the extent of his empire, the power.

She wasn't into power like CJ. And she certainly didn't have his ruthless streak. But that doesn't mean you couldn't do just as good a job, an insidious voice inside her head said. She shook her head vigorously. No! Her whole life would change.

She needed to see Steve and talk it all through with him.

A noise intruded into her thoughts: a horse cantering towards the cemetery. Billy Wontow slid from the saddle in a fluid movement and opened the cemetery gate.

"Hi. You're up early," he said as he sat cross-legged opposite her.

She gave him a lopsided smile. "Couldn't sleep."

He nodded gravely. "Not surprising. Big news last night. Everyone amazed, but most were pleased." He held out both of his hands to her and said simply, "Welcome."

She didn't hesitate to grasp his and for a moment she looked at his dark, gnarled buckles covering her paler ones. She looked into his eyes. "You knew, didn't you? About the Aboriginality."

He shrugged. "Yeah. Alison and I knew pretty soon. We can always tell our own." He grinned at her confused expression. "Don't ask me how. Guess it's the spirit singing to us or something."

"I'd like to know more ... about my birth mother. Lucia said she was abandoned at a mission when she was very small. I don't know how to go about it."

"Doesn't matter, Francey. You know who you are and we know you're one of us. That's all that matters."

"I guess so." She sighed. "I ... I'm having a few problems getting used to the idea of being CJ's daughter. All my life I thought I was Italian, now I'm the part Aboriginal daughter of a multimillionaire. It's hard to make the mental adjustment. It's like I've gone through some strange, not altogether pleasant rebirth."

Billy looked away to the dry pasture, waiting for winter rain. "CJ's a good bloke. Tough, but fair. You'll make a good boss lady one day, don't worry, it'll all work out." He got up, strode over to his saddlebag. He took out what appeared to be the Sunday paper. "Look, you've made the big time already."

He spread the front page out in front of her to show the picture of herself, and one of CJ emblazoned with the headline – THE MAN WITH THE GOLDEN TOUCH ACKNOWLEDGES LOVE CHILD with a Roy Preston by-line.

"Oh, no."

Billy laughed at her dismay. "Oh, yes. You're a celebrity now."

As per CJ's instructions, all the interested parties – Shellie, Les, Natalie, Francey, and out of courtesy the Spinettis, sat in CJ's study at the time he'd appointed – an hour after breakfast.

"This won't take long," CJ promised as he spread some papers out in front of him. Eventually he looked up and at them one by one. "Last night's revelations regarding

Francey's relationship to me have necessitated several changes to my will. I intend to legally acknowledge my natural daughter," he smiled at Francey. "My solicitor has advised me that the simplest way to do this is to write a new will with the same entitlements for everyone except for one difference. Where Richard's name was inserted as the heir to the bulk of my estate, Francey's name will now be inserted."

"May I say something?" Francey asked. What if she said it now? That she intended to walk away from everything. From CJ, Murrundi, her future inheritance, the responsibilities. She'd thought about it, long and hard. She knew what she was getting into if she stayed and in a way it would be easier to turn her back on it. She looked at CJ, and intercepted the love in his direct gaze as he waited expectantly for her to speak. Damn! She couldn't do it. In some strange, no, wonderful way she had become as bound to him as he was to her. He nodded his assent and she went on. "I don't think that's fair – to Natalie. It may have been proved that I'm your child but I've not grown up here, I've not been a part of the family ... Perhaps a fifty-fifty split would be more equitable."

"You're part of the family now," CJ's tone was firm. "I commend your sense of fair play, but I assure you, in the terms of my will, Natalie, who is already a wealthy woman, is well catered for."

"Am I?" Natalie queried. Hungover or not she would have her say. "When Richard was alive I accepted the fact that I had to take a lesser share. He was the male heir, my half-brother and I loved him. This is different. Francey's female and your illegal brat. Legally I'm not sure what the ramifications are but I feel quite strongly that I would contest such a will and let the courts judge the case on its merits."

CJ's smile was controlled. "Well, by that time I wouldn't be around to stop you but think it through carefully, Natalie. I've had expert legal advice from the top law firm in the state. As my acknowledged heir and with proof of Francey's relationship to me, all you might do is make a barrister more wealthy than he already is."

"Anyway," Shellie fussed, "I hate all this talk about death and wills. CJ's going to be around for a long time, now that he's so much better."

"But I have a right, a longer standing right," Natalie ignored Shellie's attempt to change the subject. Her fingers curled into fists which she beat on the side arm of the chair. "I've lived here all my life. My mother's money gave you the start to get where you are today."

"Which I've acknowledged," CJ pointed out. "That's why your settlement is so generous."

"You've never shown much interest in running Murrundi, or in CJ's other business interests. What would you do? Sell them all off and pocket the profits?" Les said to Natalie.

"I could get a manager in to run everything, lots of cattle stations are run that way ... as you well know," Natalie told Les tartly.

"There's a clause in my will that states Murrundi can't be sold until ten years after my death," CJ advised all of them.

Francey cleared her throat and spoke. "Look, really, this talk about wills and what happens afterwards is unsettling and unnecessary at this point in time."

"Not so," CJ interceded. "It's important that these matters are understood, by all of us."

"Oh, you think it's unsettling, do you?" Natalie snapped at Francey. "You're sitting pretty, aren't you? CJ's white-haired girl. All you have to do is hang around and be nice to him and ... and ..."

"That's enough," CJ's tone was curt. "Natalie, if you can't keep a civil tongue in your head then kindly leave this room."

"I ... I ..." Natalie spluttered, outraged by the tone of her stepfather's ultimatum. "I was just speaking my mind, that's all."

"You were being offensive and you know it," CJ returned, unimpressed. "I've had enough of it. You've been like this for months. Either change your ways or make yourself scarce. Now."

Natalie turned on Francey. "You'd like that, wouldn't you? Then you'd have him all to yourself so you could worm your way in even deeper." She stood and straightened. "If you'll excuse me, I'll go get some fresh air."

Only Les saw the look Natalie threw in Francey's direction as she made a red-faced exit. Hate and loathing mixed with an expression of sheer malice were clearly displayed. Silly bitch. Didn't she realise she was falling into CJ's trap? Making herself come over as greedy and selfish, proving how great the difference was between herself and Francey. Not that he cared. She deserved whatever she got or didn't get.

To her parents' delight, Francey drove them to the Mt Isa airport in CJ's Rolls-Royce.

"Are you sure you're going to be all right up here?" Lucia worried as they exchanged a parting hug. "That Natalie's a bitch. Be careful of her."

"Of course, Mamma. Things will be strained for a while, no doubt about that. I'm still angry with CJ and he knows it. But it'll sort itself out."

"Be happy, *cara*, that is the most important thing. The power and the money are empty tools without happiness," Carlo said as he kissed her on both cheeks. "And stay just as you are. Don't change now that you're going to be a mega-rich woman."

"I'm not mega-rich yet and I don't know ... I need time to get used to the idea, to everything."

"And your Steve. What are you –?"

"I'm going to see him as soon as your plane takes off."

"*Bene*," Carlo said. "I like him. He's good husband material," he added with a twinkle in his eye.

"Oh, Papà, you never give up, do you?"

CHAPTER TWENTY-FOUR

Francey parked the Rolls unobtrusively under several low-growing eucalypts in Steve's street, and headed for his front door. Unlocked, as usual, she turned the knob and went inside, her heart beat accelerating simply because she could hardly wait to see him. Doubts had been niggling at her subconscious since the party, growing, festering. Why hadn't he been in touch with her since CJ's announcement?

"Steve?" Francey called a greeting. She found him in the kitchen fixing a cup of coffee. "Hi!" she said, too brightly, as she gave him a hug. He hugged her back but didn't kiss her. Yes, something was definitely up!

"Hi, yourself," he answered in his deep policeman's voice. "Want a coffee?"

With the filled coffee mugs in their hands they went back into the living room. Steve waited for Francey to sit then he found a chair for himself, as far removed from her as possible. He noted that she looked tired, strung out, and a little agitated but was desperately trying not to show it. He'd never seen her like that before, not even when she'd been lost in the bush. He knew the cause. Coming to terms with being CJ's daughter and all it entailed. Frankly, it was something he wouldn't have wished hoisted on anyone he was fond of.

"Some birthday party, hey? I turn twenty-seven and find I have a new Dad as well," she began tentatively. Her smile was tremulous as she tried not to allow the insecurities warring inside her to take control. Certain, disquieting vibrations were emanating from him. Cool and contained. Worrying. Her stomach began to tie itself into knots. Where was the old Steve, the one she knew so well? The warm, compassionate, good-humoured guy she had fallen in love with. *This* Steve was acting like a virtual stranger instead of the passionate lover he'd been a couple of nights ago. She desperately wanted and needed the old Steve to resurface.

"Yeah," he shrugged his wide shoulders. "I guess joint congratulations are in order. It's not every day you hear that you're closely related to a multimillionaire."

"It's taking some getting used to, believe me. I'm not sure I –"

"Well, I think it's great," he interrupted, averting his eyes so he didn't look directly at her. "You fit right in. It'll work out well, I'm sure. CJ's got a worthy heir and you have the chance to be the mega-successful businesswoman you've always wanted to be."

Highly tuned, she listened to the nuances in his tone. Again, cool, distanced, as if they were discussing an absent third party instead of herself. Support and understanding was what she had come here for. She wanted to pour out her feelings about the doubts and uncertainties she felt inside, and the awesome responsibilities that would arise some time in the future. She valued his opinion, needed his affection and what was she getting? "Mr Cool" and his remote analysis. Why was he behaving this way? Was it her fault? She firmly believed that the best approach was a direct one. Ask!

"Steve, what's wrong?"

"Nothing." He shrugged again, deliberately nonchalant. "I couldn't be happier for you. You have a great opportunity, Francey. Think of all the things you can do in the future, with CJ's money behind you."

"Yes, I know that," she said impatiently. "But ... it won't change us, will it? I mean what we have together is too important, too precious." There, she'd said it, got it out in the open. Now she waited, almost afraid to breathe, for his answer.

"Oh ..." he began consideringly, as if only now giving it some thought. "I think it's bound to change our relationship. It'd be unrealistic to think otherwise. You're going to be one hell of a busy lady 'cause I'm sure that now you've been acknowledged as CJ's heir he'll up his training program. You'll be dealing with important businesspeople. Rubbing shoulders with politicians, the rich and famous, and jetting to all manner of wonderful places, I imagine. I doubt there'll be much time for *us* in the future."

"That's crazy." The hard knot in her stomach tightened. What was he trying to tell her? "We'll make time. We have in the past."

"Which hasn't always been easy," he stated. "Things have changed, Francey, whether we like it or not. CJ's announcement saw to that. Surely you see it too?"

"*I* haven't changed and what I feel for you hasn't changed," she said stubbornly.

Francey tried to ignore the terrible fear that was beginning to spread through the tightness in the pit of her stomach, through her limbs to her very soul. Up to now they had always been on the same wavelength, she could always tell what he was thinking, feeling and vice versa. Now she didn't like what she was hearing nor did she understand the vibes coming from him. Steve was distancing himself from her and she couldn't understand why. She loved him and she thought he loved her with the same depth of passion. Maybe – the thought brought a crushing pain to the middle of her chest – she'd been wrong.

"Is it because I'm part Aboriginal, not Italian?"

"Don't be bloody silly. That has nothing to do with it," he bit back, hiding the hurt that she might even consider such a possibility. He took another sip of coffee, his dark eyes clashing with hers, and when he spoke his tone was hard. "Face reality, Francey. You've moved upwards, into a very elite and different circle. It was fine when you were Francey Spinetti, architect – at a stretch we were kind of on the same level. Can't you see that everything is different now? You're going to be incredibly wealthy one day – I never will be. I have my pride, you know. I don't want people saying: 'Oh, look at Parrish, he's latched on to Francey because of her money. What's the male equivalent for a gold-digger? The same – gold-digger!'"

"That's ridiculous!" she shouted, despair replaced by anger. Another part of her life, the status quo, what she'd come to expect between them, was falling apart. *No,* she cried inside, dismayed, disappointed and confused by his reaction. She couldn't let this happen to them, what they'd had together was too good. Somehow she had to make Steve see that. "People do it all the time. Rich people marry not so rich people. It's what you feel inside that counts. Not the money, not the trappings."

"Not around Mt Isa," he said succinctly. "People love to gossip, believe the worst. It's the same everywhere." He'd seen it here and in Sydney, he knew he was right and that Francey had to be a touch naive to believe otherwise. God, he hated what he was doing to them but wasn't it kinder to make the cut now rather than later when their feelings were more deeply engaged? If he had to be strong for both of them then he damned well would be even if it meant that she'd hate him for the rest of their lives. Somehow, right now he didn't know how, he would live with it.

In silence she stared at him, unable to believe what she was hearing. He wasn't making any sense. Didn't what they feel for each other count enough to outweigh the imbalances? It did as far as she was concerned. But then, she suddenly realised, maybe from Steve's angle things were different ... and he had his pride. Litres of it! Pride had made him walk away from a career in the NSW Police Service instead of toughing it out ... Could it make him walk away from her too? And ... then there was the remote possibility that maybe, with her rose-tinted glasses on, she had imbued him with qualities he didn't really have.

Well, she decided, it was time to ask *the* question, find the bottom line. "Are you saying that we shouldn't see each other any more?"

Try as he might he couldn't look her in the eyes again. "Maybe that would be a good idea, for a while. Let things settle. Give ourselves time to rethink our relationship and where we want it to go."

"I thought we both knew where we wanted it to go," she murmured, trying to keep the dismay out of her voice. Don't let him do this to us, a voice inside her head said.

Steve was the best thing that had come into her life. She loved him and had intended to plan a life with him. She had thought that was what he wanted too. Perhaps she had been wrong about that.

Oh, God, had she made yet another mistake about a man and misjudged the depth of his feelings? All at once she had to get out of his living room – before she began to cry. She had her pride too and something deep inside her couldn't let him see how much she was hurting.

"I ... I'd better go," she stammered as she got to her feet.

She wanted to say so much, to plead with him to work their way through the difficulties together, but she glimpsed the set expression on his face and knew it would do no good. He had decided she wasn't right for him or he wasn't right for her and in his policeman mind that's all that counted. Damn him to hell. In fact, damn all men ...

Steve sat in the chair as if he had been turned into stone. He was numb from head to toe but he'd done it. Turned her away from him. He didn't feel good about it. He hurt. Immeasurably. For himself, for her, for what might have been and never would be. For the lonely days and lonelier nights, years, ahead of him.

Shit, his breath expelled in a low, growling sigh, he might as well take that transfer to Brisbane. Make a new start somewhere else.

Cruising around town in the Range Rover, CJ spied the Rolls parked near the Verona Hotel at dusk. He went up to the reception desk and asked if anyone had seen Francey. The clerk told him she had booked a room for the night. At first the clerk hadn't wanted to tell CJ which room, that was hotel policy, but after a fifty dollar note subtlely passed across the counter, coupled with CJ's explosive countenance and an indirect threat to his job, the clerk quietly stated the room number. He further redeemed himself by offering the information that he'd seen her five minutes ago in the bar, talking to Lisa Dupre.

Francey looked the worse for wear. Her dark hair flew wildly around her face and her eyes were puffy from crying. CJ took a deep breath and, sensing the tears were not for him, approached the table where the two women sat, deep in conversation.

"Francey, Lisa, how nice ..." he said cordially as he moved one of the chairs and sat at their table.

"CJ, I was just trying to talk Francey into having dinner with me and Pierre," Lisa said. Her eyebrows lifted meaningfully as they both studied a Francey they had never seen before, a Francey out of control and half drunk.

"Don' wanna eat, jus' get me 'nother drink," Francey slurred as she acknowledged CJ with a nod of her head.

"I'll see to it," CJ said and snapped his fingers for a passing waiter's attention. "Three coffees, please and make one black," he ordered as the waiter came within earshot.

"Wait a minut'," Francey objected. "I wanna whisky, the best." She tried to look steadily at CJ but her eyes wouldn't stay focused. "I learnt that from you, CJ, nothin' but the best – Johnny Walker Imported, thank you, waiter."

"Coffee," CJ countermanded and motioned for Lisa to make her excuses.

"Well, I'll be off. Pierre's waiting for me in the dining room. If you both change your mind, please join us."

Francey gave Lisa an uncoordinated wave then stared at CJ. "Don' want bloody coffee. Need 'nother drink."

"I suggest we continue this discussion in your room. Shall we?" CJ said firmly.

Francey stared narrow-eyed at him for a moment until she remembered the well-equipped mini-bar there. "Sure, why not?"

Once inside Francey's room CJ sat her in a chair. "Now, young lady, what has brought this on?" He hoped, rather desperately, that she wasn't reacting to the fact that she was his daughter. The thought that the reality might have driven her to drink caused him great anxiety.

"Personal." She got up and went over to the mini-bar. Deftly screwing the top off the Johnny Walker bottle she poured it into a tumbler and drank it down straight, barely shuddering this time. Hard liquor wasn't usually to her liking, the most she ever had was a light white wine, but she knew the stronger alcohol would achieve the aim of making her insensible faster.

"That's enough." CJ's tone was harsh. He made them both a strong cup of coffee and gave her a cup. "This is what you need. Francey, we have to talk and there's little point in us trying to when you're half under the weather."

"Wannabe wholly under th' weather," she retorted. Her head was beginning to ache and spin at the same time. And she had this queasy feeling in her stomach too. When had she last eaten? Couldn't remember. Wasn't important. Who the hell cared?

"What brought this on?" CJ asked.

"It's personal."

"Oh, a man." He could only think of one man capable of causing her such distress. "Steve Parrish, hey? What's he done, two-timed you?" Somehow he couldn't see that happening, Parrish didn't seem the type.

She could tell him, she realised. He was her father after all. "No. Worse. Dumped me." Without consciously thinking about it she began to sip the coffee. "Said it couldn't work out between us because ... 'cause ..."

"Because you're CJ Ambrose's daughter?"

"Right. Th' bastard. I hate him."

"I'm sorry. Do you blame me? I mean, if I hadn't said anything, gone public ..."

She gave him a funny look. "Wha'! Why should I blame you? Steve's th' one with th' prob. I said it shouldn't make any difference if we care for each other. He says it does."

"I see. It's hard to fight a person's perception, isn't it?"

"Damned right it is," she muttered with feeling.

"Perhaps I should talk to him."

She shook her head adamantly. "Wouldn't do any good. I know Steve," she sighed sadly, "too well. He's the kind of person tha' once he makes up his mind, that's it full stop."

"Then maybe you have to face the fact that he didn't care as much for you as you did for him."

She'd thought about it but the reality of him saying the words out loud was just too much. Tears began to roll down her cheeks. "I know ... That's what hurts. I ... I seem to have a knack for falling for the wrong men."

CJ noted that she'd finished her coffee so he made her another one. She was sobering fast anyway, talking the problem through seemed to be having that effect on her. By the end of the second cup of coffee she still looked terrible but was at least coherent.

"I thought that we needed to talk, about last night. About everything," he began. "I knew you wanted time to make the mental adjustment but I'm really anxious for us to get over this ... difficulty ... and become close again. Can we talk?"

"We are talking," she said simply, a wary smile lighting her face.

"Why don't I order dinner for us, room service, hey?"

"Sure. Sounds good." She doubted that she could eat much but if it made him happy ...

While they waited for room service they began to talk, or rather CJ did most of it and Francey listened.

"I have to explain about Mary. It's difficult to admit you were wrong about something, that you made a big mistake in your life. At least it's always been that way for me. I did back in Coober Pedy. I loved Mary and I should never have left her but back then I was obsessed ..."

"Obsessed with what?" she interjected, instantly interested.

"It goes back many years, to my childhood. I was just a youngster when my grandfather lost our property, Amba Downs. I loved that place. My Dad would take me mustering on his horse, practically before I could walk. I knew every hectare of the land. I had expectations. One day it would come to me. But we lost everything and were forced to lead a pretty nomadic life." He grinned. "Almost like the Aboriginals. We'd go from job to job, town to town. Mother was never strong, she didn't last long living that kind of life, but before she died she instilled in me the dream of the Ambrose's having their own place one day. It became my consuming passion. As I grew, everything I learnt and did, the money I could save, was all directed at achieving that goal.

"The opal mine worked as a short cut for me, a way of making my dream come true earlier than it might have. Of course Mickey and I were damned lucky to come across a vein that made us rich. When Mickey died I got the lot." He shook his head and when he looked at her there was incredible sadness in his eyes. "They always said I was a lucky bastard." He was silent for a moment or too, remembering. "You see, I know it's hard to understand but Mary wasn't part of my dream. I loved her in my own way but I honestly couldn't see us having a life together. She was so young, so naive –"

"Good enough to sleep with though ..." Francey interrupted sagely.

"Yes," he admitted. "She was a sweet, innocent girl. I guess I destroyed that innocence without consciously meaning to. She never meant to get pregnant, you know. She was on the pill but I guess something happened, or didn't happen. Maybe she forgot to take it one day and didn't tell me. Poor Mary. She'd never had a real family, she was brought up at the mission and the other kids and the nuns there were the only family she knew. She so wanted to belong ... that's partly why I think she wanted the baby."

"A family should include a father too," Francey pointed out, her blue-green eyes studying him closely, seeing the play of emotions on his face and through his body language.

"You're right. Only I was so caught up in the obsession of making my dream come true, I didn't think about *her* dreams." He expelled a sigh. "Selfish bastard, that's what I am."

"You won't get any argument from me on that score."

"I honestly thought she'd find someone else. Someone who would be more suited to her ... and they'd be a family. I sent her money, you know, enough to set herself up. To buy a house and invest the rest to bring in an income. She sent the cheque back to the bank, wouldn't take a cent."

"Too proud to, I expect." Francey knew it was so. It fitted the mental image Lucia and Carlo had given her of Mary Williams.

"I guess so. Anyway, when I got back to Townsville I worked hard to get her out of my head and my heart. Brenda, I convinced myself, was the right type of wife for me. Brenda and her inheritance would be an asset to me as I made my way in the world, Mary and a baby would have been a burden. I know that's cold-hearted and I apologise for it, but it's the truth. Mary couldn't have coped with the social aspect, or understood or been interested in the business side. Brenda was, always. But I tried to check on Mary. I had someone check out Coober Pedy, but they'd lost track of her. So I took the easy way out and assumed that everything was okay."

"It wasn't though, was it?"

"No. I had no idea she was ill with that blood problem. But at least you can't blame me for causing that."

Their meals arrived and strangely, Francey found that she could eat. A couple of hours before she'd thought she would never want to eat again, yet here she was, tucking into a huge New York cut steak. Was her returning appetite a sign that her heart wasn't really as badly broken as she'd thought?

"Tell me about my mother. How did you meet? What did she do? I want to know everything about her. About your romance with her."

They talked till midnight. CJ told her all the things he could remember about Mary, the little things about her life growing up at the mission. And in doing so the chasm that had stretched between them since the party was bridged.

CHAPTER TWENTY-FIVE

Francey leant back in the first-class seat aboard the flight to Sydney, closed her eyes and relived yesterday's successful conclusion of yet another business seminar at the mini conference centre. The pledges for investment capital had come hard and fast once they'd detailed the success of stage one of Cooktown's Jasmine project. Still a year away from completion, stage one was fully subscribed, as Nikko, head of the Yakismoto consortium had predicted it would be.

The trip south was partly to scout out several promising business leads CJ had come up with which, if genuine, would allow the Pac-Asia Investment consortium – the ink on yesterday's contracts was still wet – to break into the lucrative Sydney property development market. And, of course there would be time to check the building progress of CJ's mansion at Kirribilli and for a lightning visit to see her parents.

Since the party, CJ had piled on the work, telling her it was the best thing for a broken heart. Her smile was wry at that remembered remark. His opinion wasn't shared by her but at least keeping busy kept thoughts of Steve and the accompanying pain around the region of her heart to a bearable minimum. She'd heard that he had asked for a transfer to Brisbane, which was a mixed blessing. In a way it would be a relief to know that she wouldn't bump into him on the streets of the Isa but the fact that he'd be further away only intensified the pain of her loss.

On arrival at Mascot she was whisked off in a limousine to her first business appointment. This set the pattern for the first day and a half. After that and successfully negotiating an option on land for a resort complex north of Katoomba, with the intention to build an artificial skiing complex on the site as well, she purposely made time for her parents. They went to see the progress of the Kirribilli house, and then had dinner at Edna's Table at The Rocks.

"You are spoiling us, *cara*," Carlo said as he sat back after dessert and tried to be polite by not burping, a habit for which he was renowned after a particularly rich meal.

"Why not?" Francey responded. "You're very special to me." Which was the truth. She loved them both dearly, and that would never change. In fact, if and when she could, she would do all in her power to make their lives easier ... if they permitted it. But she wouldn't tell them that yet, they had to become more used to sharing her with CJ.

Only Lucia, more compassionate and observant than her husband, saw the subtle changes in Francey. The self-confidence, never much of a problem, was now even more pronounced, more sure. And with a mother's eyes she saw the underlying sadness too and her heart went out to her.

"That Steve," Lucia said suddenly, "he is a stupid man. Not as bright as I thought he was."

"Please, Mamma, you promised not to talk about Steve."

"Pah, I say nothing more other than to repeat that he is stupid to let a woman like you get away from him."

Carlo and Francey exchanged glances, their eyebrows raised. When Lucia Spinetti got on her soapbox, everyone beware. This they knew from years of experiencing her fiery outbursts.

"Perhaps he was right. I'm so damned busy these days. I get up at six, go full pelt all day and stumble into bed at midnight, or later, sometimes. Where would I get the time to fit Steve, or any other man for that matter, into my present life?"

"But it will not always be like this, *cara,*" Lucia said. "*You* must control the pace, find time to relax. Otherwise you will snap, like this," and to make her point she picked up a bread stick and broke it in half.

Francey nodded her agreement. "Yes. Once I get the next two projects under way, I'll definitely take some time off. That's a promise." She watched her father yawn – he was usually in bed at 8.30 p.m. when he had to go to the markets at Flemington the next day. She pretended to stifle a yawn too. "It's getting late. Come on, I'll see you home."

"There's no need. We can get a taxi."

"I want to. There's something in my old room I want to take back to Murrundi." She had just stopped herself from calling it "home" – she'd come to think of the outback homestead as her home – but stopped herself in time. Besides, it wasn't strictly true about the object, the subterfuge was necessary because of her parents' independent streak. It was hard enough convincing them that her expense account was paying for their sumptuous meal let alone anything else.

It was almost ten thirty by the time they arrived back at Glebe.

Meredith O'Connor met them in a rush of movement at the side entrance to the flat at the back of the fruit shop. "Thank goodness," she said breathlessly as she approached. "I've been waiting here for an hour and a half."

"What's wrong? Brett? Mitchell?"

Meredith shook her head. Obviously trying not to alarm Francey's parents she muttered, "I just need to talk to you before you fly back."

"Come inside and I'll make us a coffee," Lucia offered.

"No, Mrs Spinetti. It's late, I don't want to impose. Ten minutes of Francey's time is all I need." And so saying she half pulled Francey towards her parked car.

"What's this about?" Francey said with a laugh as she sat in the passenger seat of Meredith's ageing Corolla. "What a drama. Mum will be dying with curiosity to know ..."

"Sorry. I tried to get you at your hotel. They didn't know where you were dining so rather than lurk about the lobby of the Regent, I thought I'd wait here in case you turned up."

"Well, here I am. What's up?"

"This." Meredith unfolded a copy of *New Idea* and turned the car's internal light on. "Read page four."

Shaking her head with amusement at Meredith's cloak-and-dagger air, Francey did as instructed. Her breath caught in her throat as she read the headline and scanned the photos in the two page article.

CHIP OFF THE OLD BLOCK. CJ AMBROSE'S
DAUGHTER CAUSES HEARTBREAK

There were photos of herself and CJ, taken at the party. One of her and Bryan Steinberg – God knows where they'd got that from – and a photo of a woman in a wheelchair. Francey recognised the woman instantly, Cathy, Bryan's wife. In heavy silence she read the article. It was a subtle character assassination of herself with implied references that she had inherited her father's, "the man with the golden touch's" temperament by ruthlessly destroying the Steinberg's marriage and causing his wife's stroke.

"Where did you get this?" Francey asked finally.

"I've a friend at ACP. She sneaked me an advance copy. It'll hit the newsstands tomorrow." Meredith placed a hand over Francey's. "I thought you'd like to know, so you can be prepared."

Francey's head rested back against the car seat and, turning sideways, she looked at her friend. "Thanks, I think." She sighed. "I guess I now go into damage control. Damn it, I don't need this in my life right now. I wonder how they found out."

"Did you notice that there's no by-line on the piece? My guess is that the author wanted to remain anonymous. It might be interesting to find out why," Meredith suggested.

"It might." Francey sat up straight, deciding. "Well, I guess I'd better show it to Mum and Dad. I don't want them to find out through customers talking about it."

"Are you going to be all right?"

"Sure. I'm a chip off the old block, didn't you know?" Francey's eyes were suspiciously bright. "Tough as my father."

"What would CJ do in such cases?" Meredith wanted to know.

Francey thought for a moment. She knew her father pretty well and it wasn't hard to guess how he would react. "He'd probably weather the storm of public debate, do his best to ignore it, then he'd find the little shit who wrote it and give them hell."

"Sounds like a good prescription to me."

CJ Ambrose was furious. Shellie had shown him the article on Francey and his temper had risen to the boil instantaneously. Through his contacts it didn't take long to track down the writer of the piece – Trish Pentano, the sly, conniving little bitch. She'd rue the day she chose to tangle with an Ambrose … Subsequently he'd summoned Natalie back to Murrundi for a showdown, his gut feeling telling him that she had orchestrated the entire incident. But for what purpose? The answer to that question eluded him.

As he stood on the verandah waiting for the Learjet to land on the airstrip he noticed Mike Hunter foraging around the shrubs near the pool. "What's up, Mike?"

"Oh, CJ. Hi." Mike looked up and shielded his gaze against a bright wintry sun. He walked over and stood at the bottom of the verandah to look up at his boss. "I've misplaced my Swiss army knife. Can't find it anywhere. Thought it might have fallen out of my pocket the night of the party."

CJ grinned. "You and your bloody Swiss army knife. Feel naked without it, eh?"

Mike flushed. "Sure do. It's a little beauty. The things it can do …"

CJ held up his hands in supplication. "Don't tell me again. You've extolled its virtues often enough in the bunkhouse, it's a wonder every stockman on the station hasn't bought one."

"Yeah," Mike grinned cheekily at CJ, "maybe I should take up some kind of franchise with the company."

"Not on my time, you won't." CJ's gaze scanned the horizon and saw a flash of metal glint in the sky. "When the jet lands tell Natalie I want to see her in my study, immediately, will you?"

"Sure."

Natalie closed the study door and leant against it as she studied CJ sitting behind his desk. His head downcast, he appeared to be reading something while he rubbed his temples with his fingertips. She noted that the colour of his skin, usually a ruddy tan, had taken on a rare pallor. And the scar on his scalp, over which a light grey fuzz was trying to grow, was quite noticeable.

His head jerked up as the door clicked shut and without preamble he attacked. "Why did you do it? What did you hope to gain from letting your weak-minded friend Trish write such a dirty article about Francey?"

"I ... don't ..."

"Don't insult my intelligence by pretending you didn't know about it. *You* put the idea into her head, I'd bet money on it."

Seeing the pointlessness of denying it, Natalie shrugged an elegant shoulder. Dressed in Trent Nathan slacks, a silk blouse and a multicoloured Cuggi sweater she looked every inch the wealthy socialite. "Maybe I did suggest something, casually of course," she admitted offhandedly. Her grey eyes narrowed maliciously. "It's about time everyone, you included, CJ, saw Francey for what she is. A money-grubbing opportunist who doesn't care who she hurts to get what she wants."

"You stupid bitch." The expression in his eyes was deadly. "You think I didn't know about the Steinberg affair? When I have someone investigated I get a proper job done. However, I learnt the truth of the matter, not the half-truths Trish alluded to in her article. By the way you can tell her she's no longer welcome at Murrundi."

"But she's my friend ..." It began to dawn on Natalie that by exposing the perceived flaws in Francey's character she may have increased her own estrangement from CJ. She had thought, perhaps naively, that he might thank her for pointing out his *new* daughter's inadequacies, but no, as usual all he wanted to do was to justify and protect her. God, it just wasn't fair. What did she have to do to get rid of the millstone around her neck?

"She's no friend of mine or anyone at Murrundi's from today onwards," CJ stated as he stared at her. "And you need to get your act in order. I do not understand this irrational hatred towards Francey."

"Don't you?" She jumped in angrily. "She comes here and supplants Richard's place in your heart and fortune. The fortune which should rightly come to me, and you think I should be," she sneered, "*nice* to her?"

His voice thundered about the small room. "Don't say that again, ever. No-one could ever take the place of what I felt, still feel for my son. But she is my daughter, whether you like it or not and whether you approve of it or not. You will accord her that respect or else."

Something inside her snapped. "Oh, for Christ's sake. Forget the degree, forget her business acumen, Francey is a part Aboriginal illegitimate brat, that's what she really is," Natalie said boldly. "What do you think people are saying behind your back about all of this?"

"I don't give a stockman's spit what people are saying. You know me better than that. I've weathered more controversy in my life than acknowledging a love child."

She attempted a different angle. "How do you think my mother would feel about her, the product of a love affair, living here, in the house she built for us? You, Richard, Miles and I? Now you want it to go to her. Mother would turn in her grave if she knew."

CJ thought before he answered. "Maybe she would, but I'd like to think that Brenda had a more generous heart than her daughter seems to have." He looked her up and down, seeing a spoilt, frustrated woman. He wasn't impressed or moved by her pleas. "I will no longer tolerate your mean-spirited, bitchy behaviour around Francey. Do I make myself clear? Either you make her feel welcome at Murrundi and a part of the family, or you can forget that Murrundi is your home. And if you ever try to pull another trick like that article, I will destroy you." He paused deliberately to let the words sink in. "And you know that if I say I will, I will."

Natalie paled. She saw from the look on his face and his tone of voice that he meant every word he'd said. She had come to know him in all his roles. The ruthless negotiator, the knock-about guy, the head of the house, the beaming philanthropist. He had issued an ultimatum and she could either take it or ... "I see ..."

Her shoulders drooped in seeming defeat as she turned away from him. She had played her cards and lost. Instead of alienating Francey from CJ she had alienated herself from him. Too late she understood that Francey's hold was as strong as CJ's need. He needed Francey more than he had ever needed or wanted her. That, she realised, was a very bitter pill indeed.

CJ watched her go, the frown on his forehead increasing as the splitting headache took hold. The Swiss specialist had claimed that the operation to reduce the size of the tumour and the radio therapy afterwards might give him as much time as thirty-seven weeks. He did a rough calculation. Twenty-one, and now it was reactivating. How much time did he have left? Probably a month, two at the most.

He groaned aloud. The respite was over and he was sure the tumour was growing again. He could almost feel it pulsing inside his head, spreading its debilitating tentacles everywhere. His head began to spin and before he could move a step towards the bathroom he began to vomit, over the desk, and all over Trish Pentano's article.

"Hello?"

"Francey?"

"Yes. Who's that?"

"Bryan."

Something shuddered inside Francey's chest, an all too familiar, bittersweet pain. "Oh, I didn't expect. It's about the article … I'm sorry."

"How are you?"

She recognised the huskiness in his voice, he had always sounded that way when he talked to her. Her smile was a little grim as she acknowledged the truth. She could think about it now with a detachment she had yearned for desperately years ago. He was the past, buried, over. And deep down she was more concerned about how Steve might feel about what had been printed about her.

"I'm fine."

"I wanted you to know the real truth, not the distortion printed by that rag," he said. "By the way, I'm glad for you, glad that you're doing so well. Really." He cleared his throat. "My wife, actually my ex-wife, well, the whole story has been an exaggeration to say the least. Cathy had a stroke years ago, long before you and I got together. It's a predilection in the family, her mother's had several strokes."

"Bryan, I really don't think –"

"I need to tell you, Francey," he insisted. "I don't want you to feel guilty about something that wasn't your fault. The second stroke Cathy had happened six months after we broke up so I hardly think even the medicos would consider my affair the main contributing factor."

Francey sighed. She didn't want to discuss this with Bryan but she could sense that he needed to expunge it from his conscience. "How is she?"

"Much better since we divorced," his tone was wry. "Her parents encouraged her to give me the flick, you know. She and the children live with them. All one big happy family, minus me of course."

"I'm sorry, Bryan." A year ago she wouldn't have been able to say those words, now she could and mean them.

"Oh, I'm all right. I wanted to make sure you knew the truth, that you weren't the cause of Cathy's illness. I'm going to write to that damn editor and tell her she should check the facts in future."

"That's thoughtful of you, Bryan, I appreciate it."

"I ..." he hesitated for several seconds. "I just hope that it makes it easier to forgive me for what happened. It was all my fault, you know."

She smiled into the receiver. "Don't be so hard on yourself, Bryan. It takes two to make a romance. You didn't have to coerce me into your arms."

"Are you happy, Francey? I mean, is there ...?"

"Yes there is and I am." Only half a lie, she convinced herself.

"Then I'm happy for you," his voice sounded sad. "Bye."

As Francey replaced the receiver a feeling of melancholy

flowed through her. Strange how things had worked out. Bryan was alone, at least she presumed he was and she had got over him. Finally. Definitely. But where did she stand with Steve? In some weird no-man's-land, a situation that he had insisted upon. Well, she would give him a little time – to miss her, she hoped – then, she decided, if she had to she would go after him. What they had found together few people in life ever found and it was too good to walk away from, no matter how difficult the circumstances might be. But first she had something to do. She and Natalie needed to have a talk.

Shellie was enjoying a late cup of coffee in the kitchen with Barry when she heard the noise. It sounded uncannily like women's voices. Screaming.

When she investigated, she found Francey and Natalie standing on opposite sides of the table in the conservatory yelling abuse at each other.

"If you and that damn bitch girlfriend of your's ever pull another trick like that I'll tear you limb from limb," Francey threatened, her eyes blazing, her head thrown back aggressively.

"Do you think you scare me?" Natalie taunted.

"You should be scared. Half the genes in my body are CJ's," Francey raged. "And we both know what he's capable of."

"So you're a chip off the old block after all?"

"I could think of worse things to be," she paused for dramatic effect, "like a spoilt, frustrated cow who wishes she had half the talent I have, and the affection CJ feels towards me."

"You're the cow. You lead men on, tease them. Bryan Steinberg, Aden Nicholson, oh yes, I know about him. Les too and you even managed to get your hooks into Steve Parrish." Natalie lunged across the table, her arm long enough to swipe at Francey. She missed her face but her fingers, with their long painted nails scraped down Francey's forearm leaving two red welts across the skin.

"Ouch! You bloody cat," Francey retorted, rubbing at the marks on her arm; they stung like hell. "At least I'm not a psychopath, unlike you." Francey ducked back to avoid a second swing from the other hand.

"I hate you, you Aboriginal slut's daughter. That's what you are, you know, no better than that. You've ruined everything for me."

Francey kept her cool, and despite the provocation she smiled. "Aahh, then there is some justice in the world."

"Girls, girls," Shellie tut-tutted as she came into the room. "You'll disturb CJ with all that shouting." She looked reprovingly at Francey then at Natalie. "You should both know better."

"Oh, shut up, you old fart," Natalie muttered. She could feel the heat in her cheeks, her heart was pounding and a vein in her temple throbbed with unrelieved fury. She stared across at an unrepentant Francey, a self-satisfied, very confident Francey. Sure of her position in CJ's heirachy. Natalie could kill her, yes, she could.

"Such language," Shellie's eyebrows rose in shock. "Francey, I suggest you retire. Haven't you got a business meeting in town early in the morning?"

"You're right, I have." But as Shellie turned towards her stepniece, Francey said *sotto voce* to her opponent, "Don't think this is finished yet, Natalie. There'll be another time, another place."

CHAPTER TWENTY-SIX

Shellie sat at the foot of CJ's bed while she waited for him to wake. The medication Barry had given him yesterday for pain, which had rendered him unconscious for nearly ten hours, was beginning to wear off. A few minutes earlier she had poked her head around the door, seen him stir and hoped it would be a comfort for him to see her when he first opened his eyes.

She knew she had to appear unworried by the bad turn he'd had yesterday but that would be hard. Last night she'd prayed that it was an aberration and that the operation and radiotherapy he'd had in Geneva would assure a complete recovery. He was happy, now that Francey and he were getting along so well, and he'd finally been able to put Richard's sorrowful death behind him. She'd seen a softening in him too, and had welcomed it, knowing that his daughter was responsible.

Shellie had something important to tell him too, about herself ... and Barry. They were going to be married, as soon as the arrangements could be made. She tried to subdue the pang of sadness that swept through her at the thought of leaving Murrundi. She'd been here for so long.

Everyone was used to her seeing that the homestead and the bunkhouse supplies as well as a hundred and one other things ran like a well-oiled machine. But it was time to go. The opportunity for a happy life with the man she had loved for such a long time was irresistible ... and she was so looking forward to living it with him.

CJ's eyelids opened slowly, dopily. For several moments he felt disorientated, unsure of where he was but then, as his gaze focused, he recognised his furniture and a familiar figure sitting on the end of the bed, gently patting his feet under the blankets.

"How are you feeling?" Shellie asked.

He grimaced. "Like a road train's run over me."

"Barry said the after-effects of the drug would make you feel a bit woozy for a while."

"Woozy? That's an understatement. I'm as weak as a kitten."

"I'll get Alison to make some tea. That'll perk you up. And then there's something I want to tell you."

CJ knew it would take a damned sight more than a cup of tea to perk him up. He was nothing if not pragmatic. Yesterday's attack was clear evidence that the tumour was growing again. The medicos had said the treatment would only give him a brief remission: too bloody brief as far as he was concerned. There were things he had to do before ... he became as useless as a vegetable. Taking a deep breath he summoned a much needed inner strength. It was time.

"Before you get Alison to bring me the tea, Shell, I've got to get something off my chest."

Her eyebrows lifted. "Not more revelations, CJ. Don't tell me you have a bevy of children somewhere else?"

Despite himself he grinned. "No, nothing like that."

God if it were only that! "It's about the tumour, sis. You, me, we're both going to have to be brave ..." He paused, took a deep breath and finished it, "You see, it isn't benign it's malignant. Terminal."

"What?" Shellie stared at him, her gentle features contorting into an expression of disbelief as she tried to absorb the dire meaning of what he'd just said. "But ... surely, Barry can do something. I don't believe it." Thoughts of her own happy tidings fled to the back of her mind, blanked out by this unbelievable news. It couldn't be. Terminal!

"I know it's hard but it's true. Those treatments in Geneva, all they did was buy me some time."

"Why didn't you tell me before?" she murmured reproachfully, tears brimming in her eyes and then overflowing down her cheeks. Why hadn't Barry told her? Professional etiquette, she supposed. Oh, dear God, the ramifications of what this meant ... she couldn't bear to think about it.

CJ looked at her for several moments, his mouth tightening as he tried to control his own emotions. He reached forward to touch her cheek and wipe away a tear, his smile tinged with a mixture of sadness and compassion. "That's why. I knew it would cause you pain and I wanted to avoid that for as long as possible."

She nodded understandingly. "Who else knows? Francey?"

He shook his head. "Just Barry and Les whom I swore to secrecy."

"Oh, this is awful. I just can't believe you're calmly sitting there telling me you're going to, going to ..."

"Die?" He dragged in a noisy breath and his shoulders shrugged in resignation. "It happens to us all, sometime.

I've made my peace, accepted it." But he knew that it hadn't been easy. Every time he looked at his daughter and felt the joy inside him at having come to know her and see what she was capable of, he felt cheated by what life had thrown him. Because all too soon he'd no longer be around to share that pleasure and feel the warmth of her love. Suddenly his own eyes filled with tears.

"Oh, CJ …"

"It's all right. Really." He cleared his throat and brushed the tear off his cheek.

She asked the dreaded question. "How long?"

"A month. Maybe six weeks. It's one of those galloping tumours, the kind that spreads rapidly. But before it debilitates me completely, I have a lot to do and I'll need your help."

"You're going to tell Francey, aren't you?"

"Not until I have to," he told her. "She's got enough on her plate with the workload I've given her, and she's having a hard time getting over Steve."

"She'll be angry with you."

He grinned. "I know. I'll deal with that when it happens."

Natalie looked at the rug as she paced backwards and forwards in her bedroom. She stopped. Christ, she'd been stomping up and down so much she'd worn a tack in it. Hours. Inside she seethed, bubbled and boiled with frustration, half of it directed at CJ the rest at Francey, the smart-mouthed bitch. Implying she was a dyke. How had she known? She and Trish were very discreet. At Murrundi they'd taken pains to be careful, and she'd even indulged in a mild flirtation with Mike Hunter to make herself appear straight. Obviously she hadn't fooled Francey or … had someone told her? Perhaps Les.

She ground her teeth together so hard that her jaw began to ache. And that Les was just as bad. How delighted he'd looked the night of the party when CJ had made his startling announcement. She'd seen the smirk, the smugness. He'd thought it a wonderful payback. Oh, why was everyone against her? No-one cared a damn about her feelings. Except Mumsie, she had been the most wonderful, the only person in the whole wide world who understood her.

She'd do anything for Mumsie, hadn't she always? Whatever Mumsie had asked of her she had done ... so ... if Mumsie could accept Francey she would too. Her staring eyes flickered with some emotion then steadied. No, something inside her head screamed, Mumsie would never accept CJ's love child, she'd *know* it would alter her inheritance. But ... but, a shudder ran through her, her precious Mumsie was dead. A melancholy tear slipped down her cheek. There was no-one to confide in now except Trish but sometimes even Trish didn't understand.

Her eyes narrowed to dark eyelash fringed slits as her concentration jumped from one person to another. CJ banning Trish from Murrundi. The nerve of him. Hateful. Hateful! All he wanted was Francey, he'd never wanted her, only Richard and Miles, *never* her. She ran her fingers through her platinum hair as she thought about the intruder who had irreparably damaged her credibility with CJ.

She hated everything about her: her cleverness, her dark good looks, her ability to attract men and her sickening popularity. So different from herself. She didn't get on with people, so from the time she'd understood the principles – she had been in her teens – she had wielded power and money, and issued threats to get what she wanted. Francey didn't have to do that. She had the knack of drawing people to her and getting the best out of them in either a work or social situation. It wasn't fair.

Francey, the illegitimate half-caste bitch had come along and ruined everything she had planned, schemed and worked for. She had to be removed, somehow. Permanently! A thoughtful smile spread her thin lips wide across her face. What was the term crims used? Eliminated. Yes, Francey Spinetti, permanent thorn in her side, had to be *eliminated*.

She sat on the side of the bed, plucked a piece of lint off her red shirt and then she folded her arms across her chest and began to rock backwards and forwards. Yes, yes, yes. It could be done. After all, her smile was secretive, sly, it wasn't the first time she had *eliminated* someone who'd got in her way …

It wasn't her fault, it was CJ's. He had, chauvinist pig that he was, forced the situation because of his plan to leave the bulk of his estate to Richard. It wasn't fair! She remembered well the day he'd called them all into his study, six weeks after her mother's death, and told them he'd rewritten his will, leaving just about everything to Richard. She shook her head, she couldn't, wouldn't, let CJ do that to her. She deserved better. More, a more equal share of his millions. So … Richard had had to be eliminated. A small muscle flexed in her cheek as the memories came flooding back to her with a clarity that made her tingle.

Engineering the stampede had been easy, well, relatively easy. Knowing about the muster and the trail Richard and Billy would take to the cattle pens, via the waterhole, all she'd had to do was wait at the appropriate place.

A half moon had guided her through the scrubby brush to the rise above where Richard and Billy had made camp.

With a pair of infra-red glasses she checked the camp site and the cattle. All was quiet as she stole into the camp – thank God they hadn't brought dogs with them. She found Richard's saddle, half sliced through the cinch and then left as silently as she'd come.

Spending the night on the hill, not daring to drop off to sleep had been the most difficult part of the exercise … and keeping her horse quiet. She'd used a Walkman and up-tempo music to stay awake and as the half moon had waned and the sun began to show as a pale glow in the eastern sky she had mounted her horse and waited until she'd seen movement.

When Billy crawled out of his bed-roll and stirred the embers of the fire she waited, waited for a last glimpse of her half-brother, the man she was about to kill.

The rocking stopped for a moment. A single tear dripped down her cheek and she squeezed her eyes shut. Over. That was over. Done. Pangs of remorse flowed through her and her rocking movements began again, this time faster. She had killed her half-brother because he threatened her inheritance, an inheritance she thoroughly deserved. And with Richard out of the way she would have inherited it all after CJ's death.

A nerve began to twitch at the side of her mouth. Her mother's inheritance had allowed CJ to take the first few steps up the ladder to the ultimate success he now enjoyed. Without the deWitt money he may not have been quite so successful, that was irrefutable. Yes, she'd had moments of regret for having gotten rid of Richard but Mumsie had taught her that self-preservation and holding onto what was rightfully hers were the most important things in life

Dear Mumsie, she missed her so much. Mumsie would understand about Richard.

The rocking motions sped up, her breathing increasing with the pace of her movements. Francey was the real threat now and, like Richard, she had to be dealt with. She'd almost managed it before, until Steve Parrish had come along and saved her. But *she* was smart, cunning, and out here in the bush – which she knew so well – accidents happened. All the time. Maybe a snake bite. Maybe a situation where her car broke down and she was attacked and killed by unknown parties. Maybe she could make it look like her horse had fatally kicked her in the head. So many possibilities. It shouldn't be too hard to arrange something fatal for Francey. All she had to do was to work on the scenario, plan it down to the finest detail, as she had done with Richard.

Then everything would be as it was before she'd come here. She smiled, the twitch stopped and the rocking began to slow. Something to look forward to.

Billy Wontow yawned, stretched and scratched his full belly with his left hand as he moved off the verandah of the small cottage he shared with Alison. He looked up and the first rays of a wintry sun warmed his face. The sky was blue, not a cloud anywhere and as he loped along to the homestead for a meeting with CJ and Mike Hunter, he noted that the dew was heavy on the lawn around the pool. Then his dark eyes blinked and he stared hard at the water's surface.

Something was floating in the water, it'd probably been blown in by the strong wind they'd had last night. Whatever it was would sink to the bottom and make Henry, the part-time gardener and pool cleaner cranky, not that that was unusual, Henry was often cranky when people messed with his plants and such. He'd better do the right thing, fish it out before the meeting, otherwise he'd forget about it.

Moving onto the patio for a closer look before he found a length of wood to hook it out, his eyes widened as the *something* became recognisable. Holy Mary, mother of God. He made the sign of the cross even though he wasn't really religious.

It was a person, not a something. No, he corrected himself, by the way it was floating, face down, it was a body. If he hadn't recognised the platinum blonde hair he could have identified her from the red shirt she liked to wear. Natalie.

Natalie deWitt-Ambrose was dead.

CHAPTER TWENTY-SEVEN

Steve Parrish dropped to his haunches and pulled back the blanket to view the remains. Billy Wontow and Mike Hunter had removed Natalie's body from the pool and laid her at the pool's edge on a blanket with another covering her. Two other policemen, Senior Constable Neil Smith and Probationary Constable Erin Cooper stood close by, content to let Steve make the preliminary inspection of the body. The immediate family and workers at Murrundi remained indoors at his request.

With what dispassion he could muster Steve's expert gaze studied what had once been a vibrant, attractive woman. *Contusion on the left temple,* he wrote in his black, vinyl bound notebook. *Multiple bruises and indentations on each side of the neck. Contorted expression, slight bulging of the eyes. Red shirt has two buttons missing. A struggle may have taken place. Bruise above right breast. Possible rape and murder.*

He replaced the blanket and stood up, the muscle in his jaw flexing. Homicide. Never pleasant but this one ... He frowned, perplexed. Why? Who would want to murder Natalie deWitt-Ambrose? The frown deepened. First the son now the stepdaughter. CJ Ambrose was running out of relatives fast.

He looked at Neil and Erin. "We'll have to get statements from everyone who was at the homestead and in the bunkhouse last night. Did they hear anything strange or unusual? When did they retire? Did they know if the deceased had any enemies, any gossip that can be corroborated? Whatever you can wring out of them. You know the drill. We're going to need an ambulance, a forensic report and then later a post-mortem. Neil, would you get the paperwork started?"

"Sure, Steve."

Steve nodded to Erin. The short, slim, blonde-haired rookie's skin had paled and he noticed that she had swayed once or twice. "Not going to faint on me are you, Constable Cooper?"

Erin's chin lifted. "I'd like to, sir, but no, I won't."

"Good, come with me. We'll go into the house and get the proceedings started." He glanced up at the sky for a moment. A perfectly beautiful day, but not for Natalie. He stifled a sigh. "I've the feeling this is going to be one hell of a long day." When the call had come in, he'd begged Inspector Clarke to be the one to head up the investigation team even though, strictly speaking, he wasn't in the detectives section. After all, why not make use of all his Sydney experience, he'd said. Clarke had grudgingly acceded.

A heavy silence hung over the homestead as Steve and Constable Cooper entered the living room via the side verandah. Ten or so people sat around, each trying not to look at the other. He couldn't see Francey. He wondered where she was and then she entered the room from the hallway and sat on the side of an armchair, next to CJ. Her hand went around his shoulder in a gesture of affection and support. She looked strained, but bloody marvellous. His stomach muscles tightened until he made himself look elsewhere.

Steve cleared his throat and began, "This is a sad day for Murrundi. CJ, my sympathies to you and your family." He watched CJ nod silently, noting that the man looked unwell, obviously in shock. "I don't want to pre-empt the post-mortem but it's fairly evident that Natalie has been murdered, by a person or persons as yet unknown. As this will be a murder investigation I expect your full cooperation. We need to get statements from each of you. Constables Smith and Cooper will be helping out."

"What about the … body?" Les Westcott spoke up, his tone aggressively emotional. "You can't just leave her out there."

"Neil's called for an ambulance to take the body into town to the hospital. Someone from forensics or the coroner will have to examine it in order to determine the exact cause and time of death, but," he glanced at CJ and Shellie and smiled compassionately, "I'm sorry, I know it's unpleasant but it has to be faced. It appears that she died from asphyxiation due to strangulation, or a combination of strangulation and drowning. The post-mortem will tell us which. There's a contusion on the temple so she may have been stunned before –"

Lisa Dupre rose from a chair suddenly, her hand going to her mouth. "I'm sorry …" She rushed from the room half doubled over.

CJ seemed to come out of his daze. He stared at Steve. "I want to know who did this," he bellowed, a vein standing out on his temple. "Who in God's name would want to kill my stepdaughter? This is too much. First

Richard now Natalie. Good God, what's the world coming to?"

"CJ, calm down," Shellie soothed, her expression anxious. "You'll bring on a headache if you don't."

"Who indeed would want to kill Natalie?" Steve repeated the thought provoking question. His gaze roamed over everyone in the room. "That's what I'm here to find out." Then he became the professional investigator. "I want you to split into three groups. Neil can take some on the side verandah, Erin will take three people into the breakfast conservatory and I'll talk to the remainder here in the living room."

Four hours later the police officers' initial interview work was done and they'd returned to the station after cordoning off the pool for further investigation, and sealing Natalie's bedroom until a fingerprints team could go over it.

The three sat in the squad room going over their notes.

"What do you think, Steve?" Neil asked.

"It's too soon to be making pronouncements," Steve evaded. "Several people had opportunity.

Besides, someone from beyond the homestead could have got to her if she'd been outside the homestead's perimeter. Almost half the staff know the homestead's security code anyway. It's my guess she was outside, maybe taking a walk when it happened. Rape may also be involved. So, suspect-wise, it's wide open."

"What about motivation?" Erin asked.

Steve grimaced. "I don't know, nothing's obvious so we're going to have to dig for it. Get more background information on all the people at the homestead. Maybe one of the men was having an affair with her and the relationship went sour. I've heard that Les Westcott was keen on her a while back, and I'm sure most of us have seen her flirt with Mike Hunter, Sam Bianchini and a few others."

"Or maybe one of the women. You've heard the rumours, haven't you?" Neil said quietly. "She was supposed to have been a lesbian. Rumour has it she and that journalist, Trish Pentano, lived together. Could be a jealousy motive. Jilted female lover."

"Good point," Steve commended, "worth noting in your report as a possibility."

"You know the one who I reckon has the best motive?" Erin ventured. "Francey Spinetti."

Steve, who'd got up to make himself a cup of coffee, spun around sharply. "Why?"

Erin, with the eagerness of one new to the job, crossed the reasons off on her fingers. "Opportunity – she lives at Murrundi. Motive number one – with Natalie out of the way she inherits CJ's entire estate. Motive number two – Mrs Kirkby let it slip that Francey and Natalie didn't get along. I mean *really* didn't get along. And motive number three – means. Francey and Natalie are roughly the same height and build – Natalie was probably a little lighter, weight-wise. They'd be pretty evenly matched in a fight and if Natalie was stunned beforehand, strangling her would be easy for a woman of Francey's size and fitness."

Steve didn't speak. What could he say? Young Erin was spot-on. She'd said all the things he'd thought from the moment he'd stood beside Murrundi's pool. He just nodded and walked out of the room.

The first time Francey and Steve met face to face at the homestead was awkward. It happened two days after

Natalie's death when Steve accompanied a two-person fingerprint team from Brisbane.

Francey walked out of the large office from which CJ ran his business empire and almost collided with the man she loved. Startled, both jumped back.

"Steve. Hello." Francey recovered first.

Steve stared at her, he couldn't help himself. She was all dressed up in a cream long-sleeved power suit which showed the colour of her skin to the best advantage. Her bouncy, curly hair bobbed around her face and dangling gold earrings swayed as she moved her head slightly to the side. Cream patent leather heels accentuated her slender legs and in her left hand she carried a leather attache case. Under her other arm were several rolled up building plans. He'd never seen her look more beautiful or more desirable.

Francey saw the two men working in Natalie's room and curiosity plus the desire to stay close to Steve for as long as possible, made her ask, "What's going on?"

Steve pulled himself together. "Routine. We're pretty sure Natalie wasn't killed in the room, but we're just sifting through everything. You know, for clues. Anything that might give us a lead on her murderer."

Francey nodded. "It's awful," she said softly. "I can't believe anyone would want to ..." Her eyes widened. "Why?"

"I don't know. Yet."

Francey thought for a moment then said. "I'll be honest with you, Steve. Natalie and I weren't best buddies, far from it in fact."

"Under the circumstances, I think you should be careful what you say," Steve cautioned, hoping the officers in the room hadn't heard her admission.

"I have nothing to hide. I didn't kill her. We didn't get along, but the resentment came from Natalie, not me. She simply couldn't accept me as CJ's daughter and all that goes with it."

"Okay." He tried to change the subject. "Where are you off to?"

"Cooktown. Les is flying me up."

"You won't be away long, I hope. I've probably more questions to ask both of you."

"We'll be back tomorrow morning. The construction company's started on stage two of the Jasmine project and a few glitches have to be ironed out."

He didn't want to hear about her business exploits, they reminded him of the gulf between them. "How's CJ coping with all this?"

She shrugged. "You know CJ. He plays his cards pretty close to his chest. But deep down I think he's quite upset. We all are." Partly from guilt, she thought but didn't say. Not too many people at Murrundi had been overly fond of Natalie; she was a difficult woman to like. But none had wanted her dead she was sure of it.

From beneath her long lashes she studied him, trying to see a softening, a warming towards her but in some ways he was just like her natural father, poker-faced and controlled. One never knew precisely what they were thinking or feeling unless they wanted you to. It was driving her mad. She missed him like crazy, could hardly get a decent night's sleep for wanting him and here he was, "Mr Cool" as usual, seemingly unaffected by their break-up. Her chin set in a stubborn line. She wasn't giving up though, on him or them. Somehow she would make him see that they belonged together.

"Hey, Steve," the taller of the two officers called from the room. "Here's something interesting."

Francey peered over Steve's shoulder as he turned to look at what the man was pointing to. The room was a mess. Drawers had been checked and emptied, the sliding wardrobe door was wide open. Papers, letters and documents were strewn over the bed. Shellie would have a fit when she saw what they'd done.

On top of the mess on the bed lay a rifle which had been wrapped in an old linen skirt. Using a pencil, the man turned the rifle over then upended it so that the barrel pointed towards the ceiling. He put his nose close to the barrel and sniffed.

"Hasn't been fired recently," he pronounced. "What's the model?" Steve asked, though he had a premonition what it might be.

"A Stinger. The type a girl'd use," the shorter man said.

"Don't put a finger on it," Steve warned. "It's possible that it was planted. Tag it and have it checked for prints. And, I want the bore checked for a match with a ballistics report that's in my file at the station."

The taller man shrugged. "Okay, no problem." He looked past Steve to where Francey stood. His eyes glistened with voyeuristic appreciation. "Hey, love, think we might get a cup of coffee around here? We're going to be a while."

Francey's eyebrow arched. "Sure." Macho cops! Who did they think she was, their servant? "Down the hall and across the living room, the door on the left is the kitchen. Help yourself."

Steve grinned as he turned back to her. Winking his approval he then saw Les Westcott, decked out in a tweed jacket, woollen tie and moleskins striding towards them.

Typical bloody squatter gear but, grudgingly, he had to admit that on him it looked good.

"Francey, we'd better get a move on." He nodded sombrely to Steve. "I'm glad you're here, Steve. I've a question. When are you going to release Natalie's body for burial? There's the funeral to organise, you know."

"Tomorrow, I believe," Steve's response was to the point. He didn't like the way Westcott put his arm proprietorially around Francey's shoulders. Damn, he didn't like it at all. He waited until the man had turned away then he said, "Les, when you and Francey return from Cooktown I'll want to talk to you, to both of you."

Les swivelled back around, his gaze fixing on the policeman. "We've already given statements. What more do you want?"

"In the light of other emerging facts to do with the case, it's likely that I'll need to interview you both again. We can either do it at Murrundi or in Mt Isa. Which do you prefer?" he said formally.

Les Westcott made an exasperated sound. "We're both as busy as hell, Parrish, as I'm sure you know."

Francey intervened, placing her hand on Les' arm. "Steve's only doing his job, Les. We want to give him all the help we can, don't we?"

Steve almost smiled. The appeal in her voice, the look on her face, who could resist it? He was pretty sure Westcott couldn't or wouldn't. After all, one day she would be his boss in the truest sense of the word.

"All right," Les returned stiffly. "We'll do it here. I'll call you when we get back." He glanced first at Francey then Steve. "Okay?"

"Fine." Steve watched them walk away, his hands clenched at his side. What had he seen? His thoughtful gaze remained on their departing figures. It had been just a glimpse, but the expression in Westcott's eyes before he'd disguised it was crystal clear. The man was head over heels in love with Francey. His dark eyes narrowed even further. Why hadn't he cottoned on before? His hands balled into impotent fists at the sudden realisation. Jesus, he was supposed to be a good cop, a top detective in his day. Shit. What had he done? Gone and handed her to Westcott on an invisible silver platter. Stupid. Bloody stupid!

CJ emerged from a room down the hall and beckoned to him. "Hey Steve, may I have a word with you? In the study."

The day after Natalie's funeral the symptoms relating to CJ's tumour began to escalate. Dr Barry Ryan ordered him hospitalised so that he could monitor the medication and make him as comfortable as possible. Outside the private room in the Mt Isa hospital, Shellie and Barry stood talking quietly.

"It won't always be like this, Shellie. As the tumour grows other symptoms will take over. The headaches will become less intense, but there'll be other problems. His whole system, the vital organs will begin to break down." He sighed. "All we can do is medicate him for the pain and keep him comfortable."

Shellie wiped away a tear, she'd been prone to teariness since CJ had told her of his condition. "I don't know if I can take this, love. First looking after my father, then helping nurse young Miles and then Brenda, now my own brother. It's too much." Suddenly the urge for a drink almost overwhelmed her. Alcohol blurred the problem, made life bearable. Oh, she was tempted ... but she wouldn't. She had Barry's support, he'd help her through her weaknesses.

"I know it's hard," Barry comforted. "But you and Francey are all CJ's got now. You have to be strong for him and your niece."

"Francey's on her way in," Shellie said. "I left a message with Lisa and as soon as she and Les get off the plane they'll be here. I'm going to tell her."

Barry frowned. "CJ said he didn't want Francey to know yet."

"For God's sake, she's not stupid. Don't you think she's going to put two and two together? Besides, he's her father, she has a right to know. And for other reasons too. Francey has to start to prepare herself to be in command."

Barry didn't look convinced. "I don't know. CJ's not going to like it."

Shellie gave an impatient shake of her head. "For once in my life I don't care what CJ likes. My niece should know and if I have to be the one to tell her then so be it."

Francey sat on a utilitarian chair at the side of CJ's bed watching him and, periodically, all the monitoring equipment that was attached to him. Terminal. *Dying*. The fingers of her right hand came up to stroke her forehead, trying to ease the pain away. She didn't, still couldn't believe it, even though Barry had confirmed Shellie's confession ten minutes ago.

For a couple of seconds she closed her eyes and remembered the first day she'd come to Murrundi and her initial impression of CJ. Her mouth curved in a fleeting smile. She'd been frightened half out of her wits back then. God, how everything had changed. He'd thrust her into a world beyond her imagination, given her challenges that had pushed her beyond the limit of her own self-belief and capabilities, and she had triumphed and grown.

She had come to love him long before she'd known he was her natural father. And now, her eyes watered, she was going to lose him ... before they'd had the time to experience much of a life together. CJ might see the situation as a great cynical joke on himself and life, but she didn't. Her heart, all the way down to the depths of her soul had been devastated by what Shellie had told her. Dying. CJ.

The thought of something, a rogue something; blood, tissues and other matter growing uncontrollably inside his brain, taking over and squeezing the life out of him, turning him into what? She couldn't bear to think about it. But even so a wave of helplessness rushed through her. There was nothing she or anyone on earth could do. "The man with the golden touch" and all he'd accomplished, it had seemed larger than life. How could she, how could anyone who knew him accept what was to be his fate?

She struggled mentally to find a level of acceptance, and wished she believed more strongly in her faith – that might give her some degree of succour. And then she thought about another thing, with his passing, and God knows she didn't want to think about it but she had to, the mantle of responsibility for Murrundi and all his enterprises would fall to her. She wasn't ready. There was still so much to learn. Sensing a movement from the bed she looked up. CJ lay there studying her in much the same way as she had often caught him watching her in the past.

"You're awake," she said superfluously.

He nodded, and then his gaze probed her features deeply. "You know?"

Her hand reached out to cover his and she nodded affirmatively, suddenly unable to speak because her throat had constricted with emotion.

"It's all right, you know." He smiled at her. "I don't want you to be sad for me. I've had a good life." He chuckled weakly, "Damn it, I've had a great life. Done just about everything I wanted to. How many people can say that before they go to meet their maker?"

"But it's so unfair. We were just … just …"

"I know." His expression was understanding. "My only regret is that I won't be around to spoil my grandchildren." He frowned suddenly. "No more tears though. That's an order now."

With a last sniffle she struggled to comply. "I'll try."

"And here's another. I'm not coming back to this place." He looked about the room. "Ugh, I hate hospitals. If I have to fit out a hospital room with all the paraphernalia and staff at Murrundi, I'll do it. I'm not going to die in this sterile place."

Francey bit down on her lower lip as she struggled to swallow the lump in her throat. She agreed. "Okay."

He grinned at her agreement and then made an effort to perk the conversation up. "Now tell me how you got on in Sydney, the Blue Mountains project. It's going to set other developers back on their arses, I feel it in my bones."

The four-person investigation unit sat around a table half covered with a variety of files and reports. It had been eight days since Natalie DeWitt-Ambrose's death and they'd come together to collate and discuss the various pieces of information they had accumulated since the homicide, and to plan future moves.

Steve looked briefly at the papers in front of him then spoke, "The post-mortem report places the time of death between 11 p.m. and 1 a.m. It states that the cause of death was asphyxiation due to strangulation. No water was found in her lungs. Also, there's no evidence that she'd been sexually assaulted. And according to the doctor performing the autopsy, the contusion on her temple could have caused a light concussion, enough to stun or render her unconscious.

"So, we know how she died but not where. Her clothing showed signs of a struggle. Torn seams and two buttons were missing from her shirt. She could have been killed by the pool and her body thrown in to make us think, initially, that she'd tripped and maybe drowned. However, it seems more likely that death occurred elsewhere and her body was dumped in the water afterwards." He glanced at the man opposite. "Okay, Glen, what have you got?"

Detective Glen McAlpine, a slim man whose face was a mixture of angles and planes, with a receding hairline shuffled his paperwork. He had been seconded to the original three-person investigation unit to give them a hand with what was becoming a major homicide investigation.

State and even interstate newspapers had sent a sprinkling of journalists to cover the story and the funeral, and to interview just about anyone in the Isa who had a tale to tell about the Ambrose family. They'd made some interesting copy – especially with the news of Francey's association to CJ still fresh in the public's minds – for the Sunday editions.

Glen McAlpine opened a folder. "I interviewed Trish Pentano in Brisbane, the day before yesterday. She more or less confirmed that Natalie had been under a lot of strain for several months, longer than that, actually, over a year – because of CJ's relationship to Francey Spinetti. The fact that CJ said Francey would be the major beneficiary of his estate seemed to play on her mind. Natalie, according to

Ms Pentano, hated Francey for usurping her position and had been doing all she could to cause a rift between Francey and CJ.

"Pentano's no psychologist, but she's known Natalie for years, even before they had a relationship. She thinks Natalie had emotional and maybe some mental problems that could go back a long way. Symptoms such as moodiness, rages and illogical behaviour began to manifest themselves after her mother's death, and later on after her half-brother's death. Ms Pentano thought Natalie had a persecution complex and felt very insecure, even with all her wealth. She also confirmed that Natalie was a lesbian and had been since the age of fifteen.

"Oh, yes. I picked up the report on the Stinger rifle while I was in Brisbane. It's a match for the bullet you dug out of that tree where the stampede took place. They dusted the rifle too. The only fingerprints found belonged to the deceased."

"So Natalie could have orchestrated the stampede," Erin said in a wondering tone as she flicked a strand of hair off her forehead.

Steve's pencil drummed thoughtfully on a notepad. "That's a strong possibility but we may never know for sure. She had means and opportunity – knowing the area so well – but I'm stumped for the motive. Why would she want to kill her brother?"

"Money?" Neil Smith suggested.

Steve shook his head. "I'm not sure. She was already a very wealthy woman and would have been wealthier when CJ died. If greed, money, was the motive why wasn't CJ her target?"

"A fight, perhaps? She and Richard may have had a row over something," Erin suggested.

"That's possible," Steve agreed. He looked at Neil. "What have you got on Mike Hunter?"

"I did a background check, the usual. He was regular army for ten years, did a stint in a commando unit. Later he bought a property in western NSW and married. Three years ago things got tough for him and the bank took over his property. He also split with his wife. She divorced him and went to live in Wollongong with the kids. He was pretty bitter about the loss of the station and the family split. Apart from that he seems a regular kind of bloke. The stockmen at Murrundi consider him a good boss. According to a couple of the men he had a thing for Natalie. They reckoned she was just having a bit of fun with him, that she wasn't serious."

"What about the Swiss army knife found at the crime scene?" Steve asked.

"Mike identified it as his. He claims he lost it the night of Francey's birthday party," Neil added succinctly. "We've only his word for that, of course, even though CJ said he'd seen him looking for it around the pool."

"Maybe he was just saying that. Or, maybe the killer found it and planted it by the pool to incriminate Mike," Erin said. "Alternatively, if Mike met Natalie the night of the murder and they argued, with his army background he'd be capable of stunning her and then strangling her, maybe losing the knife in the struggle."

"What else have we got?" Steve asked.

"Les Westcott doesn't have an alibi for that night, neither does CJ's daughter," Glen said.

"Westcott was known to have been in love with Natalie," Neil informed everyone, "according to rumours in the station's bunkhouse and general opinion around the Isa. It's only hearsay, I guess, but Lisa Dupre said Les was furious when Natalie gave him his walking papers about eighteen months ago. He keeps it pretty quiet, but according to Lisa Westcott's very ambitious and wants to run CJ's whole show eventually. The man considers himself CJ's unofficial son even though there's no blood relationship."

Steve groaned inwardly. And he'd given the man a free hand with Francey, fool that he was. "You said he has no alibi for the night of the murder?"

"Westcott says he went for a drive into town early on, then came back and listened to a couple of CDs and went to bed," Neil said.

"Hhmm, that isn't much of an alibi," Erin agreed. "The post-mortem put the time of death at close to 11 p.m. Francey Spinetti said she worked on some drawings till about ten thirty and then retired," she said, looking down at her notes. "But here's something interesting. According to her Aunt Shellie, she and Francey had fought the night before. Mrs Kirkby had to break them up."

"Did Francey physically threaten Natalie?" Steve wanted to know, his heart was getting heavier by the minute. One didn't need a genius IQ to see where the possibilities were leading.

"Shellie said she said something like ..." Erin looked at her notes, "This isn't finished. There'll be another time, another place." She glanced at Steve. "One could interpret that as a kind of future threat." She stopped for a moment, then added, "There's more. Evidently, before that Natalie and CJ had a run-in the night of Francey's party. Francey came along and tried to break it up and collected a slap across the face from Natalie. I did a background check on Francey Spinetti. She took karate lessons at her father Carlo's insistence because he was worried about her going out doing amateur photo shoots by herself. So," she concluded, "she too would know how to stun a victim."

"Sure," Steve agreed then tried to move the topic away from Francey. "Are you implying that even CJ could be a suspect?"

Glen looked up from his paperwork to ask, "What motivation would he have?"

"I don't know ..." Erin said slowly. "Unless ... and this comes from out of left field. Did he suspect that Natalie had been instrumental in Richard's death? Revenge is a strong motive for murder." She checked her notepad. "According to Mrs Kirkby, Mr Ambrose had a bad headache the night before the murder and had been sedated. Statements taken the day after the murder said Mr Ambrose did some paperwork in his study then retired. He spoke to no-one either personally or by phone so he had opportunity too."

Nodding, Steve ran his hands through his hair in an abstracted fashion. "It seems that we have a few suspects with opportunity, means and motive. At least three, maybe four." He looked at his team and summarised, "So far you've done good work, but now we have to dig deeper, work on a solid motive. Find the right suspect and home in on them. Got it?" He watched them all nod their heads solemnly and then slowly file out of the room. But he sat there tapping his pencil on the table top.

In his mind one suspect was shaping up better than all the others and it was the one person he hoped wouldn't – Francey Spinetti. And the worst thing was that he could do little as an officer of the law to focus attention elsewhere.

CHAPTER TWENTY-EIGHT

Steve Parrish's expression was grim as he climbed the front steps of Murrundi's homestead. The country grapevine had disgorged the news of CJ's condition to all and sundry. Terminal. He didn't doubt the accuracy of the gossipers who'd passed the word on; they rarely made a mistake. But even so, it didn't seem possible. CJ and Les would have had the best doctors in the country double-check the diagnosis. The muscles around his heart contracted as he thought about what it meant to Francey to find her father and have so little time with him. She'd be coming into her inheritance a damned lot sooner than everyone thought, but he didn't envy her her position. Living up to CJ's reputation and memory, and carrying on his empire would be one hell of a job.

His thoughts moved to Les Westcott. The phrase "waiting in the wings", came to mind. Good old dependable Les would be more than willing to help Francey assume the mantle of control over CJ's holdings. His gut twisted in a mixture of plain old-fashioned jealousy and another emotion, something deeper. The thought of Les touching Francey made him steam, really steam.

He stopped and stared at Murrundi's front door. His

vision became distorted and blurred as the pain intensified into a wave of anger. *Les and Francey*. The idea was so unpalatable his stomach threatened to turn over. He straightened to his full height and squared his shoulders. Get a grip, he admonished himself. You're the one who walked away, old son. You let her go. He let his breath out slowly. No use belly-aching about it or wishing things were different. You've only yourself to blame.

He rattled the door knocker furiously.

Shellie answered the door. "Steve! How nice. Do come in. Everyone's in the conservatory having a morning tea-cum-business meeting."

Everyone turned out to be CJ, Les, Lisa Dupre and Francey.

"Steve, may I get you something?" Shellie asked as she moved towards the well-stocked traymobile.

"A coffee'd go down well. Thanks."

Subtlely, through long dark eyelashes, Francey studied Steve as he took his coffee and sat at the table, diagonally opposite her. For weeks, she had prayed to receive some relief from the longing she felt for him when he intruded into her thoughts, something that happened often. Too often! Now, seeing him looking fit yet very businesslike, she knew her feelings hadn't changed. She cared, deeply. Every nerve in her body had gone on full alert the moment she heard his voice and she had to exert maximum self-control to stop herself staring. God, it was awful to feel this way and know the feelings weren't reciprocated. Perhaps she should find a reason to get out of the room, away from him and the cloud of unhappiness that hung around her like an invisible shroud.

"I take it this isn't a social visit," Les said without preamble, his dislike for the policeman showing.

"You're right." Steve dug his fists into his trouser pockets to hold back the urge to smash one into Les' complacent face. He struggled against the impotent rage that welled within him towards Westcott, even though half his anger was self directed. He'd been a fool to let Francey go and now he knew it. Too bloody late, of course.

"What can you tell us?" CJ asked.

Steve looked at "the man with the golden touch", barely able to disguise the shock he registered as he studied CJ. The man had aged twenty years since the last time he'd seen him. He had gone bald, had lost a lot of weight and his skin tone was unhealthily pale. His eyes were different too, dull, as if he was heavily drugged. A wave of compassion moved through Steve as he noted his obvious deterioration. It wasn't pleasant to look at.

CJ sat next to Francey in an automated wheelchair. Steve's roving, seemingly casual glance then took in Francey's features. She'd lost weight too, and she had a distant air about her, as if her mind were on more weighty matters.

"Well?" CJ prompted.

"Yes. Ummm, our investigation's coming along. The team have been …"

"I don't want to hear that police bullshit," CJ suddenly exploded. "I want to know whether you're close to arresting Natalie's murderer."

"We're following several leads, sir. At present that's all I can tell you."

"Are you saying we're all suspects?" Francey spoke for the first time, her tone formal.

"It's routine, Francey. You were all present the night of the murder so technically, according to police procedure, you all had opportunity. However, I'm not pointing a finger at anyone in particular, I just want to reduce the options."

"You're not giving out much information, Steve," Francey complained. "I think, as Natalie's family, we have the right to know everything, especially which way the investigation is heading."

"I'm telling you as much as I can. Until I know where the case is heading it's best not to divulge a lot of half-truths and assumptions. That's how I've operated in the past and such a system works well."

"What about the Stinger rifle you found in Natalie's room?" Les asked.

"What about it?" Steve tried to evade the answer but knew he couldn't.

"Come on, man, give," CJ insisted.

Steve shrugged his shoulders. "Okay. Forensics matched the rifle found in Natalie's room with the cartridges found near the stampede site."

"Are you implying that Natalie fired the shots that killed Richard?" Francey, ever the frank one, asked outright. On the outside she appeared calm, cool – just like Steve – but on the inside her emotions were in turmoil. Looking at him, talking to him, the sound of his voice, *everything,* was affecting her more than she had ever thought possible. Being this close to him physically but worlds apart emotionally was unbearable but she bore it because to stand up and leave now would tell them all how much his disaffection was hurting her.

Steve shook his head. "I didn't say that and probably we'll never know for sure," he admitted with a rueful grin. "It's possible the rifle may have been planted in Natalie's room by a person or persons unknown."

"Were there fingerprints on the rifle?" she probed on, dissatisfied. Why didn't he come right out and say it, tell them everything, she wondered. Deep down she sensed a reserve, as if he knew more than he was letting on.

"The only prints we found on the rifle belonged to Natalie."

"Then isn't it reasonable to assume that Natalie fired those shots?" Francey persisted.

Steve stared at Francey and purposely kept his expression blank. "It may be reasonable but a court of law may not regard such evidence as conclusive."

"So, we'll never know who fired those shots for sure?" Francey's voice dropped and became quietly contemplative.

"I think not. I'm sorry."

She glanced at CJ and her arm crept around his shoulder. "This is unnecessarily upsetting for CJ." She appealed to Steve. "He's not well, you know."

Steve nodded. "Yes, I do know."

CJ bristled. "Don't write me off just yet, any of you." He shrugged away from Francey's grasp. "Can't sit around gasbagging all day. I'm going to my study. Work to do, you know."

They all watched CJ steer his wheelchair from the room.

"Well, what is it you really want, Parrish?" Les demanded aggressively.

"I'm here to go through your original statements again. Perhaps each of you may have remembered something extra. I'd like to talk to you one by one."

"Damned inconvenient. We're trying to run a business here, you know." Les grumbled.

"Les," Francey's eyebrows rose. "Steve has a job to do, like all of us." She looked at Steve. "Perhaps you'd like to speak to people in the dining area, or the conservatory. Who would you like to see first?"

*

As Steve walked back to his four-wheel drive he ran a hand through his dark hair, tousling it about his forehead. Four possible suspects in the case but as things were shaping up, with motive and means, the woman he loved – Francey – looked to be suspect number one. From the investigations already carried out and double-checking today what people had said, it was obvious that she had the strongest motive, no alibi, as well as means and opportunity. Damn!

Probationary Constable Erin Cooper sat on the other side of the table, facing Steve Parrish, her gaze locked expectantly on him. He glanced across at the station's most junior officer. Erin was champing at the bit with eagerness. Her first criminal investigation and she clearly loved every minute of it. She'd make a good officer once she curbed her over enthusiastic attitude, he thought.

"What about Francey Spinetti, Steve? Will you bring her in for questioning?"

Damn it, he didn't have a choice and he knew it. "I guess we'd better," he said, somehow disguising his reluctance. "Erin, ring Murrundi and arrange it. CJ may insist on her having legal representation for the interview."

"Do you want me to collect her?"

"Yes. As soon as possible."

"What's this all about, Steve?" Francey, dressed in blue jeans, a pink angora sweater and an accompanying frown which marred the smoothness of her forehead, asked as she sat on the proffered chair opposite him.

Steve shrugged to hide his nervousness. He also noted that Francey, in her typical up-front manner, had declined the opportunity to have a solicitor present. Maybe that wasn't smart. "Are you sure you don't want a brief here to advise you?"

Her eyebrows shot upwards. "Why? Will I need one?"

"Francey, this is an official investigation into Natalie deWitt-Ambrose's homicide," he said formally. "Recent investigation has lead me to believe you may have had some involvement." He stared at Erin who had just turned the video camera on. "Constable, read Miss Spinetti her rights."

Francey's gaze jumped from Steve to Erin as the young woman read the official sounding words. What was going on? Steve looked so ... uncomfortable, as if he'd rather be anywhere else than here, opposite her. And Natalie's death? The mental query rushed through her, why did they think she knew anything about it? It was very confusing. Still, exposure over the last twenty months to CJ's tactics had taught her the value of playing things cool, and about timing. She would wait, see which way this interview went before hitting the panic button. Hopefully, she wouldn't have to. Even so, she was nervous, she couldn't help it and the inside of her mouth was going dry, her blue-green eyes unconsciously widening in anticipation.

"We have evidence that a struggle took place before Natalie's death. There was bruising on her body, her clothes were torn. She obviously put up a fight."

Francey didn't like the mental picture she got – Natalie fighting her attacker then being overcome. It was too horrible to think about. Then another thought struck her. "Are you accusing me of murdering Natalie?"

"I want you to explain a few things, that's all." His tone was stern, uncompromising. He hated himself for it but he had to be that way, especially with the eager Erin watching both himself and Francey. He couldn't be seen to play favourites.

Seconds ticked by into a minute with Francey's thoughts in a whirl. Steve thought she'd killed Natalie – that was plainly evident. Though not versed in legal matters she had enough commonsense to realise that she was set to benefit most from Natalie's death and therefore, logically that made her the prime suspect.

"Did you see Natalie the night of the murder?"

Francey's dark tresses shook emphatically. "No."

"When was the last time you saw her alive?"

His brusqueness flustered her, made it hard to think straight. When had she seen her last? "Perhaps some time that day, probably at lunch."

"Miss Spinetti," Erin spoke for the first time. "We have a witness who says that you and the deceased argued the night before she died. Do you deny that you threatened Miss deWitt-Ambrose?"

Francey turned puzzled eyes on the young woman. "Threatened her? I don't know, I don't recall anything ..."

Erin flipped open her notebook. "On the third of September Mrs Kirkby claimed that you and Miss deWitt-Ambrose argued. You accused her of initiating a defamatory article about you in *New Idea*. You said, quote: 'Don't think this is finished yet, Natalie. There'll be another time, another place'. Did you utter such a statement, Miss Spinetti?"

"I'm not sure. Maybe." Francey's mind harked back to the fight she and Natalie had had in the conservatory. Had she threatened her? She smiled nervously at Steve. "We did row. It got rather heated. Natalie tried to scratch me."

"So you admit to the argument?" Erin pressed.

Francey frowned, then stared at the woman. "Yes, haven't I just said so?" Her gaze darted to Steve. "Is that a problem?"

Steve shuffled about in his chair. "I have to tell you, Francey, it doesn't look good. From a legal point of view you had opportunity, means and motive."

"But I ..." She shook her head. "Explain what you mean, I'm not sure I understand."

"Opportunity. You were at a Murrundi so you had access to Natalie either in her bedroom or elsewhere. Means. We know about your prowess in karate, we checked it out. It's conceivable that someone with such skills may have been able to overpower Natalie – stun her then strangle her. Motive. You argued with Natalie before her death. You were heard to threaten her *and* you would gain the most from her death," Steve said.

"Gain, how would I gain?" She asked the question even though she knew what his answer would be.

"By inheriting CJ Ambrose's entire estate. Some might consider that alone a powerful motive for murder. As well, you have no corroborating alibi for the night of the murder. You said you were working alone in your office on some plans for CJ, but you can't conclusively prove it, can you?"

Francey couldn't believe she had heard him right. Steve thought she had killed Natalie, he had all but said it out loud. How could he think such a thing? That she could be capable of killing anyone. What had happened to the love, the trust they'd once shared? She looked at him surreptitiously and saw the real Steve Parrish for the first time. He was a cold, calculating policeman doing his job to the best of his ability. Oh, yes, and he was able. More than able. Inside she felt crushed, vulnerable, all her emotions laid bare by his accusations. She wanted to crawl away somewhere and hide. Lick her wounds, regroup her thoughts, devise a defence. Later, much later, would come anger and outrage.

"I see," Francey murmured slowly. She was quiet for a moment, thinking. Then, her chin lifting and with her normally tanned skin paling, she asked, "Am I under arrest?"

Steve had enough to hold her and he knew that she knew it but a sense of reluctance surfaced and stopped him from saying yes. The last thing he wanted to do was to arrest Francey for Natalie's murder. For one thing, in his heart and despite the evidence, he didn't believe she'd done it. As well, he could imagine CJ's wrath: it would be extreme and ferocious. He'd hire the best solicitor in the state, in the country for that matter. The press would have a field day too. There would be a bloody three-ring circus so if he could avoid that for a while he considered himself duty-bound to do so.

"No. However, I formally advise you to seek legal representation. I'll make our evidence available to your solicitor on demand. Constable Cooper will escort you back to Murrundi where you will hand over your passport to her for safekeeping with the police department. Also, until advised otherwise you are not to travel outside the state of Queensland. Do you understand everything I've said?"

"Yes." She was too stunned to say more, to question, to argue. Steve's formality and the sudden realisation of the seriousness of the matter hit her like the proverbial sledgehammer, defusing her normally volatile nature and sense of fair play.

"But ..." Erin looked at her superior as if he'd gone crazy. "Are you sure, Sergeant?"

Steve stared back at her, one eyebrow raised. "Are you questioning my judgement, Constable?"

Erin backed down. "No, sir."

Inside, deep inside, Francey felt numb. Thankfully, the young policewoman didn't bother with polite conversation as they drove back to Murrundi and left her with her thoughts. She was a murder suspect. The prime suspect! Oh, God ... maybe this was a dream and sometime soon she would wake up. But no, she knew it wasn't a dream, Steve's interrogation had been chillingly real. His aloofness, his cool professionalism had been real too. That hurt more than the accusations.

In the privacy of her bedroom she sat on the bed, folded her hands in her lap and closed her eyes. *Natalie, you bitch, wherever you are I bet you're laughing.* As she had listened to Steve explain the legal reasoning back at the station all the pieces of the puzzle had fallen into place. They thought they had the evidence and, in black and white, she appeared to be as guilty as hell. All neat and tidy, according to Steve and the young constable. But ... she hadn't done it. How many times had she said so? But it didn't seem to matter, her word meant nothing, not even to Steve.

She didn't know which made her feel worse: that they thought she'd killed Natalie or Steve being so good at his job that he'd done his utmost to prove her guilt. That hurt, more than she could bear. She still loved him and that hurt too, even though she'd acknowledged that the feeling was a wasted emotion. If he'd cared for her at all, he'd have tried harder to find the *real* guilty person rather than happily wanting to pin it on her.

Damn. What was she going to do?

Steve Parrish sat on the front verandah of his home in the darkness, a glass of whisky in one hand, the half empty bottle at his feet.

Inside there was this empty chasm, he felt drained of everything other than a sense of guilt and hopelessness. Usually, when he trailed a criminal, a killer, a burglar, anyone who'd broken the law, he'd feel exultation as he closed in for the arrest. His team had done a good job on all the suspects. He'd forced himself to congratulate each of them for their efforts. He shook his head remembering young Erin's expression as he'd said Francey could go. She'd probably had to bite her tongue not to argue the point with him.

He closed his eyes and the vision of Francey's strained, white face drifted into view. The way she'd looked at him before she'd walked out the door – like he was the lowest thing on two legs. God Almighty, that's how he felt right now – lower than a snake's belly.

It was no comfort at all that he'd just been doing his job. He wouldn't get too many thanks from the local people either. Francey Spinetti had become popular around the Isa and what could he expect from CJ? Most likely an all-out war!

Steve downed the rest of the whisky and poured another. A good night to get quietly, profoundly drunk. As he sloshed some whisky onto the floorboards he knew he was already halfway there. Great!

Distantly, he heard the phone ring. His massive shoulders shrugged and he muttered into the darkness. "Whoever you are, piss off."

The phone kept ringing. Every ten minutes it rang for about a minute then stopped. Eventually the repeated calls began annoying him so much that he stomped inside and snatched the receiver the next time it rang.

"Parrish? CJ."

"I'm off-duty, CJ," Steve slurred.

"Yeah, that's what they told me at the station," CJ's voice thundered down the line. "Look, get your backside out to Murrundi first thing tomorrow morning, and bring another officer with you."

Steve scratched his head and tried to concentrate. "Why?"

"Just bloody well do it. First thing. Right?"

CJ's receiver crunched down and the sound jarred his eardrums enough to make Steve utter an expletive, "Shit." The old man had a flea in his ear about something. Of course! Francey had no doubt told him of her interview at the station.

A crushing wave of sadness worked its way through his limbs into every region of his heart and then his body and soul. Jesus, where'd he left the bottle?

CJ Ambrose sat bolt upright, propped up by five pillows that the nurse fussed over in an attempt to make him more comfortable. He hated being dependent on others, hated it to the depths of his being but circumstances had decreed that he employ a round-the-clock crew of specialist nurses to care for him. Until a week ago the women at Murrundi – Shellie, Alison Wontow, Lisa and Francey – had taken turns at nursing duties. The experience of caring for someone terminally ill had taken its toll on them, especially Francey and Shellie. On the day his legs gave up on him completely and his eyesight got so bad he couldn't read anything he'd deemed it time to call in the professionals.

An oxygen machine, a medication tray on his bedside table and other equipment about which he knew or understood little made his masculine bedroom resemble a pseudo hospital room. He clucked his tongue in disgust at what he'd been reduced to.

"That'll do, Rose," he bit back the gruffness, "I'm fine."

"How are you feeling? Do you need some medication?"

"It's bearable. No thanks." Whatever Barry Ryan had prescribed for him either made him woozy or knocked him right out. He expected Steve Parrish soon and he knew that he'd need all his faculties working at their best for what he proposed to tell him.

"I'll go get a cuppa then. Buzz me if you need anything." After a final assessment of her patient, Rose Welling, the morning nurse left the room.

CJ let out a sigh. Peace. The fussing drove him almost as crazy as the tumour which was slowly causing a deterioration of his body and mind. And lately, as well as everything else, he'd begun to forget things, important things. He knew she and Pearl and Marta were only doing their jobs, and being paid handsomely for it too, but sometimes it became a bit too much.

He leant his head back against the linen pillowslip and peered blurrily at the bedside clock as he closed his eyes. Parrish should be here soon, until then he had some time to think ...

CJ studied the policeman who stood at the end of the bed watching him. He reckoned he'd come to know Parrish reasonably well over the past twelve months or so. With his inclination to analyse he thought he knew what made the man tick, what he'd accept, what he wouldn't. Knew too that Steve had fallen head over heels in love with his daughter and had walked away from the relationship because he couldn't handle the idea that one day Francey would be a multimillionairess. Damn fool. He was straight as a die though and whip smart in every other way, and before his race was run he hoped he'd see the light about

Francey too – that they were meant for each other. CJ'd fought the idea at first but now he knew it to be right for both of them.

The other policeman, Neil Smith, obviously uncomfortable, tried to look inconspicuous as he stood like a sentinel just inside the bedroom door.

"Take a seat, Steve." CJ pointed to a straight-backed chair near the bed.

"Thanks, but I'm fine standing, CJ."

CJ frowned furiously at the younger man. "Take the bloody chair, will you. I don't like you towering over me."

Steve shrugged and the movement woke up his hangover headache. He groaned silently as the erratic throbbing began around his temples. Moving the chair close to the bed he sat and waited. CJ had summoned him and the way he felt he had no inclination to indulge in polite conversation, even with a dying man.

"I guess you're wondering why I asked you to drop by?"

"I'm sure you'll get around to telling me," Steve replied. He had a fair idea that it had something to do with Francey's interview at the station. He wasn't looking forward to being the recipient of CJ's ire.

"Okay." CJ took a deep breath and his gaze locked onto Steve's. "I wanted you here because ... I've a confession to make regarding my stepdaughter, Natalie ..."

The way CJ said the words made Steve focus his attention on the older man. What was he getting at? A confession. What kind of confession?

CJ took a deep breath. "You see, I killed her. I'm the one you're looking for."

CHAPTER TWENTY-NINE

Steve jerked to an upright position in the chair. "What? Say that again?"

"I murdered Natalie. The rotten little bitch killed my son. I found out about it and I wanted to make her pay, the same way Richard paid – with his life."

Steve glanced at Neil and indicated that he should take notes on what was being said. "You sure you know what you're saying, CJ? What you're admitting to?"

"You mean do I have all my faculties because of this tumour growing inside my brain? Hell yes. I might be dying but I'm not *non compos mentis*, yet. I know what I'm saying, know what I'm confessing to and, no, I don't want a lawyer. Not yet."

Steve made a low whistling sound through his teeth and leant forward. "Tell me what happened? All of it."

"All of it ..." CJ lay back against the pillows and wiped beads of perspiration from his forehead. "Well, it started when I overheard Natalie on the phone in her bedroom – she'd left the door slightly ajar – talking to someone, probably that Trish Pentano. She said she had to get rid of Francey because she threatened her inheritance and that it wouldn't be hard … like it hadn't been difficult to get rid of Richard. That's when it hit me. It was her. She had fired the shots and caused the stampede. I'm not sure why, I guess we'll never know for sure, but maybe she resented the fact that not long after my wife's death, I rewrote my will leaving the bulk of my estate to Richard. I organised a trust fund, a generous one, for Natalie – she'd be comfortable for the rest of her life."

CJ shrugged his shoulders. "Obviously Natalie didn't think I was going to leave her enough. She secretly resented the will and decided she wanted all of it. To get it," his voice caught emotionally, "she had to get rid of my boy. You know, she could easily have ridden out unnoticed and returned looking as if she'd just come from her routine early morning ride. She knew where they'd be camping too because she's familiar with the stock routes. The scheming, rotten bitch. I got so angry. I wanted to go in and confront her straightaway, but I didn't. I needed time to think about it."

He gave Steve a meaningful look. "God, you've no idea how hard it was to be civil to her once I knew what she'd done. After her death your finding the rifle and her fingerprints on it confirmed to me that she'd been responsible for Richard's death.

"I should have guessed before then. You see, when Brenda died Natalie went a little strange. Shellie and I thought it was grief until I realised that she had always been highly strung and very dependent on her mother. I believe her mother's death unhinged her mentally. She's been getting stranger ever since. Trying to strand Francey in the bush, her unrelenting hatred towards her … that's not the behaviour of a normal person." He paused for a moment's reflection. "I got my chance to accuse her soon enough, the night after

I'd had an attack. All day I'd lain in bed getting over the medication. Some time after dinner, I heard the French doors of her bedroom open – I knew she was going out for a walk, she often did before she went to bed. I got up, followed her and confronted her near the pool."

"Did she admit responsibility for Richard's death?" Steve asked.

"I accused her of it, but no, she laughed and said I was silly to think such a thing. I guess that's when I snapped. As I recall, I hit her and she fell to the ground. Then my hands were around her throat, pressing down. She struggled, tried hard to pull my hands away but the more she did the tighter I squeezed. I held on until she stopped struggling." His expression was concerned as he looked at Steve. "I experienced no sense of remorse and I still don't. I felt I'd done the right thing. Natalie was a sick, evil woman who didn't deserve to live. She'd taken away the best thing in my life, my only living son, and I … I felt justified in doing what I did."

Steve's gaze narrowed on the dying man. He sounded sincere, and it kind of made sense. Rough justice according to the law of CJ Ambrose, and so typical of the man to do his own dirty work. "What did you do then, CJ?"

"We were near the pool. I rolled her into the water and went back inside. I thought people might think she'd hit her head, fallen into the pool and drowned."

"Why didn't you come forward and tell me straightaway?"

CJ moved restlessly against the pillows. "Time, Steve, time. I don't have much left. I thought I'd wait, see which way the investigation went –"

"So, when you saw that it looked bad for Francey you decided to own up?" Steve interjected.

CJ nodded. "She's innocent. You know Francey. Do you really think she's capable of murder?"

"In my line of work I've seen people do extreme things under extreme conditions. Almost everyone is capable of committing murder if the circumstances are right."

"Take Francey out of the equation. I'm the guilty one, I did it. What more do you want me to tell you?"

For a moment or two Steve didn't answer. Relieved that Francey was off the hook he couldn't think of a single question. CJ's confession changed everything. The woman he loved now had a timely reprieve but … something niggled, some small sense of doubt, just below the level of his consciousness. CJ's account of the murder was pat, almost rehearsed. For Christ's sake, cut it out. You've got your man. Don't make unnecessary waves.

"I think I'd better get this to Inspector Clarke. You'll have to come into the station to be formally charged, but in your condition …"

"I can do that, I'm not totally incapacitated. Today. This afternoon. I've spoken to my solicitor in Brisbane and he's recommended a top criminal lawyer. Les is flying him in this afternoon." CJ grinned at Steve and Neil. "Besides, it's not like I'm well enough to do a flit, is it?"

"I guess not. Well, if you'll excuse me I'll go call Inspector Clarke."

"Yes, do. Use the phone in Lisa's office. Oh, would you ask her to come and see me. I need to organise some things."

Like telling Shellie and Francey and Les. Waves of exhaustion moved through his body, draining him. The telling had taken more out of him than he'd thought it would. He wanted to sleep, which he did increasingly as each day passed. Another sign that the tumour, with ruthless efficiency, was taking over. Barry had said that was part of the pattern as his body slowly and inexorably began to shut down – like an overworked engine. But not yet, he prayed, he still had a few things to do.

Francey stared hollow-eyed at the pile of newspapers spread across the coffee table in the living room. The headlines were permanently etched into her brain.

THE MAN WITH THE GOLDEN TOUCH
LOSES IT DYING AMBROSE CONFESSES: I
KILLED MY STEPDAUGHTER

POLICE CATCH MULTIMILLIONAIRE.
"NO-ONE IS ABOVE THE LAW," SAYS
INSPECTOR REG CLARKE

Looking up from the papers as Les came into the room with two cups of coffee she made a space for them on the table. Thank God for Les. He had been CJ's strong right arm for years and now he had become hers. Yesterday afternoon, Les and a lawyer CJ had brought in to represent him, Colin Maxwell, had accompanied CJ to the police station to make a statement. He was charged, fingerprinted and due to his illness he had been released on bail of half a million dollars. The excursion had exhausted CJ. These days it didn't take much to do that. He'd been in bed ever since, mostly sleeping, and stubbornly unwilling to discuss his confession with her or anyone else.

"How did the newspapers get onto this so fast?" Francey queried, her expression puzzled as she skimread a recount of Natalie's murder and the subsequent investigation.

"I wouldn't be surprised if CJ tipped off his mate Roy, which got the ball rolling."

"I don't believe he did it, Les," she said with a shake of her head. "CJ didn't kill Natalie, he couldn't have." Her expressive gaze reviewed the headlines then returned to him. "I know what made him confess, he wanted to protect me. But as I, too, am innocent, the gesture's wasted." Her eyebrows lifted questioningly. "What are we going to do about it?"

Les remained silent for a while. "I don't know if there's a lot we can do. Maxwell says it's all pretty straight forward. CJ has made a confession and the police have accepted it. What he said appears to tie in or concur with their investigation and I guess they debated whether he was confessing to get you off the hook and rejected the idea. Besides, with CJ's health deteriorating fast, Maxwell's certain the case won't even go to court." He grimaced. "Which probably suits the cops too. Saves the expense of a trial."

"But ... don't you think it's all a bit too neat?" Francey ruminated, half to herself. "The revenge angle, payback for Richard's death. I don't believe he knew that Natalie organised that stampede. I think CJ put two and two together *after* her death – when the rifle surfaced – not before it."

"Maybe, but as Steve admitted, we'll never know why or if she really did the deed. She and Richard may have had a serious row over something. Siblings often do. We know that Natalie had strange mood swings too so it's possible." His gaze locked onto her harried features as he reminded her, "Look what she tried to do to you in the bush. I think it's reasonable to assume that Natalie, if pushed, could have been capable of murder."

Francey shook her head. "I still don't believe this," she gestured towards the newspapers. "Nothing will make me believe that CJ killed Natalie. Nothing." Suddenly she had to blink back a tear, in fact, several tears. It seemed as if she was involved in an ongoing nightmare. CJ dying was a daily, moment to moment pain she coped with as best she could, but it was unconscionable that he'd go to his grave a murderer. It just wasn't right. She knew one thing, she had to do all in her power to stop that stigma being attached to her father's name. Her only problem was finding someone to help her? Steve!

He'd been so cool and controlled towards her since the party. Almost like a stranger. She missed the old Steve ... so very much. The next instant her jaw squared and her chin tilted at a stubborn angle. To hell with her pride and waiting for him to come to his senses, she would go and see him, ask for his help, beg him if necessary. Tonight, after dinner.

"It's natural for you to think him innocent, you're his daughter and you love him," Les interrupted her train of thought. "But you, we, have to be realistic. I'm sorry to sound repetitive but CJ's adamant about his guilt and the police are satisfied. The best we can do at the moment is to limit the press from turning this into a media circus. We mustn't let it get out of control. For years several journalists have bayed for CJ's blood, now I'm sure they think they have him." He expelled his breath in a sigh. "The fact that he's dying may not grant him impunity from their antics, but at Murrundi at least they can't get to him physically." He thought for a second or two. "However, they might try to harass others who work here, looking for a story angle. You know what they're like."

She didn't have Les' years of experience in dealing with the press but Francey agreed with him. "We'd better talk to everyone. Could you organise it? Bring the staff into the conservatory before dinner and I'll address them, let them know what's going on and tell them to be wary."

"Sure."

Les relaxed in a cane chair on the side verandah of Murrundi's homestead as he watched Francey back the station's Range Rover out of its space. She had seemed preoccupied over dinner, more so than usual considering the circumstances. He wondered what she was up to? He could tune into her moods easily nowadays, that's how he knew she had something on her mind. She was so much like CJ it unsettled him sometimes. The same stubborn streak, the same determination. And when she got an idea in her head she didn't let go. Just like old CJ.

As he stroked his jawline the stubble rasped against his fingers. His expression in the near darkness was contemplative. He'd keep a close eye on Francey over the next week or two, as CJ deteriorated. Stay close to the homestead. Most of all he didn't want her trying to organise anything that would upset the status quo. Hell no, he'd worked too hard to make it so.

Les smiled complacently at his own cleverness and then congratulated himself. So far it had all gone to plan, his plan. Getting CJ to confess to Natalie's murder had been easier than he'd thought. The old man, being so sick, had been more amenable than he normally would have been. All he'd done was plant the idea in his head that if someone confessed to the murder then Francey, the prime suspect, would be off the hook. And what did it matter to CJ? He only had weeks to live, that was obvious from the look of him.

He shook his head and swallowed hard to rid himself of the sudden lump in his throat. Christ, he hated to see the old man go down this way. The CJ he knew and remembered had always been so strong and vibrant. A man who'd tamed his part of the outback to his will and who'd created a formidable reputation and a business empire to match it. He loved him like the father he'd never known and, if he had ever thought about how CJ might die it wasn't like this – a slow extinguishment of life and energy. He'd expected him to go out in an explosive fashion like a shooting star.

Les was a fatalist and he marvelled at how things had in the last month or so fallen into place for him. He'd always been ambitious though he took great pains to hide the fact from everyone. Initially, that's what had driven him to want to marry Natalie. She'd been the easy and quick route to eventually controlling CJ's empire – even if Richard had lived. Natalie's half-brother had always been easy to manipulate.

He'd been fond of Natalie in his own way, been prepared to put up with her shallowness and her moods. He shook his head as he remembered that night, almost three years ago, she had told him of her sexual preferences and refused his offer of marriage. He'd seen his dreams start to fall apart. All the years of sucking up, learning the business, ingratiating himself and making himself indispensable to CJ and Richard to get the inside track into the family had been in vain.

Until Francey came along and turned out to be CJ's daughter. What a stroke of luck. He was in the race again and this time he'd win it now that she'd sorted herself out with Parrish. The man was a fool. He hadn't been able or willing to handle the *new* Francey. Good! Now all he had to do was to play it cool and to wait. Soon nature would take its course with CJ, and Francey would need him more than ever – he was the only person, apart from Lisa Dupre, who knew the ins and outs of CJ's empire.

Then it would only be a matter of time before she fell into his arms and he married her. He grinned into the darkness as he relished what was to come, the imagined feel of her in his arms, in his bed. His body hardened at the thought of her melting against him, and a wave of impatience raced through him. He wanted her now, badly. Steady on. He calmed himself slowly, allowing a few erotic fantasies to filter through his mind as he did so. Patience was what he needed at this point, and to have stayed on for so long as CJ's whipping boy he was certain he had plenty of it.

Another thought came to him as he turned the collar of his jacket up against the evening chill. If Francey had killed Natalie, would it matter to him? He debated the pros and cons of that for a minute or two and then decided. No. The bitch had, most likely, killed Richard, his best friend. She'd got what she deserved.

He got up from the chair and went back into the living room. Time for a chat with CJ before bed.

Francey pulled the Range Rover into the kerb on the opposite side of the road from Steve's house. All was in darkness and his car wasn't parked under the carport. She glanced at the clock on the dashboard. 8.15 p.m. With a sigh, she turned the radio on and settled back into the padded seat to wait.

A myriad of thoughts raced through her head as the quiet of the country town enveloped her. She hadn't thought about what she would say to Steve, or how to frame her request for him to continue investigating Natalie's murder. Somehow, she had to make him believe that CJ and herself were innocent. The people close to CJ did not believe him capable of murder. Sure, he had a reputation for being ruthless in business, and she'd seen examples of his anger on many occasions ... But murder was a far cry from being a hard-headed and sometimes bad tempered businessman.

All day she had fielded phone calls from local people, from politicians and colleagues, including Nikko Yakismoto, from her parents and even Meredith. They'd all rung to express their concern over his confession. Lucia and Carlo wanted to come up on the first plane to be with her but she had convinced them not to. She loved them dearly but coping with CJ's business, his imminent death and now the furore in the media was as much as she could deal with at present.

Her patience was rewarded when an hour later Steve's blue Ford utility turned into the driveway and parked. She waited until several lights were on inside before she left the Land Rover and crossed to the front door. She had a key but didn't consider it appropriate to use it so she knocked on the timber door and waited to hear his approaching footsteps.

"Francey." Steve's surprise was genuine and his eyes opened wide as he recognised her.

"Hello, Steve. May I come in?"

"Of course." He stood back to let her pass and as he did, a whiff of her perfume assailed his nostrils. She looked so beautiful. He wanted to touch her desperately but instead he thrust his hands deep into his trouser pockets to control the urge. Why was she here? What did she want? He followed her down the hall into the lounge room.

"Can I get you something? Coffee, wine?"

She smiled. So formal, so tense. "A coke would be nice." A good stiff whisky would have been better. She thought it might give her a touch of courage to say what she wanted to say.

Steve returned with a glass of coke and a beer for himself. He sat in one of the chairs and sipped at his beer. "What can I do for you, Francey?"

Her second smile was tremulous. "This is … awkward," she admitted. "I … I feel like an intruder, that I'm imposing, but you're the only person I felt I could turn to, could ask for help."

He shrugged. "I'm a policeman, it's my job to help people."

She almost winced. He sounded so impersonal. Then her words came out in a rush. "It's about CJ. I know he's not guilty. He couldn't have killed Natalie even if he says he did. It, it's just a …" she groped for the right word and couldn't find it, "he thinks he has to protect me, you see. That's why he said he did it." Her blue-green eyes appealed to him. "Steve, surely, you don't believe, I mean, you have reservations about his confession, don't you?"

He had, but to admit it wouldn't be professional. "Did you kill Natalie, Francey?"

Her eyes widened. "No!" She sighed. "Look, I know there's some heavy circumstantial evidence against me, motive and all that, but I didn't kill her."

Steve leant forward in the chair. "I'd like to help, really. It's just that …" He stopped, thought, and then said, "I have to go by the law. CJ made a confession and it seems believable. Inspector Clarke, myself and a police department psychologist discussed the possibility of him confessing to protect you, but after due consideration we rejected it."

"Why?"

"We'd already made certain enquires as to Natalie and her relationship with CJ. For years there's been an obvious

482

estrangement. So, for years, the dislike had been building between them. Then there's the circumstance of Richard's death. First it appeared to be an accident, everyone accepted that until I questioned the possibility of it being deliberate. Who would gain the most from Richard's death? Even though she's quite wealthy, the obvious person at the time was Natalie." He stopped for a few seconds to study her. "Although we could never prove it in a court of law she most likely orchestrated Richard's death. CJ's a passionate man – everyone knows that – and when he somehow learnt or guessed at Natalie's possible culpability, he sought revenge. I'm sorry, but under the law revenge is often regarded as a near perfect motive for murder."

She'd heard this before, from Les, and read it in the newspapers too. "You had other suspects: Mike Hunter and Les and who knows else? Perhaps someone else could have been on the property that night."

"Who?"

"Oh, I don't know. A stranger. Someone just passing through. Maybe Natalie disturbed him and he killed her. We hear about such happenings in the papers practically every day."

Steve rolled his eyes. "You're clutching at straws now, I think."

"I'll clutch at whatever helps me prove that CJ isn't guilty."

"Look, Francey, I'm sympathetic, however, I need something more tangible than wild ideas. A hunch, a clue, facts, something more definable. Otherwise …"

"Oh, Steve, CJ's going to die and I don't want people to remember him as a self-confessed murderer. He deserves better than that."

Steve ran a hand through his hair. Francey Spinetti was one damned stubborn woman, but he already knew that. Why couldn't she accept the fact that CJ had confessed, rather nobly, he thought, to keep her safe. "I don't want to argue the point with you, it's just that I don't have anywhere else to go with this case that doesn't put *you*, instead of CJ, in jeopardy."

Her eyes snapped with anger. "So, this is the easy way out. It's easier, no, more comfortable, for CJ to appear guilty than to do some hard work and really find who did it?"

"That's not fair and you know it. I've worked my arse off on this case."

An uneasy silence rested in the room between them. Francey was getting nowhere and she knew it. She glanced across at him, saw his tight features, the expression unreadable. So typical. She missed the old Steve. The Steve who'd dropped his guard to her and had pulled down the emotional walls between them. The Steve who cared. Her heavy sigh was eaten up by the quiet in the room. She had wasted her time by coming here. He couldn't be moved or changed. Accepting that she got up and put her glass on the coffee table.

"Look, what I can do is to go through all the paperwork again. Maybe we missed something," he offered, not wanting her to go. Then he too stood up.

"Would you?" Her face brightened noticeably, her heart skipping a beat at his sudden closeness. "Thank you." It wasn't much but it was better than nothing.

He walked her to the front door and opened it wide. They stood in silence looking at each other, neither able to bridge the gap which had risen between them. For what seemed an eternity but was in reality only several seconds they stared at each other.

As Francey turned away she whispered, "I miss you."

Her close proximity was driving him crazy. He could hardly think straight and his muscles and nerve endings were so finely tuned he thought he would burst. He'd have to be made of solid granite not to be affected by her beauty, the sad expression in her eyes. And then, in one of those rare moments of clarity he realised that what he felt for her transcended all else, including his stupid male pride. Her expectation of great wealth and her relationship to CJ wasn't important. What mattered was *them*, that they should be together. It had taken him a while to see the light, but how could he make up for the mess he'd made of their relationship through his sense of insecurity? He'd painted himself into a corner from which there looked to be no easy escape.

With a great deal of effort Steve got control of his feelings. "I didn't quite catch that," he said as he swallowed hard to loosen the emotional lump lodged in his throat.

She touched his cheek briefly, blinked back a tear. "Doesn't matter, it wasn't important."

Steve stood silhouetted in the open doorway and watched her walk all the way to her car, get in and rev the engine. There was a singular, coherent thought which ran through his mind as she drove up the street: you never appreciate what you've got until it's out of reach. So true, so bloody true!

Billy Wontow stood with half-a-dozen other stockmen on the ground below the verandah of Les Westcott's cottage. As he listened to Les give the orders for the day his dark eyes caught a glint of something bright stuck between the floorboards of the verandah. Rays from the early morning sun were picking up a flash of light.

"Billy. That Braford bull we bought last month, Maestro, has damaged some of the stockyard fence uprights. We'll be needing those yards at the end of the week so move him to one of the outer paddocks then fix the fencing. Then I want you to take one of the bikes and check on how that experimental herd of camels has settled in."

Lucky sniggered. "Yeah, Billy, put on your Lawrence of Arabia cape when you do that, will you."

Les grinned briefly. "Don't scoff, Lucky. Camels are an up-and-coming export meat market. In a couple of years it'll be a nice little money earner for Murrundi."

Ignoring Lucky's remark, Billy dipped his weather-worn hat in acknowledgement, "Right, boss."

Other men were assigned their duties and started to amble off in several directions but Billy, characteristically curious, wondered what was caught between the floorboards. He shuffled off more slowly than usual, waiting for Les to head towards the homestead. Once Westcott was out of sight Billy headed back to the verandah and, using his penknife, dug the item out from between the boards.

Billy checked his find. A small white button with an edge of gold around it – that's what had caught the light. Squinting, he placed the button in the palm of his hand to study it. He'd seen this type of button before. Where? His forehead puckered in a frown of concentration. He blinked several times as it came to him. On the shirt Natalie had been wearing when she'd been fished out of the pool. Two buttons had been missing, he remembered. His level of curiosity multiplied tenfold. What was the button doing here, on Les' verandah?

He glanced about to make sure no-one was around, got down on his hands and knees and loosened a piece of lattice put there to discourage small animals from making the cooler under-space their home. He then crawled under the verandah which, in traditional Queensland fashion, was almost a metre off the ground to allow for better ventilation. For twenty minutes he grubbed around the soil and found an assortment of cigarette butts, old nails, pieces of metal and lolly wrappers that had been blown under during strong winds. Close to giving up on the second button he moved a piece of white paper and a small round object slid onto the ground. The second button!

Billy almost whooped with glee. With care he placed the two buttons in the top breast pocket of his shirt and fastened the flap. Before he emerged, he checked again that no-one loitered around the yard and then he headed for the stockyards.

Work first, he decided. Then a trip into town. Steve Parrish, he reckoned, would be mighty interested in what he'd found.

Steve sat among a pile of files scattered over the length and breadth of his desk. Funny, he mused as he sifted through the paperwork in Neil's file on the deWitt-Ambrose case, if one eliminated, say, Francey and CJ, and applied logic of probable motive or lack of it to the other suspects, the one who appeared to have the strongest motive to get rid of Natalie was, in his opinion, Les Westcott.

He tapped his pencil on the top of a file as he thought. There was an air of smugness about the man. As if Westcott was privy to information no-one else had. That had niggled and annoyed him ever since the investigation had begun.

Neil had assembled a substantial dossier on Westcott. Some hearsay, some of it facts which dated back almost twenty years. The overall picture was that of a quietly ambitious, intelligent, very determined man. Over the years Westcott had worked his way through promotion at Murrundi into CJ's confidence and apart from Francey, was the other most important person in CJ's business empire. People around the Isa said he'd once been in love with and had wanted to marry Natalie. Neil's information included the purchase of an engagement ring from a Mt Isa jeweller. And wasn't it logical to believe that by marrying Natalie Les would assure himself a place in the Ambrose heirachy. No marriage had occurred and Neil had noted why. Natalie simply wasn't interested in a heterosexual relationship.

More facts had emerged. According to banking information requisitioned by the police department, Westcott was a wealthy man in his own right. Steve's eyebrows lifted in envy of the man's healthy bank balance. No doubt judicious investments over the years, assisted by inside knowledge via CJ, had made him financially independent.

And Steve personally knew that Westcott wanted to be romantically involved with Francey.

So, if he put all the pieces together, what did he have? Suppositions, possibilities and a man who coveted CJ's business empire and, perhaps desperately, wanted it for himself. Now, the easiest way – the only way in fact – to get it was through marriage to Francey Spinetti. But how did that work as possible motivation to kill Natalie? He tapped his pencil again on the top folder, thinking through the possibilities.

Les could have perceived Natalie as a threat to his plans. The woman was emotionally unstable and getting worse. She had tried to dispose of Francey once, she might try again. Also, Natalie would inherit part of CJ's estate on his death but if she died before CJ, the entire estate went to Francey. This would make marriage to Francey a very attractive proposition indeed.

Yes, motivation was there and like the other suspects Les didn't have an airtight alibi for the night of the murder. He stroked his jawline, this line of investigation looked promising ...

His head shot up as someone knocked on his office door.

Neil poked his head around the half open doorway. "Steve, Billy Wontow wants a moment of your time."

"Send him in."

Billy shuffled into the office and plonked his lanky frame down into the seat Steve pointed to.

"Good to see you, mate," Steve welcomed him. "Want a tea or coffee?"

"Not gonna be here that long," Billy's reply was laconic. "Got something for you." He fished the two buttons out of his top pocket and placed them on the desk blotter. "You recognise them?"

Steve frowned, thought for several seconds, "Natalie's shirt, I think."

"That's what I reckoned too."

"Where did you find them, Billy?"

"At Murrundi. One was stuck between the floorboards of the cottage where Les Westcott lives, the other had fallen through the verandah into the dirt."

"You're sure that's where you found them, both of them?"

"Too right, mate," Billy said with a grin. "I've got enough dirt on my clothes to prove it."

Steve grinned back, elated. Maybe, just maybe ... "Billy, I'll need you to make a statement about where you found the buttons and then I want you to do me a favour."

Billy's dark eyes narrowed. "Sure, Steve. What do you want?"

"Keep the information about the buttons to yourself. Don't tell anyone, not even Alison. Can you do that?"

"Sure, mate. No problem."

An hour later Steve assembled his investigative team in one of the station house's interrogation rooms.

"Are you serious?" Erin Cooper said boldly, "you want to reopen the case on the strength of the two buttons Wontow found?"

"We have a confession from CJ Ambrose, remember?" Glen McAlpine put in.

Steve held up both hands. "I know, I know. It's a slim lead but it's evidence that throws a new light on things. The whereabouts of the buttons tell us that Natalie was at Westcott's cottage the night of the murder. Possibly that's where she was knocked unconscious and strangled. Her body may then have been moved and dumped in the pool."

"You think Wontow's telling the truth about where he found the buttons?" Neil asked.

"I don't have a reason not to believe him. Why would he lie? He's not the sort to want to get into trouble with the police, or to simply make mischief," Steve argued.

"One might assume that he's fiercely loyal to CJ and Francey," Glen supposed. "Maybe he found them somewhere else and is trying, in his own way, to protect them."

"I don't buy that, and neither did Inspector Clarke. He's all for going ahead with this new line of inquiry," Steve stated firmly. He didn't add that both he and his superior saw the wisdom in trying to clear CJ Ambrose's name while not incriminating Francey. Neither policeman was comfortable with either Ambrose's seeming involvement in the murder, so checking out another possibility was well worth the effort.

"Westcott's a pretty cool customer. He'll say it must have happened while he was out." Erin put in. "That was his alibi, wasn't it, driving around in his car?"

"There's other circumstantial evidence which puts Westcott under suspicion," Steve said and listed them for his team.

"Okay," Neil nodded his approval, "how do we go about it?"

"As Erin said, the evidence is pretty slim so to make it stick we'll need to get a confession from him." He ignored their doubtful expressions and hastened on. "The inspector suggested I wear a wire and record an interview with him. I think I can get him mad enough to admit that he killed Natalie." Steve then added, "He and Francey are away at the moment, up in Cooktown. They're due back this afternoon which gives us time to get organised." He grinned confidently at them all. "I want this bastard, let's go get him."

Shellie sat in the same chair recently vacated by Rose, the morning nurse, watching CJ sleep. It broke her heart to see her brother go downhill like this. There was so little she could do; little that any of them could do other than make him comfortable. She smiled at nothing in particular, secretly amazed at how close they'd become over the last six weeks. Like they had been as children as they'd roamed the outback with their father while he tried to find work. Even back then, as a youngster, CJ had possessed a rare vitality and been driven to succeed at whatever he wanted to do.

The way he was handling the frustration of his situation evoked her deep admiration. The old CJ would have roared like an enraged bull, stomped about swearing and generally made everyone as tense and miserable as himself. It was almost impossible to imagine a world , her world, without CJ's larger than life presence.

For the umpteenth time she thanked God for the strength of Barry's love. Without it who knew where she'd be? She gave a little snort – probably up to her armpits in booze. Francey would be all right. She'd come through this dreadful time with her strength intact. She had plenty of moral and emotional strength to see her through the grief and later, the healing process.

"Shellie," CJ's voice was husky with sleep. "Is Francey back yet? There's something I want to tell her."

"In an hour or two. Les just radioed Lisa that they'll be leaving Cooktown within the hour."

"Sis," CJ half whispered, "I want you to make me a promise. When I'm gone marry that doctor of yours and move away from Murrundi. You deserve your own life in your own home – you've spent too many years in other people's houses. I'm sure it's what Barry wants."

Shellie shook her head. "Please, I can't think about that, it's too … too …"

"Morbid? Hell, Shellie, I have no delusions. Life will go on with or without CJ Ambrose. That's the order of things, you know. And this damned illness, by the time it's done with me I reckon I'll be ready to go anywhere to escape the pain, the boredom, the isolation of it."

"Do you need something for the pain? Shall I get Rose?"

"Not yet." His grin was half smile, half grimace. "After I talk to Francey, then Rose can medicate me.

Now I know what a damned pin cushion feels like and it isn't good."

Shellie's mouth twitched despite herself. CJ's wry humour in the face of his predicament amazed her. Just another sign of him trying not to give in to the inevitable, she supposed.

"You can do something for me if you plan to just sit there."

"Of course. What?"

"My eyesight's pretty bad, I can't focus for long periods of time. Those letters on the table, would you read them to me?"

"I'd be pleased to. I'll get my glasses."

All CJ could make out was a blur moving towards the door and disappearing out of sight. His poor sister, how she was suffering. Everyone was, himself included. But soon he'd be free, and so would they.

CHAPTER THIRTY

The police van pulled in around the back of the homestead and parked under the long carport. Steve Parrish checked his watch as he stepped out of the van. "CJ's plane should land in the next ten minutes. Lisa Dupre knows about the operation, she'll keep everyone inside. Erin, I want you to monitor the recording device." He turned to Neil Smith. "You'll be backup in case anything untoward happens. Take the point at the end of the drive and watch for the plane. Whistle as soon as it comes into view."

"We'd better do another audio check, Steve." Erin suggested. "Walk about and talk or sing while I check the levels."

Steve did so and after he'd got the thumbs up from Erin he joined Neil.

They didn't have to wait long for the sleek aeroplane to come into view. The jet circled over the property then lined up with the airstrip and began its descent.

"Wow! I'd sure like one of those little toys," Neil exclaimed with envy.

"You or I couldn't afford the annual fuel costs, let alone the leasing arrangements," Steve quipped. "Okay, I'm off.

I'll try to catch him just outside the hangar. Westcott won't be inclined to talk if there are witnesses around so I'll send Francey into the house." He mentally crossed his fingers that she would cooperate without question.

It was a reasonably paced six minute walk through the vegetable garden, around a couple of machinery sheds and by the first lot of stockyards to the airstrip. The Learjet, model 31, had just reversed into the hangar space, ready for the next take off as Steve reached the outer perimeter of the area. He could feel himself sweating and knew it wasn't caused by the weather. He wanted to nail Westcott so bad he could taste it but since the inspector had approved the plan a sense of apprehension had been growing inside him. He couldn't afford to screw this one up. He knew that his track record wasn't great and so much hinged on a successful operation. His credibility, his quest to bury the past and even his future happiness were on the line.

As he watched the door open and Francey come down the steps he was close enough to see the delight mirrored in her eyes as she recognised him. She walked towards him, briefcase and, as usual, a bunch of rolled up plans under one arm. He barely had time to admire her shapely legs in the miniskirt, part of the white linen power suit she wore with the aplomb of a catwalk model, before his brain shifted into gear.

"Steve," her tone was breathy with surprise. "I didn't expect …" But oh, how she had hoped he'd be there, that somehow, miraculously, they could work things out.

He strode up to her and took her in his arms. Finding her lips wasn't difficult and kissing her was like receiving the key to the gates of heaven. He held her close to him and as he felt the warmth and softness of her mingle with his body he almost lost his focus. She felt so good, and it had been so long ... Eventually sanity resurfaced and he pushed his head back from hers. Out of the corner of his eye he saw Westcott come down the plane's steps and falter, his mouth agape. He noted that as usual the man was dressed in his country squire gear and clutched a black attache case in his right hand.

"I love you," he whispered to Francey then continued with obvious urgency. "Don't ask me any questions, just pretend you're ecstatic about all this." He kissed her again. "Now I want you to head for the homestead and don't look back. I'll tell you what this is all about later." There were so many other things he wanted to say, that he'd been a prideful fool, that what mattered was them being together – but now wasn't the time. He'd eat humble pie when he'd attended to Westcott.

"But ..." Francey's huge eyes widened. "What's going on?" She was desperate not to move out of the circle of his arms; it felt so wonderful to be there.

"Please," Steve groaned, and using his eyes he tried to communicate the urgency of the situation. "My love, for once in your life don't question anything, just do as I ask." Seeing her frown, he added softly, "Clearing CJ may depend on it."

He stepped away from her and gave her a playful pat on the backside. When he spoke his voice was loud enough for Westcott to hear. "Yes, darling. We'll talk about it at the homestead." Then, he whispered the order through gritted teeth "Go, and don't look back!"

Controlling her puzzlement but tuned in to the unusual vibrations which emanated from him, Francey did precisely as she'd been told: she kept walking. What is he up to? she wondered. And that kiss. What did it mean? What she'd hoped – that everything was okay between them? Well, she wouldn't let him get off that lightly – Steve Parrish had some explaining to do.

For several seconds as she covered ground she dwelt on the sheer power of his kiss, how her knees had gone weak and every nerve ending she possessed had burst into life and sent pulsing messages of awareness throughout her body. Steve. Being in his arms again was glorious as was the ardour of his kiss. And how she wanted to believe his declaration of love.

Steve had never said that phrase aloud before. Her lips curved in a smile despite her confusion. She wanted very much for it to mean that he'd realised how strong his feelings were, but was astute enough to sense that the scenario seemed planned. Again, as she continued towards the homestead, she asked herself ... why?

Steve glanced back at Francey to be sure that she'd put some distance between them then he tried to regroup mentally. With difficulty. The singing in his veins, the burst of joy that had raced through him at her spontaneous response to his kiss was hard to forget. Everything was going to be all right between them, her response told him so. Now, to the task at hand.

"Westcott," Steve greeted his quarry. There would be no pussyfooting about. He'd spent hours working out a plan of attack. "We need to talk." As he spoke he studied CJ's right-hand man. Les appeared to be having difficulty curbing his anger, a situation no doubt brought about by seeing Francey in Steve's arms. A nerve in his temple had begun to throb uncontrollably and Steve saw his shoulders square under the tweed jacket – a dead give away for tension. Good, he wanted him off balance.

"I don't think we have anything to talk about," Les muttered dismissively as he tried to sidestep him.

Steve blocked his path. "'Fraid we do. We can do it here or at the station. Your choice."

"All right." Les' saturnine features set in a bored expression. "What is it now?" He glanced over the policeman's shoulder at Francey's departing figure. She was almost to the fodder barn and in half-a-dozen steps she would be out of sight and hearing. Another sweeping glance told him that no other workers were within view. He affected a casual stance, his left hand sliding into his trouser pocket. He waited for Parrish to speak.

"New evidence has come to light in regard to Natalie's murder," Steve began. "These," he pulled out a small plastic envelope which contained the two buttons and dangled them under Westcott's nose, "were found under the verandah of your cottage. I want you to tell me how they got there?" He swallowed the nervous lump in his throat and tried to forget about his sweating palms. It was time for confrontation and this time there would be no repeat of what had occurred years ago.

Les snorted. "How the bloody hell would I know? I wasn't there, remember. You have my statement."

"A statement that can't be corroborated. We've only your word that you were driving around aimlessly in your car. I put it to you, Les Westcott, that the night of the murder Natalie came to your cottage. You both argued. You lost your temper and hit her, then strangled her." He stopped for a moment to let Les digest his words. "You see, Les, we've worked up a profile on you. We know about your ambition to control CJ's business empire and how you thought that by marrying Natalie you'd be one step closer. But she wasn't interested, was she, Les? I think that recently you perceived Natalie as a threat to your long-term plans and that's why you got rid of her."

"This is preposterous!" Les guffawed. "You'd never prove any of that in a court of law and you know it. Besides, CJ's confessed to Natalie's murder. All this supposition is a waste of my time and yours."

"Maybe but at least I'll thwart one of your ambitions. Once CJ's gone you'll want to marry Francey. It's now the only way to get the control you want." Steve's sweeping arm encompassed the property. "Well, you won't be the one to marry her, old son. I will."

With narrowed gaze he watched Les' features tighten. That had gotten to him. A sheen of perspiration began to dot the man's forehead. Instinctively he knew that Westcott was remembering him embracing Francey. He felt his senses sharpening ... just a little bit more and he'd crack. But he wasn't out of control. Yet. "We've patched things up, as you just saw. Shame, isn't it?" He grinned aggravatingly at him. "All those years, scheming to get your hands on what CJ owned. It'll never happen. And you can make sure of another thing, once I'm ensconced at Murrundi with Francey it'll be goodbye Les Westcott – for good." A muscle began to throb in Les' jaw as he thought this new development through. Was Parrish telling the truth about him and Francey or was it a bluff? He shook his head slightly, trying to clear the confusion, the doubts. This couldn't be happening, he told himself, for he had planned every step with such care. He looked at Parrish and wondered ... could this dumb ass copper be about to destroy everything? No, his determination firmed, he wouldn't let that happen.

"I hope you've made contingency plans," Steve went on, almost conversationally. "We know you've stashed plenty away over the years you've been with CJ. In fact, I just might have his accountant check the books. Maybe you've helped yourself to a couple of million you shouldn't have."

Les's hand shot out of his pocket, the index finger prodding Steve's chest. "You stupid cop." His heavy breathing mixed with an escalating anger became lost in the vastness of the land around them. "If I did what you said, do you think I'd be stupid enough to leave a trail for someone like you to follow?"

"Probably not," Steve conceded. Christ, he hoped Erin was recording all this, including his own increased heartbeat. "You're smart, Westcott, I'll give you that. Your plan almost succeeded. If it wasn't for me all you had to do was bide your time, be nice to Francey. She might have married you eventually." He repeated, "You're smart, no doubt about it. I'll bet you've got away with murder too. Natalie's. How did it happen?" His tone turned conspiratorial. "Did she come to your cottage and tell you she'd changed her mind about marrying you or ..."

Out of nowhere a thought came to Steve. "Maybe she came to ask you to help her kill Francey. We've assumed that she wanted to because Francey stood in the way of her total inheritance. There was a fight and you lost control. Is that how it happened, Les?" He didn't take his eyes off Les' face. He watched a shiftiness come into his eyes and saw his mouth tighten with anger. The needling was starting to get to him. Good.

The policeman's goading and the self-satisfied smile on his face made Les' anger rise another notch, to near boiling point. Suddenly he recognised his immediate problem – Parrish! On no account was this cop going to ruin his plans, his dreams, when they were so close to fruition. Frustration and blind, uncontrollable rage churned together. He couldn't let that happen, not when he'd worked so damned hard. He deserved his reward – CJ's millions – for the years of servitude and kowtowing.

"Yes, damn you," Les yelled, in an explosion of unexpected emotion. He furtively scanned their surroundings, no-one was in sight. He knew what he had to do now. "You're not as dumb as I thought you were," he admitted in a mercurial reversal to momentary calmness.

"Natalie came to me. She looked a mess, eyes half glazed, probably doped up, features twitching. Said I had to help her take care of Francey and if I did we'd split CJ's fortune between us. Then, in a crazy, disjointed speech, she told me that she'd caused Richard's death, that she'd killed him because CJ was going to leave him everything and she didn't think that was fair." He shook his head and then continued. "The woman was certifiable, almost foaming at the mouth. She thought she was clever though, that no-one would discover the real cause of the stampede." He paused again to study Steve's face. "You found those cartridges and started an investigation because she was too damned lazy to get off her horse and pick them up. She never could attend to detail," he added with a disdainful curl of his lip.

A strange gleam came into Les' eyes. "I got very angry when she told me about Richard. You see, I loved him; he was my one true friend. He didn't deserve to be trampled to death." He stopped talking, reliving the scene in his mind.

"So ..." Steve prompted, unable to believe how well the interrogation was proceeding. He'd managed to push the right buttons and Les was blurting it all out almost as if he was at confession. "That's when you killed Natalie. You got so angry you lost your temper?"

For several seconds Les stared owlishly at the policeman, and blinked as if his thoughts were elsewhere. "Oh, I knew what I was doing. I considered it a community service. I saved the courts the problem of dealing with Natalie. I smacked her across the face and she went crazy. Came at me with her fingers curved like talons. I hit her again and this time my fist connected with her jaw. She fell to the ground and just lay there." His smile reflected pure pleasure. "Then I knelt down, put my hands around her neck and squeezed every scrap of life out of her."

"After which you carried her to the pool and rolled her in," Steve said helpfully, for the recording device's benefit.

Les' eyes narrowed as in his mind he went back to the night it had happened. Reliving it was giving him the same sense of satisfaction, of rightness. He nodded and stared momentarily at the plastic bag in Steve's hand. "That's when the buttons must have come off her shirt. When I dragged her across the verandah and down the steps."

"I guess you were the one who placed Mike Hunter's Swiss army knife near the pool to incriminate him."

He nodded. "And I encouraged CJ to confess to the crime to save Francey. That was easy – he wanted to protect her."

Steve hoped Erin had got every word. They had him. A wave of satisfaction raced through him. He'd mentally agonised whether he had the balls to pull the interrogation off and it had gone so damned well – almost to textbook. The weight of the past, his failure to close, began to lift off him ... at last. He'd known that Westcott's temper would get the better of him one day and now the man's powder-keg fuse had finally betrayed him. With difficulty he controlled the elation and instead began to feel something else, a vague sense of discomfort. Westcott was too smart and had confessed to the crime too easily, as if it didn't matter. As if he wasn't worried about being arrested by him. Then came the words ...

"Now I have one last person to deal with," Les' tone was soft, menacing. "You."

CHAPTER THIRTY-ONE

Before Steve could block the move Les swung his attache case in an arc and struck Steve in a blow to the side of the head with enough force to knock him off his feet and onto his back. Instantly Les fell on top of him and used his knees to press Steve's forearms to his body, preventing him from moving. He unlatched Steve's gun, took it out of its holster and pointed it in his face. Then he rolled off him and stood up.

"Get up."

"So you've got my gun, what do you plan to do? Shoot me, here?"

"Don't think I wouldn't like to," Les snarled. Too late he realised that his lapse of self-control had almost brought him undone.

"Do you think I came alone?" That should make Neil and Erin run to the hangar at full pace. How long would it take them to reach it? Three, maybe four minutes.

"You're bluffing."

"Am I? Two officers are at the homestead waiting for me. I said I'd be about twenty minutes. They'll come looking for me soon." He had no intention of revealing that he was wired. That might tip Westcott's temper over the edge again, something he didn't want to do because he had control of the gun.

Francey, back at the homestead and standing by the open police van, gave a squeal of alarm as she realised what had happened. For the last five minutes she'd stood in a state of shock listening to the conversation between the man she loved and Les Westcott, occasionally shaking her head in amazement as the truth of Natalie's and Richard's murders were revealed. Thank God, CJ wasn't there, he'd be devastated.

Erin looked at Neil. "Steve's in trouble. Westcott's got his firearm."

Neil nodded as he stepped out of the van, away from the recording. He looked at Francey. "Can you monitor this for us?"

She nodded. She'd become used to various pieces of electronic equipment on the property and in the Learjet. "Please, go," she said, her tone urgent. She watched the two sprint off in the direction of the hangar, her heartbeat thudding in her chest. Please, God, she silently prayed, don't let Les hurt him.

"I don't believe you," Les scoffed.

Steve shrugged. "Suit yourself." He was busy watching Westcott's every move, hoping for a weakness, a lapse in concentration. Anything that might allow him to snatch back the gun and the advantage.

Les tried to think clearly. Could Steve's words be another bluff, like his reconciliation with Francey, or was Parrish telling the truth? A wave of heat suffused his body and his stomach muscles rippled, knotting hard. What were his options? Kill Parrish. Yes. God, he wanted to, so much. The policeman had made him lose control, got him to admit to Natalie's murder, so he had no choice. But, he could save the situation; he could win, providing he got rid of Parrish and no-one knew about it.

Les motioned Steve forward with the gun. "Walk in front of me, to the plane."

"Going for a plane ride, are we?" Steve spoke the words casually but inside he was anything but. Hell, where were "the troops"? A sense of déjà vu washed over him as he stumbled unenthusiastically towards the Learjet. Him, a professional had allowed himself to be caught off guard. Shit! Hadn't he been down this road before, a couple of times? His brain went into mental replay: with Karrin in Newtown and then in that liquor shop. He remembered clearly what had been whispered behind his back. Parrish hasn't got what it takes. Parrish can't finalise a situation. Parrish can't function under stress.

Maybe they'd been right. Westcott certainly had the upper hand at the moment and if Neil and Erin didn't come in time … The man was a criminal, a murderer. Now he was about to make his getaway and he was powerless to stop him.

"You'll never get away with it, you know."

"Oh, no? Once we're on that plane I can go wherever I want to. Did you think I wouldn't have a contingency plan?" He prodded Steve in the back with the gun's barrel. "How do you feel about a free-fall at six thousand metres – minus a parachute – over some remote outback area? Quite possibly your body will never be found, and it'll look as if you've just disappeared. The authorities won't know where to look for you."

Steve didn't care to answer the question about free-falling, so he remained silent.

"Westcott!"

A shot rang over their heads and lodged in the plane's fuselage.

Les pushed Steve forward then swivelled around to see two police officers sprinting towards them, their guns drawn. Damn! Parrish hadn't been bluffing. He hesitated for a second, unsure of the distance and an unfamiliar gun. He took aim and fired two rounds, and whooped with satisfaction as the male officer dropped to his knees, hit in the thigh. The other officer knelt to render assistance.

Les began to shudder with repressed rage. All his plans and his dreams had been undone by this dumb copper. Escape was now his only option even though his confession to Steve would be just his word against the policeman's. Damn Parrish. The man was smarter than he looked. *Kill him*, a voice inside his head encouraged. His eyes narrowed in speculation. There'd be witnesses – the two cops – and he knew how the police worked, they never gave up if you killed one of their own.

Les' preoccupation with Neil and Erin was the diversion Steve needed. Ducking at the waist as he turned, he lunged at Les and caught him around the legs. All those tackles in the police rugby league team hadn't been in vain, he thought as the rangy man toppled to the ground expelling a grunt of pain and dropping the gun. They rolled around on the dusty earth, each trying to land telling blows. Steve's fist made contact with Les nose, hard enough to cause a trail of blood to run down his cheek. Then Westcott's elbow caught him in the diaphragm. Winded, he fought for breath but managed to get another fist onto Les' jaw before his opponent brought his right fist up in a powerful uppercut.

Steve saw stars and shook his head, trying to stop the spinning sensation. His muscles began to dissolve and he could feel his body going limp as he fought against the enveloping darkness.

As Les scrambled to his feet he swore under his breath. Forget Parrish, he had to get away. He glanced back at the two officers. The man lay on the ground but the female continued to approach, cautiously, her gun at shoulder level in front of her. Further back he saw Francey running towards the action. He stared at Parrish, the man was on all fours, trying to reach for the gun. Shit, he'd got his hand around the butt. No more time, he decided.

Another shot buzzed close to Les, spitting up particles of red earth. He saw that the policewoman had dropped to her knee and was taking deliberate aim. "Stop Westcott!" Erin's yell carried on the afternoon breeze. "I'll shoot."

Survival, the most primitive instinct came to the fore.

Les straightened up and raced towards the plane. He leapt up the steps two at a time but as he was about to disappear inside another shot rang out – so close the noise almost deafened him. Searing pain ripped through his left shoulder. His hand went up to investigate and came away wet. For all of two seconds he stared at his bloodied hand. Then he groaned as the pain accelerated through his shoulder, his back and down his arm. Parrish had shot him, the bastard. Grimacing he pulled the Learjet's door shut and stumbled to the cockpit. Within seconds the jet's twin motors roared into life, and the plane started to taxi onto the airstrip.

Steve struggled to his feet and shook his head in an attempt to stop the ringing in his ears. Westcott's blow had almost rendered him unconscious. He saw the plane moving along the tarmac and heard the engine building to full throttle. How far could a .38 bullet travel, he wondered? Maybe a thousand metres. Hell, he couldn't remember for sure. With legs apart, arms out in front of him and raised to shoulder height he fired, aiming for the wings because he'd heard somewhere that that was where the fuel tanks were situated. He emptied every round into the plane.

Erin, breathless, reached his side. "Are you all right?"

"Yes," Steve's tone was brusque. "The bastard's getting away though." Like the other times. A future vision of his colleagues whispering that he'd failed again drove him to the point of fury. "Give me your gun!" He grabbed it and emptied the remaining may have entailed. And maybe he'd never see his bullets into the jet as it picked up speed along the strip. "Shit, he's going to make it." Gritting his teeth he closed his eyes in an attempt to block out the reality of Westcott's escape. *Another failure.* His shoulders slumped in defeat and for the life of him he couldn't think of a word to say. Almost against his will his eyes opened and he watched the jet reach maximum speed, take off and ascend in a straight line towards the horizon.

"We got everything on tape, Steve. His confession. Francey heard it too." She patted him on the arm. "No-one could have done better, you know. You're lucky he didn't kill you." And then, ever the efficient cop, she added, "We should contact Interpol as soon as we get back to the homestead."

Steve would not allow himself to be consoled. He shrugged Erin's hand off his arm. "*Better* wasn't good enough," he retorted, his tone bitter. He'd failed. Again.

Les Westcott sat at the plane's controls waiting for his heartbeat to return to some semblance of normality. The taste of bile half choked him and with it a disappointment so complete it almost robbed him of his remaining strength. He thought of the shoulder wound, it would need dressing. It would have to wait until he got onto autopilot. Banking the jet he made a final sweep of Murrundi. It was the last time he would set eyes on the place that had been his home for twenty years. No more for him the cut and thrust of big business deals, and no more Francey and all that son, Mark, either.

The one thing he deeply regretted was that he hadn't finished off Parrish. His good hand fiddled with the instrument panel, making adjustments. He'd been damned stupid to let Parrish rile him sufficiently to lose control. The smart-mouthed bastard, with his astute prodding had got the better of him, *and* he'd been eaten up by jealousy when he'd seen Francey in Parrish's arms. The way she'd raced towards him, like a damn homing pigeon, a rapt expression on her face. She'd never looked that way at him. He swallowed the bile of envy and his one capable hand tightened on the wheel as he fought down his frustration, tried to get himself under control. Think. He must think ...

First, he had to accept what had happened, that there could be no going back. But he could have a future ... A smug smile crept across his face. He'd always been the type to think things through carefully and leave nothing to chance. He may have banked on getting control of CJ's empire one day but he had been cautious enough to make alternative plans should something unforseen happen.

His money – two million – was safe in a Swiss bank account and he'd bought a modest villa in Buenos Aires just in case. All he had to do was organise a new identity, perhaps some plastic surgery too. He had contacts who could put all of that in motion, and then he'd be able to spend the rest of his life in reasonable luxury, there was enough money for that. Yes, a new life and a new identity. He, Les Westcott, would have the last laugh on CJ, Natalie and that damned Parrish.

He could feel his left arm going numb and a river of blood had begun to drip onto his trousers and the seat. He shook his head to dispel a sudden wooziness – he was losing too much blood. Just two minutes more then he'd be able to attend to the wound.

He started a reverse bank and noted that the controls were responding sluggishly. He frowned as he studied the dials on the instrument panel, they were going crazy. Then the jet began to lose altitude and the revs began to drop. What the hell? He stared at the fuel gauge, the indicator flickered and nudged empty.

Shit. There had been no time to refuel the Learjet after the flight from Cooktown. And those shots of Parrish's ...

With his good hand he fought the pull on the wheel as the plane's nose dropped, and then with a sickening cough the starboard engine spluttered and died ...

Francey was out of breath by the time she reached Steve. "Oh, Steve, thank God you're not hurt." She threw herself into his arms. "I was so scared. Les, who would have imagined?" She stared up at him and brought a hand up to stroke his cheek. "I thought he'd kill you."

He smiled crookedly at her. "I thought so to."

Ignoring Erin's presence, Francey asked, "Did you mean what you said before?"

"About loving you?" He forgot the battering he'd taken from Les, how much his jaw hurt and pulled her close until their thighs, stomachs and chests touched. She felt glorious against him and he never wanted to move again. "You bet. You've got it all on tape, Miss Spinetti."

She smiled and cocked an eyebrow at him. "And what you said to Les, about us getting married?" Steve was all right. Better than all right. Wonderful. She couldn't tell him that she had been so afraid when the two police officers said that Les had his gun, and intended to kill him. The blood had almost frozen in her veins with a fear so great she never wanted to experience such a feeling again.

"God, that's on tape too." He let a mock groan escape his lips. "Guess I'll have to or you'll sue."

"Steve, look," Erin interrupted. "The plane. Something's wrong with it."

Relief rebounded through Steve as he squinted up at the Learjet. The shots! Some had found their mark. The plane's nose had come down, it was out of control.

As they watched he allowed a wave of exultation to move through him. He'd survived Les' attack and now he honestly felt that he'd got his man, sure that the combination of wounding him and firing at the plane had caused it to go out of control. And contrary to his previous thoughts about failure, he now knew he'd succeeded. He was going to get Westcott, one way or another.

He stared at the twisting plane, watching the spiralling plume of smoke trail from its engines as it nosedived. He knew that Les wouldn't have time and there wasn't enough height for a parachute, even if he could make it to the door. Memories of the past and his deep-rooted feeling of not having what it took, slipped deep into his subconscious hopefully never to resurface. The bogey was off his back, dead and buried.

The jet came down in almost a straight line, engines whining at first then cutting out to leave an eerie silence as it disappeared behind a small foothill. Seconds later a loud explosion followed by a trail of smoke proved the obvious.

No-one spoke for several seconds. Then they looked at each other. Each had been holding their breath as the jet plummeted to the ground.

"Guess you'll need a new plane and a new pilot," Erin murmured to Francey.

Francey gave the woman a cold stare then turned away. "Oh, God. Poor Les."

"*Poor Les* was a murderer," Steve pointed out, his arms tightening around her. "He planned to coerce you into marriage so he could control CJ's businesses. You heard me state that to him and he didn't deny it. And Natalie, no matter whether we liked the woman or not, he killed her in cold blood. He would have killed me if Erin hadn't fired at him."

"I'd better check on Neil," Erin decided and began to jog back to where Neil lay on the ground.

Francey waited until the policewoman was out of earshot. "You're right of course, but it's hard to believe. Les, a murderer! I mean, he was always so pleasant ... so agreeable, like a brother or a relative. Almost." Unbidden into her thoughts came the night in the kitchen when he'd tried to force himself on her. Why hadn't she suspected something then? Even so, comprehending it all now in a matter of minutes was difficult. She shook her head. "It's like there were two of him. One that hid inside the other."

"Yes," Steve agreed. His gaze returned to the coil of smoke which continued to rise skywards. He rubbed his jaw where one of Les' wild punches had found its mark. "The real Les surfaced today and he's received the same justice he delivered to Natalie – jury, judge and executioner."

"CJ will be so upset. He thought of Les as a kind of unofficial son." Then, as if thinking aloud she added,

"Such ruthless ambition, people around here are going to find it hard to believe. And the things he knew about CJ's business, he'll be hard to replace."

They turned towards the homestead and Steve's arm slid around her waist. He smiled as she leant into him, their hips and thighs touching as they walked. After a dozen steps he stopped and turned her to face him, his hands encircling her waist. His mouth hovered a few centimetres away from hers until he couldn't bear it and he kissed her long and hard.

"Miss Spinetti, soon to be Mrs Parrish," a wicked gleam lit his eyes, "stop worrying. You're CJ Ambrose's daughter and I, as well as countless others, have every confidence that you'll manage your coming inheritance with the same enterprise and success as your old man."

"You think so?" she asked tentatively as she settled into his embrace. There was much to do and still so much to learn. She kissed him back. Such happiness to look forward to as well, a lifetime of it.

"I know so."

EPILOGUE

News of the drama at the hangar and Les' subsequent death had a detrimental effect on CJ's health, as Francey had predicted it would. A week later he slipped into a coma from which he never woke. His funeral was held on a late spring morning with only a few close friends and relatives – the Dupres, the Spinettis, Shellie and Barry, Francey and Steve and the stockmen of Murrundi. The press weren't invited and for once they allowed the family to mourn in private.

CJ Ambrose, "the man with the golden touch", was laid to rest in the small cemetery on Murrundi beside those he loved, his and the others' graves shaded by the spreading, protective branches of the peppercorn tree.

A week later, Steve found Francey sitting on the grass by CJ's grave, he knew she came here every day to think, have a little cry too, he suspected, and to *talk* to her father. A foolscap pad rested in her lap, a filofax was by her side. She appeared to be lost in thought. Instinctively he knew she was thinking about CJ. Over the past week he had watched her trying to come to terms with the loss of the father she had known all too briefly, and the enormity of the business empire she now controlled.

"Surveying your realm, hey?" He greeted her with a kiss as he sat beside her.

"More like trying to reorganise it. Getting everything to function efficiently with reduced manpower, or to be politically correct, personpower."

She had spent hours, days, trying to figure out how to run CJ's empire without him and Les and have it work like clockwork so that she and Steve could have a reasonable life together. Consolidate and delegate were the only options as far as she could see. She believed that she simply couldn't manage his multitude of interests any other way.

"CJ left me with some unfinished business," she understated the facts. "Maybe he wanted to test me or to keep me busy, I don't know." She expelled a sigh. "Natalie's estate has to be organised and there's the Jasmine project in Cooktown, which isn't finished. I don't want to relinquish control to Nikko Yakismoto if there's a way around it. Plus there's the Arts Museum in the Isa. The mayor is exerting pressure to have it built posthaste, in time for next year's festival. The project's funded and designed but someone has to supervise the building of it." She took a breath, "As well, we've received approval for the resort complex in the Blue Mountains and there's the half completed house at Kirribilli and a new breeding program for Murrundi using two Braford bulls, plus the experimental camel herd and –"

"What about our wedding?" he reminded her gently.

"Let's elope," she said with a grin, but then frowned as she thought of Lucia. "No, Mamma would never forgive me."

"Then you'll just have to delegate more work."

She rolled her eyes skywards. "I agree. That's what I'm trying to work out."

He looked at the pad and the many lines of scribbling. "So what have you got?"

Francey studied her handiwork. "I'm going to elevate Mike Hunter from foreman to manager of Murrundi, he's more than capable. He can oversee the breeding program without any problems too. I've asked Lisa and Pierre if they'd like to move into Les' cottage and if both of them would help me manage the other projects. Pierre can appoint someone in the trade to be manager for the Cooktown project and he'll supervise the building of the Arts Museum." She looked up at him. "By the way, it's now going to be called the Ambrose Memorial Art Gallery. There'll be a studio and living quarters for a permanent artist in residence because that was a dream of CJ's wife, Brenda, according to Shellie." She smiled as he nodded his head approvingly. Then she went on, "That leaves me with the Blue Mountains proposal and the house in Kirribilli."

"And what are you doing about Natalie's estate? I suppose she was worth a tidy sum."

Francey frowned. "Shellie and I have been in something of a quandary over that, but we think we've come up with a reasonable solution. Natalie's will was made four years ago, pre-dating Richard's death. She left everything to him so ... in due course, it reverts to being part of CJ's estate. We've decided to lease her art galleries to Hugh O'Leary and Trish Pentano who've both expressed interest in them. Her estate will take a percentage of their profit and when that accrues it will be added to the estate's cash reserves which will fund a trust for talented, struggling artists. That's appropriate, don't you think?"

"Very." More than Natalie's behaviour deserved, he thought but didn't voice the opinion.

"Oh, I almost forgot," she said in a rush. "I talked to Roy Preston today. You remember him? CJ's journalist mate."

"Yes, he was at your birthday party."

"He wants to write CJ's biography." Her eyes, green in the bright daylight, glistened with unshed tears. "Isn't that wonderful?"

"You bet. I'm sure it'll be a fine testimonial to his life." Steve could see that she had worked hard to bring some order into her screamingly busy life. "So, when do you think we could find the time to get married and have a half decent honeymoon?" As he asked the question he took her left hand and turned it over to allow the diamond engagement ring he had recently placed there to catch the sun's sparkle.

"This coming January, the fifteenth," Francey, who'd been ready for the question, said with a smile. She looked up at the brilliant blue, cloudless sky and then across the pastures of yellow grass bending in the afternoon breeze. "It'll be stinking hot so most of the guests will probably end up in the pool."

"Good. That'll fit in well with my resignation."

"What resignation?" Surprise mirrored itself in her features. She stared at him expectantly, waiting.

"From the Queensland Police Service." He draped his arm around her shoulders and pulled her closer to him. "I've had some time to think too. All the projects you're involved with are going to need custom designed security set-ups. As a cop I know a thing or two about good security. I thought I'd start up my own business. What do you think?"

"It's a marvellous idea." She was silent for a moment or two, digesting his plan.

Steve's disclosure, his desire to be an active part of what her life was going to be like helped lift a weight off her shoulders. She turned away from him and blinked back a tear – she'd shed so many since CJ's death and her sense of loss went deep, to her very soul. So much had happened in her life since she'd met him. He'd been the catalyst that had turned her life upside down and made her change direction. He had introduced her to a very different world, to her past, her heritage and to her present and a future with Steve.

She wished she had known Miles and Richard. The sadness of having half-brothers she'd never meet hurt, immeasurably. And there was CJ himself. Learning to love and respect him, watching him deteriorate and then, finally, to lose him before they both had the chance to know each other really well had created an emptiness inside her that would take a lifetime to get over.

Still reflecting, her blue-green eyes looked past the homestead to the land, *her land*, which stretched as far as she could see. A tentative smile lifted the corners of her mouth. She'd lost a good deal, but had gained so much. At a cost. In life there were always costs, she realised. CJ had left her some legacy, she acknowledged. A link to the land and to the people in her employ, and she knew there would be times when the tasks would be onerous. Her smile widened a little, her confidence growing. With the combination of CJ's blood – minus his ruthless streak which she hadn't inherited – and her mother, Mary's, she would prevail.

Her thoughts snapped back to the present, to the man she loved with all her heart and soul. "What do you think about us spending several months a year at Kirribilli and the rest at Murrundi?"

He nodded in agreement. "That'll work – the best of both worlds. Eventually my security business will take me all over the country. Guess I'm going to be busier than I thought what with that and learning how to fly. In fact," he gave her a sly glance, "I had my first flying lesson today. It was great!"

"Flying! Whatever for?"

"Well, you've lost your pilot." He chuckled as he admitted it, still unrepentant over Les' demise. "You told me once before that it was efficient time management to fly from point A to B to do business. There's no reason why I can't do it. Of course, it'll be a while before I graduate to a Learjet, but I –"

She stopped him with a long, deep, passionate kiss. When they finally broke apart she glanced at CJ's polished marble headstone. Her father would be pleased. Everything was going to be fine. One day as she'd sat by his bed, CJ had said that she and Steve would make a wonderful team. She had always known they would.

Together they could make CJ's vision and their own hopes, ambitions and dreams come true ... their way.

THE END

Acknowledgements

Thanks to my dear friend and literary agent, Selwa Anthony, for her continuing encouragement. To my editors, Deonie Fiford, Rod Morrison and Laura Harris, for their much appreciated editorial expertise. To Lucy Tesoriero, Mabel and Bernard Pasfield and to Karen Davis, Senior Constable in the NSW Police Service. The SA Department of Mines and Energy, and with gratitude to Dr Kenneth Oey for the sharing of his medical knowledge.